M. L. H. Stent
December 96

COMBAT AND COMPETITION

DAVID INCE
DFC, BSc.

*Mark
With my very best wishes
David
8.12.96*

NEWTON

First Published in Great Britain by
Newton Publishers (1992)
P.O.Box 236, Swindon SN3 6QZ, Wiltshire

Copyright © DAVID INCE (1992)

All rights reserved. No part of this publication may be produced, stored in a retrieval system, or transmitted, in any form, or by any means, electronic, mechanical, photocopying, recording or otherwise, without the prior permission of the publishers.

This book is sold subject to the condition that it shall not, by way of trade or otherwise, be lent, re-sold, hired out or otherwise circulated without the publisher's prior consent in any form and without a similar condition, including this condition, being imposed on the subsequent purchaser.

Every effort has been made by the author and the publishers to trace owners of copyright material. The events described have been cross checked wherever possible and the author apologises for any errors or omissions which may have arisen.

ISBN: 1 872308 23 6

PRICE: £15.95 U.K

Printed by:
    Unwin Brothers Limited
    The Gresham Press
    Old Woking
    Surrey GU22 9LH

With my father Major Douglas Ince MC TD on his return from Italy, 1944.

FAI Diamond Gliding Badge

III

No. 4 COURSE, 1946

Sqn.Ldr. W.D.K.Franklin D.F.C.	Sqn.Ldr. K.C.M.Giddings D.F.C.	Flt.Lt. J.G.Haigh	Sqn.Ldr. T.F.Neil D.F.C.	Flt.Lt. R.S.Flight D.F.C.	Wg.Cdr. M.E.Blackstone D.F.C.	Gp.Capt. R.C.Hockey D.S.O., D.F.C.	Flt.Lt. N.F.Duke D.S.O., D.F.C.	Sqn.Ldr. D.R.Turley-George D.F.C.
Sqn.Ldr. P.J.Garner	Sqn.Ldr. K.A.Major D.F.C.	Sqn.Ldr. P.G.Evans D.F.C.	Flt.Lt. D.A.C.Hunt					

Flt.Lt. P.R.Fowler	Sqn.Ldr. E.F.S.May	Flt.Lt. P.P.C.Barthropp D.F.C.	Lieut. D.P.Davies D.S.C., R.N.V.R.	Lieut. R.B.Mancus R.N.V.R.	Lieut. H.C.N.Goodhart R.N.	Lieut. P.G.Lawrence M.B.E.	Lieut. K.R.Hickson R.N.
Lieut. P.S.Wilson R.N.	Lieut. J.F.Rankin D.S.C., R.N.	Flt.Lt. D.A.Taylor D.F.C.	Flt.Lt. E.L.Heath	Flg.Off. H.J.Dodson		K.A.Butler	

Sqn.Ldr. R.F.Martin D.F.C.	Flt.Lt. D.H.G.Ince D.F.C.	Flt.Lt. W.H.Else	Mr. J.R.B.Spink B.Sc.	Flt.Lt. F.R.Arnold	Sqn.Ldr. W.R.Morris A.F.C.	Sqn.Ldr. H.G.Hastings A.F.M.	Wg.Cdr. H.P.Powell A.F.C.
Gp.Capt. H.J.Wilson C.B.E. A.F.C.	Mr. G.M.Humphreys B.Sc. A.I.P. A.F.R.Ae.S.	Flt.Lt. L.H.Tolchard	Flt.Lt. F.E.Clark	W/O. C.Rutter M.B.E.	Mr. S.I.R.Nicol B.Sc.	Flt.Lt. P.R.Cope	Flt.Lt. I.D.Crozier	Flt.Lt. A.E.Marriott

Flt.Lt. G.E.C.Genders D.F.M.

CONTENTS

Chapter	1	CLOUD PAVILLIONS WHITE	1
Chapter	2	MARKING TIME	5
Chapter	3	PRELUDE TO BATTLE	21
Chapter	4	TYPHOON	37
Chapter	5	WINTER IN FLANDERS	57
Chapter	6	DYING REICH	75
Chapter	7	BALBOS AND BOOZE	99
Chapter	8	IN A QUANDRY	115
Chapter	9	A KIND OF APPRENTICESHIP	135
Chapter	1	CHARIOTS OF FIRE	153
Chapter	11	A TESTING TIME	171
Chapter	12	ELONGATED BALLS	195
Chapter	13	FRONTIERS OF WHAT?	213
Chapter	14	OLD WARHORSES	233
Chapter	15	FULL CIRCLE	249
		EPILOGUE	I
		GLOSSARY	III
		INDEX	IX
		HOW A GLIDER FLIES	XV

LIST OF ILLUSTRATIONS

NUMBER   PAGE

Author and his father.	III
No 4 Course ETPS, 1946.	IV
Skylark III.	VII
193 Squadron Normandy, 1944.	X
257 Squadron Crews, Normandy, 1944.	4
Gloster F5/34.	between 22 and 23
No 80 Course EFTS, Neepawa, 1943.	between 22 and 23
In a Harvard, Calgary 1943.	36
Killy in his Typhoon.	between 38 and 39
'My dear the Flak.'	between 38 and 39
Sir Winston Churchill, with members of 146 Wing.	56
Vianen Bridge, before and after.	74
Targets, Castle Bijen Beek and Ammunition Dump.	98
Me 109G and Typhoon of 193 Squadron.	152
Another Balbo to come.	170
Hunting Clan, Xmas party 1953.	194
Bungy Launching.	232
Charles Wingfield.	between 234 and 235
Olympia 419 and Dereck Piggot Distance Record.	between 234 and 235
EON Olympia 403 and ASW 20.	between 234 and 235
Formation Flying.	between 234 and 235
National Championships 1963.	between 234 and 235
Gliding Championships 1957 and 1987.	
Germany 1963 and Old Warhorses.	between 260 and 261
More Old Warhorses.	between 260 and 261

Skylark III - National Championships, 1957.

ACKNOWLEDGEMENTS

So many people have helped with this book that it is impossible to name them all. But my special thanks are due to Mrs Rosemary Bromley who has guided me unerringly since the first tentative efforts appeared on paper. To Air Vice Marshal Sandy Hunter who has supported and encouraged me throughout the whole project. To Chris Thomas, Typhoon historian par excellence, who steered me through the intricacies of the Public Records Office. To Brigadier Timbers, Secretary of the Royal Artillery Historical Trust, who corrected erroneous memories about the 27th (Army) Field Regiment in 1941. To Sebastian Cox of the Air Historical Branch, the staff of the reference library at the RAF Museum and John May A.R.P.S. who worked wonders with a set of elderly dogeared photographs.

To my old Typhoon colleagues and good friends Jimmy Simpson, Arthur Todd, 'Killy' Kilpatrick, Ronnie Sheward and Pinkie Stark I am particularly grateful - together with those of 197 Squadron, especially Allan Smith, Derek Lovell, Geoff Hartley, Bob Gibbings, Roy Allan, and the late Bruce Gilbert. Their reminiscences and those of Ben Gunn, last chief test pilot of Boulton Paul Aircraft, have helped to fill many an important gap in the sequence of events. The gliding story owes as much again to the memories of Harry Midwood and Wally Kahn, spanning between them a period of over four decades.

My gratitude to Ron Howard too, who recently retired as Chairman of GEC Avionics, for his invaluable contribution to the chapters about the aircraft industry.

Without my wife Anne the whole thing would have been quite impossible. She, it was who insisted that I learned to use a word processor, who put up with the endless disruption to meals and family life, and corrected the manuscript again and again.

Last, and not least, my thanks to Tony Roberts of Newton Publishers without whose assistance it might never have seen the light of day.

FOREWORD
by
Air Chief Marshal Sir Christopher Foxley-Norris
GCB, DSO, OBE, MA, CBIM, FRSA.

As the title indicates, this autobiography is divided into two parts; the author's active service in World War II and his postwar involvement in the aviation industry and gliding.

The first part of the book is largely devoted to operational flying on Typhoons in 1944-5. This story has of course been told before, but David Ince's highly graphic and gripping narration adds a new flavour. The ground attack fighter played a large, indeed a decisive part in our victory in Europe. The fact that we enjoyed air supremacy, to which the Luftwaffe's exhaustion on the Eastern Front had contributed much, enabled us to tilt the balance of victory, albeit at forbidding cost in casualties.

After the war, Ince was faced with a difficult choice between a permanent commission in the RAF, which he was pressed to accept, and a career as test pilot. He chose the latter but in the event chronic sinusitis curtailed his development flying and he turned to marketing and general management, and to gliding, the latter becoming his true love. His descriptions of soaring flight, particularly in top competition, are enthralling.

Less happily, his years in aviation bear witness to sharp bickering between prima donnas and vested interests; and, most notably, to the constant and deplorable interference of totally unqualified politicians such as Duncan Sandys and Healey. As long as our aircraft industry and military preparedness remain in such hands, there will be, even in more peaceful times, grave cause for anxiety.

Having to some extent been involved in most of these activities, I much enjoyed this book and can strongly recommend it.

193 Squadron Normandy, July 1944 (photo by Author). Standing left to right: ----, 'Socks' Ross, Mike Bulleid, Charlie Hall, Jim Darling, 'Boots' Brown, Rod Davidge, Johnny Button, Bill Switzer, 'Killy' Kilpatrick, Ben Lenson, Jimmy Simpson, 'Toddles' Pratt, Jimmy Fishwick, 'Mac' the Adj. Kneeling centre: Stan 'Chiefy' Carr. Seated left to right: Colin Gilmour, 'Wee Mac' MaCartney, ----, ----, Al Sudgen, ----, Bill Hurst, 'Hap Pratt, 'Sack' Bilz, Gus Gough.

Left to right: Hap Pratt, Jimmy Fishwick, 'Killy' Kilpatrick, Al Sugden, Johnny Button, Jimmy Simpson, Author, Jim Darling, Bill Switzer.

x

CHAPTER ONE

CLOUD PAVILIONS WHITE

We crowded round the operations map, sweating in the heat, as Johnny Button briefed us for the attack. The aiming point was the middle of a tiny village, overlooking a wooded escarpment, some 25 miles inland from the Normandy beaches.

"We'll run in this way and go down to port. Remember our boys on the ground are very close, ready to go in. No, repeat no! undershoots are permitted!"

The sunburned face, under its mop of curly dark hair, looked at us thoughtfully. He glanced at his watch:

"Press tits at fourteen thirty – Good luck chaps!"

Nothing to it really, just 35 minutes chock to chock and back in time for tea. I glanced at the others. Some of them had been with the squadron for a long time. Did they feel as I did, fulfilled beyond my wildest dreams, flying a Typhoon to war? Did they savour the preflight tension, the challenge and uncertainty of every sortie, and in the background always, fear to be mastered? Questions which were never asked – although for most of us the answers would have been in the affirmative. Beyond any shadow of a doubt we were the lucky ones.

I look back on that period of my life and recall the words of another airman[1].

The fact is I enjoyed the war..... it became my driving force because it had a purpose and I accepted the risks, the excitement of combat, survival and retrospect..... We all did..... with faith and courage, so that the sense of belonging to a great service in its hour of triumph lifted the spirit.....

In from the coast a belt of well developed cumulus reached upwards, dazzling white. Where they merged together the clouds formed deep canyons of clear air, framing a distant landscape of sunshine and shadow. They grew higher, closing in on the formation until we were flanked by walls of shimmering vapour – sitting ducks for the gunners waiting below. And with the thought a salvo of black oily bursts materialised from nowhere as the aircraft moved into echelon for the attack.

"Bassett Leader going down now!"

Another salvo of 88s came closer still – shredding and gone in a moment. In the same instant we were plummeting earthwards, strung out down the sky, gunsights tracking onto the target as it emerged

COMBAT AND COMPETITION

from the shadows far below. A picturesque almost alpine scene – wooded heights, tortuous winding roads and a deep gorge – bathed in brilliant sunshine. And there the similarity ended. Where the village had once been was just a vague cruciform shape, its outline merging into a sea of rubble. A charnel house of pulverised limestone and flickering fires where a Panzer unit had dug in its tanks and guns.

An umbrella of white shell bursts formed over the ruins, a lethal, seemingly impenetrable, screen. Then the diving aircraft were through and still unscathed – cannon smoke trailing down the sky – each pilot conscious of the tracer rising lazily upwards and accelerating violently towards him, willing himself to press home his attack.

Bombs gone. Moments later they erupted across the target area. There was an angry red explosion – and a new and violent fire began to rage amongst the wreckage. The enemy gunners redoubled their efforts and the air was torn by a maelstrom of flak. The dark cloud base, low above our heads, tilted crazily as we weaved and jinked in the gloom trying to evade the glowing, deadly, firefly streams. And time stood still.

Then, suddenly, it was all over and we were back in sunlight, climbing hard, moving into battle formation and setting course for home.

The I.O.[2] was waiting, pacing up and down, as the aircraft taxied in. A typical academic, with steel rimmed spectacles and a map tightly rolled under his arm, he must have found our light hearted banter difficult to accept. Yet he listened patiently enough and quietly inserted his questions.

"So it had been ABTA[3]? – and with what results.....?
"What else had we seen.....? and the flak.....?"

That was our cue – and we responded as always with a touch of the Noel Coward's – brave and ever so slightly effeminate:

"The flak Gwyn! My dear the flak!..... and the noise!..... and the people!....."

And somehow honour was satisfied, even if we said it too often in those far off days, for only those who had been there knew what it was really like.

Time to spare a thought for the Canadians working their way up the escarpment against those dug in tanks, and the superb panzerfaust and infantry firepower of the German Army. Would that we had hit the defenders really hard. As for us, driving back to our tents in the orchard, less than a mile from the sea, there was a passing moment of

CHAPTER ONE   CLOUD PAVILLIONS WHITE

euphoria. Relief at returning without loss and the warm feeling of life and survival until next time.

> *And they are fortunate, who fight*[4]
> *For gleaming landscapes swept and shafted*
> *And crowned by cloud pavilions white;*
> *Hearing such harmonies as might*
> *Only from Heaven be downward wafted*
> *Voices of victory and delight.*

Colin Gilmour tells the tale to 'Wee Mac' Macartney left and 'Sack' Bilz.
On the right Bill Hurst and Johnny Button.

Wg Cdr Johnny Baldwin briefs 257 Squadron, Normandy, 1944.

CHAPTER TWO

MARKING TIME

On my father's farm a mile or so below Hadrian's wall, in the mid nineteen twenties, we never saw an aeroplane. When the lenticulars of the Pennine wave arched across the sky, as they must have done since the beginning of time, there were no sailplanes to challenge their rising currents. Nor as yet were there any messages for me in the pattern of the clouds above.

We lived to the sounds of pipeline milking. Twice a day the yard across the lane, where Boodie worked with his cows, echoed to the clack of pneumatic pulsation and the clatter of aluminium buckets. In summer there was haymaking on the fells and at harvest time great mugs of tea and wedges of bread and butter – family and helpers sitting amongst the stubble below the slats and belts of the threshing machine. An idyllic existence for a small boy. Brought to a sudden and unhappy end when farm and livestock were sold and we moved to Glasgow.

Glasgow in the thirties was full of disturbing images. Squalid tenements and shawlie womenfolk gossiping in the doorways. The unemployed, standing around in their cloth caps and mufflers, at every street corner. Their poverty, seen for the first time, was an affront. Made worse by the tragedy that so many of them were survivors of the War.

1914–18 touched me first at Prep School. Aysgarth, in the Yorkshire Dales, a marvellous escape from Glasgow for nine months in the year. Like Hugh Dundas[1] I too discovered the *Times History of the Great War* in the school library. Before long I had become totally absorbed by the bitter struggle and my childish ambitions to be an engine driver soon gave way, Biggles-like, to the images of an aviator.

Flying became an obsession. I had to experience it for myself. Eventually a member of the Renfrew Flying Club agreed to take me up.

Ex RFC and partially disabled in his right arm, he was anxious to assure me that he could cope in the air. But I was far too excited to listen. Caught up in the ritual which was to become so familiar in later years and the precisely repeated words of command:

"Switches off! – Suck in! – Throttle set! – Contact!"

Unless you have experienced the tang of burnt oil and the slipstream in your face – and felt the transition from bumpy take off to smooth flight and itched to get your hands on the controls – you've never

COMBAT AND COMPETITION

lived. So it was with me, on that summer afternoon more than half a century ago, as the Gipsy Moth lifted into the air and swung northwest across the Clyde.

Other memories come crowding in..... with my friends John Slatter and Peter Holmes, beside the duty pilot's van, watching the yellow Hart trainers flying circuits and landings. We had been amongst the first to join the new OTC[2] Air Section at Cheltenham College, belonged to the same House, and shared a love of flying. Our visits to the FTS[3] at South Cerney were intended to instil a basic knowledge of radio, armament, and navigation. But we escaped from the stuffy lecture rooms at every opportunity.....

..... at summer camps where we were soldiers again, puttied and blancoed replicas of that earlier war, our make believe battles on the scrub covered slopes above Tidworth enlivened by the presence of an occasional Audax or Hector. Local army co-operation squadrons demonstrating the art of air support. So highly developed it was said that some of the aircraft were even being flown by army officers seconded to the RAF.....

..... above all the stolen afternoons at Hucclecote, home of the Gloster Aircraft Company, surreptitiously photographing the Gladiators and Henley target tugs on production test. And the golden day when Frank McKenna, the General Manager, whose son was also at Cheltenham, took me round the factory.

In the flight shed was Gloster's latest, the F5/34, a unique opportunity to explore the cockpit of an eight gun monoplane fighter. I sat there trying to take it all in, surrounded by the aroma of cellulose dope and hydraulic fluid, grasping the throttle lever – hand on the spade grip – head in the clouds.

A few days later I watched as the elegant prototype accelerated across the grass airfield, tucked its leggy undercarriage out of sight, and climbed away into the autumn sun, far out over the Severn estuary. From then on a career in the Royal Air Force became my dearest ambition.

In a matter of weeks circumstances beyond my control were to change all that. At No 1 Central Medical Board in London I failed the eyesight test.

However war was fast approaching and there must be some other way. Back in Glasgow once more I applied to join 602 Auxiliary Squadron. After meeting the CO, Sqn Ldr Farquhar, it seemed likely that I would be accepted, but there was another medical to face. When

CHAPTER TWO   MARKING TIME

he had completed his examination, the M.O.[4] looked at me thoughtfully and shook his head:

"I'm afraid you could never land a Tiger Moth, let alone a fast fighter like a Gladiator, and as for low flying you'd kill yourself."

Strange that he should say Gladiator when the squadron was replacing its Gauntlets with Spitfires. Was he, by deliberate choice of words, seeking to underline how far I fell short of the standards? To deter me from ever trying again.

It was the beginning of a long period of frustration. If I couldn't join them perhaps I could shoot them down! - and mindful of my father, then commanding a searchlight battery, I applied for Anti-Aircraft and Coast Defence. But the Army rightly considered that Ack Ack and CD was not for youngsters and sent me to Field Artillery.

Life in a training regiment was mostly spent on the parade ground, grinding in new recruits, as practised by armies everywhere. This tiresome introduction to the military life happened to coincide with the run up to Dunkirk, and we almost failed to realise its significance until our 1918 style eighteen pounders were taken away to help re-equip the returning troops.

The growing risk of airborne invasion brought a change of scene, to Yeadon, for airfield defence. A party of the longest serving trainees, those who had been at Harrogate for almost three months, together with several NCOs and an officer, moved into the empty RAF quarters and prepared to hold out against all comers.

From our main defensive position, on a hill overlooking the airfield, the place looked like a morgue. 609 Squadron, the local auxiliary unit, had left to take part in the aerial battles over southern England and the Avro shadow factory, which would soon be producing Lancasters in their hundreds, only existed on paper.

For company we had three local brickies. Large, muscular, beer bellied and totally idle. They were supposed to be building the pillbox in which we might have to fight for our lives, and theirs too, come to that. But they were not bothered at all until the Sergeant Major made some very pointed remarks about putting his bayonet where it would hurt!

Our weapons were pretty limited. Rifles, Molotov cocktails, and the crudest imaginable dummy gun on which we continued to practice our drills. That the latter - which had been constructed from the wheels, axle and shafts, of an old farm cart, surmounted by a rusty length of

COMBAT AND COMPETITION

stove pipe – would have deceived the enemy seems highly improbable. As for machine guns, there were none at all.

The domestic site and sleeping quarters were on the edge of Otley, a small Yorkshire textile community, where the pubs were friendly and the locals enjoyed their beer. They responded with enthusiasm to the victories against the Luftwaffe in the south, and there were some mighty parties.

One of our number, himself a local, found temptation all to great, and arrived regularly on our nightly stand-to parade rather the worse for wear. Although he managed to conceal this fairly well his little weakness had been spotted by our detachment commander – an unpleasant character, with a permanent chip on his shoulder, who was always looking for some unfortunate on whom to vent his spleen.

And so on an August evening, after the air battle had gone rather well, the defenders of Yeadon were treated to an episode of high comedy. Our hero, trying desperately to avoid swaying, confronted by his officer who knew that he had cornered him at last.

"Gunner Bloggs you're drunk!"

"Me? – not me sir!"

Incredibly he had pulled himself together and was standing rigidly to attention. Then the faintest trace of a smile as, in his drunkenness, he almost succumbed to dumb insolence. So they stood, facing each other at close quarters, officer and man, a ludicrous tableau, as the daylight slowly faded, until the Sergeant Major's voice broke the silence in scarcely veiled tones of contempt.

"Dismiss the parade sir?"

– and we fell out in the darkness – collapsing in silent, helpless, laughter.

The Army moves in a mysterious way and a batch of OCTU[5] postings came through with little evidence of any selection procedure. The 'lucky' ones transferred to a requisitioned hotel in nearby Ilkley, wore white bands on their forage caps, and started to learn how to be officers and gentlemen for the duration. No gun drill now, but there was plenty of PT and route marching, to help make good the ravages of life at Yeadon.

It was back to school with a vengeance, lectures and tests, and a need for at least some 'homework' in the evenings. An introduction to the mysteries of MT included motor cycles – on one of which I nearly wrote myself off – and driving instruction on heavy vehicles with crash gearboxes. When, years later, I bought an Alvis 12/50 big port

CHAPTER TWO   MARKING TIME

beetleback, attracted by the bunch of bananas exhaust, the experience proved invaluable.

Amongst the more durable memories of Ilkley, was a stand-to early one September morning, on one of the rare occasions when church bells were rung during the war. It lasted for hours and hours and no weapons were issued, not even rifles and bayonets. Were we to fight those German paratroopers with our bare hands for God's sake? Nobody could tell us what we were supposed to do. Even when the parade was eventually dismissed, and confined to camp for the rest of the day, there was no explanation.

When the course ended, in time for Christmas leave, three of us had been posted to the 27th Field Regiment stationed at Melton Mowbray. We were joining a regular unit, which had been evacuated at Dunkirk, and about to become its first wartime trained subalterns.

The officers of 24 Battery lived in a requisitioned Edwardian house which served as the mess. Due to a shortage of rooms a few of the most junior, which included the new arrivals, were billeted out. We probably enjoyed greater comfort than our seniors, but as a way of breaking down barriers it was not a good idea.

To prewar soldiers like Major Mead, the battery commander, and Aubrey Buxton, the senior captain, the arrival of two 'temporary' and very raw second lieutenants must have been viewed with misgiving. Their attitude, quite unconsciously, tended to suggest that they regarded us as inferior beings. Whilst the new arrivals, for their part, had little enthusiasm for peacetime customs and courtesies and were inclined to find their amusements elsewhere, given the least excuse. An uneasy relationship – which gradually improved as we came to respect the traditions of the Regiment.

The first of many moves to come ended close to the Yorkshire coast after a long detour westwards for practice firing in the Brecon Beacons. Out on the ranges, particularly in the mountain top OPs[6] the cold was unbelievable. Mine was the last shoot before dark, at the end of a long day, and it was hardly a roaring success. Every ranging shot seemed to land out of sight, on the far side of some distant ridge, to the detriment of my slender reputation. It was hardly fair because we had been fortifying ourselves at intervals with neat whisky, trying to keep out the cold, and mine as I said was the last shoot – and the light was failing.

Hedon, a few miles to the east of Hull, was a pleasant change from the rigours of South Wales. It marked the beginning of a period during

COMBAT AND COMPETITION

which the Regiment was to lead a nomadic existence in the coastal areas of the East Riding. Our arrival coincided with the height of the blitz and, although there were frequent air raids, the pubs and clubs in the town centre were still doing a roaring trade.

One night, for no good reason at all, the subalterns of 24 Battery left their favourite spot at an earlier hour than usual. The first bombers arrived overhead as we reached the mess, and the nocturnal hate seemed worse than usual, but nothing much happened at Hedon. Just a few sticks of incendiaries in the grounds and the pressure waves of an occasional landmine. In the morning it was a different story, with all the signs of a major disaster. A pall of smoke hung over the city and an acrid smell of burning filled the air.

Later in the day, with Spitfires and Beaufighters cruising overhead to drive off any Hun reconnaissance sorties, we took a truck into town. It was a distressing sight, houses blackened and burnt, others with their interiors open to view – floors teetering, treasured possessions exposed for all the world to see. Whole streets were cordoned off, restricted to military and rescue vehicles, and dust covered figures toiled in the wreckage or struggled with landmines swaying lethally on the end of snagged parachutes.

Approaching the scene of our early departure the previous night almost nothing was recognisable, hardly a building was standing, just masses of scorched and shattered rubble. I thought of the others who had stayed on, of the cheerful band to whose music we had danced on many an occasion, and turned sadly away.

A mile or so down the road from our mess was the headquarters of a balloon barrage unit. Running into some of them in the local pub, they invited us over for drinks on the following evening.

As it happened the Luftwaffe had chosen to go elsewhere that night and the little gathering in the Romney hut turned into an almighty thrash. Inciter in chief was Flying Officer Len Harvey, ex heavyweight champion boxer, who set a punishing pace. A splendid boozy occasion, just the tonic we all needed after the events of the last few days. But it still hurt that there was no way in which a Field Regiment could hit back at the enemy bombers. Even our balloon flying hosts, with their ungainly charges, were playing a part in the air defences.

When the RAF announced that aircrew volunteers were being sought from the Army it seemed entirely appropriate. In point of fact it was an obvious reaction to the situation developing in 1941. Greece

CHAPTER TWO MARKING TIME

and Crete had fallen, ground fighting was limited to the Western Desert, and the air war against Germany had become number one priority.

Should I try again? The standards might be lower now or less rigidly enforced. There might even be a way round that part of the eyesight test which had caught me out before. This time luck was on my side. A touch of deviousness, a sympathetic medical officer, and I was through.

But there were more hurdles to come. A few months passed and then an official letter arrived. It informed me that:

"RAF aircrew needs have now been fully satisfied, and all further transfers from the Army have been suspended..... Volunteers are invited for training as Army glider pilots."

Which was not the idea at all!

What to do next? – and then I remembered those prewar seconded Army officers flying Audaxes and Hectors. Was it still possible? – a visit to the adjutant's office to look through KRs[7] and ACIs[8] – and there it was, in amended wartime form. ACI 152/40.

The object of the scheme is to produce for Army Co-operation Squadrons a number of pilots who are also trained as army officers.....

It was necessary to have a minimum of 18 months commissioned service in the Army before seconding to the RAF. Another eight months to go. Better than never. I applied at once and was accepted. The game was still on.

Whilst I had been pursuing my lonely fight much had been happening to the Regiment. Shortly after the heavy air attacks on Hull there was another invasion flap and we moved up nearer the coast. Our elderly, much modified, 18/25 pounders were run into rivetted and camouflaged emplacements a couple of miles inland from Withernsea. Trail arcs were dug and false angles of sight computed to give the old guns some much needed extra range. An OP was located in the cliffs overlooking the sea. Fixed barrage lines were established. For weeks on end there was stand-to at dawn and dusk. The legendary 1 Corps of which the Regiment was then part, spearhead of the British Expeditionary Force in 1914 and again in 1939, had set the stage for one battle which never happened.

Soon new equipment began to arrive. 25 pounder gun/howitzers, more potent and flexible than the old 18/25s which they were replacing – Morris and Guy Quads, powerful, toad like, four wheel drive gun tractors – proper military vehicles to replace the

COMBAT AND COMPETITION

requisitioned cars and vans – new and better radios. We were beginning to look like professional gunners once more.

Our commanding officer, Lieutenant Colonel Dorling, no doubt enthused by this revival in our image, decided that it could be improved even further. Thereafter each troop, until then identified by its letter in the rather dreary phonetic alphabet of the period, *Ack, Beer, Charlie.....* became known as *Attack, Battle, Challenge.....* As he said, when he was putting the idea over to us:

"Do you really want to go into action calling yourselves Charlie Troop?"

When these names began to appear on our vehicles we were subjected to a fair amount of ribaldry from other units in the area. They were a bit of a mouthful on the radio. But we found a way round that and soon began to take a pride in being different as well as better. With hindsight our Colonel knew his public relations.

From time to time we pulled out of our gun pits and took off on manoeuvres. Once, when so engaged, our newly christened 'Challenge' Troop was caught by the RAF. Out on a flank, standing at the ready with megaphone and director, I watched the Quads come to a halt and the crews tumbling out, swinging guns and limbers into action.

As they did so the sudden snarl of diving aircraft almost swamped the words of command and four Spitfires came slanting down out of the sun. Twice they came back, eight cannon and sixteen machine guns, against just one Motley[9] mounted Bren on a 15 cwt truck. It was an unmistakable message conveying the savage potential of fighter ground attack.

I first met Pierre in the bar of the Beverley Arms. He wore a pilot's brevet and the word 'Belgium' on the shoulders of his blue tunic. We had much in common. Waiting for an event which would change our lives.

For Pierre it would be the liberation of his country, whilst I could hardly contain my impatience at the delayed start to pilot training. Our chance meeting turned out to be the first of many.

Once he took me up in a Blenheim, far out over the North Sea. It was grey day, with occasional shafts of feeble sunshine penetrating the cloud. The water below looked cold and uninviting, lumpy and streaked with wind lanes. We flew on and on in silence, and then:

"This is the nearest I can get to Belgium, it must do for now, but one day I shall fly above my house again."

We turned back towards the ranges off Flamborough Head, emptied

CHAPTER TWO   MARKING TIME

our guns into the angry sea and came home through the rain and low cloud of an approaching warm front. Pierre never lived to make that flight of his dreams. When the end came on a last shipping strike, I pray that it came quickly. Now only the memory remains and his name, with all those others, on the Memorial above Runnymede.

Soon after Hitler turned his armies loose on Russia the Regiment left the Yorkshire coast. A visit to the ranges at Larkhill more than made up for Sennybridge the previous winter. When my turn came to control the shoot it was immaculate. Even against moving targets the rounds of gunfire were hitting every time. As the instructors said, it showed great promise or, more likely, just beginner's luck!

From Larkhill we moved into suburban south London and then on again, to Rye Harbour on the Sussex coast, breaking our journey at an ancient country house overlooking the Weald of Kent.

In a scene that was almost Dickensian we sat down to our evening meal by the light of an immense log fire. The sap crackled and banged, the port circulated to an aroma of wood smoke, and the atmosphere was relaxed and friendly. A final turn around the rose garden failed to break the spell. It was one of those nights when the sky pulsed with stars and the sounds of patrolling aircraft seemed to be magnified a thousand times in the frozen stillness. America was in the war and the German Army had ground to a halt in front of Moscow. My departure to the RAF was drawing near. I retired to bed contented.

The approach to Rye Harbour on the following afternoon and our spirits fell with every mile that passed. A flat and dreary landscape which looked like the end of the world, and the first sight of our destination was not much better. A small railway siding, an isolated cluster of mean looking houses and rusty sheds overlooking the quayside, and beyond, two hundred yards or so towards the sea, a Martello tower.

Our quarters were totally uninsulated and icy cold, there was barely sufficient accommodation, little to do and nowhere to go. Fortunately, thanks to my enthusiasm for unofficial modifications, I was otherwise engaged. After the episode of the four Spitfires, I had been looking for ways of strengthening our anti-aircraft defences, and had found a possible answer in the Motley mounting itself.

Comprising a rotating seat, to which was attached a spring balanced arm carrying a single Bren gun – the design was such that additional guns, up to four in total, could be added by the simple expedient of cannibalising other mountings. There were problems of course, such

COMBAT AND COMPETITION

as how to operate the multiple triggers and counterbalance each extra gun, but none were insuperable.

To cut a long story short, we built a prototype double Motley, took it to the ranges near Dungeness, fired it against a number of balloon targets and proved that it worked. The next step was to assemble a total of four double units and install them in weapon pits, with a landline to the Observer Corps post in the Martello tower. After further practice firing the gun crews were thoroughly drilled in aircraft recognition and we were ready to go.

For three weeks, during a period of almost continuous frost and east wind, we manned those guns from before dawn until dark. There was an occasional alert – but we never saw a thing or fired a shot!

We made two more trips to the ranges. The first was to try out my 'piece de resistance', a quadruple Motley unit, on which the guns were to be fired and reloaded in successive pairs. Unfortunately the inertia of four Brens was too great for any normal gunner to handle. What we really needed by then was a couple of four gun bomber turrets with a hydraulic power take off driven from a stationary engine!

The second occasion was an official demonstration of ground strafing with cannon and machine guns. A party, which included officers from all over the Command, watched as twelve Hurricanes systematically demolished a line of old cars and lorries. Even with empty petrol tanks, and no fires or explosions, it was most impressive. The silence, as we moved around afterwards inspecting the results, was tribute enough.

Shortly after we left Rye Harbour I was sent to Aldershot on a messing course. Amongst other things we learned how to generate surprising amounts of heat for cooking in the field using old engine oil and water. At the abattoir a poleaxed bullock and the infantry officer standing next to me collapsed at the same time. He recovered quickly enough, but how on earth would he cope in battle!

The best part of that course was to learn just what could be done, by keen and conscientious cookhouse staff, using standard army rations. From then on I made it my business to watch what went on and urge the cooks to do better. I suspect that I was a pain in the neck, but they were put on their mettle, and soon started to take a renewed pride in their culinary skills. My colleagues were quietly amused, but it really was rather satisfactory.

By early spring the Regiment was under orders to move overseas. A quick check revealed that, if I left the UK, my secondment to the

CHAPTER TWO   MARKING TIME

RAF now only three months away would automatically lapse. The whole process would have to start all over again – 6 months after arriving in India – where it was rumoured that the unit was going. An appeal to the Colonel and fortunately reason prevailed. I was posted Officer i/c Home Details.

Amongst the forty or so who remained behind was Adam de Hegedus, Hungarian journalist, writer and student of human nature. In a book[10], published about three years later, he accused me of running a Commando regime.

He was absolutely right. It was important to keep a mixed bunch of men, including several known criminals, occupied and out of mischief. As most of them were posted afterwards to the Artillery Depot at Woolwich, where conditions were reckoned to be tough, my so called Commando training can have done them no harm at all.

For my final spell of Army life commonsense triumphed splendidly over bureaucracy. I was to be attached to an Army Cooperation squadron for unspecified liaison duties. It was an admirable solution. In the event it turned out far better than I dared hope.

Twinwood Farm, on the edge of a low plateau overlooking the river Ouse, had once been considered as a municipal airport for Bedford. Now a satellite of Cranfield, home of 51 OTU[11], it was used for night fighter training and shared by 613 Squadron to which I was about to report.

Parked on the dispersal pans were a number of Mustang Is. In day fighter camouflage, with a large black and white Panda head on the forward fuselage, the Mustangs looked clean and fast – very different to the Lysanders of yesterday. Further enquiries revealed that the Squadron had a Tiger Moth, a Master III and a Battle on strength.

From then on, whenever conditions were suitable, I was airborne in the Tiger. 'Smudger' Smith and Reggie Trapp, a golf professional from Newton Abbott, were my unofficial instructors. Despite the pressures of Mustang training they were generous with their time and, before long, I was almost ready to go solo.

One day, during the usual midday lull in Bisley circuits and bumps, the Squadron Commander took me for a check. After stalling and spinning we returned to the airfield where, using the triangular patch of grass between the runways, I managed to pull off some reasonable landings. As we taxied in I heard his voice through the Gosport tubes:

"Technically there's no reason at all why you shouldn't go solo, but I can't send you off. I do hope you understand. I'm very sorry."

COMBAT AND COMPETITION

It was disappointing, but I did understand. Just to imagine the aftermath of an incident with the Squadron's Tiger, flown solo by an unqualified Army officer, was enough! Never mind. My day would come.

In all I must have flown about 50 hours, more than half in the Tiger. Reggie, who was elected aerobatics instructor, nearly put me off for life by pulling an inordinate amount of 'G' on the recovery from his first demonstration loop. He apologised profusely, explaining that he had not aerobatted a Tiger for some time, and thereafter all was well.

A few weeks later he invited me to spend a weekend with him and his family in Devon. They were kindness itself, and the meals were unbelievable – even to the clotted cream – they must have been saving up their rations for weeks. At lunch on the day we left I watched him sitting there, his wife and children around him, and thought of the time, not far distant, when he could be taking his Mustang into action. And I thanked my lucky stars that I was still single.

Apart from one trip, wind finding with the Battle, the rest of my flying at Twinwood was in the Master. On each occasion there was some allegedly important communications purpose. Smudger was up front but I did most of the flying, and practised pilot navigation, from the rear seat. It was pleasant, bowling along at 180 mph behind the smooth running Wasp engine, learning one's way around England.

Once we were trapped by weather at Snailwell and I was able to see a Typhoon at really close quarters. 56 Squadron, commanded by the same Hugh Dundas of my Aysgarth days – 'Cocky' to his friends – was first to be equipped with the new fighter. They were suffering from a spate of engine failures, and had lost another pilot on the afternoon of our arrival. He had tried to stretch his glide and stalled in just short of the boundary. Although there was no fire, the remains were not a pretty sight and, in the mess that evening, the Sabre's reliability was the subject of much adverse comment. However I had seen enough of the Typhoon. If possible, it was for me.

On another cross country we were already aboard for the return flight and the aircraft was being refuelled by a WAAF. As the bowser moved off she sat on the starboard wing root and replaced the filler cap. Then she slid towards the trailing edge, right over the blade shaped undercarriage indicator, and we had visions of a major disaster.

Fortunately all that happened was an expression of great surprise on her face and a massive tear in the crutch of her battledress trousers. She explored the damage, her standard issue 'passion killers' clearly

CHAPTER TWO   MARKING TIME

visible, then clutched herself together grinning sheepishly as Smudger ran through starting drill. It was a hilarious return trip on what turned out to be my last flight with the Squadron.

613 had been marvellous. They had welcomed me from the start as one of themselves – insisting on sharing their aircrew meals with a wingless 'Brown Job'. More important, they allowed me to prove to myself that, whatever the medicos had said in the past, I could land an aircraft.

As a result I was able to face the pressures of Grading School[12] with that major uncertainty resolved and some useful flying experience under my belt. I shall always be in their debt.

13 ITW[13] was a happy interlude, in good company, the South Devon coast at its autumn best and Torquay still preserving much of its prewar charm. We were an unruly course, seconded Army officers or RAF aircrew remustering as pilots, out for a bit of fun, and a determined not to conform.

The honours were pretty even. We defeated the officers outright. They had little enough experience and no idea how to handle us. The NCOs were made of sterner stuff, the drill sergeants in particular adept at conveying statements like "You horrid little man..... SIR!" – without ever putting them into words.

It was a pity that our first trial of strength had to be with these professionals, but it was almost inevitable. The idea of drilling again like a bunch of rookies was offensive. Perhaps we could encourage them to have second thoughts by putting on an immaculate performance! So that the whole thing would be seen as a waste of time.

Unfortunately we counted without 'Nobby' Clarke. Lanky and seemingly uncoordinated, with rather bent features, Nobby was an odd ball. Giving an impression of cluelessness which he elaborated by expressions such as "It jolly is!" and "I jolly won't!" A natural comedian who was accident prone. Never, let it be quite clear, in an aeroplane. But quite deliberately as part of the image.

Early one morning, just as we were getting well into our stride as the faultless drill squad, Nobby had a genuine and disastrous accident. He saluted to the left with his left hand. Our instructors had a field day – suggesting that if one highly trained officer could make such an error there would be others. Bad habits, picked up on war service, must be eradicated. On second thoughts our special course might be in need of even more square bashing than usual. The message was clear. We had lost!

COMBAT AND COMPETITION

In reality the drill instructors were a good bunch, who took pride in their work and earned our respect. At ITW, dealing with aircrew trainees impatient to be on their way, they had an unrewarding task.

In the classrooms we battled with the intricacies of navigation, stripped and rebuilt the .303 Browning until we could do it blindfold, and sweated to make twelve words a minute at Morse. Meteorology, with hindsight, was treated surprisingly in the abstract. For our future safety in the air might well depend on a good practical understanding of the subject – and particularly of frontal systems.

Almost from the moment of our arrival a state of warfare had existed between Pat Garland, at thirty six the old man of the course, and the Commanding Officer. The latter, portly and slow witted, was no match for Pat's rapier like charm and determination. When his brother won a posthumous VC, attacking the Maastricht bridges, Pat decided to transfer to the RAF. Now en route to Mustangs it never occurred to him that he was well past the age at which most fighter recce pilots would be retiring from ops.

As the weeks went by the relationship between Pat and the CO got steadily worse. Matters came to a head one Saturday night when the regular pub crawl, returning to base, found that the bar had just been closed. Pat's bete noir had clamped down – and there he was, large as life, smiling at our discomfiture. When he refused to reopen the bar there was near mutiny.

The next morning Pat put his troops to work and shortly after dark everything was in place. A light fingered character had dealt with the lock on the french windows to the CO's office. A large and smelly ewe, 'borrowed' from an unsuspecting local farmer, had been herded in for the night. And just to be sure that she was comfortable we left her with a supply of hay and water and a large amount of straw bedding.

It was a great pity that the CO's reaction could not be recorded for posterity. But it was enough that the whole course was summoned to view the results, presumably in an effort to get someone to talk, and to see for ourselves that the wretched man was speechless with rage. He left no stone unturned in his efforts to find the culprit. Every vehicle on the place, service and civilian, was checked for sheep droppings, and the local farmers all received a visit. But he drew a complete blank.

Around this time the seconded Army officers acquired a collective name. It may well have arisen from the episode of the sheep. Maybe

CHAPTER TWO   MARKING TIME

it was intended as an expression of admiration. Maybe not. Less offensive sounding when spoken in the Scottish vernacular we adopted it as a sort of backhanded compliment from our RAF colleagues. From now on we were the "Broon Fockerrs!" – BFs for short.

My most vivid memory of ITW concerns a game of rugger, BFs versus the rest. We gathered on the sports field, down by the Grand Hotel – white shorts and coloured tops, Red for the Army and blue for the RAF.

About halfway through the second half, when we were all beginning to feel the strain, there was the snarl of an unfamiliar aero engine and a Focke Wulf 190 streaked low overhead and pulled up into a steep climbing turn.

Everyone scattered and dived madly into the boundary hedge, regardless of thorns and scratches, as the Hun fighter lined up. Cannon and machine guns winked viciously. The cover was thin and we must have been clearly visible in our sports kit. Yet he missed – his shells raking the turf some yards away. Then he was gone, swinging up and round for a second pass.

I cringed to the ground, convinced that my last hour had come. But no, the same thing happened again – and then, as he pulled up, a flame appeared under the fuselage. He continued climbing and jettisoned the canopy, simultaneously rolling inverted, but the nose dropped before he could get out. Later we learned that a bombardier from the nearby coastal battery, armed with a single Lewis gun, had shot him down – and probably saved our lives into the bargain.

A few weeks later we were on our way to Desford, near Leicester, exchanging the mellow South Devon air for the harsher feel of approaching winter.

No 7 EFTS[14] had become a Grading School. A filter through which those who passed were accepted into the Empire Air Training Scheme and those who failed could be 'Returned to Unit' without further cost to the taxpayer.

Grading involved some twelve hours flying, mostly dual, and two 'Flying Aptitude Assessment Tests'. In addition we understood that it was necessary to go solo in less than ten hours.

Messing and sleeping quarters were in a hut which had once belonged to the Leicester Aero Club. The interior was reminiscent of an ocean going yacht gone to seed – grossly overheated and ill ventilated. But sleep came easily after a day in an open cockpit.

We were fortunate with the weather. It was anticyclonic throughout

COMBAT AND COMPETITION

the whole of our course, and the fog usually cleared to allow several hours of intensive flying. A brisk walk across the airfield to the sound of Merlin engines, as Reid and Sigrist readied their latest batch of Spitfires for testing, made a pleasant start to the day.

Then the pressure was on. You pushed your way into the crowded flight hut, scrambled into your flying kit, and attempted to corner your instructor. There was a bit of 'first come, first served' about it all, particularly after you had gone solo. With luck you might even persuade him to book you out in a spare Tiger, after a quick dual circuit.

Memories of Desford are of calm cloudless days, with hardly a sign of turbulence, and the haze so thick in the circuit that it was barely possible to see the assembly sheds against the winter sun. Overhead, and on the approach, the place swarmed with Tigers. An occasional Spitfire would sweep low over the field, pull up steeply, lower its wheels while still inverted and roll out on a precise curved approach all the way to touchdown. A glimpse of what the future might hold if you made it.

All the BFs got through and my time at Twinwood Farm paid off handsomely. But it would be almost three months before our training got under way once more on the far side of the Atlantic.

CHAPTER THREE

PRELUDE TO BATTLE

The Empire Air Training Scheme was an outstanding achievement. In Canada alone the basic facts were impressive enough. The first course opened in April 1940, four months from a standing start, and by mid '43 the number of schools had risen to ninety two.

Even more remarkable was the way in which the standards of flying training and airmanship were maintained in the face of such a huge expansion. So much depended on the instructors and it was they, above all, who made the system work. Locked in for the duration as a result of age, or skills which could not be spared, the great majority would have given their eye teeth for a posting on ops. Their contribution has never been properly recognised.

Roy Waigh was one of them. He commanded one of the flights at 35 EFTS Neepawa, to the west of Winnipeg, and I was incredibly lucky to have had him as my instructor. For nothing, before or since, has had such a positive influence on my flying. A modest man, not much given to small talk, Roy was married and lived off the station. I never got to know him socially. Even so, in the short time that we were together, he was much more than just a gifted instructor. In the ways of the air and of airmanship he was my guide, counsellor and friend.

It was Roy who introduced me to the snow covered airfield, and the winterised Tiger Moths with their canopies and skis. I flew occasionally with other instructors. But it was he who took me through the whole range of exercises, who set the standards, and taught me to be analytical about my flying.

Neepawa. Where the skies were brilliant blue, and the snowfields bright and clean. Where the sun always shone and we flew morning noon and night. It was not unusual to be airborne three or four hours a day, for several days on end, and I once managed to put almost five hours under my belt. There was a freshness about EFTS. An awakening sense of discovery almost like early childhood. As if life was starting all over again. Twinwood Farm and Desford had become part of an earlier era. And always my growing passion for the air beckoned me on.

Climbing out over the prairie for a session of aerobatics. The atmosphere was clear as crystal. The checkerboard landscape stood out against the snow, extending far beyond the horizon. Here and there a group of grain elevators, or a township, bordered the railroad track.

COMBAT AND COMPETITION

Otherwise there was nothing. Just miles of open country, devoid of cover, the heartland of Canada's cereal farming in the iron grip of winter.

Four thousand feet and a stall turn to start the sequence. Hold the dive and pull through into a loop. Up and over. Another loop. And again. Pushing the learning curve. Aware of the CFI's[1] test to come. Now a slow roll – horizon, snow and section lines slewing horribly across my vision.

Bloody awful..... I could almost hear the familiar voice ringing in my ears:

"More top rudder! – Keep the stick forward!"

The next one was better. And the next. But I must talk to Roy about my slow rolls.

A change to forced landings. Cut the throttle and swing earthwards in a long descending arc. You're getting too close to the field! Remember to warm the engine. Your still too close! Another quick burst of power. Down and down in a long slipping turn..... You're too high!..... More sideslip!..... Then up and away before the snow can catch your skis.

My chosen field, exactly one mile square and flat as board, was too easy by far. But there was no alternative, they were all the same, hundreds of them, as far as the eye could see.

A first crack at low flying. On an afternoon when Roy was feeling benevolent. Real scenery, for a change, in the foothills of Riding Mountain. A fascinating sense of speed, as the countryside flooded past like a river in spate. Features on the surface – a farmhouse, a group of tall trees, or a sudden escarpment – rushed at you destructively.

We all longed for the day when we could practise it on our own. But the RAF knew better. They understood the dangers, the impetuosity of youth, and the deadly temptation to fly ever lower. Our time would come at OTU and not before. Unauthorised low flying was, and still is, the most heinous crime in the book. It could finish your flying career in a number of different ways. All of them unpleasant. Better by far to rely on the presence of an instructor.

Amongst that album of memories there is a vivid picture of night flying. The last landing at the end of a session. With my eye well in and my finger out. Crosswind on the final turn. Flares guttering against the snow. Green all the way on the Glide Path Indicator[2]. The round-out neat and precise. The touchdown smooth as silk. It was a

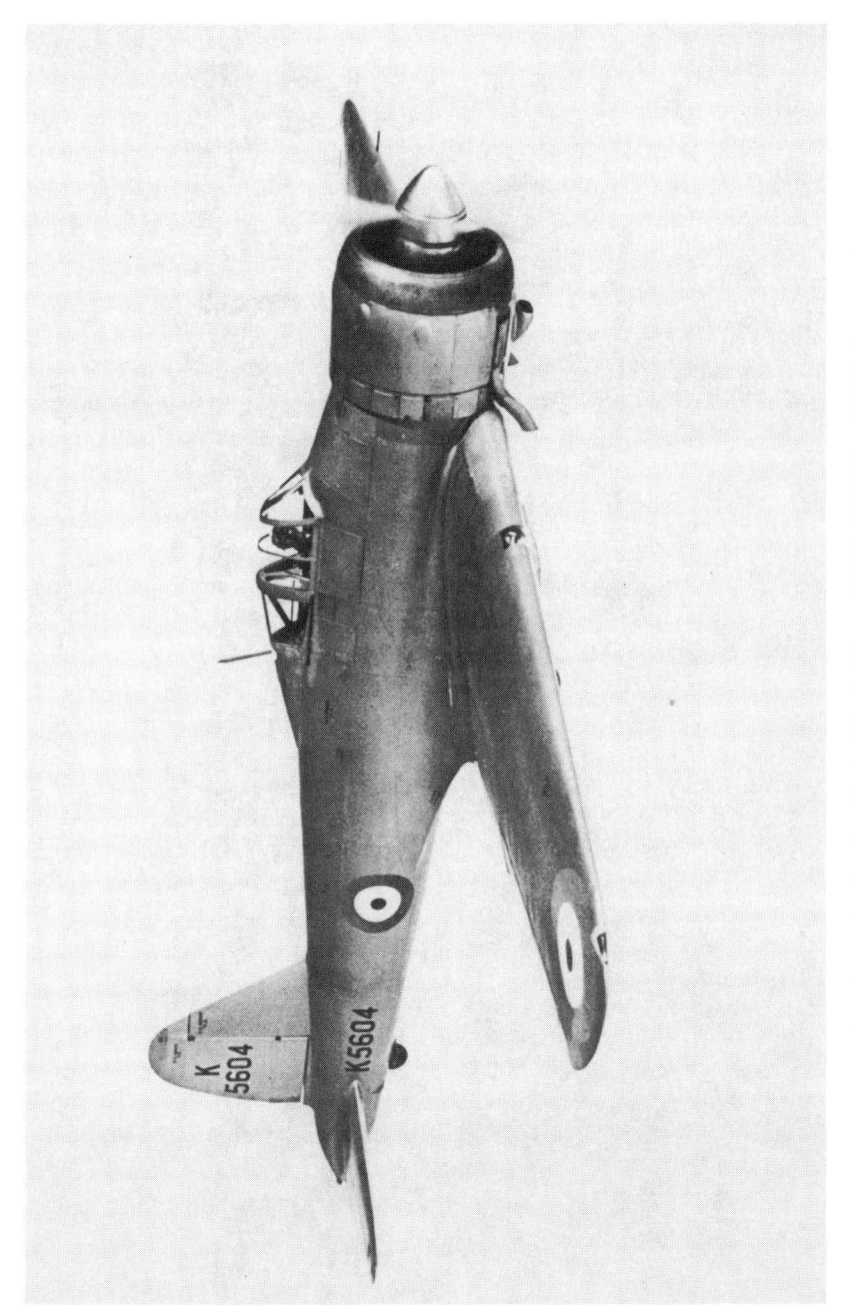

Hand on the spade grip - Head in the Clouds. Gloster F5/34, 1938 (Photo British Aerospace.)

No. 80 Course, 35 EFTS Neepawa 1943. Seated left to right: Lt Ian Stewart, Author, Instructors Fl Lt Roy Waigh (centre) and Sgt Sankey (3rd from right), Lt Geoffrey Bensusan (next right) and his two colleagues are in army uniform.

CHAPTER THREE   PRELUDE TO BATTLE

rare moment of near perfection. I felt like a god and the mug of hot chocolate, on my way to bed, tasted like nectar.

Pride comes before a fall. And mine happened soon afterwards. One evening, towards the end of the course, the mess was almost deserted. Just the three BFs – and an instructor who invited us to join him in a drink. After several double whiskies, he announced that he had to carry out an air test before dark. He must go and do it forthwith. Would one of us like to join him?

It seemed a good idea at the time. But his air test soon developed into an impromptu aerobatic display. His loops and rolls got lower and hairier. Apart from the risk of sudden death, this performance could mean curtains for two flying careers. There was no difficulty in feigning immediate and violent air sickness and to my great relief he took the hint. Never have I been so glad to step out of an aircraft.

On the following morning, as we walked together across the snow covered tarmac, Roy looked steadfastly into the distance:

"You were flying yesterday evening." It was a statement, not a question.

"Yes, Roy," I said, "and it wasn't much fun."

We had arrived at the aircraft. He turned and studied me carefully, more in sorrow than in anger:

"That's what I thought. I hope you'll never do it again."

The weather broke only once during our stay at Neepawa, with a blizzard which lasted for several days. Apart from that one occasion we rarely suffered from much in the way of wind. Which was just as well. Skis on an icy surface could be tricky, and it was sensible to keep a close watch on the sock. Taxying, even in moderately gusty conditions, rapidly became impossible as the aircraft slithered sideways and weathercocked out of control. For the airmen, who rushed out to hang on the wing tips, the combination of cold, slipstream, and wind chill must have been quite horrendous.

During the final week of the course, in the midst of cross countries, winter suddenly gave way to spring. There were problems in landing away because some of the destination airfields thawed out faster than others. Our Tigers were back on wheels while Neepawa was still covered in snow and my first ever runway landing occurred solo on an out and return flight to another School. I was completely thrown by the dark ribbon of tarmac, in total contrast to the surrounding snow, and held off much too high.

A quick burst of throttle saved the day, and fortunately Tigers are

COMBAT AND COMPETITION

strong, but it was an untidy arrival to say the least.

Two weeks later we gathered outside the hangers to arrange ourselves for a photograph in front of the obligatory aeroplane. No 80 course was over.

Rolling across the prairie, on the journey to Vancouver, Canadian Pacific provided the usual comforts. The big coaches equal to the best of Pullmans by day and the upper and lower bunks, which swung into place when required, were as comfortable as one could have wished. In the mornings, after a relaxed night between freshly laundered sheets, there was that unbelievable breakfast – blueberries and cream, eggs sunny side up, flapjacks and honey, rounded off with excellent coffee.

Then, if so disposed, you could repair to that chauvinistic delight of the North American railroads, the club compartment. A retreat where male passengers could take their ease undisturbed by the ladies. It certainly brought out the worst in our colleague Lieutenant Kenneth Morris. On his first and only visit Kenneth pushed open the door, stood for a moment like some latter day Goebbels, to whom he bore more than a passing resemblance, peered through the smoke, homed in on the spittoons and said loudly:

"How absolutely disgusting!"

We tried to convey silent apology to the other occupants and hustled him out before he could do any further damage. But relations were strained for the rest of the journey.

After leave in British Columbia we returned through the Rockies to Calgary, home of 37 SFTS[3], to find that most of the BFs – sent to different places for elementary training – were together again. A few of our fellow pupils had come straight from American flying schools where they had failed to make the grade. As was customary, and frequently successful, they were being given another chance in Canada.

Some of their stories were quite extraordinary. Trainees on the most junior course were required to eat 'square meals' – following a dogleg route from plate to mouth. Marching round the perimeter track in full kit and parachute during the heat of the day, or sitting on the 'T' after flying was over, were typical punishments for quite trivial offences.

Instructors often shouted in the air and threatened physical violence. Maybe this worked with the average American trainee, and their system seemed to produce plenty of the 'right stuff' during the

CHAPTER THREE   PRELUDE TO BATTLE

war, but it went down rather badly with our chaps.

In contrast to this brash American scene I was singularly fortunate, once more, in the matter of instructors. Ossie Ossulton had almost never been known to raise his voice in anger and his easy manner concealed a highly professional approach. He had remarkable way with him – which pushed and encouraged his pupils and yet, almost paradoxically, exercised a powerful restraint on their youthful exuberance.

We set out to master the Harvard's complexities – variable pitch propeller, retractable undercarriage and flaps – sitting in the cockpit and running through the drills until we knew them by heart. First solo came up in less than five hours and we were soon well into the new training programme.

The Harvard had a tailwheel with a very small positive castor angle and a rudimentary form of steering. The makers, North American Aviation, obviously approved of this arrangement because it appeared on the Mustang in a slightly different form. Described in the Pilot's Notes thus:

Steerable tailwheel, this springs into engagement with the rudder so that, when taxying or in gradual turns it can be used for steering. If a sharp turn is made, the tailwheel can spring out of engagement, this will occur more easily if the stick is not held back.

What they did not explain was that if a swing started on landing and this was corrected by differential braking – which in turn caused the pilot to apply an unintentionally large rudder angle – the tailwheel could unlock and precipitate a ground loop! It sounds worse than it really was. But for all that it was a feature which I did not like. In other ways the Harvard was pleasant and easy to fly. Our Mk II version was said to have a more docile stall than the Mk I. It still spun very positively and would do splendid flick rolls.

Shortly after going solo in the Harvard I visited the largest store in town. To my surprise they could supply sun glasses made up to your own prescription. Better still, one of the frames on offer looked almost identical to the standard service issue. I had solved the problem of flying in spectacles without being found out.

As the course progressed some of the flying took place from Airdrie about a dozen miles north of Calgary. A dry featureless sort place where you could sunbathe between flights, and take photographs round the airfield, which would have been out of the question back at base. After a night flying session it was customary to sleep there and

COMBAT AND COMPETITION

the round trip was sometimes completed with an early formation practice on the way home.

Hardly a tremor in the air. Not a cloud in the sky. The climb out steady as a rock. The mud brown hills, bordering the prairie, looked parched and dusty – the mountains beyond in strong relief against the distant blue. Each time the formation swung into a turn the morning sun came flooding across the cockpit, blinding you with its glare. Working hard to hold station beside the leader you were aware, as always, of his instructor watching you like a hawk. Distrusting. Ambivalent. As if warning you to keep your distance and in the same breath challenging you to do better.

Later, whilst we sweated to fly accurately in the heat and turbulence of the day, small cumulus filled the sky. When the air was more unstable those harmless fair weather clouds grew into thunderstorms which swept across the countryside in the late evenings. It was in such conditions that Ian Stewart lost his life.

Flying night circuits from Airdrie he got caught in a line squall, blinded by heavy rain and low cloud. His aircraft must have been thrown around by the violent turbulence, toppling the gyro instruments and disorienting him completely. He ended up in a spiral dive from which there was no recovery. A few days later six of his fellow BFs were pall bearers at his funeral.

Incensed at the instruction to carry his coffin at the 'trail' instead of shoulder high, to avoid offending the locals, we had argued strongly against it:

"To hell with Canadian practice" – we had said – "Ian was our friend, not their's." But the Station Commander was adamant.

It was an arid service, in a soulless modern church and the committal was hot and dusty. A sad waste of a young life. We took ourselves back to the mess for one of our better parties, a spontaneous gathering of the hard core BFs, in farewell to the first of their number to get the chop.

After that we needed a break – and what better than Banff, just 80 miles away in the Rockies. It had looked marvellous on the trip to Vancouver and the reality was even better. The spacious Banff Springs Hotel, a huge echoing edifice reminiscent of Southern Germany, was comfortable and uncrowded.

Lazing around a swimming pool was never my idea of fun. But this one was fed with hot mineral waters and the glass walls looked out at the Cascade Mountains. Besides which we had brought a good supply

CHAPTER THREE   PRELUDE TO BATTLE

of rye whisky. Alcohol and altitude are a heady mixture often, in my experience, without the penalty of a hangover. For much of the time I was gently inebriated and totally captivated by British Columbia. Even to the extent of thinking about bush flying there after the war..... If there was to be an after the war!

When we got back to Calgary an army of graders and road making machinery was hard at work, building a runway to the west of the airfield. The first Airacobras and Kittihawks started to use it before it was even finished. They came straight in from the south in loose gaggles, without any pretence of a circuit, and were gone in the morning before we were up and about. Their numbers increased day by day and soon there were bombers as well. Aid for our Russian allies and tangible evidence of the massive production capacity of the American war industry.

With the end of the course in sight the pace quickened. Formation flying, navigation and gunnery were the order of the day, together with long sweaty sessions under the hood. Anson sorties were an unwelcome chore, more appropriate to navigator training, and the staff pilots were given to practising evasive action whenever one of the 'hands' went aft to relieve himself. The BFs evolved a punishment to fit the crime. An ambush in the dark and a jug of iced water delivered precisely into the front of the perpetrator's trousers.

Just after the final flying tests my logbook was taken away. It would be returned, bound in leather, on Wings Parade. The custom at Calgary for those who came top of the course. I thought with gratitude of 613 Squadron, of Roy Waigh and Ossie..... It was very much their show.

At Moncton, waiting for the next boat home, I spent much of the time with David Tomlinson. Already making a name for himself on stage and screen, his past had caught up with him, and he was being urged to leave the RAF and return to acting. He could, they said, make a greater contribution to the war effort by playing in patriotic films, and yet he desperately wanted to fly on ops. We talked about it often during those idle weeks and I argued that, as an actor, his knowledge of the RAF and service flying would be invaluable. And so it proved to be, for his portrayals of aircrew, in later wartime releases, were quite masterly.

When our sailing orders came through it was the Queen Elizabeth again, sailing from Halifax, and crowded with American troops bound for Europe. With some 15,000 on board the enlisted men had to share

COMBAT AND COMPETITION

bunks, on a rota basis, which must have added considerably to the discomforts of the voyage. Meals were served in an endless series of sittings, and we soon got brassed off with the nonstop tannoy messages:

"This is the third call for dinner. All with white cards form your line."

In fact there was only time to provide each passenger with two meals a day. So the wise made up a bacon butty at breakfast, to fill the midday void, then slept and read the long hours away until the next call came round.

All day long, a mass of American soldiers surged round the halls and stairways. Little groups huddled in every available corner playing poker or shooting craps. The air reeked of cigars and the decks were littered with empty tins of coke. Fortunately the weather was calm and for much of the time our presence was concealed by thick banks of fog. Even so it was a voyage to be ended quickly and we were glad when the ship reached her anchorage in the Clyde.

Many years later I read an account of the Queens' trooping activities during the war. With such huge passenger loads they were alleged to be barely stable. Had an enemy appeared violent evasive action would have been quite impossible. Sometimes it is just as well to be ignorant!

It would be better to draw a veil over the period of enforced idleness at Harrogate, the worst time of all. A brief interlude with the Aircrew Officers School at Sidmouth, a sort of post graduate ITW, helped to keep us occupied. Escape and evasion had been added to the syllabus and, amongst other delights, we were shown how to break the neck of a German sentry with his own coal scuttle helmet. It was said to be very easy, but practice was forbidden!

Small arms training was also included – to help us play an effective part in airfield defence – but not to increase the fire power of friendly resistance fighters should we be shot down amongst them. Our duty in those circumstances was to evade and get home. Not to stay and fight.

As we practised with rifle, bayonet and sandbag dummies, and carried out firing practice on the Sten, that explanation began to sound less and less likely. Maybe there was a more sinister purpose behind our spell at Sidmouth – like a last minute transfer to the RAF Regiment or as infantry reinforcements for the second front. Difficult to judge, because we only knew the RAF side of the story, and mostly by rumour, but it was discouraging enough.

The surplus in single engined pilots was now so great that the vast

CHAPTER THREE   PRELUDE TO BATTLE

majority, apart from the BFs who were lined up for Fighter Recce, come what may, were likely to become reinforcements for Bomber Command. Worse still the AFU[4]/OTU pipeline was running in excess of squadron needs and we might be stranded at Harrogate for months on end.

From the moment of our arrival at Peterborough these fears were all forgotten. A first glimpse of the airfield on a frosty December afternoon – yellow sodium lights in the dusk, Masters on the approach like geese against the sunset – was more than enough. The BFs were back in business.

No 7 (Pilot) Advanced Flying Unit was a place of contrasts. In the depths of a British winter, our flying hours built up even faster than they had done in Canada. A tribute to the way in which the unit was run, the standards of aircraft serviceability, and above all to the instructors.

On the other hand there was little evidence of objectives and there were no progress tests.

At first I wondered if the sole purpose was to keep us in flying practice, until an OTU, somewhere, was ready for another intake. And yet, if you looked closely, there was a pattern. An emphasis on air to air camera gun sorties, practice interceptions, and attacks on 'enemy bombers' to prepare the up and coming fighter boy for his traditional role. Even curved approaches were set up on the Master, with 23° of flap, to simulate the lift/drag characteristics of a Spitfire.

Conversion to European conditions was taken seriously and the need for night training brought an introduction to the joys of Two Stage Amber[5], known as 'Sodium Flying'. The former was largely a matter of navigation, learning to cope with a mass of ground detail, poor visibility, the absence of section lines, and a careful introduction to the hazards of a maritime climate.

Sodium flying turned brightest day into darkest synthetic night. It was an unpleasant exercise and, like most of us, I disliked it intensely. For a start I could not wear my sunglasses with their hidden corrective lenses, although this was more of an irritant than anything else. The sodium goggles were cumbersome and uncomfortable, and their tunnel vision caused problems in locating the flarepath. Fortunately we were never subjected to it again after leaving AFU.

After my inexperienced encounter with the Master at Twinwood Farm it was surprising to realise that it cruised a good deal faster than the Harvard, and had a much higher rate of climb. The stall with

COMBAT AND COMPETITION

wheels and flaps down, and the rear canopy raised, demanded respect – as the aircraft flicked inverted without any warning – and the heavy ailerons were a disappointment.

There were many reminders of a changed world. Not least in the crowded East Anglian skies of USAF daylight ops and Bomber Command air tests. Day after day the P38s[6] from nearby Kingscliffe assembled overhead, squadron by squadron, before winging their way to war. We watched them returning – seeing the gaps in their ranks.

One came home with an entire engine missing. Difficult to imagine how such a massive object could have broken away without total destruction. He passed low overhead, long after the rest of the wing had landed, escorted by his wingman and another.

On clear nights East Anglia was lit up by a vast array of bomber airfields. Each one, with its flarepath and circle of lead-in lights, resembled a faintly glittering compass. They created a welcome landscape in the darkness. You could tell when it was like that, long before your turn to fly, by the relaxed atmosphere in the crew room.

When marginal weather coincided with the heavies taking a break you groped around, beacon flying, and worried like hell if the flare path disappeared. With good reason too. No nav aids. Dubious radio and, unlike the bomber boys, ours was no Drem[7] lighting system. We had to make do with a few gooseneck flares[8], on a grass strip, and the river with its constant threat of fog was only a mile away.

Amongst our instructors at Peterborough was Alf Warminger, an ex Battle of Britain pilot, in due course to become Sheriff of Norwich. Although neither of us knew it at the time, Alf was a future gliding colleague who, like myself, would still be active more than 45 years later. I flew with him on a couple of occasions and it was he who briefed me for my first flight in a Hurricane. The most clapped out aircraft ever. It had been built in 1938.

One day cruising southwards in that old Hurricane I managed to stalk a P38. The air was full of brickwork smoke, burnt blanket smelling muck, and the visibility at cloud base very poor. Easy to creep up behind him until my propeller was only feet behind his tail. I sat there, looking along the length of the twin booms with their big airscoops and down through the transparent rear of the humpbacked canopy, and wondered if he had fallen asleep. Suddenly he rolled onto his back, faster than my ancient steed could ever follow, and pulled away in a long vertical dive.

As I levelled out another twin boom shape slanted across my bows.

CHAPTER THREE   PRELUDE TO BATTLE

But this one had a bulbous fuselage and no propellers. The de Havilland Spider Crab, forerunner of the Vampire. I watched in fascination as it swept upwards and out of sight.

The Hurricane was a reminder of operational flying to come. An idea which proved too much for one member of our little band. The fumes in the cockpit made him feel faint, yet no one else was affected, and carbon monoxide checks revealed nothing amiss. Quite suddenly he vanished.

'Returned to Unit' – the ultimate disgrace. Was he LMF[9]? Had he deliberately applied for a pilot's course, to spin out the time before he had to face the enemy, hoping that the war might be over by then? His fellow BFs would never know.

The rest of us were off, soon afterwards, to a satellite of 41 OTU on the Duke of Westminster's estate south of Chester where the approach was totally different to anything which had gone before. After a dual check on an elderly MkI Harvard it was assumed that you knew how to fly. Type conversions were to be made with a minimum of fuss. Demonstrations were brief and to the point. Given the basics you were expected to work things out for yourself.

Spring had come. The scent of new mown grass filled the air. On the Welsh mountain peaks the last of the snow had gone and the banks of the Dee beside Eaton Hall were ablaze with daffodils.

A springtime of wonderful memories. Soon after our arrival a batch of Hurricane IIcs arrived straight off the production line. With their metal skinned wings and more powerful engines they were better than anything we had flown before. The four unfaired 20mm cannon looked suitably functional. And the essence of their newness – unblemished cockpits, smooth control mechanisms and the aromatic mixture of factory fresh materials and recently applied dope – was an added pleasure on every flight.

There was something immensely satisfying about the rugged feel of a Hurricane. The sturdy wide track undercarriage, the straightforward handling and the commanding position from which you viewed the world at large. So what if it was slower and less elegant than the Spitfire! This was a man's aeroplane – in which you would have been content go to war. But the Hurricane's fighting days were almost over. I recalled the Typhoons of 56 Squadron, which had so attracted me almost two years before. Yet how could the Hurricane's successor play any part in my future, as a seconded Army officer, indelibly labelled 'fighter recce'?

COMBAT AND COMPETITION

Fighter recce – for a start our navigation had to be improved until we could find our way to an exact position and it had to be straight in and out again, otherwise you greatly increased the risk of being caught by flak or fighters. 'Pinpointing' was easy to set up, given a large scale map and a prewar tourist guide. It was an exercise that came in two versions. Start out with a map reference and bring back the description of a building or other feature – or the reverse, with a photograph to look at beforehand and a defined area in which to search.

For Tac-R[10] training we could hardly have been better placed. The roads south from Glasgow and Liverpool, and to the west of Birmingham were carrying large numbers of troops on their way to the concentration areas for 'Overlord'[11]. These military convoys were used to teach us the principles of medium and low level tactical reconnaissance. Valuable as this undoubtedly was, it was curiously open ended. There was little evidence that our reports were being monitored by instructor check sorties, or in any other way.

Nor were we given any serious training with ground troops using camouflage, or in minimising the risks from flak or, for that matter, in being bounced by 'enemy' aircraft. For the latter an occasional sortie by one the instructors, with an otherwise idle Mustang, would have been more than sufficient to keep us on our toes.

One hot and hazy afternoon David Hurford and I were briefed for a practice Tac-R sortie. By now we had put in some 20 hours apiece on the Hurricane. Flying it was becoming second nature. Even selecting undercarriage 'up' – which meant changing hands on the stick – had become a practised art.

Our departure was neat and tidy, no porpoising to spoil it, as the wheels tucked themselves away. We moved quickly into battle formation, riding the turbulence, climbing through the murk, into air which was calm and clear. The haze layer, falling away beneath our wings, had a well defined upper surface. It veiled the landscape in shades of purple and bronze, and thickened into the distance, until it became another horizon hiding the earthly one below.

Our task, searching the roads along the Severn valley, would not be easy. But, before long, there was something very different to distract us.

Interference on the radio. Faint and disjointed at first. Then louder and unbroken. The great rolling cadenzas filled my earphones. Beethoven's Emperor Concerto. An unforgettable experience which I shall treasure always.

CHAPTER THREE   PRELUDE TO BATTLE

I pulled closer to my companion. Watching the powerful hump backed shape and the spinning disc of the big constant speed propeller as he drifted towards me. David, in the rostrum of his cockpit, visibly conducting with his left hand!

"Where's your baton, David?"

We dropped briefly into the murk, towards the river bridges below, looking for signs of movement and his reply echoed my thoughts:

"Absolutely super! - shall we turn back and hear the rest?"

The nobility of the heavens seemed all around us, as we cruised on, accompanied by those fading sounds from another age. And the magic of our Hurricanes added to the spell. Winging across the years.....

The Luftwaffe knew how to use the power of music to motivate its pilots in their great defensive battles over the Fatherland. Just as today's America Cup contenders, with their modern audio systems, apply the same techniques to blast and hype their way to victory. Easy to understand after that memorable experience above the river Severn.

Low level Tac-R was something else again. Down on the deck, you hugged the contours, watching for power lines, checking your track. In a Tiger Moth the countryside had flooded past like a river in spate. With a Hurricane it became a raging torrent. Slowing as you lifted briefly over some obstruction, accelerating violently as you dropped close to the ground on the other side. A familiar illusion which never failed to excite. Low flying was and always will be an addiction, an exhilarating pastime, requiring skill and absolute concentration.

The lethal temptation, to fly lower still, was always present. There was an issue of 'Tee Emm'[12] to remind us all about it - with a picture displaying the remains of a Hurricane. A trail of wreckage littered the length of an open field and, where it ended, a larger collection of debris surrounded a battered Merlin engine and a bucket seat. That the pilot, incredibly, had survived almost unscathed was beside the point. The total disintegration of his aircraft was enough.

An isolated line of wooded hills marked by the ruins of Beeston Castle, guards the eastern boundary of the Cheshire plain. On many a day we hurdled that ridge aiming for the distant Victorian outlines of Eaton Hall. Then, as the Dee glistened through the trees, hard back on the stick and into the circuit, curbing the Merlin's song. In the wake of our passage a rich dairy farming countryside, large estates and well set up Georgian houses. Long after the drum roll crescendos of our low flying Hurricanes have become a distant memory they will still be there.

COMBAT AND COMPETITION

Once, on my own, I was contour chasing near the borders of Shropshire and Offa's Dyke. Where mountains give way to wooded hills and castles mark the scenes of ancient wars. Suddenly I came on a long unbroken ridge, the edge of a lofty plateau, which stood high above its surroundings facing west. Something about it made me look closer – and there on top was a blister hanger, locked and silent, and the faint impression of a landing ground in the heather. Slowing down I could almost sense the powerful wind striking that escarpment and the fragile sailplane shapes, poised in the updraft overhead, as I had seen them at Sutton Bank before the war.

A moment more to absorb the scene, and then out into the valley again, back to the world of Tac-R, and the roads leading south towards Hereford and Gloucester..... Other times and other skills..... I vowed that some day, somehow, I would be back.

The Hurricanes were equipped for oblique and vertical photography and after a single Harvard sortie, to demonstrate the technique, you were sent out on your own. It was an effective approach – because each exercise produced its own immediate results, wet prints to study whilst the flight was still fresh in your mind, and this led to a rapid improvement in skill.

Our instructors had their moment of fun, demanding a vertical pinpoint of Ince Hall, a decaying country seat, which they had unearthed on the Wirral peninsular. The photographs were duly displayed, with captions suitably worded, to suggest a close family connection. It could hardly have been further from the truth!

Sqn Ldr Majumdar was our mature student. A prewar Cranwell cadet he had returned home, to early command of No 1 Squadron Indian Air Force, where he had won a DFC fighting the Japs. Proud in the best sense of the word, a powerful character, Karen Krishna Majumdar had given up a staff appointment and dropped a rank in order to broaden his experience by flying on ops in Europe. A splendid man. In the words of that earlier war 'One would have been happy to go over the top with him.'

But that was hardly the situation as we taxied out together and lined up for take off. Combat was almost the last exercise before our conversion to Mustangs and, to my delight, I had been chosen to joust with this formidable adversary. Drawing the short straw perhaps – but there was much to be gained from such an encounter.

Fifteen thousand feet – and we were rushing towards each other almost head on. A brief glimpse of a grey-green shape standing on its

CHAPTER THREE   PRELUDE TO BATTLE

wing tip, as it hurtled past in a violent turn – and the sudden onset of 'G' – vision momentarily fading. Within moments we were locked into a winding match, throttles wide open, pulling on the limit..... and this man was good! Almost ten years my senior and he was doing his utmost to reel himself in my tail.

Escape from that turning contest was almost impossible, although both of us kept trying, for our aircraft were equally matched. And so, as our height drained away, we worked and sweated, and endured the 'G'. Only the threat of cannon shells was missing as we strove to break each other's will. After what seemed an age, but was probably only a matter of minutes, our battle was deemed to be over. Inconclusive perhaps – but for me at least, as we clambered down from our aircraft and walked across to the NAAFI wagon for a much needed mug of tea, it had been a valuable experience.

My adversary went on to complete a tour with 268 Squadron, collecting a bar to his DFC, and then returned to India. Soon after I was saddened to hear that he had lost his life in a flying display.

Mustang flying took place at Hawarden. We were allowed rather less than two hours general handling, and then it was all gunnery, for a further eighteen hours. Surprising because the Mustang was a very different aircraft to the Hurricane – heavier, faster, and with large area camber changing flaps. It had a low drag wing, long range, good if rather bland handling and a clean very roomy cockpit with excellent instruments and secondary controls. However it lacked the RAF's standard blind flying panel and the seating position, although more 'G' tolerant than its British counterparts, did not feel quite right. Like sitting in a bath, hardly the way to go to war, and not conducive to the harmonious relationship which I had so enjoyed with the Hurricane.

Perhaps I was biased, but there were other reasons too. The combination of toe brakes and tailwheel lock, which I had first encountered on the Harvard, made its presence felt quite early on. It happened when the lock broke at touch down and I ended up going backwards down the runway at about 80 miles an hour.

More to the point the Mustang was not as manoeuvrable as a Hurricane, our Allison engined versions were underpowered, and we received only limited advice on the use of flaps in combat.

If nothing else these features required time for practice. Which hardly happened at all.

In a Harvard - 37 SFTS Calgary 1943.

Debriefing - Left to right: Bill Switzer, Bunny Austin, Johnny Button with Air Liason and Intelligence Officers.

CHAPTER FOUR

TYPHOON

Lee-on-Solent, home of the Naval Spotting Pool, was occupied by no less than six squadrons – two from the Royal Air Force, equipped with Spitfire Vs, and four Fleet Air Arm units flying Seafires. It was crowded and uncomfortable. But that hardly mattered to the reinforcements from Hawarden who had arrived, full of enthusiasm, ready to play their part in the Normandy landings.

The CO took a different view. We had received no training in Naval Bombardment and he was under strict instructions to conserve the flying hours on his aircraft for maximum effort during the invasion. They were not to be used for type conversion. We were grounded. Not allowed to fly a Spitfire until we'd flown one!

Wandering disconsolately around the dispersals I ran into John Irving who had trained with us in Canada. He had joined one of the squadrons from a Spitfire OTU and was cleared to fly escort. It was hard to bear.

During those pre-invasion weeks, with the station almost cut off from the outside world, its occupants were involved in their own private battle. Pilots deprived of the delights of Pompey[1] were apt to live it up in the bar. Elderly staff officers regarded the wardroom as a civilised place and objected to the inroads into their precious supplies of gin. Some even expected to find the paper of their choice neatly folded beside their recognised breakfast places. We considered such practices arrogant in time of war and did our best to disrupt them. One way and another the navy was certainly different.

Geoff Hartley thought so too. He was the senior flight commander and had led the two RAF Squadrons on their move to Lee-on-Solent. On arrival he had made himself known to the duty officer who looked him over and asked him if he was in charge. Geoff agreed that he was – to which the response went something like this:

"You chaps had better watch it here. There's a limit on wardroom bills for those below the rank of Lieutenant Commander."

Geoff, a Yorkshireman, whose relaxed and affable manner belied a forceful personality, was absolutely livid. He got his own back, night after night, by arriving at opening time with his pilots. They bought tots of gin in advance of consumption, stored the contents in a jug, and so prevented the Navy's limited supplies from falling into the wrong hands!

The surrounding area was packed with troops preparing to embark

COMBAT AND COMPETITION

for the invasion. Security was tight. There were signs galore – "Do not loiter. Civilians must not talk to troops". The Spitfires, which we were forbidden to fly, were being painted with black and white stripes. History was in the making and, unless something happened soon, we would be left sitting on the sidelines.

Fortunately our plight had been noted and we were posted to Cranfield for Spitfire conversion. The Mark V with its clipped wings and low altitude blower – unkindly described as 'Clipped, Clapped and Cropped' – was my favourite at first. But the Mark IX, more potent, especially at high altitude, grew on you with experience even if it had lost something in the purity of its handling due to the increased torque and gyroscopic effects of the more powerful Merlin engine. Both were a joy and we lived in a world of our own, for days on end, quietly hogging the hours.

On the last sortie from Cranfield I went on a solo battle climb, upwards through sunshine and shadow, until the cumulus dwindled into the distance below, and the supercharger thumped as it changed gear. Soon half of Southern England lay spread beneath my wings. The South Coast and the Isle of Wight were clearly visible, and my thoughts returned briefly to the invasion, wondering what the future had in store.

On the way home a familiar airfield came into view its runways and dispersal areas shimmering in the heat. There was no sign of activity, no aircraft in the circuit, perhaps they were all asleep. Temptation stirred. My Spitfire was unmarked. They would never be able to track me down.

I came out of the sun diving fast and low, battering the crowded dispersals with sound and sweeping upwards again in a sustained vertical roll. It was immensely satisfying.

I never took a Spitfire into battle. But the memories remain, bright and beautiful, like the summer skies over Bedfordshire where, for a brief moment, I learned to fly and love it.

Just before we were due to return to Lee-on-Solent there was a change of plan and we found ourselves en route for 84 GSU[2] at Aston Down. A pity in one respect that we never returned to those spotter squadrons. It would have been a splendid line shoot for the BFs:

"We are Army officers, seconded to the RAF, who hold commissions in both services and direct the fire of naval guns!"

As for the naval bombardment sorties, according to Geoff Hartley, they got off to rather a bad start. The first targets to be engaged were

Killy in his Typhoon at B3 St Croix Sur Mer, Normandy, 1944.

Flt Off Ben Lenson - with crew - whose bombs destroyed
Vianen bridge in January 1945.

"My dear the flak!" Johnny Button CO 193 Squadron, Normandy 1944.

With Pete Langille (Centre) and Jimmy Simpson (Right), Normandy, 1944.

CHAPTER FOUR   TYPHOON

coastal gun emplacements and armour piercing ammunition was used exclusively, even for ranging. After a number of pilots had returned from shoots over the invasion beaches, with nothing seen, they started to use H.E.[3]

Naval spotting then became a much more rewarding activity. The large calibre high explosive shells were easy to see, the opening shots were usually close to the target, the corrections were rapid and precise, and a salvo produced the most satisfying results. In fact the whole thing worked so well that it was quite possible to continue hitting enemy tanks and transport as they struggled to escape.

Aston Down supplied replacements, pilots and aircraft, for the squadrons of 84 Group 2nd TAF. Scattered around the airfield were Spitfires, Austers, a few Ansons and the Typhoons which, above all, I wanted to fly on ops. Perhaps this was the moment to make it happen with another last minute type conversion. Speed was essential – before any fighter recce postings came through. I sought an appointment. The Wingco would see me after lunch.....

My arguments were well rehearsed. Based on an index finger which had been mangled in an accident some years before. This, with some truth, was a decided disadvantage when pulling 'G' on a Mustang and attempting to press the trigger on its pistol grip control column at the same time. A problem which did not exist with the spade grip and thumb firing button on British fighters – ergo what about a transfer?

I spoke carefully, avoiding any reference to my Army background, and the Wingco listened in silence. Then he looked up, staring me straight between the eyes, as if seeking the truth. Was there the faintest hint of derision in his expression. Did he think that I was LMF? Should I be on my way within the hour to wherever they sent such unfortunates? For an awful moment I thought that I might have overplayed my hand – and then at last:

"The Typhoons have been suffering casualties. They need reinforcements. Would you.....?" A wintry smile crossed his face.

"Yes sir! I would like that very much. When can I start?"

I felt myself grinning like a fool.

Before the afternoon was out I had presented my credentials at the Typhoon flight and found an aircraft to explore. Now I was seated high above the ground, pilot's notes in my lap, absorbing it all.

The Typhoon was massive. At seven tons almost double the weight of a Hurricane. An aggressive shape with its thick slightly cranked wings, deep chin radiator, and 20mm cannon. The cockpit and seating

COMBAT AND COMPETITION

position betrayed its Hurricane ancestry and I felt immediately at home. There were some attractive features too. The sliding teardrop canopy gave a superb all round view. The undercarriage and flap controls were located conveniently on the left and the gunsight had been arranged to reflect directly on to the armoured windscreen.

On the following morning it was the real thing. The bang of a Coffman starter and the engine coughing, hesitating, spewing sheets of smoke and crackling into life. A marvellous sound – like a multitude of thrashing chain drive transmissions. Taxying out, conscious of the instruction to wind on full port rudder trim, to watch the powerful swing to starboard...... and I was off.

What a splendid brute of an aircraft. At $+7^4$ and 3700 rpm the sense of power was exhilarating. The acceleration fairly pushed you in the back. There was quite a lot of vibration which got much worse when the spring seat bottomed under positive 'G' – and rumour had it that the Typhoon's natural reverberations could lead to infertility!

It was a wary introduction to the fighter of my dreams. The sheer size and weight, and the performance, demanded respect. Aerobatics took up a lot of sky and the spin was quite violent. But confidence came fast, and all the time an inner voice kept urging me on:

"You're going to war with this one! Learn to fly it to the limits – like you did with the Hurricane!"

Downwind in the circuit and the yawing effect from the undercarriage was quite pronounced. There was a marked increase in drag when the big twenty four cylinder engine was throttled back and the flaps were very powerful. Steep approaches would be the order of the day. But not this one. I came in sedately, using plenty of power, and wheeled her on with her tail high in the air.

Within a couple of weeks I would be ready to join a squadron. Except that I had never practised dive bombing or rocket firing. It was obviously essential to learn as much as possible from other members of the GSU's Typhoon flight while there was still time.

As for my fighter recce training perhaps it might help to compensate for a lack of experience in weapon delivery. Much later, after many months on ops, with an Armament Practice Camp behind me, I reckoned that I had been no worse off than those who had followed the 'normal route' to a squadron. Their OTUs had concentrated on Typhoon conversion with typical 'fighter' emphasis and insufficient attention to target finding and ground attack.

Air to ground on the Severn ranges, down on the saltings near

CHAPTER FOUR   TYPHOON

Weston super Mare, and the Typhoon was obviously an excellent gun platform even in rough air. You soon came to terms with the rudder loads needed to avoid skidding in a dive – essential to prevent the shells drifting sideways – and to counter the asymmetric effect of an occasional stoppage. The flat trajectory and visible impact of the 20mm ammunition made for rapid aiming adjustments and accurate shooting. It was a satisfying start.

In addition to the standard mix of gunnery, formation, combat, and low flying there were a couple of dive bombing sorties without bombs. By quizzing the others beforehand, and following them carefully through each simulated attack, a basic drill began to emerge.

Run in was at 8000ft, with sections in finger four, changing to echelon at the last minute. The formation leader rolled almost vertical as the target disappeared below his wing, allowing the nose to fall away until he could bring his sight onto the aiming point. Properly executed this was a precise and comfortable manoeuvre which would line up the target exactly on the desired heading – important if it was a bridge or a ship, with only minimum positive 'G' adjustments to centre the gunsight bead.

'Aiming off' was required to compensate for the trajectory after release. As the Typhoon pundits put it:

"Continue the dive until approaching a height of about 4000 feet, pull through the target, pause briefly and press the tit. If the dive is shallower pull through further and pause longer."

Once again there was a marked difference between the well understood techniques of flying training and the less certain approach to applied flying. My unofficial and impromptu conversion to ground attack was in no way an OTU. However it highlighted, yet again, the limitations and the problems of operational training.

Almost immediately after my defection to ground attack one of the fighter recce squadrons began to re-equip with camera carrying Typhoons and I was rostered to deliver the first of these to Odiham.

There was a deep depression heading in from the Atlantic but the warm front, so the Met man said, was not expected to cause any problems until mid afternoon. Through the window behind him, as he sat over his charts, the cloud was thickening fast and the windsock pulled and trumpeted.

If I was to make Odiham today, whatever the local experts might think, there was no time to lose.

Airborne soon afterwards I wondered if the most ancient Typhoons

COMBAT AND COMPETITION

were being quietly dumped on an unsuspecting fighter recce! This one was down on performance and there was a great deal of vibration. So much in fact that it seemed prudent to keep a close watch on the engine.

The weather got steadily worse, with sudden flurries of rain, and the tops of the Berkshire Downs were already in cloud. A brief diversion eastward and it should be possible to take the Thames valley through to Reading. What a stupid idea! The hills closed in on either side and I was reduced to creeping along with 30^0 of flap and the canopy wide open. The cockpit was no longer insulated from the miserable world outside. It was cold, wet, full of exhaust crackle, and altogether less secure.

A Walrus loomed out of the murk ahead going in the same direction. He seemed to be standing still as I squeezed my way past him. If the weather became really impossible he could cut the throttle and drop down onto the river below. Lucky old Shagbat!

The cloud over Reading was lower still and the rain had become a deluge. Flying a circuit to pick up the line to Basingstoke, trapped above the roof tops, was sheer claustrophobia. In my anxiety I missed it first time and had to go round again.

After that it was easier, following railways through the flat countryside. Only the Sabre, rough as ever, in contrast to the exhaust which crackled reassuringly through the open canopy, and a few overhead power lines stood between me and my destination. Except at the very end. The airfield was on rising ground. It was touch and go once more as I slid round a minimum altitude circuit, drifting in and out of cloud, and dropped thankfully onto the sodden runway.

268 Squadron were not best pleased with their new acquisition. It was clapped out, heavy with added armour, and down on range compared with their Mustangs. A few days later the engine which had vibrated its way from Aston Down finally gave up the struggle. On subsequent deliveries one felt distinctly unloved. Each Typhoon was just another embarrassment to be tucked away in a corner of the airfield until they were forced to use it.

In the midst of these trips to Odiham I was summoned to meet Denys Gillam, then Group Captain Commanding 20 Sector, at his Tangmere headquarters.

At first he seemed withdrawn – almost to the point of diffidence. But the interview soon revealed a very different man. The steely determination was unmistakable. You would cross him at your peril.

CHAPTER FOUR   TYPHOON

His questions were searching and to the point. Why had I joined the Army and then seconded to the RAF? Why the switch from fighter recce? How many hours on Typhoons? What experience of bombs and RP? At last he seemed satisfied and pronounced my fate – a posting to one of his bomber squadrons.

Hurn, when I got there was warm and peaceful. The air was full of New Forest smells and the drowsy murmur of insects. The war seemed far away. As the evening shadows lengthened the airfield began to stir, watching and waiting. And suddenly they were back, eight or twelve at a time, sweeping down across the threshold, the noise of their engines shaking the ground.

Moments later they were strung out high on the downwind leg, curved approaches swinging into a tightly spaced stream landing. It was stirring stuff.

My first social occasion with 193 Squadron remains a vivid memory. Watching them relax, in the bar of a New Forest pub, with their tankards held close to the shoulder – mark of the clan to which they belonged.

As a newcomer you sensed the camaraderie and the elitism of a fighter squadron at war. Thrown together at a dramatic moment in time they had become comrades in arms, respecting each others' skills and buoyed up by the mutual confidence which comes from sharing the risks of battle. Bonds, stronger than any discipline, which could turn a bunch of young pilots into something much greater. It happened time and again.

Johnny Button the CO, in non regulation dark blue shirt and silk scarf, battle dress cuffs turned back at the wrist, was the timeless fighter leader, dominating them all with the strength of his personality. So like a throwback to 1940 that you half expected to see his blower Bentley parked outside the pub!

That evening I met two other members of the squadron who would remain lifelong friends. The first, Charlie Hall, when it was my turn to buy him a drink, answered in pure Colonel Chinstrap (from a popular BBC Series of the day). A deliberate, slightly inebriated:

"I don't mind if I do."

Typical of this chubby extrovert, with his unruly moustache, that he should wish to put a stranger at his ease. Jimmy Simpson did too, in a different way. A Londoner, born and bred, he was more mature than the rest. His manner was direct, almost blunt, but the integrity and strength of purpose were unmistakable. There was a sensitivity

COMBAT AND COMPETITION

too, a feeling for the needs of others. An ideal man to introduce you to ops.

Seen from above, on my first sortie, the beachhead was an awesome sight. The narrow coastal plain, looked like a vast construction site, littered with dumps – tanks, guns, bridging equipment, ammunition and fuel – the whole paraphernalia of war. ALGs[5] added to the congestion, their open dispersals and makeshift runways visible for miles. Huge highways had been bulldozed across the countryside, swathes of bare earth swarming with traffic, each convoy throwing its curtain of dust high in the air. Until, as they neared the battle area, the vehicles slowed and the telltale clouds subsided.

To port through the thickening haze a brief glimpse of Caen, shattered buildings open to the sky, the flicker of distant fires, and as suddenly the bocage countryside below was empty, devoid of movement, threatening.

A brief command, a swift formation change, that familiar rolling entry to the dive and our target lay below. Cannons thumped – and thanks to those training sorties at Aston Down the rest came almost automatically – pull through, pause and press the tit. A quick glance back to check the bomb bursts, then it was over, and we were climbing steeply away.

What an anticlimax. There had been no sign of the enemy. No fleeing soldiers, no flak, even the bombs looked puny. I felt cheated. All those years, waiting and training, just for that. Later I would see more, but never much. Enemy skills in camouflage and concealment, except on rare occasions when they were forced to move by day, were too good by far.

Such had been the pressures to move the squadrons to France that the landing grounds were operational within range of enemy guns and sometimes under fire. An advance party, flown in by Dakota, was reduced to living in foxholes for more than a week. Eventually the Huns were pushed back, the rest of the Squadron arrived, and they became aviators again.

As the situation improved 146 Wing and its four Typhoon Squadrons (193, 197, 257 and 266), soon to be joined by a fifth (263), settled in at St Croix sur Mer. B3 had a single PSP[6] runway, laid across the stubble, and an orchard where our tents were pitched amongst the apple trees.

The shattered casemates of the German beach defences, beside the

CHAPTER FOUR TYPHOON

airfield, looked out across the coast towards Arromanches and Mulberry – a scene of never ending activity with men and materials continuing to flood ashore.

Wing Ops was located on the edge of the orchard in two trailer vans parked close together, covered in camouflage netting, their awnings protecting the briefing area from the worst of the weather. Here, if not airborne, were to be found Denys Gillam, now commanding 146 Wing, and the Wing Leader. Here too were the army/air liaison and intelligence sections. This was the nerve centre – where sorties were planned and the squadrons were briefed – situated on the boundary between the two parts of our lives. The orchard and the air.

A large scale map under perspex showed the whole beach head and the battle areas. It was covered in chinagraph markings – the bomb line, inside which nothing must be attacked – and the enemy units beyond. Crack divisions, SS and Panzer, stiffened the defences. The elite of Hitler's Armies.

In Normandy they faced a stronger enemy, who possessed devastating air superiority, and we could not but admire their tenacity and courage as they strove to hold the line.

The enigma of the German nation, their fanaticism, their willingness to fight and die for such an evil cause, occupied many a conversation with Neville Thomas. Usually in the late evenings, catching up on his battle map. It was a subject which fascinated us both, but we never reached any conclusions.

'Tommy', the Senior Intelligence Officer, was old by our standards. He must have been at least 35! and the future bank manager was just beginning to show through. Very much at the centre of things, shrewd and capable, he had learned to keep his own counsel. Just occasionally he might unburden himself, to an audience of one or two, especially if there was a bottle around. Because Tommy enjoyed nothing better than a quiet session with a few intimate friends.

The orchard at St Croix sur Mer will always recall the legend of Reggie Baker. For it was there at dusk, after his grave had been found, that Jimmy Simpson told the story again. A Wing show which he was leading, late in the day, had run into intense flak. Hit and diving almost vertically out of control he had called his squadrons – calm and confident on the radio – and turned them away from the murderous barrage – in the last moments of his life.....

As Jimmy's voice died away the bursting shells were all around

COMBAT AND COMPETITION

us..... and the glowing streams of tracer..... and a single Typhoon hurtling earthwards..... What a way to go!

Those who were privileged to serve under his command recall an extrovert, hell raising Wing Leader. Who feared no man, had no respect for bureaucratic authority or stupid senior officers. His voice on the telephone, through the canvas walls of his office on the airfield:

"Baker! BAKER!..... B for Bastard!..... A for Arsehole!..... "

When the occasion demanded he had his own phonetic alphabet!

Above all they remember his last show. And those whom he led on that occasion have a more personal memory. The groan which went up at briefing when he announced that they would be going in at 4,000 feet, and his response, so poignant in retrospect:

"What's wrong! – Do you want to live forever?"

A very gallant gentleman. He was awarded a posthumous DSO.

Before we turned in, Pete Langille, 'A' flight's tall gangling Canadian, told me another story. About Jimmy's battle to get on ops. Difficult enough, after two years at Cranwell instructing on twins, without the horrendous crash which he only just survived. He was unconscious for almost a fortnight, with no memory of the flight on which it had happened, or of anything else immediately beforehand. But Jimmy was tough and we were singularly fortunate that we had acquired him or, more correctly perhaps, that through his own determination he had managed to acquire us.

That night was typical of many. Silence in the orchard, just a faint rumble of gunfire in the South, the distant explosions throwing a curtain of light across the horizon. Before long we slept. Moments later, or so it seemed, all hell broke loose.

An air attack on the beachhead and, as usual, the occupants of the orchard were in more danger from the defences. A tent and bedroll offered no protection from shell splinters and as these rained down, you sweated it out in bed, tin hat protecting head or crutch. The alternative, braving the chill night air to sit upright and protect both at once, was unthinkable!

Sleep returned briefly as the air attack died away only to be interrupted again by the arrival of a heavy calibre shell. Others followed at intervals as the enemy kept up his nightly hate. The gun in question was eventually located in a railway tunnel near Pont L'Eveque. A low level attack by 197 squadron, led by Johnny Baldwin who had taken over as Wing Leader, effectively blocked both ends of the tunnel and stopped that bit of nonsense for good.

CHAPTER FOUR   TYPHOON

For the most part, in July and early August, we hammered away at the enemy around Caen and westwards. Strongpoints, troop and tank concentrations, headquarters, fuel and ammunition dumps. There was a wild and savage beauty about those sorties which lives forever in the memory. Beauty and death.

Down below were the killing grounds of Normandy. Marked by lurid bursts of flame, and tenuous clouds of smoke, which drifted across the woods and fields and shattered, stricken, villages of the Bocage. Beauty and death in the choreography of wheeling, diving, aircraft – in the lazy rising tracer and the clouds of bursting shells – in the last stricken moments of a friend. Usually in silence. Sometimes a few words of shocked surprise, suddenly cut off. Like 'Wee Mac':

"I've had it! Second tour too....."

One day a huge bomber stream came sweeping in from the sea. For almost an hour it darkened the sky, a procession of Lancasters, Fortresses, and Liberators – escorted by Spitfires – on their way to pound the enemy positions around Caen. The start of Operation 'Goodwood', another round in the fight to break out of the beachhead.

We watched in awe – and then sudden concern, as a Liberator went out of control in a dramatic sequence of tail slides and stall turns. In moments the orchard was full of silent figures, willing the crew to bail out, and praying that their aircraft would hold together until they did. When the first parachute emerged, and the rest followed, there was an audible sigh of relief. Until we saw that the falling bomber was scything back and forwards amongst those helpless swinging figures. After half a dozen heart stopping passes it fell away below them and disappeared from sight.

Soon afterwards the weather broke, and became completely non operational for days on end. The attack petered out in a morass of bomb craters, mud and rubble on the northern outskirts of the city. Once again the resilience and tenacity of the Germans had been remarkable – and there were growing doubts about the wisdom of using strategic bombers in this way.   It seemed too much like Monte Cassino all over again.

Non flying weather and we were off to explore the local area – Jimmy Simpson, Pete Langille, and myself – and at the wheel, 'Killy' from Ulster, Fg Off Kilpatrick, perhaps the only pilot known to have survived after losing the tailplane of his Typhoon.

To warnings of fifth columnists and snipers in the rear areas we buckled on our pistols, and set off at suicidal pace, while Pete and

COMBAT AND COMPETITION

Killy argued about the route. Jeep trips were always spiced with danger. But this one was like some manic motor rally as our driver, slithering on the muddy surface, weaved between tanks and lorries to a steady accompaniment of:

"T'is this way Pete. It is indeed! Get out of the way you fat bastard!"

To Jimmy and myself, hanging on grimly in the back, it was soon apparent that there would be little opportunity for sightseeing. Whenever we entered a village, Killy remarked that there might be a sniper in the church tower and his foot would go down even harder on the accelerator. Eventually, on the way back to B3, he was persuaded to stop in the middle of Banville and again for a photograph beside its damaged church.

No manufactured goods of any sort were to be seen in the village shops. But there was plenty of local produce – cut off from its traditional markets in areas still occupied by the Germans. Butter by the kilo, big discs of Camembert, even bottles of raw Calvados from under the counter – in exchange for a few cigarettes – if you were lucky.

The locals were mostly old men, women and children. The others had gone to forced labour or underground with the Resistance. Those to whom we spoke seemed bemused. A few were almost hostile – others not unfriendly, glad that the Germans had gone, but still cautious.

For us the breakout from the beachhead was a foregone conclusion, simply a matter of time. The Allies had almost total air superiority and overwhelming material resources. The enemy was forced to move under cover of darkness or face almost total destruction by day. For the inhabitants of Normandy it was very different. They had experienced the Germans triumphant in 1940, had suffered four years of occupation, and now the Anglo-American forces had ground to a halt. Not surprising if they were still worried about the outcome.

The Prime Minister's visit could hardly have been in greater contrast. One day, as the weather began to improve, a Fiesler Storch appeared low in the circuit. Harry Broadhurst, AOC 83 Group, under whose command we were temporarily operating, had arrived with Winston Churchill.

We gathered round him as he climbed out of the aircraft, seeing the familiar figure in raincoat and nautical cap, pleased that he was on the beach-head and had found time to visit the Wing. Winston was in

CHAPTER FOUR   TYPHOON

his element, splendidly informal – full of deliberate mispronunciations and good humour.

"We've got that bastard Hitler and his Narzees on the run..... one more good heave should shee them orf for ever."

He spoke from the heart, with a marvellous feel for his audience, as if rolling back the years to take part in the battle himself. Inspiring and deeply moving. When the time came for him to leave, and Denys Gillam called three cheers for the Prime Minister, we cheered him to the echo.

With the return of flying weather the Americans broke out southwards from the Cherbourg peninsular. As they went over to the attack the left flank of the advance swung east in a giant hook to take the Germans in the rear. To Tommy's dedicated map watchers it was frustrating that the British and Canadians were making so little progress against the enemy divisions massed against them in the Caen sector.

A few days later the map showed an astounding change, with a massive German thrust aimed towards Avranches. Most of Panzer Group West was being thrown into an all out drive, to cut off the advancing 3rd US Army from its bases in the north. Amongst them were those same crack German divisions which had been holding the line around Caen. Admire them we might and yet one of our worst fears was that of being taken prisoner by an SS unit. Bad enough, as a ground attack pilot, to be captured by front line troops, but to fall into the hands of the SS, with their reputation for unbridled brutality, would be a thousand times worse.

It happened to Killy in the closing stages of the battle for Mortain, when the Typhoon squadrons were locked in combat with the panzer spearheads, and through sheer guts and that deceptively carefree Irish manner he turned it to good account.

Hit by flak near Vire he forced landed half a mile behind the German lines and managed to evade the enemy foot patrols by hiding under a tank for almost four hours. From this exceedingly dangerous position, with the crew moving around a few inches above his head, it was perhaps fortunate for him that he was seen by a German officer, and forced to surrender!

Despatched to Luftwaffe HQ, with an escort of two riflemen, travel was only possible at night and the overcrowded roads made progress very slow. For nearly a week he was on the move – collecting a number of American POWs in the process. On the sixth day, close to

COMBAT AND COMPETITION

an SS Headquarters which was being dive bombed almost nonstop, Killy's little party took refuge in a ditch, where they were joined by a further five, very demoralised, German soldiers.

Killy, as he subsequently described it, turned on the propaganda machine and persuaded all the Huns to surrender, and pose as his escort, until they reached the allied lines. After further adventures, which included bluffing an SS officer, stealing a lorry, and ending up with an even larger 'escort' which had swollen to twenty seven, Killy finally made contact with an American unit and hitch hiked his way back to B3 – just nine days late. A valiant effort part of a long and courageous tour for which he received the DSO.

The sortie on which Killy went down was an armed recce with bombs against the rear areas of the Mortain salient. Led by Bill Switzer, commanding 'A' Flight, it proved frustrating beyond words. The search area was surprisingly untouched by war. Yet only a few miles to the west, where the ground attack squadrons had just delivered a decisive blow against the panzers, the countryside was devastated and strewn with the debris of battle.

We tracked back and forth across the gentle rolling wooded contours. But the Hun was lying low after his battering on the previous day and so Bill brought us down and down, trailing his coat, until we were less than a thousand feet above the ground. Eight Typhoons, in two sections of four, cruising in battle formation – asking for trouble – until Killy was caught by a sudden burst of flak and called out that he was heading home and an imminent forced landing.

For almost half an hour more we sweated it out, hunched in the heat of our cockpits under a cloudless sky, willing Killy to make it, until shortage of fuel brought an end to the fruitless search.

Frustration turned to anger when we were told to bring our bombs home. Yet Bill was probably right. An astute enemy commander might well have pulled his forces back during the night, after the disaster at Mortain, in order to reduce the risk of encirclement. And we had seen absolutely nothing to attack. Better to save our bombs for another time.

A few days later I was flying number two to Bill. It was a dawn show, and he was trailing his coat again, low to the south of Caen. Suddenly the tracer came hosing up and he was hit by the very first burst and started to burn. I shouted at him to bale out, but there was no sign of a parachute, and his aircraft dived vertically into the middle of a large wood where it exploded on impact.

CHAPTER FOUR   TYPHOON

But Bill was still very much in the land of the living. He had fallen into the trees, not far from the burning remains of his aircraft, his parachute opening in the nick of time. Concealing himself as best he could despite a broken leg, which he strapped with his dinghy thwart, Bill survived in the middle of a major battle. He was picked up eventually by our advancing troops, still alive, by which time Jimmy Simpson had taken over the flight.

As the enemy fought to extricate his forces, after their failure at Mortain, the occupants of the orchard at St Croix sur Mer were involved in a battle of a different sort. The log which straddled the crudely screened trench behind ops was crowded with miserable figures cursing and groaning. Fortunately there was plenty of Kaolin and some lucky chaps seemed to remain immune. As a result we were able to keep going, near enough at full strength, although the same could hardly be said of our physical state.

Pride of place in the story of Normandy dog must go to Doc Horn who organised a supply of sanitary towels. Stockpiled at B3 they were to be used for a purpose which their designer, even in his wildest dreams, could never have foreseen. It amused us hugely to imagine the enemy reaction had they ever captured and examined a pilot equipped with one of Doc's secret weapons!

Speed was of the essence and they were delivered immediately thanks to the 'beer run', a well established service with origins of a different nature.

Dust on the beachhead landing grounds in the early days had caused a spate of engine failures. Vokes produced a simple carburettor air intake filter and an emergency modification programme was put in hand. Units based in France flew their Typhoons back to England, a few at a time, and these were soon returning with two firkins of beer apiece on their bomb racks.

The beer run continued, long after its primary purpose had ceased to exist, by the simple expedient of rostering an aircraft on a round trip to Tangmere at regular two day intervals. Pilots changed over at the far end, giving each the benefit of a short leave in England, and the obligatory barrels were loaded up for the return flight.

Doc's sanitary towels travelled by the same route packed into the gun bays of our beer barrel bombers.

The enemy forces trapped in the Falaise pocket fought desperately to escape and there was a brief resurgence of German fighter activity in an attempt to stem the savage losses which were being inflicted on

COMBAT AND COMPETITION

them from the air.

The Wing reacted with a number of fighter sweeps and there were a few encounters with 20 and 30 plus 109s. However our main role continued to be that of ground attack directed increasingly towards the escape routes back to the Seine.

As the ground battle went mobile 146 Wing's 'Bomphoon' squadrons expected an instruction to change over to rockets. There were two important advantages. Drop tanks could be carried in addition to RPs, which increased the radius of action, and the rockets themselves were considered to be more effective against targets – particularly armour – on the move.

Johnny Button and Allan Smith of 197 Squadron fought against the idea – arguing that the Wing must be able to respond instantly, with bombs, even under the most fluid battlefield conditions. The Luftwaffe's re-appearance was further justification for retaining some Typhoons with bomb racks as they were faster, and more manoeuvrable, than those fitted with rails.

While the two Squadron Commanders were making and winning their case, I was briefed by the Wingco to accompany him on an armed recce.

In the cockpit and five minutes to go. Five minutes to run through the familiar drills, deep breathing on oxygen, feeling the tension that stems from the challenge of a compelling and deadly sport, its excitement and its uncertainty – the very essence of operational flying. And this sortie had an extra twist. My number one was the top scoring Typhoon pilot with thirteen and a half kills.

Johnny Baldwin seemed such an unemotional man, so very different from his colourful predecessor, yet his skill and his unruffled confidence was an inspiration to all around him. In the air you sensed an exceptional and considerate leader. A veray parfit gentil knight.

How, I wondered yet again, had I come to be flying with him alone? Perhaps as a belated comeuppance for an indiscretion on a fighter sweep south of Paris. Sprog of the lot I had been first to answer his question on the radio. Identifying a bunch of impossibly distant specks with the words "Mustangs Bigshot" – and then having to sweat it out!

Whether that was the real reason was of no importance at all. What mattered most, as Jimmy Simpson put it bluntly:

"If you're flying with the Wingco on his own – you'd better have your finger well and truly out!"

CHAPTER FOUR TYPHOON

Ground crews swarmed over the surrounding aircraft preparing them for the next sortie. Most of them were stripped to the waist, tanned and fit as never before – thanks to Adolf Hitler – although they might have put it differently! Some were draped with belts of 20mm ammunition, others, working under the wings, were fitting drop tanks. Today, again, there would be no bombs.

In the background, where Stan Carr's 'office' and 'workshops' were located in a cluster of camouflaged tents, a chorehorse chugged softly away – pleasantly soporific in the warm sunshine.

Stan and his boys. They never let us down. Highly skilled, improvisers and scroungers par excellence, they kept our aircraft serviceable under the most daunting conditions. Up to every legitimate demand we put upon them and, as I was to discover in the months ahead, a few more besides.

Senior NCOs like Stan Carr were the backbone of the Service. Ex Desert Air Force. Still in his early thirties. Behind a deceptively relaxed exterior Stan possessed an iron determination, and he ran his crew like a veteran. To us he was always relaxed, polite and helpful. Nothing was too much trouble. Stan and Joe Hickey, his right hand man, identified totally with the Squadron, and we with them. 6193 Servicing Echelon was 193 Squadron, whatever officialdom might say[7], and they supported us magnificently.

The muffled crack of a Coffman starter on the far side of the airfield was a reminder of more urgent matters. Careful strokes on the cylinder pump. Press the starter and booster coil buttons. The engine coughed and burst into life. The two Typhoons taxied out to meet at the runway threshold, clattered onto the PSP tracking, and took off together in a gathering storm of dust.

We turned east, crossing the twin waterways of the river Orne and the Caen canal, catching a glimpse of Liseaux Abbey in the distance – brilliant white – almost luminous. A dramatic outline far removed from the ugly scenes of devastation which lay ahead. For the enemy had been forced to move in daylight and was paying the price.

The roads leading across the open plain were littered and blocked with wrecked and burning transport. Columns of smoke hung in the summer sky. In the midst of all this carnage more vehicles, of every sort and description, motorised and horsedrawn, continued to straggle out from the hilly countryside to the south east. These were the survivors, who had fought their way out of the trap at Falaise, only to face annihilation from the air on their final dash to the Seine.

COMBAT AND COMPETITION

But before we turned our attention to the roads there was something else. The Wingco's voice sounded in my ears:

"Bigshot going down now – enemy gun position."

As I followed, searching the ground ahead, bare earth showed faintly through camouflage netting, revealing the telltale outlines of newly dug weapon pits close to the bottom of a reverse slope. 88s probably, part of some hastily assembled battle group, ready to fight it out to the bitter end defending the flanks of the retreat. A dangerous trap set to catch the advancing Canadians as they topped the crest ahead. But lack of time had prevented adequate concealment and, in revealing their position, the Huns had given us an opportunity to hit them first.

Cannon smoke trailed back suddenly from the Wingco's Typhoon and his first burst ripped viciously through one of the crudely camouflaged emplacements.

No time to take in more as I opened fire on another, seeing the flash of exploding shells in its shadowy depths, followed by a burst of flame. Back on the stick, and a gun barrel, long as a telegraph pole, slid into the glowing arc of the reflector sight. The cannons thumped again. A fleeting impression of crouching, stumbling figures engulfed in a carpet of firecrackers – then up and away.

As we swung hard to port the flak came up, late and inaccurate. Moments later we caught a half track, accompanied by a large lorry, skulking along the edge of a wood and both erupted in flames. There seemed to be ambulances everywhere, threading carefully amongst the wreckage on the roads. All were plastered with huge red crosses. Difficult to believe that every one was genuine. But we left them alone. There were plenty of other targets.

A couple of days later 193 Squadron went visiting on the ground. Released from ops for 24 hours we scrounged a 15 cwt truck and headed south. The roads were almost empty and we made good time, stopping only to check our way in the middle of a small village.

Or rather it had once been a small village. Now, like so many others, it was just an open cross roads, surrounded by shattered houses and piles of rubble. Here and there an odd balk of burnt timber, a broken picture frame, a dirty remnant of curtain – all that remained of a small community which had been caught in the whirlwind of destruction. Yet not quite all. The sound of drunken song, and before we could locate its source a swaying figure emerged from the ruins and came reeling towards us. This survivor, gently and happily inebriated,

CHAPTER FOUR   TYPHOON

produced a bottle and demanded that we toast every conceivable aspect of 'la Liberation.'

As the road climbed towards Mount Pincon we looked back, savouring the warmth of his raw Calvados, and saw him standing there, a lonely scarecrow, waving to us from the desolation of his home.

Mount Pincon was a shambles. In and around the orchards and homesteads the spiked and shattered guns stared blindly out across the slopes which they had failed to hold. Abandoned equipment, empty ammunition boxes, the jetsam of battle lay everywhere. The remains of a classic defensive position, where the Germans had fought to the death, until overwhelmed at last by sheer weight of numbers and superior firepower.

Here the dead were already buried, each temporary grave marked by a rough wooden cross, with a few hastily scrawled words, under a steel helmet. Even the aroma of death had begun to fade and the predominant smell was of burnt and pulverised buildings with a touch of farmyard manure.

Not so as our truck jolted and rumbled on down the winding roads to the south and east of Falaise. The sickly sweet odour grew steadily worse, until it dominated the senses, and there was no escaping its dreadful embrace. Surrounding us on every side was the reality of what had been happening, down there in the bocage, inside the ring of steel which had closed and tightened around the German Armies in Normandy. It was like a vision of the apocalypse.

From Trun to Vermoutiers ran the awful highways of death where the retreating columns had been cornered, and systematically destroyed, as they tried to escape. Stalled nose to tail they had been devastated by nonstop air attack, on roads swept by torrents of artillery and mortar fire, until hardly a living creature remained. We climbed down from the truck and walked among them in a valley still as the grave itself, where no birds sang and nothing moved except the flies and maggots. They lay where they had fallen, amongst the debris of their broken weapons and ruined vehicles. Some were hideously torn and disfigured, or charred and blackened until their shrunken corpses were hardly recognisable as those of human beings.

Others lay seemingly untouched, calm and peaceful, handsome in death, their sightless eyes staring forever into space. The horses were the saddest sight of all. Unable to escape they had been mown down where they stood. Their bodies swollen and distended, their noble

COMBAT AND COMPETITION

heads grimacing in rigor mortis, pitiful beyond words.

The scale and the horror of it all was almost too much to take, and it was a thoughtful little party which returned to St Croix sur Mer that night. Yet there was hope too. For we had seen the twisted symbols of Nazism broken in the dust. Entrails of a defeated army. The victory at Falaise had struck a massive blow for freedom.

Churchill surrounded by members of 146 Wing in Normandy, 1944. Gp Capt Denys Gillam (foreground), Flt Lt Davidge and Fg Off Kilpatrick (to his left in peaked caps).

CHAPTER FIVE

WINTER IN FLANDERS

The defeated remnants of the German armies in Normandy took another severe mauling from the Typhoons as they struggled across the Seine. The retreat degenerated into a rout. There was no coherent line of defence as the enemy fell back in disorder towards the Pas de Calais and the Belgian frontier. And the ground attack squadrons, operating at maximum range from their beachhead airfields, harried them from dawn to dusk.

Johnny Button had gone on rest and Guy 'Plum' Plamondon, a French Canadian, had taken over the Squadron. On the last day of August, leading eight aircraft on armed reconnaissance he caught an enemy convoy out in the open between Arras and Douai. Trapped on one of those poplar lined roads which run straight as a die across the plains of northern France without a hedge or a scrap of cover in sight.

Plum placed us perfectly. We swung into line abreast and dived towards them, drop tanks tumbling away. A motley collection of military and commandeered civilian vehicles, some horsedrawn, they were crawling along in the heat and seemed oblivious to their fate. When they spotted us at last a few wild bursts of flak came – but it was all too late. The wagons at the front and rear were knocked out almost simultaneously, and many more were caught on the first pass, trapping the remainder. The flak trucks were swamped. The return fire died.

We came in again, taking out most of the rest and, as we pulled away, nothing moved on the road below except billowing flames and clouds of dirty smoke. We had accounted for 22 vehicles and reduced a whole column to ruins in a matter of minutes.

The next sortie, another armed recce, further up the Pas de Calais, was briefed to cross the Channel and land at Manston. Approaching the search area the German radar echoed in our headphones:

"Yoy...ing... Yoy...ing... Yoy...ing..." An incessant message. The radar sounds grew more demanding. Easy to picture the long gun barrels swinging far below, the high velocity 88mm rounds slamming home, a swift succession of muzzle flashes above the emplacements, shell bursts erupting around us...... And then we saw a gaggle of Lancasters ahead, attacking a heavily wooded position, their giant bomb bursts marching through the trees.

Further north we shot up a couple of heavy MT a few miles inland from Boulogne. Then a horse drawn wagon appeared charging along

COMBAT AND COMPETITION

a country lane frantically seeking cover. Caught by a burst of cannon fire it stopped abruptly in the entrance to a large field. I looked back and there tucked in around the perimeter were the wagon lines of an enemy transport unit:

"More targets under the trees Bassett Leader! and Jimmy Simpson, encouraging: "Roger Dave, lead us in."

Cannon shells scythed amongst them and there were rearing horses, falling horses, dying and panic stricken horses, absolute chaos. The field was in the bottom of an awkward hollow and I hung on too long with my second burst and almost mushed in. Pulling up rather shaken as Felix Cryderman came through on the radio – loud and very upset:

"You bastards can do what you like – I'm not attacking no more horses today – or any other f****ing day!"

And Jimmy, calm and understanding:

"OK Black Three – stand off and watch our backs."

Moments later we had reduced another enemy unit to absolute ruin. But who could take pride in such a massacre of defenceless animals. For Felix, the Canadian lumberjack, who had lived and worked with horses all his life, it must have been hell. Yet the German Army depended on them and it was our job to destroy their transport.

Jimmy's voice again – flat and deliberately unemotional:

"That's enough chaps. Time to go home. Bassett Leader setting course."

All was peaceful as we passed low over the chalk cliffs, keeping well clear of Boulogne, before climbing out over the sea. The late afternoon sun gleamed on our canopies and reflected across the water. Dungeness looked as if you could reach out and touch it.

There was only one salvo, but it was enough. The familiar oily bursts blossomed right across the formation. Several aircraft were damaged and Jimmy's Typhoon began to stream glycol. The heavy batteries at Boulogne must have been tracking us from the moment we settled into the climb and had fired with great accuracy. Jimmy sweated it out, as his coolant slowly drained, and we tucked in beside him, hardly daring to breathe. But his engine kept going and he made it back to Manston and a normal landing.

We were inside the nearest local within minutes of opening time. The beer tasted splendid. Just what was needed to wash away the dust and stink of Normandy and drown the images of those dead and dying horses. It was a long and boozy session.

Shortly afterwards long range tanks, and round trips via Manston,

CHAPTER FIVE WINTER IN FLANDERS

were not enough. We became birds of passage, moving from strip to strip, trying to keep up with the pace of the advance. Until the Wing stopped briefly at Lille/Vendeville and went into action against the German garrisons defending the Channel ports.

A forecast of non flying weather led to a spontaneous night on the town. The liberation was very new and everywhere 'les Aviateurs Anglais' were warmly welcomed. Some hours and many drinks later we came across a vast emporium with swing doors reminiscent of a Western saloon. Inside was a large room with a sunken floor covered in sawdust. On the far side, standing with her back to the bar, was the most remarkable creation – an Amazon warrior in the flesh – and what flesh! The skin tight black leather bra and pants showed off her well endowed shape to perfection and the force of her personality was positively elemental.

She strode across the sawdust towards us, brandishing a whip and sadly, as she came nearer, the image changed. The flesh was just too substantial and the beautiful face was hard and demanding. This harpy took one look at Felix – in build apart from the obvious differences they were not dissimilar – and decided that she had found a soul mate, or at least a mate for the night. She threw herself at him with glad cries of "Mon Dieu – quel magnifique!" and the like. To which Felix responded ungallantly "Christ I'm off."

In the end we persuaded him to stick around as the rest of us were more than curious about the goings on in this very strange establishment. Felix was scared to death. He only recovered his confidence when there was a burst of machine gun fire out in the street. That was something he understood and could cope with!

Having no wish to become involved with a bunch of trigger happy Frenchmen, who seemed at one in their determination to eliminate the hated traitors of France, we returned to the jeep and drove back to base.

The following day, wandering around nursing our hangovers, Charlie Hall and I found a German bomb dump. The 250kg bombs had been fitted with screamers, four to a bomb. The thought occurred to us that we might fit a larger version to our Typhoons. Stan Carr organised several prototypes, and they kept us amused for days. But the idea was quickly forgotten when we moved to Armament Practice Camp at Fairwood Common.

The APCs[1] provided range facilities, a supply of practice bombs and rockets, aircraft servicing and rearming. The rest was up to the

COMBAT AND COMPETITION

squadrons. For those like myself, who had been forced to learn on the job, it was a golden opportunity.

Dive bombing, so far, had been a matter of trial and error, and the continuity provided by four practice bombs, on frequently repeated sorties, was an enormous help. The steepest possible attack, pressed well home, proved to be the most accurate. Gravity drop was minimal and the compensation required, by pulling the nose through the target, was correspondingly less. From then on it became my standard technique.

Low level bombing practice was too easy. It failed to simulate the weight and inertia of a high explosive bomb. On ops we had to release them into a pretty substantial object, or make the final approach in a shallow dive, otherwise they were liable to ricochet. A few 500lb casings filled with concrete might have been useful for training.

Practice RPs were fitted with 60lb concrete heads. Accurate flying was essential as they were highly sensitive to slip or skid. Range and angle of dive were equally critical in order to get the correct gravity drop. To help with the latter the graticule of the standard reflector sight was rotated in azimuth, until the image on the windscreen had been turned through 90^0. The inner (top) end of the lower range bar became the RP aiming point and the range bar control itself was recalibrated in angles of dive 30^0, 45^0, 60^0 etc. Thus providing an adjustable sight line, raising the aircraft nose as the dive became shallower and vice versa.

As practice brought improvement my own sortie averages came down to six yards with RP, seven yards low level, ten yards dive bombing, and twenty two yards flying number three in a section attack. What the others achieved individually I never discovered, because there were no published results, but the Squadron average was better than twenty five yards low level and thirty yards dive bombing. A reasonable basis on which to go back to war.

When we caught up with the Wing at Antwerp the enemy was still holding out in the northern suburbs of the city. The docks had been captured almost intact and the fight was on to clear the way for shipping. The Germans, well aware of what was at stake, were doing their utmost to prevent this happening. They hung on doggedly, even on the south bank of the Scheldt estuary, where they were totally cut off.

We took our first casualty attacking the coastal batteries at Breskens. It happened with sudden and unexpected violence. Fire and

CHAPTER FIVE   WINTER IN FLANDERS

flame mushroomed amongst the diving aircraft, only to be snuffed out in an instant, leaving an ugly pall of smoke hanging in the air. A voice said "Hap's bought it!" and at the same moment the smoke swirled and faded – revealing a few unrecognisable bits of debris. They tumbled lifelessly away, and disappeared for ever as we concentrated on the target.

No one else was touched except the CO, who took the full force of the explosion, as his number two blew up. His ailerons were almost immovable and one undercarriage leg hung down uselessly, wrenched and twisted out of line. Yet he got back to Antwerp, landing last of all. The damaged leg collapsed and he slewed off the runway. His aircraft was a write off.

Some days later I accompanied Jimmy Simpson to Ops, sneaking a preview of the target, as he prepared to brief 'A' Flight for a low level show. Neville Thomas climbed down from his van and joined us. He looked decidedly angry and out of sorts, not at all his usual urbane self, and muttered about the unspeakable bastards we were going to attack.

Eventually it all came out. The Canadians had overrun an enemy position, in the immediate vicinity of our target, and found the body of one of their soldiers who had been captured on the previous day. And then, barely able to contain his rage, Tommy looked at us and said:

"Those filthy Huns had hung him over a fire and roasted him to death."

For the first and almost the only time, as Jimmy headed the Jeep along the peritrack, I felt hatred and loathing for the enemy troops who were shortly to be at the receiving end of our guns. A feeling that would not go away..... that got worse as I ran through the familiar drills..... swamping all rational thought.....

Down below it looked just like the photograph. A pillbox surrounded by a network of trenches – sodden, treeless, and low lying – beside a narrow lake with the river beyond. A bleak and cheerless place to die in agony.

We came in slowly. Eight Typhoons with sixteen one thousand pound bombs. Hell bent on revenge. The pillbox filled our gunsights – smothered in bursting shells. The first section was through. Bombs gone and eleven seconds to go. Eight muddy explosions. And another eight. A direct hit. Others cratering the spidery network of diggings. We went back again and again. Ferocious, bloodthirsty, strafing runs.

COMBAT AND COMPETITION

Hammering the damaged pillbox. Raking the trenches from end to end. Willing our shells to tear such a monstrous enemy to shreds. Until the ammunition ran out and our cannons clattered into silence.

It was Jimmy as usual who called us to order and we cruised home, through the quiet autumn skies, drained of emotion.

A successful attack on the coastal batteries at Flushing brought the Wing three useful recruits from the Spitfire equipped naval bombardment unit to which I had been posted before D Day. It so happened that Geoff Hartley had been controlling a shoot with HMS Warspite against the same target. But the guns could not get it right and salvo after salvo pitched uselessly into the floodwaters around the gun emplacements. When the Typhoons appeared, and plastered them with bombs, it was the last straw.

On landing Geoff applied for an immediate transfer and encouraged Bob Gibbings and John Irving to do likewise. There was a continual need for Typhoon pilot replacements and the last attempt to recruit them, from the Spitfire squadrons of 2nd TAF, had not been very successful. So they were welcomed with open arms and put through a rapid conversion course with some genuine bombing practice. Geoff and Bob joined 197 and John went to 263 where he learned all about RPs by firing them in action!

There were other sorties to the north of Antwerp. Close support for the troops fighting their way towards the Dutch border. Destructive attacks on tiny hamlets. Picturesque little places, hugging the canals, their gardens bright with marigolds as we swept low overhead. On a fine evening you could still see them from the circuit. Burning houses, angry red in the gathering darkness, and the smoke trails hanging low.

I almost bought it on one of those sorties, climbing in line astern, close to the airfield. Just a brief glimpse of a shape materialising through the cloud layer high above – plunging earthwards – striking at the very heart of the formation. No question of any evasive action, and barely time to register the slender outline, as the V2 hurtled past my starboard wing and was gone.

The effect of that near miss was very odd. It created an extraordinary feeling of euphoria, almost of invincibility. The sortie had done its worst. There was nothing more to fear. Then, as if to prove the point, we ran into a particularly nasty combination of low cloud and concentrated flak – and I felt strangely remote and immune from it all!

During our time at Antwerp V1s and V2s arrived at a combined

CHAPTER FIVE   WINTER IN FLANDERS

rate of forty to fifty a day. This rose to almost eighty when the offensive was at its height, providing ample opportunity to study their behaviour.

It was said that a V2 never gave any warning of its arrival. True in a sense, but our experience was different. On a clear day the walking stick trails could be seen from the ground at Deurne, soaring upwards above the launching sites, before they vanished into the tropopause. Four minutes later, and you could almost set your watch by them, they arrived in characteristic fashion. An exploding warhead followed by the sonic boom echoing and re-echoing backwards into the empty sky.

Those with a warped sense of humour took a fiendish delight in timing them secretly and then announcing:

"V2 arriving in ten seconds!..... three!..... two!..... one!..... NOW!"

And, to make matters worse, the wretched missile frequently disintegrated en route!

As the bombardment intensified there was growing concern about our lack of dispersal. The pilots, in their terraced cottages at Deurne, were said to be living dangerously close together. A single lucky hit might knock out most of the Wing. In the end it was agreed that a number of us would be accommodated in town and 193 moved into a block of centrally heated flats.

After unpacking, as we were relaxing on our beds and enjoying the unaccustomed warmth, the building rocked violently. There was a sudden blast of air and the lights went out. Groping around by torchlight it was soon apparent that all the glass had gone, the heating had ceased to work, and the door had been thrown right across the room into the window embrasure.

We were lucky that night. Saved by the reinforced concrete structure, which remained standing when the V2 exploded thirty yards away, and the fact that we were lying down when the massive door flew over our heads. Only Bunny Austin, shaving in the bathroom, was slightly the worse for wear, his face cut by flying splinters. The dispersal scheme was promptly abandoned and 193 returned to base for the winter.

V weapons and winter quarters were evidence that we were into a new phase of the war. Everywhere from Switzerland to the North Sea the advance was slowing down. The enemy was not on his way back to Berlin, as we had fondly imagined until a few weeks ago, at least not this side of Christmas.

In our sector, on the left of the line, he was falling back towards

COMBAT AND COMPETITION

the river Maas. A natural defensive position. Stalemate seemed likely until the spring.

In the cramped cottages we were preparing to dig in as well. The tiny kitchen cum living room, which I shared with Jimmy Simpson, contained our camp beds, a couple of chairs, and a cupboard. Otherwise it was completely bare, down to the stone floor. In cold weather, even with the old stove going full blast, it chilled to the marrow. At night, huddled for warmth in our blankets, we slept fitfully as the flying bombs thundered across the sky. Occasionally, when one cut out too close for comfort, the moment of silence would be broken by Jimmy or myself with a hopeful:

"Missed again!"

There was an Me 109 production unit at Deurne with sub assembly and stores dispersed around the Napoleonic forts close to the airfield. The instrument bay was a treasure trove – its beautiful AC horizons and DC turn and slip indicators, in their sealed packs, a generation ahead of the ungainly suction driven devices on our blind flying panels. And the gyro compass, known to us only in principle, was fitted as standard to the Gustav[2].

First to acquire a selection of instruments, some of which might be useful right away, and others – well just to keep for the moment – and then to explain myself to Charlie Hall who had been watching with interest:

"Those miniature ball type skid indicators. Might improve our dive bombing if we mounted them on the gunsights. And a gyro compass would be super for navigation."

Charlie was rather offended by the thought of my gunsight modification. Until he recalled how easy it was to build up a significant sideslip angle in a steep dive. Then he saw the point. But he remained less than enthusiastic about the gyro compass. It needed power and the master unit had to be mounted in the rear fuselage which could be difficult. And then – as if reading my thoughts:

"There's enough material in those forts to assemble several brand new 109s, what about one for the squadron?"

The CO and Jimmy supported the idea. Stan Carr, without whom it would have been impossible, was delighted to take charge. A team of volunteers was soon recruited to help collect all the parts. Operation Gustav was on.

Once we strapped a complete fuselage to the back of an open truck and towed it tail first, on its undercarriage, through a maze of greasy

CHAPTER FIVE   WINTER IN FLANDERS

cobbled streets. The last leg of that hazardous trip passed close to 35 Wing which occupied the far side of the airfield. We drove gingerly past and they looked at us as if we were mad. Perhaps we were, or maybe it was just a passion for things aeronautical.

The prototype skid indicator, clamped to my gunsight by an oversize jubilee clip, was easy to use and it seemed to help. So Stan got his fitters to make up a batch for the Squadron.

The gyro compass was a different matter. As an unauthorised modification to the Typhoon's electrical system the E.O.[3] would have none of it. But one of our pilots, Bill Hurst, an ex Brat[4], decided to fit one regardless. He wired up a master unit and cockpit repeater, ran them off a battery and inverter, proved that they worked and then carried out his own installation. Every pilot who flew with it wanted one for himself. But Bill would not oblige. He was in enough trouble already with the E.O!

In the centre of Antwerp the heady post liberation days had gone forever. The New Century, a hotel which had seen its share of wild and spontaneous parties was virtually out of bounds. Crowded with base wallahs who seemed to be taking over all the best places in town.

But not, let it be said, before the Wing had made its mark. 197 Squadron, aggravated by the hotel orchestra's failure to create the right sort of music, had already distinguished themselves by decorating its members with a selection of potted plants.

By the time we felt able to go there again the base wallahs had arrived in strength and were occupying most of the upper floors, including those above the ballroom where our parties usually started. All went well until the backwoodsman in Felix Cryderman suddenly reasserted itself. Out came his revolver and his soft laughter, always a sign of danger, was lost in a fusillade of shots as he tried to destroy the chandeliers over our heads.

We shouted at him to put the bloody thing away – which he did with surprising speed, and not a moment too soon, as a bunch of indignant brass hats stormed into the room. Felix looked up at them from the depths of his armchair, wreathed in gunsmoke, oblivious to the atmosphere of menace.

"Some fat drunken Canadian pilot" he said softly "He went that way" – and then, more audibly – "serve the buggers right – most of them look shit scared."

After that we took our custom elsewhere. To 'Scabby Gabby's', the noisy saloon bar near the airfield – or to other more discrete if dubious

COMBAT AND COMPETITION

spots away from the city centre. Places where there was safety in numbers, if only to support those who might yield to temptation!

One evening these precautions were of no avail. The setting itself was innocent enough. Half a dozen of us sitting round the bar, in conversation with Madame, whilst her assistant hovered in the background. No hint of the unexpected until it suddenly registered that one of our party had been missing for some time. Madame pulled back the heavy curtains. And there, like the male lead in some erotic play, was our missing colleague in flagrante delicto with Girl Friday. We stood transfixed, trying to find words to express our...... who knows? – and then gave up, closing the curtains gently and leaving them to their pleasures.

We were dedicated party goers. It was part and parcel of squadron life. A way of unwinding at the end of the day. Celebrating a successful show, trying to forget, or when we had just lost a friend. Like the night after Pete Langille bought it attacking an enemy column – caught by flak – too low to bail out. Pete, loyal and dependable, never seeking the limelight. His courage had been an inspiration. We would miss him like hell.

Charlie's voice broke in on my thoughts:

"Another snort old man? "

And the ever watchful Jimmy, like some demonic conductor, urging us on:

"Cats! Sister's Cat's! My Sister's Cat's! Up My Sister's Cat's! Pudding Up My Sister's Cats! Black Pudding Up....!"

We bellowed it out again and again through all its lewd permutations. Helpless with laughter as the drink took hold and the mistakes became more and more frequent. Laughter which relieved and relaxed. Wonderfully therapeutic. And we knew that wherever he was Pete would understand.

That night was long ago and the memories grow dim. Was it just about Pete alone? Or all of them? The ones who never came back.

When Johnny Baldwin went on rest, 'Bomber' Wells took over as Wing Leader. His arrival coincided with a series of new developments, phosphorous incendiaries, blind bombing under ground radar control and target photography.

Our camera equipped Typhoons, survivors of the ones which I had helped deliver to Odiham in the previous June, were acquired by Denys Gillam from 35 Wing as they were about to depart for Gilze-Rijen. He could claim that he was doing them a favour. Taking

CHAPTER FIVE WINTER IN FLANDERS

over their unpopular Tiffies as they started re-equipping with Spitfire XIVs. In point of fact his Wing would now be able to fly its own photographic sorties and he would get the results quicker than before.

Gerry Eaton, a flight commander with 257, and I were the guinea pigs. Loaned from our squadrons, as and when required, to fly unescorted missions. Our FR^5 Typhoons carried three F24 cameras, one oblique and two vertical, mounted in the starboard inner gun bay. We planned to use the vertical pair only, making our target runs at about 4,000ft.

My first sortie, on 15th Army HQ at Dordrecht, flown several hours after the action, was abandoned due to low cloud and 35 Wing got in first on the following day. The Army Commander, Von Busch, was lucky to be away at the time as the target was well and truly pranged. The Dutch Resistance responded quickly with a list of casualties, and the date and place of the military funeral..... and would the Wing please oblige with another attack to finish off those who had escaped!

Going in immediately after an attack on a heavily defended target, which soon became standard practice, was character forming to say the least. Better to be part of a squadron – bombs and cannon in hot blood – than sweating it out alone waiting to plunge into a hornet's nest. Or was it?

Photo reconnaissance offered a unique challenge. That of bringing back the first real evidence of success or failure and simultaneously, not to say unavoidably, providing a measure by which the quality of your own sortie might be judged. Not surprisingly it exerted a powerful attraction.

Thoughts to encourage the loner in photo 'M', sitting high above Rotterdam, looking down on the perfection of a late autumn day. The outlines of the city shimmering softly through the haze. Black shell bursts stained the sky. The squadrons moved into echelon and plummeted earthwards. Light flak veiled the target merging into a carpet of destruction – and the diving aircraft became vague shadows darting through layers of murk and smoke.

Brief words of command, leaders reforming their squadrons, and then silence on the radio. The storm of flak died away. A pall of dust hung over the target area. My time had come.

The 88s opened up immediately, a muffled thud shook the aircraft, and oil began to smear the screen. It spread rapidly, still thin, but enough to obscure the view. The cockpit filled with fumes and the curtain of oil grew darker.

On instruments now. Fear caught at me and I strove to fight it down..... Hold the dive!..... Hold it!..... You must hold it!..... Level out and switch the cameras on!.....

By now I was down to 2,500 feet – rocketing blind across the centre of Rotterdam – at least the flak was invisible!

The return trip was agonizing. Trying to spare the engine resulted in a suicidally slow passage across the docks and I expected a direct hit at any moment. Winding the canopy open was no help at all. An alarming close up of the Dordrecht bridges, heavily guarded by flak guns, frightened me out of my skin and I was deluged with hot oil. After what seemed an age I reached friendly territory and called 'Longbow'[6] to alert the nearest airfield, Gilze-Rijen, to my predicament.

Oil continued to flood over the windscreen obscuring my goggles and, when I raised them, stinging my eyes. Time to start the approach, staying high in case the engine failed, and slightly offset to provide a view of sorts until the last possible moment. The temperatures were almost off the clock and the oil pressure falling rapidly..... Undercarriage..... Flaps..... Into the final turn.....

It was a surprisingly good landing which came to a shuddering halt alongside a group of airmen and a Coles crane. Difficult to know who was the more taken aback. But reaction was beginning to set in and I shouted across to them, "You can take it away!" The effect was rather spoilt when I slipped on the oily wing root, and ended up in a heap on the runway, fortunately without further damage.

Photo 'M' had been hit in the spinner, which was like a colander, and the constant speed mechanism had been badly damaged. The fuselage looked as if it had been painted glossy black. It was a miracle that the engine had kept going.

In the mess after a late lunch, still red eyed and stinking of oil, David Hurford, Nobby Clarke and others dropped by to take coffee. It was good to be amongst the BFs again. Even if there was more than the usual leg pulling, about usurping their role, that it served me right for fiddling my way on to Typhoons, and so on.

The dance at Deurne that evening was a great success, thanks to Jimmy Simpson. A set of Glen Miller records, which he had purloined from Heaven knows where, had been turned into musical scores by the Belgian orchestra. So we drank and danced the night away to the best of 'Big Band' sounds. Jimmy had also, perhaps unwisely, offered to

CHAPTER FIVE   WINTER IN FLANDERS

find some partners for 'Plamondon's Playboys'. Organised, as he admitted later, through a local seminary, complete with chaperon. He assured us that there were no nuns!

Perhaps the Squadron diarist was thinking of the latter as he commented unkindly that:

"......*when they appeared, there was speculation that Flight Lieutenant Simpson's eyesight might not be up to the standard which the Service required of its fighter bomber pilots.*"

Plum went on rest and Derek Erasmus, Rhodesian and a flight commander from 266 Squadron, was promoted in his place. He took over as the dreary task of interdiction – depriving the enemy of his V2 supply routes – became top priority and the impact of his arrival was timely and positive. 'Rastus' was an aggressive and demanding leader. But we could not have wished for a better commanding officer.

Day after day the clouds hung low over the sodden polders. Attempts to get through to our targets were frustrated time and again. Once we were caught running close to a narrow gap in the overcast, providing the German gunners with excellent tracking data, and our press-on CO's aircraft was badly damaged. There was outrage in his voice as he handed over the lead and we started our long descent towards the target.

I was afraid. Not so much of the enemy but the weather, which was atrocious, and for the chaps who were with me. Afraid that I might fail to find the target or bring them safely home.

Below cloud base, skirting a violent storm, reflector sights glowed ruby red against a receding wall of mist. Rain curtained the railway line. Lower still, catching the outlines of a level crossing ahead – dim original of our photograph at briefing. In the final moments we spotted a repair gang at work and raked their truck with our cannons in a single flying pass. A burst of tracer reached up to bar the way and vanished in the surrounding downpour.

More rain obliterated the scene before the first bombs went off. I pulled up into a turn:

"Bassett White Leader orbiting port three miles south of the target."

And back came an anxious: "Black Four – there's no one ahead of me!"

That was the last man to attack. What on earth did he mean? Had all the others bought it? Then reason prevailed and a quick glance confirmed that four Typhoons – and a distant fifth just visible through the murk – were closing up rapidly from behind.

COMBAT AND COMPETITION

"It's OK Black Four. I have you in sight. We're all here. Come on up and join us."

The Wing seemed doomed to endless interdiction. Targets came in every conceivable form – track, embankments, goods yards, signal boxes, junctions and bridges – especially bridges.

For the command had gone out. London had taken enough. The deadly flow of V2s to the launching sites must be cut down to size or, better still, stopped completely. The enemy thought otherwise. This was his ultimate terror weapon, shortly to change the whole course of the war, and nothing must stand in its way. When the lines were cut he drove his repair gangs with utter ruthlessness. So we went out and cut them again and again.

Interdiction was a slog. But there was one consolation. The V2 offensive against Antwerp would have been infinitely worse without it.

Sometimes an easy show produced unexpected hazards. As happened when I took a section of four to destroy a set of lock gates east of Nijmegen. An ideal target for a low level attack, no flak, and our bombing seemed to be spot on. Except that I almost collided with the target – mushing violently through the plumes of spray thrown up by my own cannon shells.

As we reformed after the attack Ben Lenson warned me that I had a double hang up[7], which explained a great deal. He was closing in for a look.

"Bassett Leader your aircraft looks OK. Your bombs too. But the fins are a badly damaged."

So what about those two little propellers, safety elements in the fusing system, had they gone too? Ben wasn't sure. I checked the selector switches, operated the bomb push continuously, and pumphandled the control column. All in vain. The bombs stayed put.

I called Craven A[8] for assistance and there was an armourer waiting at the end of the runway. He came forward as I slowed carefully to a stop and disappeared under the wings. Moments later he emerged grinning broadly and giving me the thumbs up. Panic over! The fins looked horrible. Battered and twisted, the propellers torn off, so that the detonator pistols were floating free. The slightest jar would have blown my aircraft to pieces!

With the first snows the polder countryside surrounding the Zuider Zee, which contained many of our interdiction targets, became even more bleak and secretive. Dyke and canal, villages and farms, stood

CHAPTER FIVE   WINTER IN FLANDERS

out against a covering of white. The landscape looked flatter, more vulnerable than ever to the whims of its conquerors who might inundate it again at any time. Snow storms stalked the leaden skies creating worlds of dazzling blindness.

This seasonal weather brought with it other, more significant, changes. The Luftwaffe began to appear again in increasing numbers. And suddenly, incredibly, the Hun was on the offensive, pushing forward with armour through the Eifel and into the Ardennes. On Tommy's map in Ops the enemy spearheads, and the bulge in the bomb line towards the Meuse, began to look distinctly ominous and there was even talk of a breakthrough from Liege towards Antwerp.

For the present General Winter seemed firmly on von Rundstedt's side, and the Allied Air Forces were grounded for days on end, allowing the German columns to move forward unimpeded. Our new Wing Leader, encouraged by the way in which the weather often seemed to improve after dark, began to consider night intrusion. When a Ju 88 over Deurne illuminated an American convoy, and shot it up, his enthusiasm knew no bounds.

The idea was hardly new, but the thought of ranging around those dreaded polders, in the darkness and the dead of winter, did not appeal. It became even less attractive when I found myself on the Wingco's short list. Then came the German paratroop rumour and night intrusion seemed like the lesser of two evils!

It started with a 266 show against Deelen airfield to the north of Arnhem. The place was said to be full of troop transports preparing for an airdrop on Deurne. Strategically, as part of a concerted plan to link up with the armoured drive westwards from Liege, and assuming that the Germans still had the resources, it made good sense.

266 returned from Deelen empty handed. But the rumours intensified. The Ju52s were definitely there, too well camouflaged to be seen, and the woods around were swarming with troops. These veterans of Emaal Eben, and Crete, fanatical battle hardened troops who had fought in the snows of Russia and hung on for months in the ruins of Monte Cassino, would be dropping in to beat up the pilots tonight – and if not tonight, maybe tomorrow night, or the night after.

We set up every conceivable kind of booby trap and retired to bed, fully dressed, pistols at the ready. Visions of coal scuttle helmeted giants, armed to the teeth with machine pistols and potato masher grenades, disturbed our sleep. Came the dawn, and Goss the batman trying to revive us with his mugs of hot sweet tea, but we were flaked

COMBAT AND COMPETITION

out and exhausted.

We never slept in our clothes again but there were other nights of alarm before the German advance was finally halted. As for the night intruder project it never got off the ground.

By day we continued to be thwarted by the weather. A fighter sweep towards Aachen, conducted above an impenetrable layer of mist and low cloud, was notable only for the number of engines which began to run rough after more than a week on the ground. The Luftwaffe had disappeared. And the enemy's armoured spearheads were hidden in the murk below – totally out of reach.

Stuck between that blanket of white and the cloudless vault above was to feel totally naked and frustrated. My engine vibrated horribly. Drop tanks drained. Eyes searched unceasingly for enemy fighters, or a gap in the overcast down below through which we could find something, almost anything, to attack. We came home empty handed and thoroughly fed up.

193 tangled with the Luftwaffe on Christmas Eve, and on Christmas Day as well. The first occasion was a fighter sweep in the Osnabruck area, and I was airborne as spare, determined not to miss the fun after the fiasco over Aachen. The bomb line came and went. No one turned back. I hung on, hoping against hope. The Rhine came into view – and the CO was not amused:

"Spare go home NOW!"

I was furious. But there was much worse to follow. Four aircraft turned back, with engine and other problems, minutes after my departure. The remaining four soldiered on and were bounced by 50 plus, 109s and 190s, near Enschede. One Typhoon was never seen again, and another was damaged, with no claims against the enemy.

197 in the same area fared even worse, losing two and one damaged, to twelve 190s which suffered no losses in return. On Christmas day 'B' Flight, caught by a mixed force of about 60 enemy fighters whilst attacking a train, helped to redress the balance. The locomotive blew up in a cloud of steam. Mike Bulleid destroyed a 190, another was badly damaged, and the Typhoons returned without loss.

In the evening Johnny Baldwin attended Christmas dinner as our guest. He had just received a bar to his DSO. There were speeches, and gentle inebriation set in, but most of us went to bed early.

Derek Erasmus's skill as a leader was well demonstrated in the destruction of an MT Repair Unit west of Arnhem. It was our last op of the year, with twelve aircraft, and the Squadron was carrying a

CHAPTER FIVE   WINTER IN FLANDERS

mixed load of high explosive and incendiaries. The aiming point was unmistakable, a massive rectangular roof in the middle of a heavily wooded site, and his dive was beautifully positioned and uncompromisingly steep. The bombs went off in a single rolling salvo, and the whole building disappeared in a sea of smoke and flame. Incredibly there were no near misses amongst the surrounding trees for the whole bomb load had fallen inside the four walls of the target.

We came home in a state of high elation ready to sign off with a storming squadron break. And that December afternoon – with Derek's exhortation ringing in our ears as we let down towards the airfield:

"Make it a good one chaps!"

We excelled ourselves. Tight across the threshold – pulling up one by one with controlled violence and metronome precision like guardsmen on parade – undercarriage selection from an inverted position – and the tightest steepest curved approach into a closely sequenced stream landing.

A splendid team manoeuvre. Like the Typhoon it had become part of our lives – signing off each sortie – showing the world that we were the best.

The mood changed abruptly with the news that 197's popular CO, Allan Smith, had been shot down leading a low level attack against a bridge over the Waal. It was a great loss for, by any standard, he was an outstanding Squadron Commander. His pilots reported that he had put down OK, and had run from his aircraft, so there was good reason to believe that he was alive. Even so they were devastated and attempted to mount a revenge sortie. Which was not a good idea.

All in all New Year's Eve became a pretty subdued affair.

Vianen Bridge before attack by 193 Squadron, January 1945.

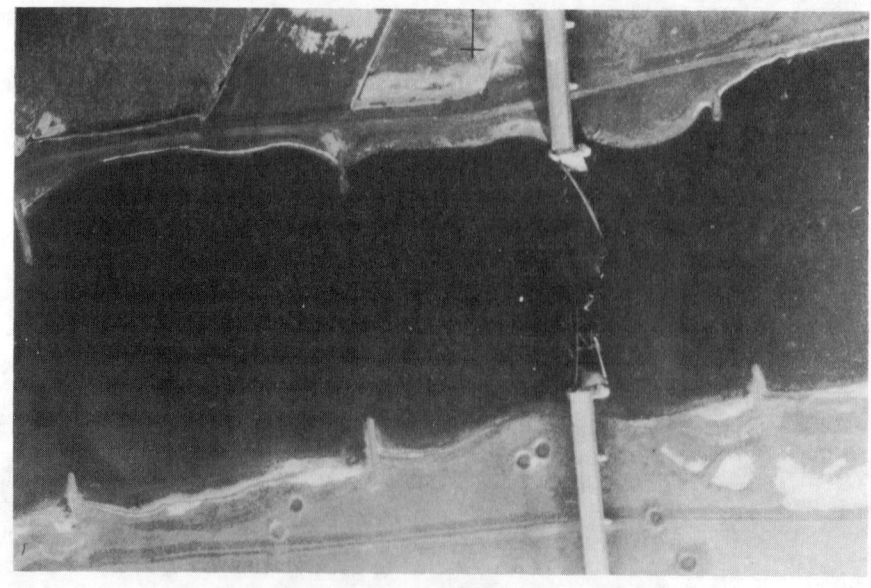

Vianen Bridge after attack by 193 Squadron, January 1945.

CHAPTER SIX

DYING REICH

The day dawned cloudless with scarcely a breath of wind and a hard frost. Perfect flying weather. But the squadrons, briefed and ready to go for almost an hour, were stuck on the ground. The runway was still being de-iced. Such a delay was unprecedented. The RAF Regiment, whose responsibility it was, had been caught out by Hogmanay and when the air raid warning sounded they were decidedly unpopular.

A train had stopped on the line beside the airfield and, when the sirens sounded, the engine driver started reducing his boiler pressure. The effect was prodigious. Great billowing clouds of white, brilliant in the low sun, which must have been visible for miles. I raced Jimmy Simpson to the top of the embankment and we confronted the culprit in his cab.

"Arretez vous tout de suite!" had no effect – apart from a mumbled "Non il est necessaire." So we drew our pistols and threatened him with instant death.

At this, much to our relief, he cut off the offending blast of steam. Simultaneously a Bofors opened fire from the opposite side of the airfield, sending a clip of shells low overhead. The driver looked very upset. But we were unrepentant:

"Serves him bloody well right! Creating a beacon like that!"

The sound of diving aircraft came almost as we saw them, a loose gaggle of Me 109s, swarming towards us above the rooftops of Antwerp. Bofors thumped, cannon and machine guns responded abruptly, and the snarl of unfamiliar engines rose to a crescendo as they flashed across the airfield, all mottled camouflage and splashes of yellow.

In their gunsights were eighty plus Typhoons, out in the open, most of them fully armed and fuelled. The target of a lifetime. Yet only the first eight carried out any sort of attack. In a single pass they destroyed just one aircraft and caused minor damage to eight others. Two further enemy formations appeared in the circuit. Flying aimlessly around at low level, they made no attempt to avoid the defensive fire, and departed to a cynical chorus of "Weave, you buggers, weave!"

Long afterwards it emerged that JG77 had put up about 100 aircraft for the attack on Deurne. Only one Gruppe of about thirty found the target, while the rest searched in vain to the north. On the way home they blundered across the V1 routes to Antwerp, where the massed ack ack took a dreadful toll. JG77 never flew again in Geschwader strength.

Within the hour we were on our way to attack a suspension bridge over the Waal. Almost next door to the one which had been Allan Smith's downfall, it was to remain standing for another three days, before we finally took it out. Ben Lenson, who was flying number two to Jimmy Simpson on the second attack, scored the two vital hits. His thousand pounders exploded on the roadway, in the middle of the main span, and the whole structure rolled slowly sideways and sagged into the water. It was a superb piece of bombing.

New Year's Day had begun with enemy fighters. For 193 it ended with intense flak, one pilot shot down in flames, and a remarkable escape. The survivor was Charlie Hall. A 20mm shell exploded inside his starboard main tank and the fuel failed to ignite. Lucky Charlie.

Charlie joined me shortly afterwards, with two other pilots, on a trip by road to Chievres south east of Brussels. There we were due to pick up four new Typhoons, part of a larger batch, being flown in by the ATA on their first Continental delivery. Chievres, until recently a USAAF base, had become the temporary home of 123 Typhoon Wing which been had moved there – in an essentially political gesture – to support the Yanks and confront the German thrust in the Ardennes.

Our Typhoons arrived at last light, just before the snow started to come down in earnest, and we were grounded. Billeted out in a country house, which even then managed to boast huge log fires, clean sheets and feather duvets. Much appreciated as the blizzard swirled outside. But it began to look as if we might be stuck there for ages.

Field Marshal von Rundstedt's spearheads continued to move westwards and the air was full of rumours, fact and fiction, like the paratroopers of Deelen. This time they included the legendary figure of Otto Skorzeny, famous for rescuing Mussolini in 1943, and now said to be leading a special force, in American uniforms, creating havoc behind the lines! Elsewhere, so the stories went, allied fuel and ammunition dumps had been overrun and blown up. An American forward airfield had been captured by tanks, the Mustangs destroyed, and most of the personnel killed or captured. It was difficult to know what to believe.

In the end we got airborne, late on the fourth day, splashing down the runway between banks of bulldozed snow and ice. The air was crystal clear and an occasional dying cumulus, pale in the evening light, drifted slowly across our track. As we headed for home the

CHAPTER SIX   DYING REICH

snowfields thinned and faded, giving way to plough and pasture, until the landscape down below took on its familiar sodden look.

Deurne lay shadowed under a huge cumulonimbus, which extended northwards as far as the eye could see, trailing low across the Scheldt – extinguishing the gleaming tracery of waterways and flooded fields. To starboard the dark wall of turbulent cloud reared upwards and the towering thunderheads, far above, were touched with crimson by the last rays of the setting sun. The awesome power and the unearthly beauty of that scene touched me to the core. All the fears and frustrations of the last few days seemed to fall away and I became convinced in some strange way that Hitler's last offensive was already over.

During our enforced absence the Me 109G had acquired RAF livery, with yellow undersurfaces, and the letter P to identify it as a captured enemy aircraft. It was almost ready to fly, strapped down on a set of jacks just clear of the ground, and Stan Carr was preparing to make the first engine run. He slipped into the cramped cockpit and ran through the drills. The DB 601 fired first time. In less than ten minutes Stan had run through the checks, operated the undercarriage and flaps, exercised the propeller, and taken the engine up to maximum boost and RPM. No problems at all. He gave his audience a delighted grin and shut down.

We had a goer, or so we thought, Charlie and I. A briefing from Chiefy, permission from our CO and the Wing Leader, a couple of Typhoons for close escort, a word to Flying Control, and we would soon be learning all about the Gustav. Sadly authority decreed otherwise and it was sent back to England, to the Central Fighter Establishment, where our previous CO was the only member of 193 Squadron to get his hands on it.

Johnny Wells took advantage of a brief improvement in the weather to conducted the first blind bombing trials, whilst I flew attendance with a photo recce Typhoon. On the run in, flying straight and level, MRCP[1] gave corrections port or starboard and a count down to the precalculated bomb release point on their radar screens. It seemed dreary in the extreme. As the bombs fell away I switched on the two vertical cameras half hoping, if the truth were told, that they would reveal a substantial bombing error.

At the end of the photographic run I went into a long dive towards Schouwen Island where the Wing had recently carried out an attack in force. A low pass and a steep turn round the target would be sufficient

COMBAT AND COMPETITION

to collect a series of pictures on the oblique camera. It was a different approach to obtain more detail and make things easier for pilots who had not been photo recce trained. When the prints came through the low obliques were excellent. The blind bombing, as expected, showed an error in hundreds of yards. But Group insisted that it should go ahead.

The enemy offensive, which had started so well before Christmas, ground to a halt. The deep salient south of Liege slowly collapsed and we were grounded once more. Cloud and mist shrouded the airfield. Snow fell, froze, turned to slush, and fell again. Some hardy souls located an indoor pool which had no heating and went swimming. 'B' flight found an abandoned American ambulance, brought it back to Deurne, gutted the interior and built in a set of wooden lockers for our flying clobber and parachutes. It was a great success.

My own activities centred around a Fortress which had crash landed close to the runway. With New Year's day still fresh in our minds I persuaded Stan Carr to remove one of the twin 0.5 calibre turrets, and we helped ourselves to several spare guns and every round of ammunition on board. The turret fitted nicely into an old German flak position close to the squadron dispersal. If the Luftwaffe ever returned we would have our own means of defence.

While we were adding the finishing touches a V2 fell apart, directly overhead. Pumps, turbines and twisted shards of metal came showering down around the sandbagged emplacement, accompanied by the familiar receding thunder of a sonic boom.

That experience led to an interesting evening with Neville Thomas. I had called at his trailer for what was intended to be a brief chat. In the end we talked far into the night, keeping the cold at bay with the help of a whisky bottle. We talked about the enemy offensive in the Ardennes, their jet and rocket aircraft, and weapons to come. We even frightened ourselves with the thought of V2s carrying poison gas and atomic warheads!

One for the road – and the moment had come to try out my latest idea, a forward facing camera installation for our photo recce Typhoons. I explained that the technique would be very similar to low level bombing. It would require no special training and should give us really close up target pictures. Tommy looked at me owlishly – we had been at the whisky for a long time:

"If you can do it Dave, and it works, Denys Gillam and Johnny Wells would be delighted."

CHAPTER SIX   DYING REICH

He paused, obviously dying to say more, and then – drink getting the better of his natural caution:

"You'll have the opportunity soon enough, Gerry Eaton is going on rest and you'll be responsible for photo recce."

Urging me to keep quiet about our conversation he went on to talk about 257 Squadron and their recent losses. Arthur Todd was about to become the new CO and I would be joining him as a flight commander.

No hang ups about that – I felt ready for a flight – and Toddy was fine. He had joined 193 in the autumn on what was probably his fourth tour.

In the weeks that followed, after he moved in with Jimmy Simpson and myself, we managed to learn a little about his background. Toddy had flown Hurricanes in the defence of Malta and subsequently against the Vichy French in Sierra Leone. Posted home to 164 Squadron, pioneers in RP ground attack, he had continued flying Hurricanes and then Typhoons, adding to his score of enemy aircraft. Sent on rest, soon after 'D' Day, he had spent the following months engine testing at Napiers.

As for 257 Squadron they were as good a bunch as one could hope to meet. Given an understanding and confident hand at the helm they should go from strength to strength.

Keen to get the forward facing camera installation under way I sought out Stan Carr yet again. We set up an F24 with a 14" lens, as far forward as possible inside the gun bay, pointing forward. It was no good. The cannon aperture was too small and cut off much of the picture. Enlarging it was out of the question. So we scrounged a 20" lens and it might have been made for the job. I left the detailed engineering to Stan and turned my attention to other matters.

When the weather improved the V2 supply routes had again become high priority. The Hun had used our enforced absence to improve his supply position. Antwerp and London were suffering badly again.

Much of the effort was now being directed at a variety of smaller rail bridges across the polders. Difficult enough targets at best, the enemy had found a way to make them more so. Sections spanning the water were rolled back along the permanent way so that nothing was visible from above. A number of bridge bombing sorties were diverted, as a result of this subterfuge, before we got wise to it. From then on, if the structure had disappeared, we concentrated on the

COMBAT AND COMPETITION

bridge approaches.

Just before my departure from 193, Rastus and Jimmy Simpson rostered me to lead an eight aircraft show. Typical of them to set this up - so that their trainee flight commander would join his new squadron with the advantage of having done it at least once before.

Lesson one - the leader should always pass his cigarettes round at the start of briefing - excellent psychology and with Jimmy's example I had been fully converted to the idea. Now, as he gave me a conspiratorial smile and helped himself from my open case, the awful truth suddenly dawned. Briefings in future were going to be a major drain on my duty free supplies. Such were the unexpected burdens of command!

On my first sortie with 257 the weather clamped at base and the squadron diverted to Woensdrecht. The night turned bitterly cold and the black painted ex Luftwaffe huts, amongst the pine woods, provided little comfort. In the morning, when Toddy briefed us for the next op, the thought of returning afterwards to our tenements at Deurne was very welcome.

Minutes later I was standing beside him when we heard the sound of a diving aircraft and caught sight of a Spitfire, plunging vertically, high against the blue. Suddenly, and with quite appalling violence, it began to recover. Both wings folded upwards and broke away. The fuselage pitched nose down again and fell headlong, throttle wide open, to crash less than a mile from the airfield.

In the silence which followed we watched the wings fluttering downwards, above the mushroom of smoke, and a voice said softly:

"Poor sod, what the hell was he up to?"
and another, as if in reply -
"It would never have happened with a Tiffie."

Had anyone spoken - or was it all in the imagination? I looked round, hoping to find the answer, as Toddy called us to order:

"Right chaps, let's get a move on, press tits in ten minutes".

A favoured explanation was lack of oxygen, an uncontrolled dive, and a violent out of trim recovery. More likely, with hindsight, that critical Mach number effects had led to coarse application of nose up trim with the inevitable tragic consequences.

The move to B89, at Mill, south of Nijmegen coincided with the opening of the assault on the Siegfried Line. We were up early. Valises and kitbags stuffed to bursting with the accumulated bits and pieces of four winter months. A last quick breakfast in the terminal building

CHAPTER SIX   DYING REICH

and the Wing was on its way, squadron by squadron, back to the world of close support and the start line of the first spring offensive.

The day was unseasonably mild with difficult flying weather. On the first op our target was obscured by cloud. As the Squadron orbited I spotted two Spitfire XIVs beating up an adjacent enemy position and Toddy chose to attack it instead. The result was impressive and quite unexpected. A massive explosion surrounded by ever expanding concussion rings as the pressure waves tore at the moist air.

Approaching Mill and a layer of stratus was already spreading rapidly across the unfamiliar airfield. The circuit was full of aircraft, trying to get down as fast as possible, and the last few unfortunates were reduced to groping around at less than three hundred feet before it clamped completely.

By midday conditions had improved sufficiently for an attempt at blind bombing, creeping up through a gap in the overcast and setting course to the north east. In tight formation – sections in finger four – dangerously silhouetted against the cloud below as we responded to the controller's instructions:

"This is Cosycot, steer zero six zero..... port five degrees..... steady..... thirty seconds to go..... twenty seconds..... ten seconds..... five..... four..... three..... two..... one..... zero!"

Bombs gone, and nothing to see. No cannon fire, no flak, no explosions down below. Just a solid layer of cloud. To a man we disliked it intensely and doubted its value. But Group and the Army seemed happy enough. Who, we wondered, was kidding who?

Late on the same afternoon the sky cleared completely and we were briefed for a Wing show against the northern hinge of the enemy line. Overlooking two great rivers, with the Reichswald forest screening its southern flank, the Matterborn feature looked almost impregnable. A fortress guarding the heart of Germany.

Now, it was under siege. The red roofed hamlets and dark patches of woodland, were being subjected to a massive artillery bombardment. Fire and flame wreathed the landscape. The smoke of battle rose high in the air and the approach roads were crowded with advancing Allied columns as we had not seen them since the heady days of Falaise. As we dived on the camouflaged positions, and the defences responded with a violent barrage of light flak, it was evident that the winter stalemate on the northern sector was over at last.

That night, long after we turned in, I caught the pulse jet resonance of an approaching V1 and wakened to utter silence. A memory of Antwerp which would haunt me, on and off, for years. In reality there was little enough to disturb our sleep. Just a faint rumble of guns, when the wind was in the east, and the familiar dawn chorus of Sabre engines.

The huts in which we slept might have been worse and they had stoves to keep us warm when the nights were chilly. But the wooden prefab buildings, at the back of each dispersal, were more like field shelters of the sort that are used for animals. Mill, like all ALGs, was pretty basic and had been completed in some haste. The PSP runways and perimeter track were surrounded by lethal acres of soft peaty soil and drainage ditches. High ridges of earth had been thrown up by the levelling operations and then abandoned. Our jeeps could barely cope. But help was at hand. The squadrons were about to be issued with Bren carriers!

The Luftwaffe only appeared twice during that early spring offensive. On the first occasion an Me 109, flying straight and level over the airfield, was caught by a section from 193 Squadron. They lined up one at a time, filling it with their cannon shells, until it responded by diving into the ground. Less impressive still was the Me 262, in fighter bomber guise, which made a hit and run attack on the next door airfield and appeared to run out of height as it headed for home.

As the Army worked slowly south they came up against stubborn resistance in the German frontier towns and villages. In reality these formed part of the Siegfried Line and many were 'liberated' in attacks which involved successive waves of Typhoons battering them for hours on end.

In one set piece attack the Wing destroyed an ancient Dutch Castle, which formed the core of a strong enemy position, on the east bank of the Maas. Bijen Beek looked magnificent. But the occupants refused to surrender and there were allied lives at stake. We took it out in a combined effort – three squadrons with thousand pounders – followed by one with RPs.

The classic outline, standing four square inside its rectangular moat, made a splendid aiming point and 257 released as low as possible with instantaneous fusing. As we pulled away, and 263's rockets rained down behind us, the place was in ruins – massive walls breached, roof fallen in, barns and stables razed to the ground – burning from end to end.

Photo recce sorties, using the close in – steep turn – technique,

CHAPTER SIX   DYING REICH

were producing some excellent results. Bill Hurst in particular had proved an apt pupil. But it was just as well that the forward facing camera would soon be available. His low obliques of a bridge near Emmerich were an example of sheer perfectionism and considerable hazard. The flak guns could be clearly seen, following him round as he circled his objective three times with the camera running!

Bill's superb photographs of a church and seminary south of Goch – which had been used by the Wehrmacht for more secular purposes until destroyed in another attack – and my less elegant close ups of Castel Bijen Beek were given VIP treatment. Both were displayed in the Prime Minister's entrance to the Air Ministry as examples of 'Classic attacks of the week'. Excellent publicity for the Wing!

One day Toddy and I were watching 'B' Flight about to set course on a late afternoon show. Suddenly one of the aircraft dropped out, with its engine cutting, and swung into the circuit. We could see that he was going to undershoot and ran for the Bren carrier. Below 500 feet and he had forgotten his bombs. Without a wireless it was impossible to warn him. Then he realised, jettisoning them live in his haste, and they exploded on impact. Moments later he dropped out of sight, wheels and flaps down, into a thick plantation short of the runway.

The carrier got there, in a flurry of mud and spinning tracks, and we were looking at the Typhoon flown by Jock Ewans. Inverted, where it had come to rest, after cutting a swathe through the saplings. And we were afraid for him because of what might happen before we could get him out.

The ground was soft, the inevitable sand and peat, and access to the site was obstructed by ditches – so that the only possible route for the crane was a long way round. In the meantime the canopy had gone, the top of the fuselage, windscreen, armour plate and pilot's head were buried in the topsoil. The hot engine creaked and sizzled gently as liquid seeped from inverted tanks and broken pipes.

We dug at the soft earth around the cockpit walls with our bare hands, and then remembered the shovels in the Bren carrier and managed rather better:

"Jock are you there?"

Of course he was – but somehow it seemed wrong to ask a man in his position if he was still alive. There came an answer too – through a mouthful of mud – full of apologies. For bending the aircraft. For being so much trouble. We dug some more, until the trim moustache became visible, and it was possible to switch off the ignition, turn off the fuel and get the mud out of his mouth. We told him not to release his harness, that we would get him out soon, and to stop apologising.

After that it was a matter of waiting for the crane, the fire tender, and blood wagon. We lay in the damp earth on each side of the upturned cockpit and Jock was passing calm, but nothing would stop the flow of apologies.

It was almost dark by the time he was out and on a stretcher. Only then did he admit to any injuries. How bad we never discovered for the doctors were noncommittal when we visited him in hospital. Then he was gone. Evacuated to England.

Jock was the Squadron's last casualty. Less than a week later – a week in which amongst other things we destroyed a troop train and a convoy of thirty trucks – we were disbanded. The AOC, when he visited us, suggested that it was due to a shortage of trained Typhoon pilots. Other squadrons were similarly affected. 257 had a proud record and would live again.....

Some of the pilots went on rest, others were posted round the four remaining squadrons. Toddy went back to the UK on Mustang IVs and the Wingco sent me up to the front as a VCP^2 Controller.

I set off, greatly displeased by the turn of events. Yet this was an opportunity to broaden my knowledge of close support and I made a determined effort to approach it in a positive frame of mind. So much for good intentions. Stuck at divisional level, on permanent standby, it seemed as if my services would never be required. Even a request to visit the forward areas, with the idea of drumming up some unofficial trade, was turned down.

After almost three weeks of enforced idleness my little team was suddenly ordered to move up, close to the Rhine, opposite Wesel. The brigade headquarters to which we had been directed was just moving into the local bank where they discovered a vast cache of wine. The slim bottles, packed in straw filled wooden cases, made a mouth watering sight. Soon after dark we began sampling them, sitting on our camp beds amongst a jumble of signal wires and the intermittent ringing of telephone handsets, until our hosts were in some danger of becoming drunk in charge.

In the morning I woke with a hangover, to the sound of mortar fire, convinced that our moment of glory was at hand. But nothing happened – except a signal from Group calling the whole thing off. The operation to clear the west bank of the Rhine was now in its final

CHAPTER SIX   DYING REICH

stages. There would be little need for VCP in the immediate future.

Much had been happening at Mill. Word had come through that Allan Smith was a prisoner of war. Denys Gillam had been posted to Group Headquarters. Partly, it was said, to prevent him from flying on ops. Not that it did much good because he continued to visit us as often as possible, borrowing an aircraft and a number two, and quietly disappearing to war. We had seen it all before while he was commanding the Wing.

Gillam was a legend. Flying Spitfires in the Battle of Britain. Bringing the Hurribomber into action. First Typhoon Wing Leader. Commandant of the Special Low Attack Instructors School. The most highly decorated British fighter pilot and undisputed master of ground attack. More than 2,000 operational sorties to his name. He had nothing to prove. Yet Mike Bulleid remembers flying with him less than a fortnight from the end of the war. No wonder that we were proud to have served under his command.

Johnny Wells, promoted to Group Captain, was now commanding the Wing and the CO of 266 Squadron, Johnny Deal, had become Wing Leader in his place.

The really bad news was that Derek Erasmus, whose leadership had done so much for 193 Squadron, had been lost on a low level attack against the main V weapon railhead at Raalte in Holland. There was a lot of cloud in the target area and hardly anything had been seen. No obvious flak or power lines. Just an aircraft, diving into the ground, after releasing its bombs. Perhaps he had been caught by an exploding tanker, hit by his shells on the run in. But even that is conjecture. His death will always remain a mystery.

193's new Commanding Officer was plump, ebullient, and prematurely balding, with a nose which must have been well and truly broken earlier in his career. 'Butch' – and the nickname matched his looks – had joined up, in the late thirties, on a short service commission and had been given command of his first Typhoon squadron back in 1942. He was posted, without a break from ops, to lead another squadron and only went on rest after 'D' Day. One way and another he had been around for a long time.

When he joined us at Mill his main preoccupation seemed to be that of playing himself into a post war permanent commission. The contrast with Derek could hardly have been greater.

Sadness at Derek's death turned swiftly to regret that 193 had not been entrusted to Jimmy Simpson. Maybe he was almost tour expired

COMBAT AND COMPETITION

– but the war in Europe could not go on for ever. His behaviour, almost his every action, revealed what the squadron meant to him, not only as a unit but in human terms as well. And he knew what made it tick. Able and trusted, popular with air and ground crews alike, he was the obvious choice. But Jimmy, still commanding 'A' Flight, was on leave and I was about to become his successor. Felix Cryderman was on a fighter leader's course and 'B' Flight had passed into the capable hands of Snowy Harrison, an Australian from 266.

My return to ops coincided with a spell of anticyclonic spring weather. The Americans were already across the Rhine at Remagen. Along our own front, north of the Ruhr, the British and Canadian armies were poised to cross this last major barrier to the heartland of Germany.

On the first sortie, leading eight aircraft on interdiction, the Rhine from 8,000 feet was only a faint glimmer through the haze. Running in on our target near Hengelo a gaggle of Lancasters was clearly visible in the middle distance, bombing one of the German border towns. On the way home I led the formation towards the bomber stream in the hope of finding some German fighters. But there were none, except for a couple of Me 163s, strange tailless shapes darting in like gadflies from high above the heavies and then zooming vertically upwards – totally out of reach.

Fortunately they did not seem to be doing much damage, but we hung around climbing gently, just in case any of them happened to come within range or run out of fuel. Meantime the Lancs stoked up a lethal firestorm. Flames roared through the doomed town, drawing air inwards from all around, and throwing a tornado of debris and red hot ash thousands of feet upwards. The core pushed straight through the inversion to produce a towering cumulus – awesome against the unbroken blue.

By the following day it was shirt sleeve weather in our Bren carriers, en route from briefing, and the sun shone out of a brazen sky as if summer had come too soon. There was a Wing show in the morning against an ammunition dump near Emmerich and I found myself, flying with Butch for the first time, leading the second section. The target was well marked by fires and explosions from the squadrons ahead and we came down through the murk adding to the conflagration with our incendiaries.

That afternoon I took a section of four against enemy troops in the area of the airborne landings planned for the following day. The

CHAPTER SIX DYING REICH

smoke filled haze was worse than ever and, as we climbed towards the inversion, its smell invaded our oxygen masks. Brick dust and burning, drifting in from the heart of the Ruhr, mixed together with more of the same from the battlefields down below. The dying smell of Hitler's Reich.

It was a satisfactory little show. The target was easy to find in spite of the poor visibility and the bombing was accurate. The flak was ferocious, as so often seemed to be the case on the eve of an Allied offensive, but we returned to base unscathed. Tomorrow we might not be so lucky for the Typhoons would be on anti-flak patrol. However Jimmy was back from leave and selfishly perhaps, for he was almost on rest, we were happy to know that he would be flying with us again.

Much later Bomber Command directed a concentrated raid on Wesel. Target indicators lit the sky, prelude to a display which belied the 60 miles from Mill. We stood in unaccustomed silence outside the officers mess, watching the distant fireworks, our thoughts on that vital strip of land across the Rhine. More particularly about the guns around it on the outskirts of Wesel. Perhaps some of them would be destroyed in this attack. Or they might run short of ammunition. One could always hope.

Gun crews in open emplacements were best dealt with using anti-personnel weapons. So the Typhoons of 193 and 197 had already been armed with cluster bombs. Whilst those of 263 and 266 were carrying thin walled RPs for maximum shrapnel effect. 193 headed the roster, with sections of four taking off every 15 minutes. We were in for a busy day.

On our patrol line it was a glorious spring morning. All was peaceful. The smoke and haze of yesterday had gone, and the dropping zone lay bathed in sunshine. At first the sky was empty, and then we saw them in the distance – a vast armada reaching back beyond the horizon – 'Operation Varsity' on its way. Soon the leading formations were clearly visible. Paratroop carrying Dakotas, followed by an endless stream of glider combinations, Halifaxes, and still more Dakotas, towing their bulky charges.

They moved like a flood tide – rolling on remorselessly to break above the gentle wooded slopes beyond the Rhine. Parachutes blossomed in their hundreds and gliders, with barn door flaps extended, stooped like birds of prey. An elite force, trained to perfection, at the high noon of its assault.

Near the limits of our search area a heavy flak battery opened fire.

COMBAT AND COMPETITION

The pattern of trenches and gun emplacements was clearly visible, hastily camouflaged, in the middle of an open field. We went in fast with our clusters, strafing for good measure. A burst of flame and smoke shrouded the site – and I could hardly hide my satisfaction:

"Good show White Section – that should keep the buggers quiet!"

A game of cat and mouse with the German gunners. Low down, encouraging them to have a go, and mostly they lay doggo until our backs were turned. When the streams of tracer came chasing up from behind, we were – as the Squadron diary once recorded, tongue in cheek:

"Not really scared of flak, just highly strung!"

Back at Mill the sections of four came and went. For a long time no losses occurred. Then a section from 'B' Flight, led by Snowy Harrison, returned without him. He had baled out amongst the gliders.

At the final count the Wing had flown a total of 88 sorties. Two Typhoons were missing, with one pilot safe and the other, Snowy, still outstanding.

'Varsity' had been lucky with the weather, which broke immediately afterwards, and it was possible to catch up on other things. Stan Carr had just completed the prototype forward facing camera installation and the first test flight proved that it worked.

For the operational trial Tommy suggested an SS Battalion HQ, in a small group of houses, which we had recently destroyed. It was ideal because 35 Wing had already taken a vertical pinpoint and this would provide a conventional target photograph for comparison.

The approach in a shallow dive was exactly like a low level attack. Even the bomb/RP push started the camera running. The results were spectacular. Showing a degree of detail which was not apparent in the previous pictures. An unexpected feature, created by the relationship between the leading edge aperture and the lens, was the way in which the centre of the shot was highlighted as if by a very powerful flash.

Examples of these first 'forward obliques' were forwarded to Group HQ. They requested 100 copies which were circulated widely. Rumour had it that 35 Wing, in the person of their Commanding Officer, were not amused. We were stealing their thunder!

A week or two later Tommy invited me into his office. A set of prints was lying on his desk. 35 Wing had fitted a forward facing camera in the slipper tank[3] of a Spitfire XIV and they too had circulated their first results. 'Death of a Hun – by Group Captain Anderson' featured a human figure caught on top of a set of lock gates

CHAPTER SIX   DYING REICH

and being mown down by cannon fire as it tried to escape. Tommy smiled at me benignly:

"Now look what you've done! You shouldn't go around stirring up Group Captains like that!"

Snowy returned after we had given him up for lost. Landing in the thick of the fighting he had abandoned his chute and been taken prisoner by American paratroops. Tall, fair haired, and wearing a 'Gott mit Uns' belt, they would not accept that he was an Australian.

Set to work unloading supplies he eventually managed to convince an officer that he was indeed what he claimed to be. Life then became more bearable. He drew a rifle and armband, dug a foxhole, and spent the time trying to pick off snipers – a lethal occupation if ever there was one! When the British armour broke through he hitched his way back to base. In his own words, his voice slurred with exhaustion:

"They were very hostile days!"

A USAAF Mustang IV made an emergency landing at Mill and required an engine change. Keen to fly anything new, I let it be known that Mustangs already featured in my log book, and that I would be happy to do the air test.

As I climbed aboard the memories came rolling back – the well engineered cockpit – toe brakes and tailwheel lock, pistol grip control column and electric propeller controls. For a moment I feared a re-run of my negative feelings about the Mustang I. But absolutely not. The Merlin 61 sounded reassuringly like a Spit IX as it crackled into life, and the big teardrop hood made a world of difference. One seemed to sit higher, more in command. I ran up the engine and waved the chocks away.

The Merlin had more power. I applied too much of it, too quickly, and maybe the trim was wrong. The big paddle bladed prop swung the aircraft to port. Maximum starboard rudder was not enough and more power would only make the situation worse. For what seemed an age I hung on grimly, as the Mustang veered across the runway, until by some miracle it lifted into the air, within seconds of mud and disaster.

After putting the replacement engine through its paces, I concentrated on the approach and landing. It was in the groove, the touchdown smooth as silk. But I felt a real Prune after that squalid take off. Tempting to have another go. Much better to leave well alone. I taxied in and returned the Mustang to its ground crew.

An impressive aircraft. In a totally different league to the Allison engined version. But the old problem, whether or not to use the flaps for manoeuvring, was still there. Almost as important, something which I had not recognised previously, the need to adjust to its greater inherent stability. Given time to know it better – nothing would have been more satisfying than a chance to fly a Mustang IV on one of its deep penetration missions.

By the time the weather improved our troops were across the Rhine in force and moving fast. One thrust had swung southwards to cut off the Ruhr and another was driving towards the north German plain, threatening to trap the enemy forces in Holland.

Time to find out what the Huns were up to. Perhaps we might even catch them on the roads again. 'B' Flight went first. Jimmy Simpson and I, each with a number two, followed soon afterwards.

Near Hengelo, accompanied by Bob Waldron, I caught a long convoy struggling eastward and we started several fires amongst the trucks. Back at base, comparing notes with Jimmy, whilst our aircraft were being rearmed and refuelled, it seemed a good idea to have another go at them before dark. Ideally we would have carried phosphorous incendiaries on all four aircraft, but there was no time for that, and only Waldron's was bombed up.

Airborne again I found myself prey to conflicting emotions. Satisfaction at catching the enemy out in the open again. Concern in the knowledge that we had never before cut it so fine in terms of daylight. And an uneasy feeling that I had encouraged Jimmy, one of the few among us who was married, to fly an extra sortie at the very end of his tour.

The light was going fast when we got to the scene and the convoy, marked here and there by fires still burning from the previous attack, was nearly invisible. Our cannon shells sparkled brilliantly in the gloom, and Bob Waldron's incendiaries spread themselves across the road in a scintillating carpet, but it was too dark to see anything else.

On the way home we headed into the setting sun. Down below the land had become indistinct. Not a light to be seen. Farms and villages lost in the purple darkness. But we flew on in sunshine, aircraft burnished with light, each propeller a disc of shimmering gold. Up here was warmth and life. We could go on forever. A few spans away the rugged shape of Jimmy's Typhoon hung motionless in the sky, his head hunched forward in familiar silhouette, and I experienced a sharp sense of loss. For this would be our last op together.

The demand for forward obliques came thick and fast. Catching up on some of the recent Wing shows was high priority. On one, which

CHAPTER SIX   DYING REICH

included a General's house and signals centre, I set out with a dreadful hangover. Jimmy's farewell party the previous night had taken its toll. Fortunately it was a peaceful trip, and for other reasons as well, because several runs were needed to capture the individual targets on film.

Napalm, that controversial weapon of future wars, came to us in preview as a converted drop tank. Nearly eight foot long, and two feet in diameter, like a beer barrel with a spherical nose and straight tapered tail. Painted a brilliant red.

Another pilot was given the doubtful privilege of dropping the first pair on the S'Hertogenbosch range – and I accompanied him in one of the photo recce aircraft. The results were disappointing – a series of nice clear photographs of a low flying Typhoon – but nothing else. The igniters, wrongly positioned, had failed to work and the target was drenched with 180 gallons of useless petroleum jelly.

Some days later it was my turn. I watched as the armourers went through the laborious process of filling the bombs, by Jerrican, through a large funnel. Twenty x $4\frac{1}{2}$ gallons per bomb, at $2\frac{1}{2}$ minutes each, almost an hour.

Boscombe Down had carried out trials with the 90 gallon version, and a smaller one as well, back in December. But no information had reached us – and I had to work out my own dropping technique. Despite their streamlined shape, the bombs had no fins, and they were certain to tumble. I decided to drop them from the lowest possible altitude.

The effect was most impressive. The fiery mass sprayed forward and upwards, in a cascade of incandescent reds and yellows which threatened to engulf my tail. Many years later I read the Boscombe Report, which recommended a minimum dropping height of 100 feet, at speeds not in excess of 290mph. However their cine film plots suggested that I was probably quite safe.

The upshot of that demonstration was a napalm strike against a strong point near Arnhem which led to my first clash with Butch. Totally ignoring the non ballistic properties of our new weapon he briefed us for a dive bombing attack. I could hardly believe my ears. Driving over to the aircraft we had a stormy discussion as I tried to persuade him to rebrief for a low level delivery. Just to make matters worse the target was partly obscured by artificial smoke and Butch revealed his indecision with a shallow dive, releasing above 2,000 feet. The bombs tumbled all over the place. But my request to lead the

COMBAT AND COMPETITION

second section in low level was sternly refused.

Butch had an opportunity to retrieve the situation later that day, going back with twelve aircraft, and a mixed bomb load. After the napalm fiasco we wanted to hit the enemy hard. This time we went in on the deck, and the artificial smoke hung about us, rolling downwind like dirty fog banks on either side – pointing the way.

When the Canadians overran the position they found the house at its centre razed to the ground. Our phosphorous incendiaries and anti-personnel clusters had wreaked havoc amongst the surrounding trenches and dugouts, and the survivors were totally demoralised. Even the earlier, inaccurate, napalm bursts had played a significant part due to their unexpected and frightening nature.

That was the first and last time we flew operationally with napalm, inconclusive but obviously potent, and possibly the only time it was used by the RAF in World War II. USAF Lightnings dropped napalm in Italy during 1945 – although where, and how often, is not clear – and the bombs used on the Boscombe trials had attachment lugs for British and American racks.

As I wrestled with the problems of napalm, Bob Gibbings was having his troubles elsewhere. On an armed recce led by Geoff Hartley he was strafing an airfield when the target blew up in his face. In his graphic description:

I found myself flying through a red hell, convinced that my last moments had come. The engine stopped, presumably from oxygen starvation, only to restart immediately I emerged from the holocaust. To my utter amazement I was still flying, and I climbed gingerly away. The windscreen and canopy slowly cleared revealing an aircraft that was almost a total write-off, leaking fuel, oil and glycol, the leading edges burst open, everything scorched and burnt.

Incredibly Bob flew on for 20 minutes climbing to 7,000 feet in the process. A few miles short of the lines he decided that there was no hope of getting home, and prepared to bunt out, jettisoning the canopy and releasing the straps. Just a little trial to make sure the system worked. He pushed the stick tentatively forward, and in a trice was half out of the cockpit, trying desperately to hang on to the spade grip.

Another minute and his battered Typhoon would have been safely back over friendly territory. Instead he was dangling on the end of a parachute being shot at by the enemy. He landed unhurt only to fall into the hands of a one eyed madman, a major from the Russian front, who threatened him with a firing squad. Hostilities ended before he

CHAPTER SIX   DYING REICH

reached a prison camp and he eventually found his way back to the Wing.

We moved onto German soil wondering what to expect. But the satisfaction was real enough as the Wing formed up and set course for Drope to the northeast of Lingen. Sixty or more Typhoons cruising low, over the homeland of a broken enemy, on a route surrounded by landmarks familiar from months of fighting. Now all was peaceful. The Wehrmacht and the flak guns had gone. But the war was not over yet. So we flew in battle formation searching the skies for danger.

In my battledress pocket was a piece of paper newly issued to every pilot. A Union Jack in full colour and a message to our Russian allies, which started with the words 'Ya Englichanin', obviously intended to increase the chances of surviving a forced landing in Russian occupied territory. It underlined the unpleasant fact that they were already besieging Berlin for there was almost total distrust of Stalin and his evil regime.

We never talked about the end of the war. To do so might raise images of survival and these could be counter productive. Better to live with what you had come to accept after many months on ops – after seeing what happened to those around you – a growing awareness of your own vulnerability and the idea that you too might not survive. Better by far to soldier on as if the odds were unchanged. Otherwise you might be tempted not to press home your attacks. It was not so much a matter of courage as a form of self protection.

At another level the end of hostilities would mean the loss of a way of life that, incredible as it may seem, many of us had come to cherish. The wonderful camaraderie of a front line squadron in which possessions and class played no part – and what mattered were basic human values – skill, integrity and trust. Add the challenge and uncertainty of operational flying and a modern, heavily armed, fighter aircraft at your fingertips. Small wonder if we continued living for the present.

As for the Germans – fanatical in defeat – we might well be faced with a period of final redoubts, of Luftwaffe remnants carrying out suicide missions. Who could tell how and when it might all end?

Allan Wyse, our last recruit, joined the Squadron just after we got to Drope. A first class sportsman and a natural pilot he had reached a Bomber OTU, flying Halifaxes, before they decided that he was too short to cope. Transferred to fighters, he had suffered the trauma of hearing that the rest of his crew had been shot down and killed on

COMBAT AND COMPETITION

their very first op. Allan seemed to feel that he had let them down. But it was no fault of his and I was very pleased to have him on my flight.

His first show with us was particularly satisfying – destroying a train which been reported south of Hamburg. We found it exactly as described at briefing, sitting in a little country station, the engine billowing smoke. Butch set up a copybook attack and we blew the whole thing to bits.

Once again Butch had shown that he could lead a very effective operation in straightforward circumstances. Yet that show was followed immediately by another, which was an utter shambles, and resulted in my last and most violent clash with him.

It was low level against an SS Battalion HQ, directed by 'B' Flight's Bunny Austin, who was doing a spell as a VCP Controller. Bunny drew our attention to the Y shaped drive leading to the target and it was clearly visible as Butch led the way with his section of four. As I prepared to follow, their cannon shells exploded around an adjacent farmhouse, and it was obvious that they were not going for the right place.

I aborted my own attack, and another argument ensued with Bunny supporting me strongly. Butch insisted that he had bombed the correct target and that my section must attack it as well. In the end, as with the napalm at Arnhem, he left me with no alternative except to obey his orders.

This time it was too much. I organised an air test and came back with a set of photographs. These showed that we had attacked the wrong target and the undamaged house, with its Y shaped drive, was unmistakable. Butch knew that he had no control of my photo recce activities, for which I was directly responsible to the Wingco, and that I would do the same again if the need arose. After that he left me to lead my own shows. And he never held it against me. It was one of the nice things about him.

Two other episodes marred my time at Drope. The first happened, landing back, after Ben Lenson had been hit in the radiator and forced to bail out in the battle area. I was worrying about him as we returned to base and failed to register a warning that there was an aircraft stuck on the grass runway. After touchdown, rolling fast, the wingtips of a Spitfire suddenly appeared very close on each side of the nose. Too late to do anything except brake hard and cut the switches. The Typhoon ran on, propeller chewing up the Spitfire's rear fuselage, pitching slowly up on its nose until I was looking down the engine

CHAPTER SIX   DYING REICH

cowling into the other cockpit.

Difficult to know what to say in such a situation. I shouted in the sudden silence:

"I'm awfully sorry old chap."

He never replied, just leapt out and ran, as if pursued by the fiends of hell. The markings on his Spitfire were Free French, the Cross of Lorraine. Perhaps I had spoken in the wrong language!

The engine was shock tested, a new radiator and propeller fitted, and my aircraft was airborne again in a matter of days. The Spitfire was a write off. Vive le Typhoon!

Soon afterwards, flying photo recce on a Wing show near Emden, the attack ended quicker than expected. Badly positioned, and trying to follow the last aircraft in before the ground defences had time to draw breath, my approach was too steep with insufficient nose down trim. Holding the dive to get the usual close up photograph I was forced to make a violent recovery, pulled far too much 'G', and passed out completely.

As consciousness returned I could hear the engine, feel the spade grip in my hand, and see nothing. Vision cleared, and the aircraft was in a gentle climbing turn to port, the target far below. Sunshine flooded the cockpit like a reprieve. And then I looked at the wings. On each side, inboard of the cannons, there was a massive chordwise wrinkle and there were missing rivets all over the outer panels.

I flew gingerly home reflecting that, even in the circumstances, the amount of 'G' had been quite phenomenal. Extra care was always needed to pull off a smooth landing in the photo recce Typhoons although the elevator felt perfectly normal on the ground. There was undoubtably something different about them. I must find out why.

Stan Carr inspected the mainplanes in silence and consulted the Squadron Engineer Officer who had been a stressman at Hawkers before joining the RAF.

In the end they decided that the spars were undamaged – the wrinkles on the inboard wing section, which was not stressed skin, were of no consequence – and new rivets would take care of the rest. After that had been done, and the wrinkles hammered flat in an effort to recover the original aerodynamic shape, photo 'C' was returned to service.

The Typhoon's rugged structure had probably saved my life. But any investigation of its unusual flying characteristics would have to wait. For much to my relief we were moving on once more. I had seen

COMBAT AND COMPETITION

more than enough of Drope.

Alhorn, B111 as it had now become, was an ex Luftwaffe night fighter station south east of Bremen. The runways, except for one which had been hastily repaired, were cratered and useless. The hangers no longer existed and the dispersals on the edge of a pine forest were crowded with the burned out wrecks. A few buildings surprisingly, including an excellent officers mess were virtually untouched.

There was little time to enjoy any of that. As the fronts, east and west, converged on the Elbe it was reported that a major German force was moving northwards to make a last stand in Norway. It would travel by sea, and embarkation was already under way, an ideal target for the Typhoons. We were up before dawn on May 3rd, to a forecast of perfect flying weather, and the news that 2nd TAF had ordered maximum effort against shipping in the Lubeck/Neustadt area. This was out of range from Alhorn, so the squadrons were to operate from B150 Hustedt, north of Celle, alongside 121 Wing under 83 Group Control.

I well remember those last hectic days of the war, not least because Hustedt was close to Belsen and 121's Wingco had just visited it himself.

Between sorties he attempted to describe what he had seen and could still barely believe. And we, for the first time, became aware of the horrors of the concentration camps.

I led two shows that day and the second, with eleven aircraft remains as clear as yesterday. It was a beautiful afternoon. Visibility must have been upwards of 40 miles, and a line of a cumulus shadowed the Schleswig peninsular to port. Lubeck bay was shrouded in smoke from earlier shipping strikes. Further up the coast, beyond Neustadt, flames suddenly erupted from an enemy airfield. The fire grew and spread feeding a huge column of smoke which drifted away inland.

Immediately ahead, in the lee of Fehmarn Island, a modern passenger vessel lay at anchor, uncamouflaged, dirty white in the sunshine – and a freighter nearby. We went down on them almost vertically, hanging in our straps, through a salvo of rocket flak and the familiar curtain of shells, the hulls expanding in our sights. Both ships were engulfed in bomb bursts, flame and smoke from direct hits, and near misses cascading them with water.

Climbing away there was an excited call on the radio. Someone had

CHAPTER SIX   DYING REICH

spotted a flying boat low over the sea. Mike Bulleid as always was quick off the mark. At full throttle – overtaking fast – an impossible deflection shot and he hit it fair and square with his first burst. By the time the rest of us got there the BV 138 was already doomed. We were supposed to be credited with an eleventh share apiece but, without question, it was another for Mike's bag of enemy aircraft. A fantastic piece of shooting.

As we left the wreckage, and headed for home, an MTB appeared zigzagging flat out. Perhaps it was on an air sea rescue mission, but the thought never crossed our minds as our cannons tore it to shreds. The Wingco's story about those poor devils at Belsen was there to spur us on. There was no mercy for the enemy that day.

Fuel was running low so I reduced speed for maximum range, and opened up the formation. The final part of the flight crossed an area of flat and featureless countryside dotted with hundreds of small woods. Difficult to know your exact position. There was a certain amount of twitch on the wireless and we came straight in to Hustedt without a circuit.

On the way home that evening we cruised into the setting sun, the air was calm and still, the last of the cumulus fading away overhead. It had been epic stuff. The chaps had done the Squadron proud. Almost as if they realised that it might be the last time. As if they intended to safeguard its reputation right to the end.

Around me was the very essence of 193. Ben Lenson, safely back from his recent parachute descent. Jimmy Fishwick, his commission just through after many months, and Bob Waldron. From 'B' Flight there was Snowy Harrison supported by a formidable quartet – all of them nudging the 200 sortie mark – Charlie Hall, Mike Bulleid, Eddie Richardson sometime keeper of the Squadron diary, and Bunny Austin recently returned from his spell as VCP Controller. And there were the new boys too. Mike Thexton, who had joined the Squadron when 257 was disbanded, and Allan Wyse flying like a veteran as my number two.

A few words on the radio and they moved into tight line astern, preparing for the let down and break. As they did so I caught a fleeting glimpse of propeller discs, golden in the sunset, and was possessed once more by that wonderful feeling. Flying on forever above a fading, dying, landscape.

Less than twenty hours later, after more shipping strikes around Lubeck Bay and Fehmarn Island, we had fired our last shots in anger.

Castle Bijen Beek attacked by 146 Wing, 21st February 1945. Shown in the PM's viewing room as 'A classic RAF attack of the week.' (Author's Low Oblique).

Ammunition dump, Zevenaar attached by 146 Wing, March 1945. (Author's Forward Oblique).

CHAPTER SEVEN

BALBOS AND BOOZE

With the end of the fighting in Europe summer had come. Marked by a spell of magnificent weather which seemed set to go on and on. Like the celebrations at Alhorn. The party to end all parties.

Each morning after the latest possible breakfast, or no breakfast at all, we took ourselves off into the surrounding countryside seeking the spoils of war. In the evenings, surrounded by a growing collection of motor vehicles, the party rekindled itself with renewed vigour. We moved indoors as darkness fell, pausing briefly for solid refreshment and thundered on into the small hours.

On the third day I shook off my hangover and went back to work. Group wanted photographs of the final shipping strikes and Charlie Hall had volunteered to come along as my number two. There was a ceasefire in force. But hostilities were not due to terminate officially for another 24 hours and Tommy, briefing us beforehand, stressed that we should take nothing for granted. Our aircraft were fitted with drop tanks, in order to make the round trip from Alhorn, and the cannons were fully armed.

We cruised low down across the rich farmland of Niedersachsen and Schleswig Holstein, past the sprawling ruins of Hamburg and the burnt out shell of Lubeck until Travemunde lay ahead. Skirting the white beaches we dropped down towards the *Deutschland* and the *Cap Arcona*, lying close together, on their beam ends in the shallow water. The vast hulls loomed large against my gunsight and I switched the camera on.

The whole of that forward oblique pass between Lubeck Bay and Fehmarn Island was a graveyard of sunken, burnt out and capsized ships. Charlie and I returned to base, well satisfied with what we had seen, happy that the Typhoons had played a major part in frustrating plans for that final Nazi stand in Norway. On subsequent reckoning 146 Wing alone had sunk more than 40,000 tons of enemy shipping.

Shortly afterwards we learned that some were prison ships, whose wretched inmates had been moved from their concentration camps in the last weeks and days of the war. Whether they were hostages for the safe conduct of their unspeakable jailers, or about to be sunk in an effort to destroy the evidence of atrocity, had yet to be ascertained. Whatever the truth our attacks had unwittingly added to their sufferings.

Back at Alhorn Felix Cryderman had grounded himself. He had

COMBAT AND COMPETITION

confronted Butch earlier in the day and refused to fly a Typhoon again claiming that it was no longer necessary and much too dangerous. From then on he ribbed us unmercifully for risking our lives, until they sent him home to Canada, which was just what he wanted. Ironically he was to be killed, bush flying in British Columbia, before many years had passed.

When the AOC visited us to present the Squadron badge, Butch was in his element, determined as ever to secure that elusive permanent commission. You could see it in his face as the band fell in and he took command of the parade.

Air Vice Marshal Hudleston's words were complimentary. But there was a dreadful sense of anticlimax. Had he really been talking about us?

Our future, and that of the Squadron was obscure to say the least. In a month or two we might be scattered to the four winds. We celebrated the occasion by getting rather tight.

The Wing was at Alhorn for barely a month, the beginning of a long period of painful adjustment, coming to terms with the idea of peace and thinking about the future. Some were attracted to the idea of a career in the Royal Air Force. Others kept their heads down and soldiered on hoping for the earliest possible release.

Charlie Hall and I explored the area together. Starting with the mess basement, which was knee deep in Nazi photographs and magazines, with a few swastika arm bands and ceremonial daggers abandoned in haste by their owners. The rest of the airfield was a dead loss. Everything had been destroyed. But a train of flat cars, on an adjacent railway line, was loaded with damaged aircraft which yielded a few more instruments for my bottom drawer. Most were Ju 188s and amongst them an almost undamaged Tempest V.

That railway line ran through the depth of a pine forest, where we tried our hands at deer stalking, lethally armed with German machine pistols.

We never actually hit anything and this highly dangerous sport came to an abrupt end when two stalking parties opened fire on each other as the quarry fled between them!

Fortunately there was plenty of flying, practising for the Victory Air Parades, and there were extra flights for the leaders too as they learned accurate station keeping between squadrons. This was a new skill and the range bars on our reflector sights proved invaluable until it became second nature. Then came the Balbos proper, sweating to

CHAPTER SEVEN   BALBOS AND BOOZE

hold station in the turbulent air, with 193's Typhoons proudly sporting their new scarlet eagle insignia. Butch was on leave and I was happy to be leading the Squadron again.

After the Victory Air Parades there were others. Until life seemed to become one long round of formation flying and parties. Photographic sorties continued, mainly to obtain information on ex Luftwaffe airfields. Following the system which we had developed in the later stages of the war, to assist in planning and layout, before the Wing moved to a new location.

On one such sortie over Oldenburg airfield I saw a couple of coxed fours practising on the Weser. The slim hulls and the swinging oars brought back memories of prewar bumping races on the Severn at Tewkesbury. It seemed like another world.

The target for my photographic sortie on 31st May was a grass airfield south of Hanover. Shortly afterwards on the 8th June, following yet another Victory Air Parade over Nijmegen this time for Princess Juliana of the Netherlands, the Wing moved to its last home at R16 Hildesheim.

Although the town itself had been heavily bombed the airfield was virtually untouched. Our aircraft were hangered and the Wing was accomodated in modern quarters.

For me at that moment the way ahead was clear – test flying if I could make it – or failing that a career in the RAF. My name had already come up on the first postwar list of permanent commissions, as a substantive Flight Lieutenant with backdated seniority. It seemed a good omen. I sat down and wrote a letter to my old friend at Glosters, Frank McKenna.

Hildesheim was an interesting place. It had been the last base for a staffel of the Luftwaffe's clandestine and special purposes unit – KG 200. From here they had operated a variety of aircraft, including captured Fortresses and Liberators. In the aircraft graveyard, apart from these, were examples of many German types, including the outstanding Daimler Benz engined FW 190D. Typhoons from 146 Wing had tangled with a couple of them briefly, shortly after the Luftwaffe's last fling on New Year's day, and found themselves totally outperformed.

From Hildesheim it was only a short distance into the Harz mountains. Driving up the rack railway, when the road became impassable, to reach the summit of Broken – almost 4000 feet above sea level – where the ruins of a hotel and the distorted aerials of a radar station looked out across the plains towards Magdeburg and Berlin.

Only the core of the hotel remained. A massive, ugly, hall and staircase. An overblown mural covered the walls, towering above its surroundings, three witches flying in line astern. Innocent enough you might think. But the Nazi artist obviously intended otherwise for the way in which they sat astride their broomsticks was powerfully erotic to say the least!

On the same trip we went further into the Mountains, searching for an underground V weapons factory in a salt mine near Nordhausen. There was nothing to identify it from outside. Just a single track railway leading into a narrow tunnel. A miserable place where V1 and V2 assembly was carried out, far under the hillside, in most primitive conditions. Inside, even on a fine midsummer's day, the air was cold and clammy.

Shortly after our visit a large area of the Harz, which included Broken and this unique plant, was due to be handed over to the Russians. However it was obvious that they were not going to get their hands on the contents. The whole place was a hive of activity, brilliantly lit, its production lines being stripped down and removed before our eyes.

The Americans in charge of the operation were extremely cagey, but they opened up when we asked them about the previous workforce. It was like the horrors of Belsen all over again. A nearby concentration camp, created for the express purpose, had supplied the forced labour. Many of the prisoners had lived and died underground. And there were regular transports to an extermination camp for those who were no longer able to work.

Due to the Allied bombing campaign much of the German aircraft industry had been moved to the east, particularly, so we understood, around Liepzig.

The temptation to see something of it was too great, and one hot and hazy afternoon I toured the airfields surrounding Halle.

At one several FW 190Ds were parked in the open and at another, Burg, a number of Mistels, those remarkable pickaback arrangements with a piloted Me 109 or FW 190 mounted on top of a Ju 88 or He 111. They were brave men who took them into battle, surviving the hairiest of take offs, and facing all the normal hazards of ground attack and a few more besides. For each unmanned bomber, crammed with high explosive, was released at point blank range by firing a set of explosive

CHAPTER SEVEN   BALBOS AND BOOZE

bolts.

Burg, although I did not know it at the time, had been another KG 200 base. Here a force of some 50 Mistels had been concentrated to carry out last ditch missions against the Oder and Vistula bridges which had fallen intact to the Soviet Armies. I wanted to land at Burg and take a closer look. But this was Russian airspace and it was unwise to hang around.

One of our chaps who inadvertently did, a Flight Sergeant, got lost and landed in the Russian Sector. His 'Ya Englichanin' form and its message was a waste of time, as none of his captors could read, and he was treated like a prisoner of war – locked up overnight with a bare minimum to eat and drink. In the morning an officer appeared and he was grilled at length. He returned a shaken man, much relieved that they had let him go, and grateful that his engine had started on its first cartridge.

It was becoming daily more obvious that our Russian allies would be very difficult bedfellows in future years, and many of us inclined to the view that we should deal with this problem now, whilst the Western military machine was still mobilised and ready to go!

With such thoughts in mind it was dreadful to stand idly by whilst a whole wing of Czech Spitfires refuelled at Hildesheim on its way home. We were forbidden to speak to them. Perhaps to avoid a confrontation or the risk that they might be persuaded to turn back at the eleventh hour. We watched uneasily as they took off for Prague and wondered what fate, or the Russians, might have in store for them at the other end.

A trip with Neville Thomas to HQ 7th Armoured Division at Cuxhaven, where his brother was CRE[1], led to a splendid evening in the mess and a monumental hangover the following morning. Something that frequently seemed to happen to those who went swanning with Tommy! It also led to Cuxhaven airfield which was a veritable treasure trove of Luftwaffe hardware.

Most of the aircraft were radar carrying night fighters, Me 110s and 410s and, seen in real life for the first time, a Heinkel He 219. High and boxlike on its stilted tricycle undercarriage, this particular aircraft carried an armament of four 30mm and two 20mm forward firing cannon. They were supplemented by two more 30mm cannon mounted in the centre section, which were tilted to fire forwards and upwards, the lethal "schrage Musik" (literally "slant Music") for stalking an enemy bomber from below.

COMBAT AND COMPETITION

Both occupants were provided with ejection seats, the first we had ever seen, and the crew compartment was heavily armoured. The straight control column, seen on earlier German designs, had given way to one which was more like the split stick on our own fighters, except that it was topped by a two horned yoke instead of a spade grip. The instruments were well up to the standard of our Me 109G at Antwerp with additional features such as an autopilot and radio altimeter. The He 219 may have been ugly but it was a formidable beast.

Tucked away in a corner, amongst all the radar antennaed night fighters, I found two gliders, a Grunau Baby and a Meise. In no time at all the squadron sent a Queen Mary up to Cuxhaven and the gliders were derigged and brought back to base. A local gliding site, which was marked on the map, had obviously been used for bungey launching and yielded nothing except an empty barn. We needed a winch, a Tiger Moth, or a Jungmeister. As we cast around for one or other of these 84 Group Gliding School at Salzgitter heard about our gliders and they were 'officially' removed. We never saw them again.

Another sad blow, the result of a clamp down on ex enemy transport, was the loss of our treasured BMW Sports roadster. We got wind of this when someone flying near Bremen spotted a check point, with a long queue of vehicles leading up to it, and a field alongside into which almost every one was being diverted and parked. In the weeks that followed they became a major hazard and any German car or truck not carrying an official permit was confiscated on the spot. The unfortunate occupants were returned to unit, regardless of rank, in the back of a 30cwt or 3 tonner. For transport around Germany, from then on, it was back to the ubiquitous jeep.

Hildesheim had one fascinating relic. A rare, and until then unknown to us, Dornier 335 single seat fighter. Tucked safely away in a small building under cover and out of sight, it seemed virtually complete.

The usual bunch of enthusiasts looked it over, noted the push-pull configuration, and tried to visualise ground angles and rear propeller clearances. We thought that it was a prototype and wisely decided that it was not for us. Although it was a decision which we took with some regret.

Apart from its unusual layout the Do 335 was an aircraft with many advanced features. Like the He 219 it had an ejection seat, very necessary with the rear propeller, an autopilot and radio navigation

CHAPTER SEVEN   BALBOS AND BOOZE

equipment. It had powered ailerons, and the front propeller had a reverse pitch position for braking. The armament once again was formidable, three 30mm and two 20mm cannon. The new two horned yoke control column was also in evidence, the horns in this case being even more festooned with well positioned controls, bomb release, cannon and gun buttons, auto pilot and radio press to transmit.

Surprisingly the Do 335 remained undisturbed throughout our stay at Hildesheim. Scientific officialdom never came to collect it or even inspect it. Yet reports, published later, suggested that RAE Farnborough, with only a two seat Do 335 to fly and evaluate, were unable to lay their hands on a single seater.

This absence of interest seems even more remarkable in view of developments at Volkenrode, an aeronautical research establishment, less than 20 miles away on the Hannover-Braunschweig autobahn. Here, under the auspices of the Ministry of Aircraft Production, a special unit was being set up, senior scientists from the UK, supported by RAF personnel, with an Air Commodore in charge[2]. Their task was to scour Germany for prototype aircraft and the key personnel associated with them, to bring them to Volkenrode, and to finish the construction of those which were still incomplete.

The team from Volkenrode should have been out and about, round the airfields of 2nd TAF, asking the units what they had seen and enlisting their aid in the search. In practice it was just the reverse. They never publicised their activities and visiting them was strictly forbidden.

A number of prototypes were out of reach in the Russian Zone. Those in the American and French Zones were almost equally inaccessible. In the end, largely through lack of trust between the Western Allies, there was no will to continue and the whole project collapsed. It was a tragedy. After the end of the war there was so much in Germany available for the taking and so much was lost.

One place which we were encouraged to visit was the 84 Group Rest Centre in the Harz mountains. On arrival at Bad Harzburg our little party debussed in a cobbled square surrounded by timber and stucco houses.

It was like being transported to a different moment in time. The streets were clean and tidy, with masses of flowers in tubs and hanging baskets. Even the inhabitants looked well turned out in a threadbare sort of way. The little town, overlooked by wooded hills, felt peaceful and secure. Bad Harzburg appeared virtually untouched by war.

COMBAT AND COMPETITION

The small hotel was airy and comfortable, with a balcony outside each bedroom, where we could relax and watch the world go by. The bar offered plenty of choice, and in the galleried dining area there was a small orchestra which played to our bidding. As the evening wore on, and candlelight gleamed softly on the long stemmed glasses, we took a great fancy to the Radetzky March. It was rousing, blood tingling, stuff. We would adopt it for the Squadron and put words to it. The unfortunate orchestra was urged to play it again and again – and the wine flowed like water – until we were almost incapable of putting words to anything.

In the morning we woke to the sound of bells and a multitude of hurrying footsteps down below in the square. The locals were out in force on their way to church.

Churchgoing on this scale no longer happened in the UK. How could we even begin to reconcile it with the Germany we had known as our enemy? The arrogant brutality of the Nazis and the horrors of the concentration camps were still too close. In the future perhaps we might come to terms with the idea that behind these outward evils there had been something else. A despairing silent majority, decent citizens for the most part, dragged down into the abyss, fearful for themselves and their Fatherland.

The shattered towns of north Germany seen from the air, or close at hand on the ground, were in unbelievable contrast to Bad Harzburg. For those who have no personal experience of the destruction wrought by Bomber Command it is almost impossible to describe the appalling devastation, the endless acres of rubble, the total absence of shops and public services of all kinds. And everywhere was just dust, more dust, and the ever present smell of burning and death.

To have seen the urban and industrial wreckage of Germany, in the summer of 1945, was proof enough of the extent to which the bomber offensive must have affected the course of the war. Those who still argue to the contrary claim, as of course they would, that the substantial growth in enemy arms production from 1942 onwards, was clear evidence of its failure.

But, and this seems to be the fundamental weakness in their case, there has been little effort to assess the further increases in output and the acceleration in new weapon programmes which would have occurred if there had been no strategic bombing campaign. The scenario might have been very different if that extra capability, and fuel, together with the resources tied down for home defence, had

CHAPTER SEVEN   BALBOS AND BOOZE

been available to the enemy on the Russian and Western fronts.

At Hildesheim my photo Typhoon investigation got under way at last. Comparison flying soon revealed that there was marked difference in the handling compared with other aircraft. You could pull 'G' much too easily, accurate slow flying was difficult, and on landing there was a definite tendency to pump handle and overcontrol in pitch. Stan Carr went right through the elevator circuit. Nothing wrong there. Friction, mass balance and elevator profile were quite normal. What else was different on these aircraft? A camera installation replacing the port inboard cannon? Extra armour around the engine and radiator?

And then it clicked. The forward armour had been removed at some stage. But the extra tail ballast was still in place. The three photo recce Typhoons were weighed. We had been flying them for months, and on ops, with the centre of gravity behind the aft limit! It was a sobering thought. The offending tail ballast was removed and, for the last two months of their lives, they handled like normal Typhoons.

As the photo Typhoon exercise ended 146 wing acquired an Anson XIX. On the strength of his time with 84 Group Communications Squadron this aircraft became Butch's responsibility and, to my surprise, after all our disagreements, he converted me onto it before anyone else.

It so happened that I had worked out a forward facing camera installation for the Tempest V – based on an otherwise unoccupied section of leading edge near the wing root. If we could make up a sample I would have a ready made excuse, or so I thought, to deliver it by Anson to the Central Fighter Establishment at Tangmere. Once there I could slip across to Glosters, to see Frank McKenna, who had responded positively to my letter.

The upshot of that particular idea was a quick trip back to the railway line near Alhorn. The train of flat cars and its Tempest was still there. We removed a section of wing, and brought it back to Hildesheim, where Stan Carr worked his usual magic. In the end I flew the Anson to Tangmere via Brussels. On board was our Tempest sample, an accompanying set of photographs, and seven passengers on UK leave.

Frank McKenna asked me to spend the night at his home on the outskirts of Cheltenham. He seemed little changed, just slightly more rotund and ruddy faced, and we picked up almost where we had left off more than six years earlier.

After his family had retired to bed he told me that there was a test

COMBAT AND COMPETITION

flying opportunity coming up at Glosters. Phil Stanbury, who was responsible for development flying on the Meteor, wished to retire in the near future.

A new single engined jet fighter prototype, the E1/44, was on the stocks and a development test pilot would be needed to take this on. Glosters would be happy to offer me the job, provided that I could organise myself a test pilot's course before leaving the RAF, and there was one due to start in January 1946.

Returning to Hildesheim I put in an immediate application for ETPS[3], hoping that it might produce the desired result, and then got on with the job in hand. There was still plenty of flying to be done, maintaining operational standards, and the squadrons were targeted at 450 hours a month.

Leading a formation low level, on a visit to the Mohne and Eide dams, the urge to divert briefly and beat up a nearby USAF base proved irresistible. Their Mustangs returned the compliment in much larger numbers, and with immaculate timing, catching us all at tea in the mess a few days later. Johnny Wells was highly suspicious but nobody said a word.

Soon afterwards tea time and tragedy coincided. A visiting flight commander from 33 Squadron, had just taken leave of us in the mess. He made his departure fast and low and attempted to sign off with a slow roll. Moments later we were looking at a mass of smoke and flames, rising from the far side of the airfield, where his Tempest had gone straight in. To have survived the war – and then that – it was such a waste.

Our first and last officers mess dance was held at Hildesheim. The dining hall was almost unrecognisable with an imported band on the balcony and the tables decorated and candlelit. Even the garden was a mass of fairy lights, as if Christmas had arrived early, and we were all in our best blue.

Sadly, apart from some slight evidence of returning civilised behaviour, it became just another thrash. Perhaps it was still too soon for most of us to behave otherwise. There was more activity around the downstairs bar, and skittle alley, than on the dance floor. Even the puking bowls, those thoughtfully provided Luftwaffe creations for the seriously inebriated, may well have been back in use.

"Herr Hauptmann! ist verboten auf weinstube. Ausgehen sie schnell nach der krankenschale. Jawohl Herr Oberst!"

To be remembered, and perhaps best forgotten as the ultimate

CHAPTER SEVEN   BALBOS AND BOOZE

party in a four month long wake to mark the passing of 146 Wing.

Came the moment of truth when we were visited by Air Chief Marshal Tedder on a whistle stop tour of BAFO[4]. He arrived by air and gathered us round him, out on the field. The occasion was difficult, for he had come to thank us and, at the same time, to explain that our time as comrades in arms was almost over. Yet he knew exactly how to handle it. His words were sincere and his touch was sure. To all who heard him then he came across as the most understanding of senior RAF Commanders.

The day after Tedder's visit there was a summons from the Group Captain. My encounter with the Free French Spitfire at Drope had caught up with me at last and there was a black endorsement to record it. In time honoured fashion the form was inserted, on the first blank page of my logbook, where the evidence could be removed for ever by means of a sharp razor blade!

As he signed the endorsement Johnny Wells looked tired, and almost bald, his alopecia worse than ever. Without a doubt his war had cost him dear. He gave me an encouraging smile, which belied his words, for I seemed to be in even more trouble. When Group had heard about my trip to CFE[5] with the Tempest forward facing camera mockup, they didn't like it at all. He handed me a typewritten note. It was my copy of a letter addressed to the Officer Commanding 146 Wing. I glanced at it hurriedly.

.....appreciated that Flt Lt Ince unwittingly short circuited the proper channels..... requested that you will inform this officer the work he is doing is very much appreciated by this Headquarters..... The signature was that of the SASO[6], Freddie Rosier.

The subject changed. 146 Wing would be disbanded in a matter of days, and 193 Squadron within the month, it was time for the usual assessments. The form was already there – lying on my open logbook. *As a F.B.Pilot..... Exceptional.....* Endorsements were suddenly of no consequence at all. At the bottom of the page there was an official looking stamp – *Fliegerhorst Kommandantur Hildesheim* – just that, nothing else, no swastikas or eagles. It seemed rather a nice touch.

Early August. 266 Squadron and its Rhodesians had already gone. Only Ronnie Sheward, who had been their Commanding Officer, was still around. He had returned briefly to take over 197 as its last CO. Butch had been posted, and I found myself in charge of 193 for the few brief weeks remaining.

In that time we were called on to give two demonstrations. The

COMBAT AND COMPETITION

first, supply dropping by a section of four Typhoons, took place on the airfield, and went off rather well. The second, organised with Group Headquarters, was to be a combination of low level bombing and napalm. Practice bombs, as many as we chose to drop – and a single live napalm delivery – provided that we could find a suitable site.

South of Hildesheim was one of those last ditch Luftwaffe airfields. We went there by road and it was almost perfect – on open ground, sloping gently up towards a sheer escarpment not far from Goslar, without a building in sight. Around the perimeter were a number of substantially complete aircraft, mostly Savoia Marchetti SM 79s and 85s, together with a few Ju 52s. We selected a viewing area for the audience, chose a suitable target, planned the run in and breakaway for maximum safety, and got down to serious practice.

If nothing else we could use the occasion to secure some good pictures of napalm. So a photographer was laid on. We opened the proceedings with individual aircraft, dropping practice bombs, followed by a section attack. The great bulk of the target, an SM 85, made it absurdly easy and the smoke vortices from a succession of direct hits were duly recorded on film.

Back at base I changed aircraft and took off again with two 90 gallon containers of petroleum jelly. They burst all over the Savoia Marchetti, erupting into a great ball of fire, which went down rather well with the troops. As for those splendid pictures of napalm in action – our photographer had used up the whole of his magazine on our practice bombs and had failed to equip himself with a spare – we had nothing at all!

On the 7th of September 1945 I led the Squadron back to England, landing to refuel at Courtrai. Sad and elusive memories. Waving the chocks away and saluting Stan Carr and the boys of 6193 Servicing Echelon for the last time. A low pass across the airfield in tight formation and Craven A's valediction on the wireless as we climbed into the distance. Pulling up into the circuit, for a final stream landing at Lasham, and the bonds of wartime comradeship seemed to be slipping away for ever.

We wished each other luck and promised to keep in touch. Then they were gone, off on leave, posted elsewhere, never to return. 193 Squadron – its motto 'to rule the earth and the sky' – had ceased to exist.

What was once 84 GSU had suffered a sea change and become the Group Disbandment Centre. In the dispersals they were doing dreadful

CHAPTER SEVEN   BALBOS AND BOOZE

things to an earlier batch of Typhoons. Wings and fuselages, stripped to bare shells, were being lined up in closely packed rows and bulldozed together, for all the world like a giant scrap bailing press. Tomorrow, or the day after, our aircraft would be under the hammer.

For my Typhoon there was a brief reprieve – back to Germany – and another napalm demonstration on Battle of Britain Day. More urgent, from a personal point of view, was the lack of any response to my application for a test pilot's course. It was essential to see Frank McKenna immediately.

I phoned him to make an appointment and obtained a landing clearance at Brockworth for the following day.

The familiar airfield, which had been such a hive of activity just before the war – with Gladiators, Henleys and the glamorous F5/34 monoplane fighter – was almost deserted as I taxied in and parked outside the flight shed. Only a few remaining Typhoons, from the last production batch, would fly from here. All Meteor testing had been moved to Morton Valence some miles to the west.

Frank's comfortable, if spartan office, was dominated by a large scale Meteor IV. A beautiful example of the modelmaker's art, with its long nacelles and silver finish, a replica of the aircraft in which Group Captain Wilson would soon be attacking the World Air Speed Record. Willie Wilson was the Commandant of ETPS and we decided that I should get in touch with him in an attempt to break the impasse.

There was only time for a telephone call to Boscombe Down before I left for Wunsdorf. It was hard going, and I had the distinct impression that he didn't want to see me, however I managed to fix a date which fitted in with my next visit to the Typhoon breakers yard.

Back in Germany 123 Wing was down to two squadrons, and these would shortly be disbanded, but at least I was among friends. Johnny Baldwin was the CO and Johnny Button his Wing Leader – and for the first time I met Pinkie Stark who was commanding 609. Short and balding, even in those days, the vigour of his personality was well complemented by a handlebar moustache, piercing eyes which missed nothing at all, and a voice which was deep bass cultivated and warm. A sterling character.

Before we flew to Volkel, the temporary base for our contribution to the air display at Ypenburg on the 15th of September, Johnny Baldwin arranged a highly unofficial discussion group. It revolved around the presence of an ex Luftwaffe Major who had turned up at Wunsdorf demanding to see the Commanding Officer. When confronted by Pinkie, who had been told to deal with him, he announced that he was a qualified pilot on FW 190s – and he wanted to fly a Typhoon! The sheer effrontery. But he was an aviator and an enthusiast – and Pinkie likewise. Only it wasn't Pinkie's decision, even if his comment said it all:

"If we ever did agree – I would escort you. My cannons would be loaded. The slightest sign of any nonsense and I would shoot you down!"

In the end he worked at Wunsdorf as a labourer. His world was aviation and he could not bring himself to give it up. Besides which he needed a meal ticket.

To invite him in, to sit and talk amongst us, was forbidden during the period of no fraternisation which existed immediately after the war. But Johnny Baldwin looked at it from a different angle. It was an opportunity not to be missed. To get an enemy view on our operations and tactics at first hand. While memories were still fresh.

The results were instructive. The German pilot had a fixation about our failure, in his opinion, to operate in much larger formations. The fact that they might have been forced into this themselves – once the Luftwaffe had lost overall air superiority – was something that had not occurred to him. And he seemed unwilling to accept the idea that large formations were essentially inflexible.

Against ground targets there was no disagreement. Speed and surprise were the name of the game. Attacks which were pressed home, before the enemy had time to take cover or retaliate, were the most effective and suffered the lowest casualties. Our Luftwaffe major had seen it again and again. As he had also seen the opposite.

They had thought our ground troops arrogant in their neglect of camouflage. The anti-aircraft fire generally ineffective – and believed that the Luftwaffe could have caused enormous damage, given more fuel and better trained replacements. As for the Typhoons, in the ground attack role they were greatly feared by the Wehrmacht, but the Luftwaffe considered that we were often easy to bounce. However, as soon as they mixed it with us, the less experienced German pilots were usually outclassed.

In the final stages of the war this had become a vicious circle with high pilot attrition rates and replacements, who had done their primary training on gliders, frequently going on ops with no more than 100 hours of power flying. As for the information from RAE[7] that the FW 190 could outclimb a Typhoon. It may have happened on 130 octane

CHAPTER SEVEN   BALBOS AND BOOZE

at Farnborough. But their ersatz fuel was a long way down on octane rating. In practice they could not do so.

Before returning to England it seemed a wise move to make my number with the CO of 35 Wing. For my Army background had caught up with me, and I was about to go back on fighter recce, posted to 2 Squadron as a flight commander.

My first and only formal meeting with Group Captain Anderson was a disaster in every sense. For a start I had good reason to be apprehensive about his reactions to my forward facing camera activities with 146 Wing. I tried to dismiss such forbodings and keep an open mind. Here was a man who had led a squadron of Hawker Hectors in 1940. Whose feats, in these obsolescent biplanes, had included dive bombing the German forces at Dunkirk. And he was still flying operationally in the last months of the war. Perhaps he would be more tolerant and understanding than I had been led to believe.

But he wasn't. He greeted me coldly and gave me a week to return my Typhoon to Lasham, put my affairs in order and report to Celle. And God help me if I was not there in time. For my part it was pray God for that posting to ETPS.

Back at Lasham they wanted my Typhoon for scrap, but Denys Gillam was the CO of 84 Group Disbandment Centre, and I was able to borrow his Tempest V for the trip to see Willie Wilson at Boscombe Down.

There had been just seven squadrons of Tempests operational during the war. We had envied them for their deeper penetration role and the air combat opportunities which this had given them in the final months. But above all we had coveted their new aircraft. They were such obvious successors to our splendid Typhoons.

The Tempest retained all the Typhoon's best features, allied to a thin, laminar flow, elliptical wing. With the maximum thickness at almost 40% chord, the four 20mm cannon had been tucked neatly away inside the wing, and the whole aircraft was painted in a smooth low drag camouflage finish.

Denys Gillam's Tempest, with his personal "ZZ" on the fuselage, looked a thoroughbred as I walked out to it that morning. The cockpit was Typhoon, almost to the last nut and bolt, and I felt immediately at home. The take off was very similar and required plenty of left rudder.

Thereafter everything was that much better, a noticeably higher rate of climb, some 20 miles an hour faster on the cruise. The spring

COMBAT AND COMPETITION

tab ailerons, felt lighter, giving a higher rate of roll, which made the whole aircraft feel more agile. There was much less vibration. Probably because the engine had been moved forward, to accomodate a fuselage tank, and its bearers no longer picked up directly on the wing root fittings. Yet, in spite of these major changes and improvements, there was still that marvellous feeling of rugged security, so reminiscent of the Typhoon.

It was impossible to resist a few aerobatics en route. These were further evidence of the improved handling qualities, compared with its predecessor, and the way in which you could throw the aircraft around. Then it was time to join the crowded traffic pattern at Boscombe Down, which required a long straight powered approach all the way to touch down. It had been a brief and happy introduction to the Tempest.

Not so my meeting with Willie Wilson. Perhaps he was being bombarded with applications for places on the next course, or under pressure from the MAP to keep the numbers down. Maybe ETPS was suffering serious staff losses from demobilisation. Whatever the reason, although he was ready to listen, he showed no great enthusiasm for my case. Eventually he put the situation to me quite bluntly. Although my application for ETPS had been received the RAF would not nominate me for the course. If Glosters wanted me that badly they must do it themselves.

Were the MAP[8] trying to get Glosters to make some financial contribution? – if so it was difficult to believe that they would agree. I flew back to Lasham rather depressed, attempted a steep curved approach, and ran out of elevator travel on touchdown making a rather untidy wheel landing.

Fortunately the Tempest's owner was not around and I went up and did some stalls and another circuit to sort out the situation. The Tempest elevator was less effective at low speeds, power off, than the Typhoon. Or perhaps there was a greater rearward movement of the centre of pressure, at high angles of attack, with the laminar flow wing. At all events it required a slightly different technique to the Typhoon, but one which was not particularly difficult to master.

A quick letter to Frank McKenna gave him the details of my meeting with Willie Wilson. He replied within days. Glosters had asked the MAP to accept me as their nominee for the next ETPS course, starting 1st January 1946, and this had been agreed. A career with Glosters was on.

CHAPTER EIGHT

IN A QUANDARY

Celle in the autumn of 1945 was a depressing place. My ex Army friends, the original Broon Fockerrs, had long since disappeared. Demobilisation was in full swing and there was little evidence of any positive activity. For the moment at least 35 Wing seemed to have lost its way. It was a sad commentary on the times.

The officers mess was still the scene of an occasional impromptu party. But there was none of the light hearted warmth and spontaneity which had illuminated our gatherings in my Typhoon days.

When the Group Captain, supported by Bill Malins, began his song and dance routine with the words:

"How're we gonna keep 'em down on the farm now that they've seen Paree?" we knew that he would soon be leaving us for the night. Then we could relax and enjoy ourselves. For Andy at those little gatherings, and on other occasions as well, managed to convey the impression that most of us were on the wrong side of the footlights. Bill Malins, the Wingco Flying, was an easier and more friendly character but it was not his show.

George Thornton, my fellow Flight Commander on 2 Squadron, had been around for some time and knew the form. He was a great ally in an uncertain situation. We played it carefully, exchanging any information that came our way, and concentrated on running our flights.

No easy task – for there was a distinct lack of enthusiasm amongst some of the pilots impatient for civilian life. Few reconnaissance sorties were actually needed and there was little attempt to define any training requirements. A fighter reconnaissance unit, with its individualistic approach, was particularly difficult to keep going in the face of such constraints and our efforts suffered accordingly. Aircraft serviceability remained surprisingly good, in spite of ground crew losses from demobilisation, but our flying programmes were always hand to mouth.

Without George, whose worldly manner concealed a warm and generous nature, life at Celle would have been a deal worse. We were only together for a couple of months, but I shall always remain grateful for his support and the way in which he helped to enliven a dreary interlude.

Almost twenty years were to go by before we ran into each other again at the Farnborough Air Show. By then he was looking a little

COMBAT AND COMPETITION

plumper, and more worldly wise, but scratch the surface and underneath was still the same old George. He had left the RAF and seemed happy enough, based at Hatfield, demonstrating business jets for de Havillands.

I always enjoyed flying the Spitfire XIV although it had lost the evocative charm of its Merlin engined forebears. The delightfully simple, almost Tiger Moth like, feel and handling had been sacrificed – and successfully – for better performance. The nose was enormous and the cylinder banks of the massive two stage Griffon engine seemed to be bursting out of their cowlings. The rest of the aircraft looked deceptively unchanged, apart from the larger fin and rudder, but the wing loading was much higher and an additional tank had been squeezed in, behind the cockpit, to compensate for the increased fuel consumption.

The Griffon sounded rough and raucous, even at cruising power, as if it was running on nails. But its handling had been simplified by a more advanced propeller mechanism. This optimised the RPM so that you could use the throttle effectively as a single lever control.

2 Squadron had the latest FR MK XIVBs, fitted with full rear view canopies and the new gyro gunsight. The latter was superb device. You tracked an enemy aircraft by holding it inside a pattern of diamond shaped spots which was projected onto the windscreen or optical flat. A twist grip on the throttle adjusted the size of the pattern, shrinking it round the target to generate a range input, and gyro precession did the rest. In a quarter attack the whole pattern moved, as you pulled 'G', automatically setting up the correct lead for deflection shooting.

It was so easy and natural to use that most pilots felt completely at home with it from the start. Lefty Packwood, one of the Broon Fockerrs, was flying a Spit XIV when he shot down his Me 109 over Gilze Rijen on New Year's day. As the first and only one of us to destroy an enemy fighter in the air I envied him his GGS[1].

As might be expected, in such a stretched version of the original design, the Spit XIV had some rather odd characteristics. Plus $12lb/in^2$ boost was the maximum permissible for take off, otherwise you were in grave danger of wiping off the undercarriage. Even so it leant over like a toy aeroplane and you had an impression of moving crabwise. Once airborne maximum climb was at +18, with +25 combat emergency – an indication of the power restriction for take off.

The torque and gyroscopic effects of the outsize engine, with its five bladed propeller, were impressive. Pitching the aircraft nose up

CHAPTER EIGHT   IN A QUANDARY

or down induced noticeable yaw and vice versa. My first attempt at a slow roll was an untidy excursion all over sky. Eventually one got better, but it was always a difficult performance.

The two position flaps, controlled by a lever like an old fashioned gas tap, had seemed quite in keeping with the Merlin engined versions. On the Griffon Spitfire they felt strangely out of place. As for the rear fuselage fuel tank, not to be used on take off, failure to empty it first pushed the centre of gravity beyond the aft limits.

Despite its idiosyncracies the Spitfire XIV was an attractive aircraft. But it was impossible not to compare it unfavourably with the Tempest V, which had none of these problems, was about 40 mph faster low down and an infinitely better gun platform.

A summons from Freddie Rosier at Group, resulted in an offer which caused me to think again about my intended move to Glosters. Meeting him for the first time I was struck by his visible scars and burns, he had been shot down at least twice during the fighting in France in 1940, and even more so by the enthusiasm and dedication of a regular airman who believed in his calling. As I listened to him, extolling the importance and the benefits of a Service career, I knew that he spoke with total sincerity and conviction.

His message was simple. My permanent commission had come through at a rank and seniority which was ideal in relation to age and experience. If I decided to stay in the RAF there would be an immediate posting, as a Squadron Leader, to the new BAFO School of Army Cooperation.

I was in an absolute quandary. In prewar days the RAF had been the height of my ambition – and here it was on offer, with the added inducement of instant promotion. On the other hand I had a strong commitment to Frank McKenna who had done so much to get me on to the next course at ETPS. Freddie Rosier was sympathetic, but adamant about the advantages of an RAF career, and insisted that it was not too late to change my mind. Eventually he sent me back to Celle with instructions to think it over carefully.

Glosters won, but it was a very close thing. If Freddie Rosier had got in first it would almost certainly have gone his way. In the RAF at war I had felt totally committed and happy. Peacetime might be different. A service career could so easily be blighted by politically inspired cuts and changes. There had been evidence enough of that between the wars and the behaviour of the newly elected Labour Government was hardly encouraging.

COMBAT AND COMPETITION

At Glosters the situation could hardly have been more different. With the Germans out of the race they were the leading company in jet aircraft development, with the prospect of strong sales at home and abroad for years to come. There would be all the engineering related attractions of development flying, the challenge of the E1/44, and the exciting new world of transonics.

My posting as a lecturer to the BAFO School of Army Cooperation would have been a challenge too. As an ex gunner officer with a ground attack and photo reconnaissance background there was much that I could have contributed. I had even begun to sort out some ideas on the subject.

There would need to be an introduction. A touch of history. Close support by fighter aircraft was not new. Strafing the trenches with machine guns and small fragmentation bombs had become a recognised pursuit during the Great War. Army cooperation had ceased to be limited to reconnaissance and artillery spotting. But not for long.....

In the years after Versailles the RAF had to fight for survival and the case for strategic air power, which helped to win the day, created a very different set of priorities. Even the dive bomber, developed as an important part of the armoury in Germany and the USA, was almost totally ignored in Britain.

RAF bomber and fighter squadrons were given perfunctory training in direct support, but this was never a primary role, nor could aircraft be spared in any numbers. When war broke out the small number of army cooperation squadrons equipped with Hawker Hector biplanes, or the more recently introduced Westland Lysander, were expected to provide whatever ground attack sorties the army might need. It was a forlorn hope.

The shock success of the Luftwaffe's close support tactics in 1940 brought about a change of heart. Army Cooperation Command was formed at home, before the year was out, with a brief to 'organise, experiment and train.'

In 1941 a mixed South African/RAF Air Component, supporting the ground forces, made an important contribution to victory against the Italians in East Africa. But it was the Desert Air Force, working hand in glove with the 8th Army in Cyrenaica, that set the pace for inter service cooperation and ground attack.

Meanwhile, back in the UK, the pressure was really on, to create and train another tactical air force in time for the invasion.

The first Order of Battle for 2nd TAF was issued on 9th December

CHAPTER EIGHT   IN A QUANDARY

1943. A light bomber group – two composite groups comprising some thirty Spitfire and Typhoon squadrons, hived off from a reorganising Fighter Command – seven Mustang equipped fighter recce squadrons from Army Cooperation Command and the same number of Auster Air OP Squadrons. It was a start, but there was less than six months to go and, in that limited time, the composite groups had to be expanded by a further twenty squadrons.

A natural lead into the next part of the syllabus. Operational training. The sheer delight at being let loose on a modern single seat fighter. Authorised low flying. Satisfaction at bringing back a good set of reconnaissance photographs. Success at air gunnery. Sorties led by an instructor who really put you through the hoops – battle formation, endless crossover turns, tailchasing and mock combat – so that you were forced to fly your aircraft to the limit. And you landed back, wringing in sweat, with a marvellous feeling of satisfaction, like the end of a hard fought rugger match.....

Those memories helped to pinpoint the strengths and weaknesses of operational training. Aerial photography, and standard attacks on enemy bombers, were effectively taught because the techniques were well defined and backed up by proper illustrated detail. Most important and valuable of all was what, much later, came to be known as lead/follow training, under the control of experienced, highly motivated, instructors.

The main shortcoming was in ground attack. This seemed to stem from the fact that the OTUs – unlike the elementary and service flying training schools which operated to established methods and standards – were always chasing a changing requirement.

Ground attack was a major change, and trained pilots were needed quickly in the run up to the invasion. It was all too much for a system geared to the output of 'straight' fighter boys.

The day was saved by such notable efforts as those of Batchy Atcherley, at CFE, and the Low Attack Instructors School, set up at Millfield, by Denys Gillam. Even so, in the opinion of many pilots, ground attack and the techniques of army close support never got the attention which they deserved.

All the evidence suggested a failure to set up and sustain a minimum OTU capability – to support it with a sound and developing syllabus – and to stop it being eroded by short term squadron needs. Continuity, however limited, even when pilots or aircraft were in short supply, would have been far better than closing units down. Operational skills and tactics were what mattered and took time to assimilate. Type

COMBAT AND COMPETITION

conversion was not a problem. But an inability to recognise the extent, and the penalties, of 'on the job' operational training certainly was.

It was said that there were plenty of fighter leaders from the Middle East who were experienced in army support. But they were hardly evident in the Typhoon squadrons of 84 Group and the terrain, in any case, was very different to that of the Western Desert. Moreover the German armies, which had become exceedingly skilled at camouflage in the face of allied air superiority, exploited those differences to good effect.

At CFE the Air Fighting Development Unit, which included ground attack, provided valuable training for fighter leaders. But this did nothing directly to develop the operational skills of the chaps they went on to lead – except by example on ops. 'Training on the job' in another guise.

Armament Practice Camps were a limited form of post operational training. The squadrons rotated through them in turn, coming off ops for two weeks at a time, for intensive RP and bombing practice. The results of each sortie were easy to measure, and the trends were generally positive, so APCs were considered to be a good thing. But just how good? For this was a highly subjective judgement, unsupported by any meaningful analysis in squadron terms.

Comparing the limited overall figures available from 193's visit to Fairwood Common in September 1944, with the improvement in individual pilot performances, is illuminating. These suggest that the average squadron dive bombing error had reduced from well over 100 yards to less than 30 yards – and the low level error from around 50 yards to less than 25 yards. A considerable increase in hitting power[2] – which was apparent from the results when we went back on ops.

There was another facet to the operational training story. By 1942, it had been established that single seat fighters were capable of handling army support and reconnaissance, which had been the preserve of light bombers and other specialist aircraft like the Lysander. Not only that but they sustained lower losses, were easier for other fighters to escort, and could look after themselves much better in combat.

From that moment it could be argued that there was a growing requirement for a new breed of fighter pilot. One who, with respect to his forebears, could navigate himself really accurately, find pinpoint locations and seek out an enemy on the ground.

Whether to reconnoitre, to photograph, or to attack was immaterial

CHAPTER EIGHT   IN A QUANDARY

in the broader training context. Those were complementary skills, which could be added on as required. Perhaps the time had come for Tactical/Army Support OTUs and frontline units to combine the functions of fighter recce and ground attack. The Typhoons of 146 Wing had demonstrated the idea, at least in part, with their photo recce sorties, and the concept appeared to offer many advantages.

Flying on ops. This was the moment of truth. Of challenge and uncertainty. Of the need to belong and be accepted. Of fear and fulfilment and the subtle awakening of squadron pride. A time to learn as much and as fast as possible, from your fellow pilots, and from every sortie. To be possessed by a determination to help the ground troops who were fighting such a bloody war compared with your own. For this was the way to success.

And success it certainly was. The evidence is there, in the war diaries of the Typhoon Wings, from Normandy to Schleswig Holstein and eastwards to the Elbe. It is recorded for all time in the signals from ground commanders at every level. Close support really worked.....

Even so there were many lessons to be learned. VCP/FCP[3] and Cab Rank, so often thought of as the ultimate in army close support, was less used in Western Europe than might have been expected.

The reason was simple. Keeping aircraft on standing patrol, waiting for orders, was inefficient and wasteful. In theory at least Cab Rank was reserved for situations involving a brief and highly concentrated succession of strikes. Such as might be required to support an attack, or to break up an enemy counter attack. In practice these conditions hardly seemed to apply. It was all rather confusing!.

'Rover', the system used in Italy[4], was a definite step forward. Each formation was briefed for a target before take off. On arrival overhead they made a single orbit, allowing the controller time to divert them on to an alternative (Cab Rank) opportunity, and this would take immediate priority. No call from 'Rover' and they attacked the original target.

Cab Rank could be very effective, but sometimes there were problems in pinpointing and identifying the target - to a greater extent than on other missions - in the absence of good 'close in' navigation features. There could be other confusions, with artillery marking using coloured or white smoke. And the enemy was not above adding to the difficulties by putting down his own decoys. Although it reduced the element of surprise, there was surely a case for air to ground

COMBAT AND COMPETITION

'pathfinder' marking of difficult targets, with smoke rockets or napalm.

There was also the question of switching the Cab Rank effort quickly to vital sectors along the front. The American tank formations, on their breakout from Normandy, solved the problem with direct radio communication between the leading tanks and the supporting 9th Tactical Air Force fighter bombers. And to avoid problems of mistaken identity they carried red canvas roof panels.

One of the constraints on close support was Tedder's 'curse of the heavy bomber'. When, as happened very occasionally, the heavies bombed short and hit our own troops the bomb line was pushed forward in a panic response. Sometimes thousands of yards. It was frustrating to be barred from attacking the enemy by an edict which bore no relationship to the accuracy of fighter ground attack.

Whenever the battle went mobile, and the ground forces started to advance, we were faced with a similar band of enemy territory in which no air attacks were permitted. And the faster their progress the broader it was. Thus, when the Hun was at his most vulnerable, forced onto the roads in daylight, the bomb line afforded him its greatest protection. It was another powerful argument in favour of direct radio communication with the forward troops.

Mobile warfare raised other problems. A rapid advance increased the flying distance to the battle area, until drop tanks became essential, creating a conflict between range and hitting power. The RP equipped Typhoons were reduced from carrying eight rockets (twelve maximum on two tier installations) to four plus two 45 gallon drop tanks. For the fighter bombers it was a question of tanks or bombs. Typhoons had been known to operate with a single 500lb bomb under one wing, and a drop tank under the other, but it was very rare.

Mobile warfare also meant more armed reconnaissance. Broadly the alternatives were to go in on the deck trying to avoid any known defended areas (not so easy in a fluid situation), or just above the light flak ceiling of 4000 feet. At this level formations of eight aircraft tended to be the norm. Low down it was better to operate sections of four, or even pairs, particularly if the weather was bad.

To pull up immediately on encountering a train or road convoy, unless you could hit it on your first pass, was simply asking to be clobbered. Much better to press on out of range and come back in a dive, line abreast, at right angles to the length of the target. These tactics enabled the whole formation to attack simultaneously - faster in and out - with a better chance of swamping the defences. Fewer flak guns

CHAPTER EIGHT IN A QUANDARY

would be able to engage each individual aircraft and even less would be presented with non-deflection shots.

Napalm, the petroleum jelly bomb, which I had used once in anger and three times in demonstration, was to become an emotive subject in later years. Had it arrived earlier on the scene, there seemed to be no good reason why it should not have become a key weapon in our close support armoury. Flame throwers were used by the armies on both sides. So why not a flame throwing bomb against enemy soldiers? A low level close support show, using napalm followed by high explosive, would have been quite devastating.

The thin walled napalm container burst immediately on impact. But eleven and twenty five second delay high explosive bombs were a different matter. Badly delivered, at low level, they bounced over or through the target.

146 Wing's 'Bomphoon' squadrons tackled the problem in totally different ways. One went to great lengths - including the study of stereo pair photographs - in order to arrive at the bomb release point in level flight and as far below the top of the target as possible. The other invariably made its attack, in a shallow dive, aiming at the base of the target. Both techniques worked well in practice and there seemed to be little to chose between them.

Air superiority was taken for granted by the allied armies. By day they moved at will, convoys nose to tail, as if the Luftwaffe did not exist. There was no attempt at concealment. 2nd TAF squadrons were concentrated on the best airfields, in large numbers, aircraft parked close together.

On the other side things were very different. Camouflage was as masterly as it was essential. Almost nothing moved in daylight, unless the Hun was in full retreat.

Once on the road his transport attempted to keep well spaced out, dashing from cover to cover. Foxholes and vehicle pits, a desperate attempt to provide some protection from air attack, had been dug into the verges alongside all the principal routes.

It was similar at night. There was no difficulty in identifying the battle zone. The lights of the allied supply columns - the Yanks were said to be by far the worst offenders - led forward until they were suddenly extinguished - and from there on was nothing but darkness.

Thinking about that lopsided environment raised all sorts of questions. For the Typhoon squadrons in particular - was it possible that we had been tied too closely to an Army which had become

COMBAT AND COMPETITION

dangerously dependent on air power? Had the wheel turned full circle, reproducing some of the worst features of the Wehrmacht/Luftwaffe relationship which had been so damaging to the German Air Force?

The answer must emphatically be no. We were part of a tactical air force and army support was our job.

The RAF had other Commands and massive resources elsewhere. Within 2nd TAF itself the Spitfires, IXs, XVIs, an increasing number of Mk XIVs, and two wings of Tempest Vs were there to hold the ring with the Luftwaffe. Sufficient to say that the Germans learned as much, when they tried to achieve local air superiority, during von Rundstedt's last winter offensive in the Ardennes.

Of course the Typhoons did get an occasional fighter sweep when the Luftwaffe was in its more active phases. But these were few and far between. Never really enough to satisfy the desire of any pilot worth his salt, flying a single seat fighter, to prove himself in air combat. Even those of us deeply committed to ground attack were not immune.

But the real point at issue, it seemed in retrospect, was the balancing act needed between battlefield air superiority and effective ground attack. For the needs of the army could best be met once the enemy air forces had been driven onto the defensive. If the Luftwaffe had been stronger in the last year of the war the pattern of Typhoon ops might have been different.

As for the Germans they had learned to live without air superiority – and that held some lessons too.

By now I suspected that my developing syllabus had overshot the boundaries of any brief which might have come my way. But it never got that far.....

The low lying north German plain, divided up by three great rivers, was never more at risk from flooding than in the winter of 1945/46. Earthworks and retaining walls, damaged or suffering from lack of maintenance during the war years, could fail at any time. 35 Wing was given the task of recording the state of the flood defences.

The forward facing camera in the slipper tank of our Spitfire XIVs was aligned some 15^0 below the horizontal, allowing a continuous series of forward oblique photographs to be taken in level flight, almost ideal for the job.

I covered many miles of the Weser and the Maas – for the risk of flooding was a Dutch problem as well. The straight sections were easy and small changes of direction could be photographed in a flat skidding manoeuvre. Sharp bends could only be followed in a steeply

CHAPTER EIGHT   IN A QUANDARY

banked turn which threw the camera wide. The solution was to terminate one run at the bend and line up for the next section before switching the camera on again.

On the last of those river sorties I felt the onset of a cold. At the time I thought nothing of it, never even realising the implications. For in rather less than a year the career on which I had set my heart would collapse with devastating suddenness.

That common cold turned into acute sinusitis, which subsequently became chronic, but I believed it to be cured after a month of treatment in the RAF Hospital at Halton. The deep ray therapy had seemed to work and I was discharged in time for my posting to Cranfield where ETPS had just moved from Boscombe Down.

We were a vintage crew on No 4 course, the first in peacetime. Amongst them were two other Old Cheltonians. Jim Haigh, who had spent most of his war with Coastal Command, had been a fellow bandsman with me in the OTC, and Dickie Martin. Dickie had achieved fame early in 1940 as the Prisoner of Luxemburg. Flying Hurricanes, with No 1 Squadron in France, he had made a forced landing and been interned. Allowed out for exercise he paraded back and forward watched by an idle and unsuspecting guard. Each day he extended the length of his walk until he got far enough away to make a successful break for freedom. 'Officer Martin' was back with his Squadron in time to take part in the Battle of France.

There were thirty three of us in all. Ron Hockey, the only Group Captain, with an illustrious record in Special Forces, was the most decorated apart from Neville Duke. Others stood out too. The hell raising Paddy Barthropp, and after $3\frac{1}{2}$ years as a POW who wouldn't be slightly mad, a warm hearted larger than life character. Pete Garner who was to lose his life flight testing the Westland Wyvern and a number of naval officers.

One eclipsed the rest. Forceful, brilliant and ambitious, with a single mindedness which would take him to the top unless he upset too many people on the way. For Nick Goodhart was one of those infuriating individuals who knew he was right and, on the rare occasions when he was wrong, could drive his opponents into the ground with the force of his arguments and his personality!

Amongst his naval colleagues were others of a different stamp. Ken Hickson urbane and relaxed, whose appearance, even in his twenties, was vaguely reminscent of a bishop. In later years, as Commandant of ETPS, his looks and manner were almost identical to the genuine article. A charming and gentle rogue – in his element knocking the arrogant off their perches.

Then there were the two Dickies, Mancus and Turley George, Navy and RAF respectively, ex CAM Ship Hurricane pilots. The similarity between them was quite remarkable. Differing only in degree, they were tall, thin as rakes, and solemn to the point of lagubriousness. The outward impression was totally misleading. Each possessed an unexpected and delightful sense of fun.

We had Cranfield to ourselves and there was a pleasant air of ordered permanence about the whole place. Quite different from the days of my hurried Spitfire conversion. In the hangers an interesting fleet of aircraft, ranging from Lancaster to Tiger Moth, with a Grunau Baby thrown in for good measure, was waiting to provide us with a sample of 'representative landplane types.' And, for the first time at close quarters, there was the exciting and unfamiliar sound of a jet engine.

Ground school could have been tough, after years away from any formal education, and I was grateful for my short spell at Glasgow University immediately before joining up. As the only aircraft industry nominee on the course I chose to sit at the back. This landed me next to Ron Hockey, where there was much to be gained by following his relaxed example.

As for Nick Goodhart he was out in front, fast on theory, faster still on the draw with his slide rule, and sometimes it even seemed as if he was trying to push the lecturer. You couldn't help admiring him. But it was hard on us lesser mortals. And in our youthful, less tolerant days, we were secretly pleased when 'Humph' didn't let him get away with it.

Humph – G McLaren Humphries – was the chief ground instructor and co-founder of ETPS who had been largely responsible for the syllabus which we were following. A small and deceptively mild mannered man, he saw through the slothful in an instant, yet he could be infinitely painstaking and tolerant with the most mathematically illiterate. Under his guidance we gradually came to grips with the theory of performance and handling, and the mysteries of data reduction. To the trainee test pilot Humph was beyond price and we held him in the highest regard.

Each morning started with lectures. After Humph the rest of the day was taken over by Sandy Powell, Chief Test Flying Instructor, and his flying tutors – with time for a sortie before lunch and more in the

CHAPTER EIGHT   IN A QUANDARY

afternoon.

Exposure to a variety of aircraft was a wholly new experience and the ability to switch rapidly from one type to another became essential. Limited conversion training was provided. But pilot's notes, and a short spell sitting in the cockpit, was the norm. If you couldn't cope on that basis it was too bad. Forget about test flying. In practice the whole thing soon became second nature and flying skills sharpened up no end.

Increasingly you became aware of the different features, the strengths and the weaknesses of each design. This awakening of a more critical and questioning approach was vitally important. The very reverse of squadron practice, where each pilot subconsciously adjusts his technique to the characteristics of his aircraft, and familiarity blinds him to its deficiencies.

Moving from aircraft to aircraft, combined with the introduction of various exercises, soon demonstrated the demands which test flying could impose. You were expected to fly a new type, on very short acquaintance, with sufficient ease and accuracy to carry out any required programme. And, as if that were not enough, to observe and record, and subsequently to report your findings verbally and in writing. No auto observers or voice recorders either at this stage in the game.

You soon discovered that the value of a test pilot, however brilliant his performance in the air, was almost akin to his ability to communicate the results of his work in concise and lucid fashion. And so report writing became a vital and major chore. Many an evening was spent working away after dinner, sometimes far into the night, extracting data from the ubiquitous knee pad with its stopwatch and grubby roll of paper. Reports followed a standard format, which became second nature, until your mind conjured up the headings as you fell asleep each night. The same headings appeared on your knee pad too – as an aid memoire for your training.

From that time onwards I never approached a new type without that same mental check list – and never walked away from it without at least some notes under each heading. If only for my own benefit I had to record my thoughts on its salient features. In a few short weeks I had acquired the habit of a lifetime.

The policy on type conversion, where for the most part we had to cope on our own, meant that we saw relatively little of Sandy Powell and his team. Although they were probably watching us carefully. This

COMBAT AND COMPETITION

was confirmed in later years, after I came to know Sandy much better, and discovered that he had got his former students pretty well taped.

Soon after the start of the course I paid a visit to Gloster's flight test department at Moreton Valence. Llewellyn Moss gave me a warm welcome and a quick tour of inspection:

"Everyone calls me Mossie," he said.

A countryman at heart, he had been a huntsman before the war, but flying had become his life. Now in his 50s he was chief production test pilot. With full order books, and a steady flow of Meteors to keep him busy, he was a happy man.

"So, you'll be taking over from Phil Stanbury. That's good I've been wondering what was going to happen on the development side."

He wasn't sure about progress on the E1/44.

"I hear that the men from the Ministry keep changing their minds. But you ought to get your hands on it sometime next year."

Had I got anywhere to live?

"Can recommend my own place, out in the country, quiet and very comfortable. Understanding landlady..... That is if you.....?"

I assured him I would be very interested.

Later, just before I left, we walked out to the Meteor which he was about to fly, and he told me about his occasional double life. Dr Jekyll was the unruly pilot beating the living daylights out of some inoffensive corner of the Cotswolds. Mr Hyde was the firm and understanding airfield manager, dealing with irate telephone complaints, who promised severe retribution as soon as the pilot returned. Mossie wasn't sure which part gave him the greatest pleasure!

He climbed into the cockpit and looked down at me.

"Let me know when you want that accomodation. See you again soon."

Back at Cranfield there were more types to get under my belt and some of them stand out still after more than forty years.

The Lancaster was a pleasant surprise. Lightly loaded it leapt off the ground in sprightly fashion and felt right from the word go. On the cruise it burbled along happily, at an indicated 250 mph low down, to the satisfying sound of its four Merlins. The handling was pleasant, the controls well harmonised, and the manoeuvrability remarkably good.

The Mosquito, on balance delightful, another aircraft in which I felt very much at home but in a different, more careful, way. Perhaps it was the memory of John Slatter, or the awareness of its high single engined safety speed, although they were really one and the same

CHAPTER EIGHT IN A QUANDARY

thing. In 1944, five years after we had last seen each other at Cheltenham, I managed to contact John again. He was on rest, married, and instructing at Bassingbourne.

I arranged to pop over and visit them before leaving for Normandy. Days later a letter arrived. It was in a strange hand. John's Mosquito had suffered engine failure on take off. They had been wonderfully happy together. She was expecting his child.

More than any other design of its day the Mosquito seemed to have two quite different personalities. The clean aircraft – fast and lively – and the other with massive drag from its undercarriage and flaps. Throttled right back, with the engines crackling and banging, the approach was steep and the speed well controlled. Similar to the Typhoon. Most satisfying.

For all that I liked the Mosquito my first love, as ever, was the single seat fighter and of these ETPS had a fair selection. The Tempest II was slightly faster than Mk V which I had flown from Lasham but I missed the Sabre up front. There was a similar loss of elevator control at low speeds, only more so, and a trickle of power was needed to three point it neatly. Years afterwards I read that squadron pilots were advised to wheel it on because of its tendency to swing. But, as far as I recall, none of us had that problem.

I had a couple of unfortunate experiences with the Tempest II. The first, when a complete starboard fuselage panel – from the engine firewall aft to the seat bulkhead – pulled off in a dive. It went with quite a bang and there was a brief dust storm in the cockpit which became very cold and draughty. Fortunately there was no further damage. After I landed, and the remains of the panel had been recovered, the reason was obvious. The Dzus fasteners had been rotated into the locking position but a number of them had not been pushed fully home.

Another time I never even got airborne. The Centaurus died as I lined up for take off. A fuel line, designed to self seal in the event of battle damage, had sealed itself internally cutting of the fuel supply.

Had it happened a few seconds later I would have been in dead trouble. More spectacular was Jumbo Genders' first Meteor landing after his aircraft had turned itself into a glider. He had suffered compressor surge and a double flame out at altitude, and had been unable to relight his engines. He came in high, fishtailing the Meteor through a series of impossible sideslip angles, and got down safely on the runway. Considering that he had never flown a jet aircraft before,

COMBAT AND COMPETITION

had no propeller braking and little idea of its gliding angle, it was a good effort.

We itched to get our hands on the Meteor and Vampire. Not only were they very different to anything we had flown before but in a real sense they were a glimpse into the future.

In my case the Meteor came first. The cockpit felt unfamiliar, with its rather upright seating position and long travel throttles, but the automatic sequencing system made engine starting easy. The rising whine of the turbines was an urgent reminder that they were burning fuel at a vast rate. There was no time to waste. I taxied gingerly, then faster, adjusting easily to the tricycle undercarriage. Aware that the Meteor's wheel and air brakes, not to mention its four 20mm cannon, depended for their operation on the contents of a single compressed air bottle. For it was still early days and there was no thrust to spare for engine driven compressors.

Sitting astride the runway centreline I listened to the turbines winding up against the brakes, watching the twin temperature gauges. Jet pipe temperature was critical on take off and harsh throttle movements were to be avoided at all costs. Failure to do so was to risk flooding the combustion chambers with fuel and wrecking the hot section.

Although the Meteor was easy to fly it was a disappointment. To be fair the main problem was shortage of thrust, and this was already in hand on the new Mark IVs which I had seen at Moreton Valence. But ours were Mark IIIs. The acceleration on take off was poor and the climb sluggish. The ailerons were heavy and the stick force per 'G' fairly high. Even a short session of aerobatics was hard work.

The approach and landing was quite straightforward, although the response to changes in throttle setting was much slower than a piston engine.

On the first occasion, misled by the splendid forward view, I touched down with the nose too high and continued to hold the stick hard back, until the aircraft pitched smartly onto its nose wheel. The tail bumper had to be replaced and there was much leg pulling.

The Vampire I also suffered from lack of thrust. But it was much more my idea of a jet fighter. The cockpit was simple and functional, with a gunsight reflecting straight onto the armoured windscreen like the Typhoon and Tempest. The throttle lever was much better positioned, with the high pressure cock conveniently close by, and the three vital direct reading fuel contents gauges unmistakably visible

CHAPTER EIGHT IN A QUANDARY

immediately below the standard blind flying panel.

I remember one morning taking the Vampire out over Woburn, where the carcases of heavy bombers, which had been flown there to be broken up, were scattered around the Duke of Bedford's estate like stranded whales.

I went higher as the sunshine weakened under the cirrus of an approaching warm front. Enjoying the smooth vibrationless ride, and near silence, which had been such an attractive feature of the Meteor. Just the gentle hiss of air sweeping past the canopy and cockpit sides.

But there was another dimension to the Vampire. It was a thoroughbred with delightful handling and light, well harmonised, controls. I ran through a sequence of aerobatics and found myself over a vast complex of earthworks and concrete runways which was the new London Airport.

The three fuel gauges stared at me accusingly. It was high time to go home. I leaned the nose down in a long shallow dive back to Cranfield, aware of the slippery feel, as the speed built up and the airflow sounds became louder and more urgent. Apart from the delightful absence of torque and vibration this greater awareness of the surrounding air was one of intense pleasures of jet flying.

Back in the circuit, low on fuel, and the nose wheel refused to lock down. I went through the usual motions, made a pass close to the watch tower, and they said it looked OK. Still no green light and the tanks were almost dry. This time I held the nosewheel off deliberately for as long as possible and all was well – although there was barely enough fuel to taxi in.

The turbine faded into silence and I climbed out savouring the heat and smell of Kerosene. As Gloster's man on the course it was embarrassing to realise that I preferred the competition. In their different ways all de Havilland aircraft which I had flown seemed to have admirable handling characteristics – Moth, Mosquito, Vampire – and the Dove too later on.

At the other extreme we tried our hands at a couple of very different gliders. Thanks to Ron Hockey, and his Special Forces contacts, a Halifax and Hamilcar came to Cranfield for several days of intensive flying.

The Hamilcar was huge, its tandem cockpits far above the ground and, on tow, the controls were heavy. My two flights were early in the day, when the air was calm, and there was no difficulty in holding station just above the slipstream. So I began to ease my way out of position in order to see what the recovery was like, in terms of control loads and response, but the Army glider pilot instructor would have none of it. Even when I explained to him what I was trying to do.

The approach and landing was quite dramatic. Having watched some of my fellow students I flew a confident circuit, positioning high above the runway threshold, lowered the vast flaps and pushed the nose down into a steep dive. There was an immediate and disapproving reaction from the back seat:

"You'll undershoot from here! Raise the flaps and go round again."

Go round again – what the hell was he talking about? Yet, once the flaps were up, it all seemed to work with surprisingly little loss of height. The landing was a joke. A headlong diving approach followed by a very determined roundout. Hard back with both hands, the speed decaying rapidly, and a creaking far below as the undercarriage took the strain.

This uncouth manoeuvre had to be initiated at just the right height. Too soon and she would drop out of the sky. Too late and you would hit the ground still going downhill at a rate of knots. Ballooning and float didn't come into it all. And we were flying an empty glider. What it must have been like, landing with a tank on board I hate to think.

We towed the Grunau Baby with the ETPS Tiger Moth and re-discovered aileron drag. A reminder that rudders still had a use apart from countering torque and coping with asymmetric power. As the thermals began to stir, there were brief opportunities to try our hands at soaring. Brief unfortunately they had to be. Because we were evaluating the Grunau as another aircraft and not in its operational role.

As if to encourage us further Kit Nicholson, a leading prewar architect and glider pilot who had served in the Fleet Air Arm, dropped in at Cranfield. He was flying a German Meise similar to the one which I had 'liberated' at Cuxhaven the previous summer. The Meise, or Olympia, was Hans Jacobs' winning design for the Olympic Games, and our visitor had flown it from Bramcote some 40 miles away. We were most impressed.

Soon afterwards Robert Kronfeld came to ETPS. At that time a Squadron Leader in the RAF, he gave a talk about the Airborne Forces Experimental Establishment, where he had been working as a test pilot. His lecture was illustrated with slides showing some quite remarkable trials. But a few of us – Nick Goodhart and myself amongst them – would have preferred a talk on soaring flight from the

CHAPTER EIGHT   IN A QUANDARY

master himself.

As the course moved towards its climax things began to go wrong again.

On each descent there was difficulty clearing my ears, and frequent pain. I was forced to carry out many of the exercises at lower altitudes. Then my sinuses flared up once more. The top RAF ENT[5] specialist tried his best but there was no permanent cure.

Frank McKenna was kindness itself. I was not to worry. He would organise a replacement whilst I must concentrate on finishing the course as it would always stand me in good stead. Back at Cranfield again I told the sad story to Willie Wilson. Hearing on the grapevine that Auster Aircraft were looking for a test pilot he arranged for me to visit them.

In the event my visit to Rearsby was a disaster. I had flown an Auster on a number of occasions and had my reservations. Derived from the US designed Taylorcraft plus, it was a potentially good aircraft, marred by a few unfortunate features such as the throttle and flap controls, and the strange geometry of the control column. Compared with a Tiger Moth or a Chipmunk the handling was disappointing. But a few modifications, and some development flying, could do a lot for its sales potential.

The MD and the General Manager seemed to think otherwise. No modifications for them. They were satisfied with the design as it was. Sell as many of them as possible into a post war market which was crying out for aircraft.

I could almost hear the words:

"There's one born every minute," as we sat together in the cramped and ramshackle company offices which had once belonged to the Leicester Flying Club.

The idea that the reputation of their company and its future markets were important – or that they might depend amongst other things on the pilot appeal of their first postwar civil aircraft, meant nothing at all.

They didn't need a test pilot. It stood out a mile. What they wanted was a hard sell demonstration pilot to get orders for the existing design, warts and all.

I travelled thoughtfully back to Cranfield, thanked Willie Wilson for his kindness in putting the opportunity my way, and explained why it was not on. It seemed unlikely that Austers would have any interest in an ETPS graduate or he in them.

COMBAT AND COMPETITION

"You're probably right," he said, "But it seemed worth a try. I'm only sorry for your sake that it didn't come off."

Pete Lawrence, one of the naval officers on the course, wanted to follow up the vacancy which had come up again at Glosters. I gave him all the contacts, but strangely nothing came of it at the time. Bill Waterton got the job instead, straight from the Central Fighter Establishment, without any test pilot training. Pete joined them in 1951 from English Electric and lost his life soon afterwards, ejecting too low, from a Javelin in a spin.

Jim Haigh was married in Bedford at the end of the course. Jumbo Genders and I were present as witnesses and we lunched with the happy couple before they left on their honeymoon. It was the last time I saw Jumbo. A modest man, and an outstanding pilot, he was posted to Aero Flight at Farnborough. He died, like Pete Lawrence, exploring the stalling and spinning characteristics of another swept wing aircraft. The tailless DH 108.

After that it was all over. Log books completed and signed up.

The Empire Test Pilots School..... Certified that..... satisfactorily completed..... Signed Group Captain..... Commandant.

Test flying had become the ambition of my life. It had been within my grasp and then slipped out of reach. The last few months had been a nightmare. So near and yet so far. Had I taken the wrong decision when Freddie Rosier had made his offer the previous summer? Jet fighters and sinusitis didn't really add up, but there might have been other routes to a flying career in the Royal Air Force.

Now it was too late and I had no ambition to fly professionally in any other capacity. Nothing more to be done except grit my teeth and pick up where I had left off at Glasgow University. As I said goodbye to my fellow graduates it seemed unlikely that our paths would cross again.

CHAPTER NINE

A KIND OF APPRENTICESHIP

There was little enough time to think about flying as I strove to get my mind into gear after six years of war – ETPS notwithstanding – and the first University sessions were tough going. But the reality hit me hard during the following summer vacation at de Havillands.

Shut away on the production line, armed with a windy drill, I longed for the Hornets and Mosquitos out on the tarmac and the open skies above.

A craving which became so acute that I finally put a call through to the chief test pilot's office. John Cunningham answered. At the mention of ETPS he asked me to come and see him immediately. Before we had time to sit down he told me that he needed a pilot for development flying. Glancing through the window, where a second high speed version of the DH108 was nearing completion in the experimental shop, he asked me if I was interested.

It was Glosters all over again. What I wanted to do most was there for the taking and permanently out of reach. I asked about Doves and Chipmunks – in view of my sinusitis – and his enthusiasm vanished.

I left his office profoundly depressed. How to face life without flying? The airlines might be a possibility. But they held little appeal and the two state corporations only seemed to be interested in pilots with a multi-engined background. That night, while the mood was still with me, I wrote to the Midland Gliding Club and enrolled on a course.

Arriving there a few weeks later was like turning back the clock several years. The blister hanger and scruffy lean to clubhouse, overlooking the escarpment, were exactly as I remembered them from my OTU days. But now the site had come back to life. There were gliders on the landing area, a couple of Kirby Tutors, a strutted Kite, and a collection of ancient motor vehicles.

The view from the Mynd has a magical quality. For it seems to reach into the very heart of Wales. Bounded to the north by a bleak range of hills which dominates the horizon with ragged outcrops of rock jutting into the sky. To the south the landscape, softer and more wooded, rolls upwards towards Knighton and Clun. Knighton – its Welsh name means 'The Town on the Dyke' – and Offa's Dyke was familiar too from many a Hurricane sortie. A mystic border region. Like the Long Mynd itself, as I came to know it better, a kind of haven in time.

COMBAT AND COMPETITION

Perhaps here, amidst these serene surroundings, might lie the answer to a broken flying career. For the first time there was hope. Time alone would tell.

That evening Theo Testar gave the course its only formal briefing. Theo was the club's chief instructor. A commercial traveller of the old school, proud of his calling, and straight as a die. His little black Austin 8, which seemed barely large enough to contain its owner, always shone like a new pin, and he likewise.

We listened to him carefully. A likeable ruddy faced man with a twinkle in his eye and a slow laugh. As he drew on his pipe and warmed to his theme we learned that he had served in the RAF as an instructor during war. Too old for operational flying he was intensely proud of his time at CFS.

He poured scorn on solo training with a selection of dog eared photographs to prove the point. 'Hairy moments at Handsworth before the war' might have been a suitable collective title. In his opinion ab initio solo training was strictly for the birds! Ha...Ha...Ha... On the Mynd it was quite out of the question. Hence the fact that courses here were only open to those with previous experience. Early next year the club would be taking delivery of its first two seat training glider and from then on things would be very different.

In Theo's squad that week there was one other ex RAF type, and a Group Captain who was still in the service. David Dick had flown Thunderbolts in the Far East and was about to go up to Cambridge. Pat Moore, quiet and rather shy, was the oldest among us and, as I discovered when we went hill walking together on the only non flying day, certainly the fittest. Like Theo he had started gliding before the war.

Pat had an almost fanatical belief in the minimum size, high performance, glider. The Windspiel, a tiny lightweight prewar German design, was his idea of perfection and he was forever trying to get an updated version built in England. He had to wait another 25 years before realising that ambition – and when the prototype finally emerged I had the task of proving it in competition – but that is another story.

While it remained anticyclonic we took turns to fly off the winch. Just over 400 feet at the top if you were lucky. Barely enough for a decent circuit in the Tutor. Basic simple stuff. But there was always the chance of a thermal. So we worked and sweated in the unbroken sunshine – retrieving cables, pulling the gliders through bracken and

CHAPTER NINE   A KIND OF APPRENTICESHIP

heather, clearing sheep from the landing area – and caught nothing!

The day after my hill walking trip with Pat Moore we woke to a different world. The bunkhouse felt cold and draughty. The clouds were scudding past and the windsock tugged querulously at its mast. The west wind had returned. Soon both Tutors were up and away. And, for the first time on that August morning, I knew what it was like to be bungyed over the edge and sense the power of the Mynd's mighty soaring engine.

Hunched behind the windscreen, feeling the surge of lift as I swung in close to the ridge and watched the rugged contours falling away below, it was enough to be flying again. Enough just to sit back and admire the view. But not for long. Soon, almost instinctively the game was on.

I must find the strongest lift, gain as much height as possible, outclimb the other Tutor. Concentration became intense, searching for the best position on the hill, intercepting each budding cumulus as it drifted across the site, above all coming to terms with the Cobb Slater variometer.

The original minature ones took up almost no panel space and were very reliable. Two transparent vertical tubes mounted side by side. In each was the vital indicator, a hollow spherical pellet, one green and one red. The faster you climbed the higher the green ball moved up its tube – spinning like a dervish on its column of rising air – a crude analogy of the glider's behaviour. Compelling stuff – but not so good when the red ball took charge and you were struggling in heavy sink.

At Camphill – where Bert Cobb and Louis Slater flew with the Derby and Lancs Gliding Club and the muse was strong – the members had composed a ballad in its honour.

I am fairy lift – and I am fairy sink
Our energy is bottled and it makes us work like stink
We're a pair of hard worked fairies
Bobbing up and down's our job
I bob up for Slater and I bob down for Cobb.

At the end of the week there was little enough to show. Just thirteen flights and less than five hours in my logbook. But the seed was sown. The challenge was there. In the fullness of time it would be mine to grasp. Instructing – cross countries – competitions – I could see it all.

For the next two summers I worked at Boulton Paul Aircraft on the outskirts of Wolverhampton. On Friday evenings, rain or shine, I

COMBAT AND COMPETITION

caught the train to Church Stretton where Teddy Proll the Polish ground engineer would be waiting with a truck.

For most of the enthusiastic young members in those days it was public transport or else and there were those who thought nothing to walking the five miles or so uphill, from the railway station, at the end of a working week. Motor cycles ranging from elderly vintage models, with angular tanks and narrow tyres, to the most modern postwar machines were popular with the less impecunious and some even aspired to four wheels.

John Holder, son of a baronet and one of the regulars, settled for three. Heir to Holders Brewery, he was learning his trade at Mitchells and Butlers in Smethwick, and his weakness for bright red motor cars of allegedly sporting performance had found expression in an air cooled Morgan.

On many a night we ran down to the Bridges Inn at Ratlinghope – the locals pronounced it 'Ratchup' – with three on board the Morgan, two in the cockpit and one astride the tail. Quite illegal. But no worse than the neighbouring farmers on their unlicensed tractors. Of course that was in the days of the friendly policeman who often visited the clubhouse and always announced his departure with the words:

"Must be off to Ratchup to see to a leaking tap!"

A country bobby of the old school, he knew that they kept strange hours under the northwest corner of the Mynd, and never failed to warn them when the inspector was on his rounds.

It was said that the Morgan would pitch forward, and end up inverted, if you braked too hard. But we reasoned that the chap riding the tail moved the CG aft. For all that it was dicey, sitting out there in the open, hanging on to the hood. Particularly so on the return journey, with John talking nineteen to the dozen, while the back end slithered around and the loose gravel underneath sounded like bursting flak.

There were frequent visitors – amongst them Sandy Saunders, a Wing Commander, full of outlandish ideas and just old enough to have been a prewar member. Sandy had a slight lisp which became pronounced when he was excited and Theo, who had taught him at one stage during his RAF training as well, recalled some of his efforts with wry amusement.

"One day, right in the middle of an exercise, under a sky full of cumulus, he suddenly spoke up 'Thir, may I thwottle back and take advantage of thith thermal'. It was as if he was quite deliberately

CHAPTER NINE   A KIND OF APPRENTICESHIP

taunting me, and I allowed my anger to show 'No Thaundeth, thertainly not, you're here to fly hith Majethy's aeroplaneth, not to take advantage of thermalth.' It certainly shut him up! Ha... Ha... Ha..."

Once Sandy was caught in the air when a sudden squall swept down on the site, blotting everything out in mist and rain. When the cloud finally lifted there he was, in the club Olympia, sitting on the bungy point. He looked up from under his beaver hat, with its RAF cap badge, and stroked his flowing moustache:

"Did you thee my blind landing?" he asked with an angelic smile.

Pride of place amongst our visitors that year were Philip Wills and Kit Nicholson with their new Slingsby Gull IVs. They had come up to the Mynd to join Charles Wingfield, the club's top soaring pilot, for a practice weekend shortly before the three of them, and Donald Greig, were due to leave for the Championships in Switzerland. It was a tragic event for the British team – Greig and Nicholson were killed in separate accidents – and Alpine soaring became a non starter at World Championships level for almost 40 years.

Later, when the news came through about Kit's fatal accident, it seemed such a dreadful waste. A brilliant architect at the height of his powers. His prewar clubhouse and hanger at Dunstable – simple, functional, and still pleasing to the eye after more than half a century – remains evidence enough of that. And the man himself. Charming and modest. Lost to us all on a mist shrouded mountain top.

Philip came back from the double tragedy and wrote a moving almost lyrical story about the death of his friends. He wrote something else too, which was totally different, about those same Championships. A word painting full of the wonders of race flying through the Alps on a superb summer's day. You knew instinctively that both came from the heart and, whether the writer realised it or not, that each gained immeasurably from the other.

The fact is that Philip could write quite beautifully about his experiences in the air – and it is through his writings that I have tried to understand him better. Yet he remains an enigma – even though he did so much for the gliding movement – leading from the front by competitive example – and in the political arena too, battling single mindedly for his sport. He had risen high in the ranks of the wartime ATA[1] and had served for a short time on the board of British European Airways. As Chairman of the BGA[2] Council and its inner management committee, subject to re-election but with no limit to his tenure of office, he held all the levers of power.

COMBAT AND COMPETITION

I remember him – who indeed could easily forget him – not only as he was during that first encounter at the Long Mynd, but over more than thirty years. Crewing for him when he won the World Championships in Spain. As a fellow competitor. As a member of the BGA Council. Fighting the Air Space corner with his invaluable support and, more controversially, when I was thrown into opposition due to my close association with Elliotts of Newbury. Maybe it is best to let the events which involved him speak for themselves.

The award for sheer eccentricity amongst our visitors must go to the Cambridge University Gliding Club. Their appearance, like Fred Karno's army over the crest of the hill beyond Pole Cottage, was improbable to say the least. First came the 'Brute' an enormous Fordson winch cum prime mover, followed by a cut down 'Beaverette' armoured car, and a number of battered and obviously unroadworthy motor cars and trailers.

As they grew nearer you could see them in greater detail. The load on the open framework trailer was mind boggling. Fuselages side by side, nose to tail, one wing and the tailplanes shoe horned inside. Externally, with touching confidence in the driver – for Heavens sake! – a wing on each side and one on top. And you wondered what sort of people would emerge from that runcible cavalcade.

On that first occasion there was a familiar face. David Dick, the only one to thermal soar on our course together the previous year, and he soon introduced me to the others. A group of people who were to become friends and colleagues on the gliding field for many years to come. Not least amongst them David Carrow, six foot four and the most extrovert of them all. You could hear his laugh from the far side of the airfield.

David was a man of parts. Squadron navigation officer on Halifaxes. Awarded the DFC. It was he whose enterprise and faith in human nature had evolved the open trailer loading scheme. Following Cambridge his career encompassed a spell at the RAE. Then a complete change of direction took him into the City and the world of insurance.

Cambridge arrivals were rarely without drama. Perhaps a trailer had been rolled, or there was a breakdown en route. Maybe the 'Brute' had turned nasty and needed sorting out before it would give them a launch. Whatever the crisis they responded with every sign of enjoyment – for this was part of the fun – and the place was alive with their voices and laughter – and a to-ing and fro-ing far into night.

CHAPTER NINE A KIND OF APPRENTICESHIP

Early in the morning, on the day after my introduction to Carrow et al, David Dick and I were bungyed off in our respective club Olympias. We kept together, climbing in the smooth untroubled lift, until we were almost a thousand feet above the hill. Airbrakes were to be the modus operandi for our little game – the leader unlocking his to create a little extra drag – and the number two using them like a throttle. At least that was the idea. For we intended to fly our sailplanes in close formation.

Within minutes we were making a neat echelon starboard, then line abreast, moving closer – responding to the familiar hand signals – a few careful turns – steeper now and less tentative with growing mutual confidence. Into line astern and back to echelon. Then building up speed for a couple of tight low passes, moving as one, sweeping along the ridge.

Soon the first feeble rags of cumulus began to form and drift back over the ridge and the smooth lift distorted into areas of growing turbulence. Accurate station keeping became more difficult. It was time to call it a day. We wound up our little show with a fighter break over the clubhouse and down in time for one of Mrs Jarrett's substantial breakfasts.

My only regret is that we failed to work it up further – or to use it for some of the air displays which came my way soon afterwards. But David gave up gliding, and our lives diverged, when he went back into the RAF.

He eventually retired as an Air Vice Marshal, after a career which had included ETPS, V bombers, OC Flying and Commandant at Boscombe Down, and a spell as Director of Operational Requirements.

Later that week Espin Hardwick, chairman and founder of the Midland Gliding Club offered us a flight in his Slingsby Petrel. A singular honor for two such recent practitioners at the Mynd. An embarrassment too, as we were invited to fly it again whenever we wanted. For his pride and joy was not all that it seemed. Without any doubt the highly cambered gull wings gave it an outstandingly good low speed performance. Marvellous in weak lift. But the penetration was negligible.

In addition the old gas bag had a strong objection to flying at more than about 45 mph. She told you so by shuddering noisily. Two enormous clear vision panels were the origin of that unpleasantness. As the speed increased they generated considerable turbulence, and sufficent sound and fury, to discourage any rash thoughts about pushing it up further. As for handling, the less said about that the better.

Surprisingly I developed a soft spot for her. Partly, I suppose, because she took me on my first real flight in wave. Over 6000 feet on a balmy, cloudless, late summer's afternoon. A gentle wave, in phase with the hill, and I sat there being wafted slowly upwards. No need to push her around or indulge in any heroics. Only on the long way down – heaving at the toggle end of a cable which held the spoilers open – did life become tedious. I dearly wanted to tie a knot in it – in more senses than one!

More likely my affection for the Petrel stemmed from her owner. For Espin Hardwick was the kindest of men. A hunchback with the heart of a lion. A successful Stockbroker who, with all his disabilities, had somehow managed to retain a charming, almost childlike, love for his sport. Not that he looked the least like a child. Indeed his strong features bore an uncanny resemblance to the buzzards which soared above his beloved Mynd.

But you only had to be there when he landed, helping him out of the cockpit, and he could hardly control his enthusiasm:

"David, its really good at the moment. There's a strong belt of lift running straight out from Asterton. It goes on and on! Take my Petrel and try it."

He was always treated with respect. Only a few long standing members, addressed him as Espin. To the rest of us he was Mr Hardwick. Whenever he appeared he was surrounded by helpers. We fussed about him, moving his glider out of the hanger and taking it to the launch point. Packing him in with cushions. It was rather old fashioned, almost feudal, but none the worse for that.

I had agreed to help Theo with Will Nadin's ATC camp at the end of the summer. Will, as Group gliding officer for the Midlands, had somehow obtained authority to use the Mynd for instructor training. My father was there too, flying as a club member, and Will generously invited him to join in. He insisted that I was doing him a favour and father was an ATC instructor. So what did it matter if his gliding school was up in Scotland?

It was a good start, and they were a friendly bunch, but I felt restless and frustrated. I had set my heart on a Silver 'C', before returning to Glasgow, and the distance leg was still outstanding.

One morning, after a cold front had gone through, the temptation became irresistible. A little persuasion and Theo agreed to run the

CHAPTER NINE A KIND OF APPRENTICESHIP

show on his own, whilst I went off in the Olympia. It was madness really. The air was much too moist and unstable. By the time I emerged from my first cloud, well downwind of the site, the sky was almost completely overcast with showers already falling here and there.

Soon I was grovelling low over Wenlock Edge, looking for a field in the valley beyond. Ape Dale it said on the map but I felt more like the proverbial donkey. How to face them back at the Mynd? The ATC adjutant had made up a special dunce's award. An oversize plaque on a rope. To be worn like a necklace. The Golden Order of 'Pull Your Finger Out'. PYFO for short. Tomorrow assuredly PYFO would be mine.

I pulled myself together. Still seven hundred feet above the hill and the lift was surprisingly constant. That grovelling business was all in the mind. Might as well put as much distance as possible behind me by slope soaring the fifteen miles or so to Much Wenlock.

When I got there it looked a pleasant little place. A cluster of houses clambering up the hillside, roof tops glistened wetly among the trees and the church steeple almost close enough to touch. But what in the hell was I to do now?

As I teetered indecisively over the town, there was a brightening in the sky upwind, as if the clouds were about to break. Behind that elusive patch they thickened abruptly and a curtain of rain hung down in thin uncertain tendrils. A developing storm cell. I tracked back a couple of miles along Wenlock Edge, dead in its path, and waited with baited breath. Perhaps there was still a chance.

With every mile it seemed to grow in vigour. A watery shaft of light and the cloud behind looked blacker still. The hesitant rainstorm was fast becoming an unbroken wall of water, obliterating everything in its path. The Wrekin's volcanic shape vanished in the downpour – and as it did so the Olympia was carried upwards in a mighty surge of lift. A glorious tidal wave of smoothly rising air which swept all my fears away. The ridge was no longer of any consequence. I screwed into a turn, watching in fascination as the green ball went off the clock.

That climb went on strong as ever, without pause or interruption, for more than 12,000 feet. In cloud and on instruments most of the way. The cockpit chilled as it entered an icy world of lightning and electrical shocks, where hailstones rattled on the canopy and the massive updraft suddenly gave way to a series of jolting sharp edged gusts.

COMBAT AND COMPETITION

No oxygen. Time to beat a hasty retreat before the cunim carried me even higher. That was easier said than done. It took minutes of careful flying, riding the turbulence, to break out under the anvil. When the ice eventually melted, and the canopy cleared, I found myself descending over a sea of broken cloud. Through the gaps ahead was nothing but urban sprawl. Acres of factory buildings. Chimney stacks belching smoke. The heart of Britain's industrial life – yet it looked strangely empty and hostile as the Olympia sank lower. And all around the showers were closing in.

I had made silver 'C' distance and gold 'C' height. Quite enough for a first cross country outing which had almost come unstuck. It seemed sensible to play it safe and land at a decent airfield.

At Elmdon they were more than kind. Treated it as an emergency – waived the landing fee – and even threw in a free telephone call to the Mynd. And the ever generous Will Nadin flew his Auster across and towed me home.

At Boulton Paul the following spring I was moved to the project office under Charlie Kenmir the chief aerodynamicist. He could add little to the published information about the fatal accident which had occurred during my absence. The two test pilots had been flying together, carrying out diving trials on the prototype Merlin engined Balliol, and the windscreen had collapsed killing them both instantly. Their replacements had been through ETPS and one of them was an old friend.

Dickie Mancus looked thinner than ever, but it was great to see him again and catch the familiar smile.

"Technical Dave! Welcome back! Charlie said you'd be looking in. Come and meet Ben."

There was a great deal of noise from the adjoining office. Its occupant was shouting – reading the riot act to some unfortunate on the other end of the phone. He hung up and turned to meet us as we walked through the door. His vitality and the sheer force of his personality filled the little room.

"David Ince" – the accent was marvellous untamed Glaswegian and he spat out the words like a machine gun – "Dickie says you've been to ETPS" – his voice shot up an octave – "And what in the hell are you doing up in the design office" – it subsided ever so slightly – "Better come over here and get some flying." He grinned at me mischieviously and slipped another cigarette into the long ivory holder – "C'mon lad, lets sit down and talk it over."

CHAPTER NINE   A KIND OF APPRENTICESHIP

That encounter with Ben Gunn was a momentous event in my life. More than anyone else he helped me survive the loss of a test pilot's career. Immediately after I graduated from University he asked me to join his team and, even after what had happened with Glosters, I found it desperately hard to refuse. A generous, larger than life character – there have been many times when his capacity for whisky has had a devastating effect on my well-being – but my affection for him remains unbounded.

Ben and Charlie made a deal. I would work in the project office, act as flight test observer on the Balliol – which gave me an opportunity to fly it as well – and carry out as much other flying as Ben could usefully organise for me to do.

The Balliol was approaching its preview handling trials at Boscombe Down and there were two problems which needed urgent attention. We tackled the airbrakes first. They were forward hinged affairs, arc shaped in side elevation, and caused an excessive change of trim. The problem was solved by progressively adjusting the relative areas of the upper and lower segments and observing the results over a range of speeds. In addition the limiting speed, brakes open, had to be measured after each modification. It was a lengthy process involving a lot of short flights.

Then we looked at the stall. The new advanced trainer specification called for buffet warning and a pronounced wing drop. And the Balliol had no warning at all. Charlie decided to try breaker strips – short spanwise blades attached to the wing root leading edges – to induce a turbulent wake at high angles of attack. These worked a treat, except that the aircraft no longer dropped a wing, the breaker strips had created such a positive root stall!

We went on to try a whole variety of shapes. Blades and wedges. Flat and hollow ground. All to no avail. With each there was ample buffet warning but the aircraft sank straight ahead with the stick hard back. In the end it went to Boscombe for its preview handling without any breaker strips and eventually won the production contract.

That was a marvellous summer. Ben checked me out on the Wellington, a batch of which were being refurbished by Boulton Paul, and the Oxford so that I could handle the communications flying. On the gliding front Charles Wingfield – who was still taking it easy following an attack of sinusitis during the previous year's World Championships at Samaden – invited me to share the flying of his Olympia.

COMBAT AND COMPETITION

We celebrated our partnership with an airborne visit to the Cotswold Club which was holding an open weekend at Staverton. Charles had an uneventful trip and I followed with the trailer. There seemed to be a sort of BGA visitation in progress because Philip Wills and Ann Douglas[3] were both there, together with Wally Kahn[4].

The weather was kind and our hosts had laid on a barbeque. It was a pleasant evening under the stars and Wally, on that first encounter, made a profound impression. Hardly surprising because he is a large and flamboyant character, well over six foot and some fifteen stone in fighting trim.

Wally and I sat over the dying embers of that barbecue and talked into the small hours. Through his not entirely unbiased comments it was possible to learn a little about the ruling caucus within the BGA. Later, when I became a Council member, Wally seemed like a permanent opposition – trying to keep the government on the rails. A man who hates injustice, fights fearlessly for what he believes to be right, and has occasionally been known to let his emotions run away with him! A marvellous raconteur and a great friend.

Up late the following morning, in the heat and humidity of a cloudless summer's day, conscious of self inflicted wounds and it was my turn to try and fly home against the wind! Charles was unyielding:

"Its only 55 miles. You'll be back in no time at all. See you there for tea."

There was no cumulus and the inversion at Staverton was less than two thousand feet. A couple of sweaty hours later and I was barely half way. Worse still, approaching Ledbury, the ground was rising up to meet me. Shortly afterwards I found myself trapped over a little valley, too low to go anywhere else, and with precious little underneath except a few narrow orchards straggling across the sun facing slopes. When all seemed lost I stumbled into a thermal, a narrow erratic affair, barely sufficient to keep me airborne and clung on grimly, winding round and round in the searing heat.

A bag of cherries helped to keep thirst at bay. I chewed them in savage frustration spitting the stones out through the clear vision panel. 'Water and fine sand only' it said in the Air Navigation Order. But there was none to jettison!

Eventually, after more than an hour, one of the many miserable trickles of rising air picked up sufficiently to lift me out of immediate danger. From the top of that climb a solitary mass of cumulus was visible through the haze. It was still working well when I eventually

CHAPTER NINE A KIND OF APPRENTICESHIP

slipped under its shadow and encountered the best lift of the day which drew me swiftly into cloud. When the ground appeared once more, and the familiar shape of the Mynd lay ahead, I had far too much height.

Down across the bungy point, out over the valley and up into a well barrelled half roll, looping downwards for a final beat up. But it was already after six on a Sunday evening without a soaring wind – and there was no one to witness my line shooting return – they had all gone home. Just Teddy Proll to greet me, his face wreathed in smiles:

"Oh my goodness, David, you make first flight to Long Mynd. I see you coming and put the kuttle on."

A few minutes later Charles rolled up beside the hanger. He had spent most of the afternoon at Staverton and had made the journey by road at rather more than double my speed!

About that time Cambridge visited us again and I heard more about David Carrow's pioneering cross country, the first ever in wave, which had appeared in the papers over Easter. He had reached 10,300 feet (ASL) over the site, and then turned straight downwind, encountering further wave lift over Bromyard and just south of the Malverns. On each occasion he had headed into wind and climbed back to 8,500 feet before continuing on his way – eventually landing on Newbury racecourse over 100 miles from the Mynd.

Many years later he recalled what happened afterwards:-

My sole objective had been Silver 'C' height and distance. As for the Kemsley Winter Cross Country Prize, I hardly knew of its existence. At least not until I got in touch with the BGA. And then there was trouble.

Geoffrey Stephenson had achieved an excellent thermal cross country, a few days earlier and his wife had ordered a new fridge with the prize money. Then this ignorant sprog from Cambridge, on his first Silver 'C' attempt, knocks his flight for a six. BGA Secretary Clowes was pretty sharp with me when I called with my barograph chart, landing certificate etc:

"Why had I kept my flight secret from poor Steve?"

He was not mollified by my comment that Espin Hardwick had immediately publicised the flight in the Birmingham Evening Post! And the deadline that year was March 20th, so 'poor Steve' didn't have another chance to do better!

Just over a month after my return trip from Staverton – Teddy and Charles got me into the air, with the aid of a rope attached to the Olympia's tow hook and a 25 knot wind on the hill.

COMBAT AND COMPETITION

It was a late start and I wasted three precious hours, trying to work round a large area of decaying cloud, instead of waiting for it to drift away downwind. A classic error which left me being blown towards the Lincolnshire coast with insufficient land ahead to make 300 km.

For the rest of that long afternoon I struggled southwards, beside the Wash, in a succession of weak and turbulent thermals which kept drifting the Olympia out to sea. A slow and hazardous journey – accosted at one stage by a playful Lancaster which kept barging through my circles in an alarming and highly stalled manner.

When I finally rounded the southwest corner of the Wash – and dug myself out of that dreadful hole at six feet per second to almost 4000 feet – I pressed on too hard and almost blew it again.

That was the worst part of the whole trip, hanging on by a thread of broken shifting lift, as fields and woods gyrated below in unpleasantly close proximity. The suspense was almost unbearable. Just one half decent thermal would be enough. By the time it arrived, and the little town of Melton Constable slid below, I was practically ready for a padded cell!

Afterwards, taking the straight line distance and my time en route, the ground speed worked out at 31 mph. The 2000 ft wind had been forecast at 28.75mph and the barograph trace indicated an average cruising height nearer 3000 ft. A balloon would have done it as fast!

The Captain and members of the nearby Caister and Great Yarmouth Golf Club were most hospitable. But they alerted the press and a couple of reporters turned up. Once they started questioning me the cat was out of the bag. Until then, following my telephone call to Charlie Kenmir before take off, I was off sick.

Two days later I arrived early for work, slid unobtrusively behind my desk, and waited for the inevitable. Charlie wasted no time at all. He marched straight across the room grinning with evil delight:

"Off sick indeed – its all over the papers – the press have been after JD and he knew nothing about it – you're in the shit!"

Moments later Ben was on the phone – "What's this you've been up to lad, breaking records[5] and things, JD wants your guts for garters! Come and tell us all about it when he's finished with you." And he rang off shouting with laughter.

J.D. North was the Managing Director. He had been designing aeroplanes before the first World War. Not that he looked that old. But he rarely smiled or spoke and it seemed unlikely that he had much sense of humour. When he walked into the project office that morning

CHAPTER NINE A KIND OF APPRENTICESHIP

I soon discovered that I had totally misjudged him. He came across to my desk, waving Charlie to join him.

"Hope you're feeling better!" There was a twinkle in his eye.

"That was a great flight! You can do that sort of thing as often as you like. Provided you let me know beforehand. Then I won't look such a fool when the papers ring up to ask me about it!"

My first Nationals, taking part as a team entry with Charles Wingfield, was a non event. Camphill, with its short winch runs and low launches, was never the easiest of thermal sites and the small fields, ringed by stone walls, were not a happy hunting ground for pilots struggling low down in marginal conditions. As luck would have it the opening days were just that – with a gentle easterly drift – carrying the brave and foolhardy out over the valley towards Mam Tor and deeper into the hills.

There were some courageous attempts, mostly by the lucky few blessed with Weihes[6], creeping away in the direction of Manchester – and later in the week, as the weather broke down in a thundery col, a day of occasional intrepid climbs. The pattern of those brief high altitude efforts was always the same. A momentary shaft of sunshine breaking the gloom to coincide with a fortunate or well timed winch launch. A fast and violent climb – inside a cu-nim which was embedded deep in the murk – and a heart in mouth descent through hail and deluging rain praying for sight of the ground.

At Camphill there were no de-rated days[7], no launching grids[8], and few tasks. You watched the sky, biding your time, hiding your intentions until the last possible minute. The whole idea was to be there on the launch point before anyone else could react. Unfair? – by modern standards certainly. Too great an element of luck? – without a doubt. Did we mind? – not at all. For those simple unfettered competitions had a spice of adventure and uncertainty which is missing today. There was more choice and much more fun for the crews.

Charles and I got it wrong that year. My logbook shows two circuits, not even extended ones, and his was no better. When the weather started to break he exercised his owner's prerogative, decided that conditions would put his aircraft at too great a risk, and grounded us both.

Although contest flying was in short supply there were other diversions. The tiny pub down below the hill at Little Hucklow did a roaring trade.

COMBAT AND COMPETITION

On most nights it was full to bursting and the rafters rang with many a traditional gliding song. They tended to be simple and repetitive but it hardly mattered. After a few rounds of beer and a rollocking melody on the piano we were off.

Old Johnny Bugger he had a sweetheart
he loved her right from the bottom of his heart
she was skinny and he liked them plump
so he pumped her up with a bicycle pump.
CHORUS:
Singing I do believe
I do believe
Old Johnny Bugger was a gay old bugger
and a gay old bugger was he.

In the way of all the best ballads it told of the subsequent events of Johnny Bugger's life. Although somehow they seemed to have got into the wrong order – and the meaning of 'gay' has changed a little over the years!

Old Johnny Bugger wasn't feeling well
he called on the doctor his symptoms to tell
Doctor! Doctor! I've a pain in my side
But before they could cure him the poor bugger died.

And finally about what he left behind him –

Old Mrs Bugger she had a queer pain
so she called for the doctor to come round again
and the doctor said now listen my dear
there's soon going to be another Bugger here.

That pub and its convivial sounds was the background to a very different tale as one of the Camphill regulars told the story of Louis Slater's wave flight the previous autumn.

Letting down over an extensive sheet of cloud, his escape hole closed and he had to continue his descent totally blind. Writing about it afterwards Louis had described the outcome in his own inimitable style:

After seeing 500 feet go by, and still no sight of anything but fog, I became slightly apprehensive. At zero my hair began to push my beret off – one eye was on the Turn & Bank and the ASI – and the other was out on a stalk through one of the holes in the perspex. Looking for rocks to hit. I was just approaching minus 500 feet when I came out into the clear over the Bamford dams about 200 feet above the water!......

CHAPTER NINE   A KIND OF APPRENTICESHIP

Louis got down safely, after diving off his remaining height and pulling up at the last moment, to land on a 45^0 slope which towered straight into cloud. Expecting to slide backwards, and damage his aircraft, he was held securely by the plantation of tiny bushes in which he had just landed. His luck had held out to the last.

Shortly after our abortive Nationals, Charles came to the conclusion that his sinuses were not improving and he decided to take a long gliding sabbatical. It was a sad end to a brief and happy partnership.

At the club we would miss his advice and experience as much as his slow, almost pedantic, turn of speech and quaint sense of humour. Charles was a delightful eccentric. Like Philip Wills he smoked a pipe and packed the tobacco into a little paper bag. A deliberate weapon in the cut and thrust of a meeting, if you used it as Philip did, spinning it out inordinately, bemusing the opposition. But not Charles. There was no guile about him.

The following year Theo Testar stood down and I became CFI at the Mynd. And Charles in a last generous gesture offered me his Olympia for the Nationals.

Gus Gough and Charlie Hall with the Squadron's Me 109G. Antwerp Deurne, Autumn 1944.

Typhoons of 193 Squadron being bombed up at Antwerp Deurne, Autumn 1944.

CHAPTER TEN

CHARIOTS OF FIRE

In the following spring – as the engineering graduates at Glasgow University waited for their degrees – the pilot employed by Elliotts of Newbury created a unique piece of aviation history.

Clearing customs at Lympne, on his first aerotow delivery flight to the Danish Air Force, he started to prepare for take off as the glider pilot hurried across the airfield to join him. Anxious to save time he connected the tow rope at both ends, applied the parking brake on the tug, and swung the propeller with no one in either cockpit. The engine started immediately, the throttle was too far open, and the brake was not on after all.

A few seconds later Towgood, that really was his name, had succeeded in destroying Elliotts' prototype aeroplane and a brand new Olympia to boot!

An extraordinary accident which resulted in the offer of a free ride to Denmark when the next sailplane was ready for delivery. And I found myself a few weeks later on tow, low over the Scheldt estuary, heading towards Rotterdam and the Zuider Zee. A cavalcade of wartime memories – rudely interrupted on the second day, at Leeuwarden, by a Dutch Meteor which came screaming in from behind when the Olympia was barely a hundred yards from touchdown.

We had been cleared in advance, and instructed to land on the runway, but glider pilots do not argue with jet fighters. I closed the brakes, squeezed in an 'S' turn to land on the grass, and the Meteor didn't even go round again.

After that we flew higher, in the heat of the day, and landed at Esbjerg to clear customs. The last leg was like a dream world. Low level once more. The Olympia hanging motionless behind the tug, while the gentle contours of Jutland slipped by and the shadows lengthened.

A nostalgic trip and an excellent way of unwinding after sitting my finals, but I doubt that Lorne Welch, in the Auster, saw it in the same light. Lorne, CFI of the Surrey Gliding Club, had experienced a very different war. Shot down on his one and only operational flight. On the first thousand bomber raid. One of the OTU crews, brought in to make up the numbers, before he had even joined a squadron.

Escaping from prison camp with another pilot they managed to break into an airfield only to be recaptured in the cockpit of an

COMBAT AND COMPETITION

aircraft moments before starting the engines. So near and yet so desperately far from freedom.

After that effort they were both transferred to Colditz where Lorne became one of the glider escape team.

That summer there were problems out in Korea. Soon it began to look as if Britain would be at war again. As things got worse our prewar members recalled the fiery horseman. According to legend he was to be seen in times of national emergency, a fearful apparition, galloping soundlessly along the Burway[1] at dusk. It was said that he had appeared in September 1939.

But we never saw him in 1950.

When I set out for the Nationals my crew chief and sole crew member, a captain in the Gloucesters, was under threat of imminent recall from leave. A great worry. But the newly acquired Alvis 1250 sports saloon seemed to be even worse. It could hardly cope with the hills and in the middle of Congleton, with the rain bouncing off the cobbles and cascading down the streets, it boiled over and gave up the ghost.

Two cheerful characters from Camphill answered our call for help. Harry Midwood and Bungy Baker. They turned up in Harry's aluminium bodied Ford V8 ex ambulance. A petrol guzzler, but great fun to drive, with quite a performance in its day.

"Silly old fool," said Harry in an audible aside, with scant regard for my finer feelings towards the marque Alvis. "Buying a car like that for towing." Then he grinned at me. "Best cut your losses and sell it here and now. There's a garage across the road." And then, with a generosity which took my breath away – "Don't worry we'll see you through the Nationals with this old bus."

And they did too, in more ways than one, because my army crewman was recalled the following day, and so Harry and Bungy became my crew as well.

On the first night I ran into Nick Goodhart, and was introduced to his brother Tony – another Naval officer. Known to my crew, ever after, as 'The Bearded One.' The two Goodharts had made a team entry in the RN Gliding and Soaring Association Mu13 and my old ETPS colleague was full of enthusiasm.

There was a different feel about this competition. The weather for a start. A strong southerly wind gusted through the trees on Eyam Edge. It swirled across the camping area, shaking the tents, and provided a brief spell of soaring on the south face before the rain.

CHAPTER TEN CHARIOTS OF FIRE

Then the fronts went through and it swung into the northwest.

We had five contest days. For the first three I played safe, trying to climb as high as possible, unashamedly ballooning downwind. On the third day there had been an optional task, a race to Boston, and I deliberately opted for the alternative – free distance and height – to avoid changing my tactics. It was a good move. I made the greatest distance of those who had elected not to fly the task, which moved me up to fourth overall.

Ambition stirred. A weak trough was expected to go through on the following day. I would sit on the hill until conditions improved and travel behind it to the coast. My flight this time would be to a pre-declared goal, earning an extra bonus. Or so I hoped. Others had done the same already, mostly to Ingoldmells, an aerodrome near Skegness.

Except that the conditions didn't improve and I got stuck on the ridge, milling around with a number of unhappy late starters. The rest had gone long ago and Ingoldmells seemed impossibly far away. So much for ambition. I could see myself landing back with a duck. And then something very strange occurred. As we homed in on another feeble thermal a length of lavatory paper materialised amongst the circling gliders – to be followed almost immediately by another – and yet another.

Sandy Saunders' secret weapon! Each time he hit a surge of lift Sandy threw a length of bumph out of the CV panel[2] and then wound his circle tightly round it. What the situation must have been like inside his cockpit I hate to think and the cavortings of his Olympia soon frightened the others away.

But not Don Brown and myself. Don was sharing the Surrey Weihe with Wally Kahn and he had been flying with great determination. We were both desperate to get away, ready to try anything, and it was just possible that Sandy's bumph might do the trick.

We harried him without mercy, confused at first by the erratic performance of his offerings, which swung hither and thither, at one moment rising in sinuous elegance and in the next collapsing earthwards. Eventually, by following the more positive ones, we managed to pull ourselves up to a height at which we could risk leaving the site.

Downwind, in the far distance, there was blue sky and cumulus. I drifted away, hanging on to the last vestiges of that elusive lift, and then turned eastwards under the grey sheet of cloud. There was

COMBAT AND COMPETITION

nothing for miles. The altimeter unwound steadily.

Somewhere east of Sheffield, well below launch height, surrounded by steel works and railway lines, all hope had gone. And then at the last moment, preparing to land in a grubby little field, I caught a thermal. It stank of burning and sulphur, but its strong turbulence carried me swiftly upwards, higher this time, before it faded to nothing.

Another long nail biting glide, and then out into the sunshine at last, running up to the Trent. A power station stood astride the river dominating the scene. From its chimneys and cooling towers a visible upcurrent darkened the sky, topped by a lone cumulus high overhead, a second man-made thermal which took me to nearly 6000 feet.

After that there ceased to be any problem. Cloud streets lined my route. Navigation was easy. The long white frontage of Butlin's holiday camp was visible for miles. I landed at Ingoldmells relieved and happy to have made my goal.

Disillusion came later. Don Brown had declared Ingoldmells out and return. He had taken a camera and notebook to record his presence over the turning point. While I was burning off surplus height, he was heading homewards again scoring more points.

There was worse to follow. Tony Goodhart had declared Ingoldmells too. Arriving with height to spare he remembered that the daily prize was for the longest time in the air. So he hung around delaying his descent and in the process found himself climbing a mile or so offshore. He then decided to have a go at crossing the Wash. After that he went on round the Norfolk coast, well on the way to Great Yarmouth, and the last 55 miles from Skegness had been easiest of all. It was the longest flight of the day.

The winds had been dropping throughout the week so the organisers, greatly daring, offered an out and return as the final task. Once again it was optional and there were few takers. Most of those in the top half dozen places took themselves off southwards in the general direction of home.

Of the others Philip Wills made a splendid attempt – rounding the turning point at Boston and getting back to within four miles of Camphill – which helped to win him the Championships again. Nick Goodhart on his first ever cross country, landed a short distance out on track, and I got lost in the murk, after a slow climb in what must surely have been the dirtiest cloud of all time. In the end I failed to reach the turning point by some nine miles.

CHAPTER TEN   CHARIOTS OF FIRE

That was the flight, or rather the landing of the officious policeman. It ended on a cricket pitch, in the little village of Helpringham and our gallant constable arrived on his bicycle as I clambered out of the cockpit.

"I'm putting you under arrest! We're at war now with them communists out in Korea – and for all I know you've flown that thing from Russia."

He didn't actually say that I was a saboteur or a spy but that was what he meant. And then threateningly, in response to my angry reaction.

"Oh you'll see the Chief Constable before you're finished." Then with even greater suspicion – " and where's the engine?"

Eventually we came to an arrangement. He took a statement. Put me under a sort of house arrest in the local pub, where I was at last allowed to use the telephone, and the landlord thought it was a huge joke. Then he went back to the cricket field, to cross examine Harry and Bungy before we all met up, to see if our stories tallied.

At the end of that contest week I was hooked. Somehow, in spite of those last two flights, I had held on to fourth place. It had been one of the most enjoyable and fulfilling experiences of my life.

After the Nationals were over Charles Wingfield put the Olympia up for sale. I went into partnership with Doc Cotton to acquire it and, with his support, decided to have a go at the Kemsley Winter Cross Country Prize. But we seemed to be out of luck that year. The weekends passed with minimum thermal activity, and a total absence of wave, until only one Sunday remained.

It was late March and bitterly cold, with overnight snow still lying, as we rigged the Olympia. RAF Shawbury had forecast unstable conditions, with a 15-20 knot northerly wind backing northwest in the afternoon. There might just be a chance. So I declared a 70 mile goal flight, to South Cerney, unaware that Geoffrey Stephenson had gone 85 miles from Dunstable to Friston three days earlier.

The first hour was a dead loss, stuck low down on the south end, unable to get away. Eventually, risking all, I made a dash through heavy sink in the lee of the hill and caught a wind shadow thermal which took me straight to cloud base. But it was already 2.30 pm. From now on would be a race against the clock.

To Ludlow was high and fast following a beautiful cloud street. Then a long glide to the Malverns where there was another thermal, an absolute corker, in exactly the right place. Between Gloucester and

COMBAT AND COMPETITION

Tewkesbury the Severn valley was badly flooded – better to turn west of track.

Perhaps the short day was already dying. In almost every direction the clouds were ragged and fading away. But wait – where the Stroud valley carved deep into the Cotswold Edge, and the sprawling town sparkled in the late afternoon sun – a burgeoning cumulus filled the sky. Good for another thirty odd miles if I could reach it in time.

I needn't have worried. Above that sunlit escarpment everything seemed to be going up. The lift was strong and smooth to almost 6000 feet in cloud. South Cerney was in the bag and more if need be. Surely it would be better to go for maximum distance now – change gear, slow down – and extract as much as possible from the tailwind and whatever else might still be around? With a bit of luck I might even make Westbury Hill.

Near Chippenham two wide and gentle thermals, almost a matter of drifting on the wind, gave me a few hundred feet between them. Lazy circles under a cold and empty sky – swinging through ghostly wisps of moisture which rose from the woods below. The sun had almost gone and my feet were frozen. Then back on a southerly heading – bowling along – as if there was half a gale behind me. Lower and lower. Faster and faster. The classic optical illusion. Near the ground the penetration seemed fantastic, but the hill loomed high ahead, it would be touch and go. Inside the cockpit there was nothing left except hope and cold and tension.

4.50 pm. Soaring Westbury on the north face, round the corner from its White Horse, which needed a good spring clean. I had arrived below the top to find surprisingly good hill lift and a last unexpected thermal.

Ten minutes later, following the Wylie valley towards Salisbury, and the light was beginning to go. There was a good field and a well set up country house close to the main road. Time to call it a day.

The wind was bitterly cold as I secured the glider. When it dropped there would be a hard frost. In the big house there was a warm welcome and I was just in time for tea. We sat comfortably round the glowing fire – my host and his wife – surrounded by their dogs and children.

"Tell us about gliding," they said. And much later, over the second sherry – "If they don't arrive soon, you'll join us to dinner."

Oh for the pleasures of cross country soaring in those far off days! When Doc arrived it was colder than ever out in the field, and the ruts

CHAPTER TEN   CHARIOTS OF FIRE

crackled with ice. We derigged quickly in the clear moonlight – and the family, hospitable to the last, insisted on a bowl of soup all round before we rolled for home.

After the evidence of my flight had been submitted to the BGA it was 'poor Steve' all over again! That splendid thermal over Stroud, and my late change of plan, had beaten his flight three days earlier by just 14 miles. Such is the luck of the game.

The Cottons lived at Madley, near Hereford, where Doc ran his country practice. They had been appearing regularly at the Mynd over the previous two years. Doc himself and his children, John, Ann and young Peter. When the Nationals came round again they were a ready made crew, and a very sound and well organised one at that. Which was just as well. In 1951 the competition would be tough. Five 18 metre gliders were entered in the individual class, including two of Slingsby's new Skys, and all to be flown by top pilots.

I got off to a good start on the first task by going early. Taking a calculated risk by creeping away at low level towards a cu-nim which was building over the Ladybower reservoir. Most of that flight was in cloud and it ended near Ripon when the ground became visible at less than a thousand feet in heavy rain. Fortunately there was a convenient sports field straight ahead and I scored third for the day.

This was followed by a race to Dunstable. Although slowest of the seven finishers it moved me up to second place. When the Championships were over Nick Goodhart, with access to most of our barograph charts, carried out a revealing analysis. Everyone had experienced a bad moment within the first hour, and mine alone had lasted for a further 90 minutes!

The next two days were hard going against the 18 metres, although handicapping helped. But the fifth contest day was an absolute disaster. There was a very strong westerly wind with a low cloud base and no thermals. So I went ridge hopping downwind, via Froggatt Edge, trying to score a few points. The outlanding was only eight miles away and the retrieve overshot. We arrived back on site to find that the rest of the field had found wave soon after my departure and many of them had got away. There was just time for another launch and I sat on the hill, furious with myself, until it was nearly dark. But the wave had gone.

Doc pulled medical rank and packed me off early.

"Time you were in bed sir, for a good night's rest. You'll be competing again tomorrow, and just remember, tomorrow is another

COMBAT AND COMPETITION

day!"

The 'sir' was a figure of speech. Spoken gently enough – but it had common antecedents with the form of address used by the drill sergeants at ITW!

Dear Doc, God bless him, he had such trouble driving at night with his thick glasses, and probably flying too, although he would never admit it.

Sadly he was not long for this world, but he was a generous friend and partner, and a super crew chief during our short time together.

On this occasion he was absolutely right – and I was motivated to fight and win the next task – an out and return to Boothferry Bridge. The first leg was a simple downwind dash, the return a hard slog into wind, as the conditions deteriorated ahead of a warm front.

Fortunately the thermals seemed to be streeting particularly well in my part of the sky, and it was satisfying to beat the 18 metres again.

On the final day, with a forecast of light winds and fair weather cumulus, the organisers set an out and return race to Derby. I started too late and on my way back the clouds slowly evaporated. At the end there was nothing left, just a marginal final glide, over the bleak Derbyshire countryside. The bluff which was Eyam Edge loomed through the thickening haze – until the trees alone barred my way to the finish line – and there was the ultimate frustration of a bottom landing.

The Goodhart brothers, alternating between Meise and Mu13, were first and second in the team class. I finished 6th in the individual class, behind four of the 18 metres and Frank Foster in the Rhonbussard, and found myself selected as reserve pilot for the World Championships the following year.

The preparations were hectic. A pre Worlds task flying match at Lasham – picking up the Sky – new radios from Pye – collecting Frank Foster's Standard Vanguard straight off the production line at Coventry. The last, my responsibility, resulted in a lengthy expense account lunch, thanks to the salesman whose job it was to hand over the car.

An ex air gunner, he meant well by the British team, even if there happened to be only one of us around at the time. When he finally poured me into a totally strange vehicle, with unfamiliar handling characteristics and a steering column gear change, I found myself wishing that his hospitality had been a shade less generous!

That episode had a strange sequel. Frank had been asked to take

CHAPTER TEN   CHARIOTS OF FIRE

the reserve pilot as one of his crew – no problem there – Frank and Pat his wife gave me a warm welcome. But with Jack, who was Frank's crew chief, the initial relationship was less easy. When I delivered the Vanguard to his home, he decided to test my driving ability. Supper dragged on and on, until there was hardly time to make the twenty or so miles to catch my train from Banbury, then he tossed over the keys.

"You drive," he said, "but you'll have to go like the clappers."

Difficult to resist such a challenge – I knew the Vanguard better now and used all its performance. By some miracle we got there intact with a couple of minutes to spare and I hope he was thoroughly frightened!

We drove more circumspectly on the way to Madrid. Even more so after seeing Lorne Welch's combination jack-knifed amongst the poplars in southern France. It emerged later that the trailer chassis was not symmetrical. Fortunately no one was hurt and the damage was minimal. Now they were mobile again, somewhere ahead of us on the final leg of the journey.

Castile at last and the bare plateau felt like an oven. The villages which looked so picturesque in the distance were little better than collections of hovels with families and livestock living together under the same roof. The poverty was shockingly obvious as we wound our way through the narrow streets. After a while we began to wonder what was in store for us at the other end.

The airfield of Cuatro Vientos, a few miles south of Madrid, seemed to confirm our worst fears. It was hardly better than a huge overgrazed paddock, more dust than grass, with a windsock and a couple of tiny hangers. A newly completed headquarters building, and an elegant swimming pool, stood nearby in magnificent isolation.

That swimming pool was a godsend in the heat. Protected by its massive walls from the dirt and dust outside we swam and sunbathed and drank sangria – and sometimes chatted to the other teams. It was here that the implications of a German entry, the first since the war, struck me most forcibly. I found it interesting and by no means unacceptable.

But the presence of Otto Skorzeny, and of Hannah Reitsch who was competing in the two seater class, was a different matter entirely. Many Nazis had taken refuge in Spain at the end of the war and the legendary Skorzeny – who had been rather a worry when our Typhoons were snowbound at Chievres in January 1945 – had settled in Madrid. With his black eye patch and close cropped hair he

COMBAT AND COMPETITION

certainly looked the part.

As for the Third Reich's famous woman test pilot, you had to admire her for skill and courage, even if she was a bit of a self publicist. Watching her in animated conversation with Skorzeny it was impossible to believe that she was beyond politics. She had too many friends at the top. Seen for the first time she looked tiny, and fragile, with an air of suffering. Yet it was difficult to feel any sympathy.

Much more to my liking was Willi Scheidhauer, ex chief test pilot to the Gebruder Horten in Germany. A comfortable and warm personality. When Rheimer Horten moved to Argentina, and continued developing tailless aircraft, Scheidhauer had gone with him. And the Argentine team in Madrid was equipped with two of the latest Horten XVs.

There was an fascinating RAE report on Horten. The two brothers were primarily interested in gliders and thought nothing of diverting German government funds, allocated for military aircraft, to finance the development of new and better sailplanes. Most impressive were the Horten IV and VI, with a level of performance years ahead of their time.

Best of all was the story about the Mustang laminar flow wing. When the technical details and test data were circulated to the German aircraft industry, the first thing the Hortens did was to build a laminar flow version of the Horten IV.

So I badly wanted to talk to Scheidhauer, even if he had almost no English and I had as little German and when the opportunity came we managed to communicate surprisingly well:

"In Horten Segelflug" - presumably he meant the Horten IV - "I make fourteen times the gold C height and eight times the distance."

He was quite unselfconscious about his missing fingers explaining that he had lost them through frost bite, on the end of a parachute, after his glider had broken up in a cu-nim. As for the handling of these high aspect ratio flying wings, he agreed that they were different, but a good pilot soon got used to them.

Most marked was the lack of directional stability and damping in yaw. If you got into difficulties you used both drag rudders together and individually they were more than adequate to cope with the aileron drag. He could definitely recommend the prone position. Although somewhat tight for space it was very comfortable, even after many hours flying, and he was a heavy man!

It was the Horten IVb, with the Mustang derived laminar flow

CHAPTER TEN   CHARIOTS OF FIRE

wing, which interested me most. Scheidhauer confirmed the RAE report that the performance had been much improved but there had been some problems with longitudinal stability and control. Horten's military aircraft commitments had prevented any further work on this project before the end of the war.

Came the first contest task – free distance – and Frank, in common with the majority, chose to go north. Towards the end of the day, as conditions deteriorated, the combination of our radios and high performance tow cars was so effective that most of the British crews were well up with their pilots. And thus we were part of the tragedy which ended all his hopes.

It happened in the hills near Calatayud, on the road to Zaragoza. As we rolled along underneath him the temperature dropped sharply, the clouds grew dark and threatening, and the wind veered through 180^0 in ugly strengthening gusts and flurries of rain.

Suddenly Frank came up on the radio calling urgently for information. In one of those dreadful misunderstandings Jack responded:

"Blowing down the hill" – and Frank interpreted it as – "Landing down the hill."

By the time we saw what he was up to, downwind and downhill, it was far too late. He didn't stand a chance. Thrown against a telegraph pole, his Sky was almost a write off, and he was out of the running.

For me at least the awful anticlimax of that event was saved by the fact that Philip Wills needed crew reinforcements. So Ann Douglas as team manager, in a decision for which I shall always be grateful, asked me to help him.

It wasn't that simple. How do you come in, as an outsider, to assist a husband and wife team who have been a contest winning combination for years? How, with an enigmatic personality like Philip, do you play yourself in as a replacement for two close friends who have fallen by the wayside? It seemed to me then, and I still believe it was the right approach, to do everything possible to help, where help was needed, and otherwise to keep firmly in the background.

It became a deliberate routine. First of all to ensure that I bore the brunt of the rigging and heavy lifting. Then, while we were chasing Philip with the empty trailer, to adopt a more passive role. Leaving the driving and radio to Kitty unless she asked for help. Forcing myself not to interfere, keeping an eye on the navigation and fuel state, for petrol pumps were few and far apart.

In fact the navigation was easy. For every contest day found us on the road to Zaragoza – fast and straight for the first few miles – soon giving way to winding gorges and hairpin bends up through the Guadalajara mountains – and from then on twisting and turning endlessly through the high Sierras.

Mine was the privilege of the return journey – briefly one of the champion night rally drivers of Spain! – for this was the time when I could make my best contribution. Once again our radios and Standard Vanguards gave the British a head start over the other teams, and I saw it as my task to get Philip back as fast and as safely as possible. The comfort and handling of our excellent estate cars was such that I only remember disturbing him once. It happened as I acted to avoid a Unimog[3] and trailer coming the other way, on a tight corner, and slid on a patch of gravel. His sleepy voice came from the back, not chiding, but with gentle conviction:

"Careful David, you've got a very precious load."

And it was too. For there was just one more day to go, and Philip was in the lead.

Then suddenly it was all over. Philip was World Champion. He had flown like a man possessed and it had been a great privilege to crew for him. Under the pressures of winning his occasional preoccupations were hardly surprising. I began to wonder if my reservations about him were unfair. Then, shortly after we got back, Lennox-Boyd the Minister of Transport and Civil Aviation threw a reception for the team and Philip, reverting to his political self, was distant as ever.

On the journey home from Spain I kept thinking about my conversation with Willi Scheidhauer and the laminar flow Horten IVb. Why, I wondered, were no laminar flow projects being developed in the UK? But I was wrong. There were already two of them on the stocks.

The Slingsby Skylark appeared first, arriving at Lasham in the following spring, an attractive if somewhat severe looking design with a slab sided fuselage and a 13.7 metre fully skinned three piece wing. No 1 BGA test group, to which I had been co-opted, approved of the handling and the good rate of roll and it was duly issued with a certificate of airworthiness. But we reckoned the wing loading was too high and so it proved to be. Tony Deane-Drummond, known as D^2, who flew it in the 1953 Nationals to a very creditable third place, had problems on weak thermal days.

CHAPTER TEN CHARIOTS OF FIRE

In 1954 when Camphill hosted the World Championships, and the British weather did its worst, Geoffrey Stephenson flew a new laminar flow version of the Elliott built Olympia – the Olympia Eon IV. Rumour had it that he, like Tony D^2 with the Skylark, was unhappy about the low speed performance. When I visited Camphill with Anne Burton, my wife to be, we saw the Olympia IV, and I talked to Steve. His rather guarded reaction to my questions suggested that there might well be some substance in the stories about it.

One pleasant surprise on that trip to Camphill was Fred Slingsby's generous loan of his new Eagle two seater for the first week of our honeymoon which we had planned to spend at the Long Mynd. The Eagle was being flown in the World Championships by the Welches – Lorne and Ann Douglas having married earlier in the summer. And, quite unknown to them, we were already in touch with the Reverend Marcus Morris, editor of the 'Eagle', a boys' magazine published by Hulton Press, who had agreed to use it for a new publicity stunt.

The magazine would run a series of competitions and the winners would be awarded with free flights. We would look after the glider and take it from venue to venue round the country on a succession of weekends throughout the year. Anne was a journalist, and in PR, which was a great help in dealing with the somewhat devious minded editor and she had more ideas in the pipeline. Slingsby was in the picture too – well pleased about the publicity which it would bring to his company.

With hindsight the establishment must have been gravely offended that we had acquired an attractive perk without consulting them. They took action while we were away on our honeymoon and control of the project passed to Ann Welch. But there was more to it than that. With our elder daughter, Virginia, soon on the way the loss of the Eagle seemed to spell the end of any competition flying in the immediate future.

So I got myself onto the tug pilots' list at Lasham and we acquired a pre-war grocer's van to serve as our weekend accomodation. Quite unroadworthy, the outer shell mostly held together by its paint skin and we slept on the floor. It was all we could afford at the time.

July 1955 – we were installed on a concrete hardstanding near the clubhouse, with Virginia just six weeks old, and I was busy aerotowing in the pre-contest period – when a sort of miracle landed on our doorstep.

Not that he looked the least like one. In an elderly Harris tweed

COMBAT AND COMPETITION

jacket and grey flannel bags, he looked careworn and very middle aged, with the clumsy hands and rough hewn features of a countryman. He spoke diffidently – yet his words were marked by a strange underlying arrogance – and I remembered where I had seen him before. At Welford Airfield, in the autumn of 1949, when I had flown in from Hereford to evaluate the Eon Baby for the Midland Gliding Club.

Jim Cramp, the Luddite, as he called himself – and it was a very apt description – chief inspector of the aircraft manufacturing department at Elliotts of Newbury. He had come with a message from Horace Buckingham his Managing Director. The Olympia IV was mine to fly in the Nationals if I was interested.

Interested? I'll say I was. What if it was rumoured to be a lead sled. I had nothing to lose, and it would be marvellous to get back into competition flying again. But there were complications, such as a retrieve car and crew to be organised, and only four days to go.

"No problem," said Jim – with all the uncertain authority of his position, but for once mercifully he was right – "Elliotts will take care of all that."

Anne was enthusiatic too, and so – though I little realised it at the time – there began an association with Elliotts of Newbury which was to be one of the most challenging in my gliding career.

My partnership with the Olympia IV started with a bang, straight up to 10,500 feet off a winch launch, and back down again within the hour. The first soaring flight in ten months and it was an absolutely corking day, with almost no lid on the instability and a surprisingly dry air mass.

I landed back for a quick bite – as the sky sprouted bouncing infant cu-nims in every direction – and my head was filled with thoughts of height diamonds for tea.

Anne had been flying dual and I rejoined her at the launch point. We parked Virginia in her pram near the end of the runway, which was not in use that day, and walked across onto the grass to prepare the Olympia for its next flight. Something prompted me to look up in the direction of the approach and there, to my utter horror, was a Hunter, wheels and flaps down, in the final throes of an emergency landing.

"The baby – oh my God!"

We started to run towards the pram, but it was too late, and we just clung to each other in agony for our child. The Hunter sank out of

CHAPTER TEN   CHARIOTS OF FIRE

sight, into dead ground beyond the threshold of the runway, and a cloud of dust shot upwards as it hit the stubble. There were several brick piers, part of the wartime lighting system, on the extended line of the runway. Perhaps they would wipe off the undercarriage and it would arrive sliding out of control on its belly.

With the thought it came bounding into sight – intact and rolling fast, across the boundary – over the peritrack – and then, blessed relief! onto the grass parallel to the far side of the runway. We reached the pram as the Hunter came to a stop far out in the middle of the airfield and there was Virginia, still out to the world, peacefully asleep, as if nothing had happened. It was a shattering experience and I had no wish to fly again that day.

A pity really because Derek Piggott climbed to over 24,000 feet later in the afternoon – and I had to wait a further 23 years to get my third and last diamond[4] for height.

Three days later and the opening task of the Nationals was free distance. My first flight was an outlanding 8 miles away near Dummer. A fortunate quick retrieve and the second failed to connect. I began to wonder about those lead sled stories. The third launch was long after five o'clock but it gave me a fast climb, straight off tow, high into cloud. After that several widely spaced thermals, and a 15 knot tailwind, took care of the first 50 miles, well beyond Salisbury.

Past Blandford Forum the remaining cumulus vanished, but to seaward of track there was a pronounced thickening in the haze. It looked like a different air mass. A sea breeze front? I steered gingerly towards it and was rewarded with bits of intermittent lift which carried me on to Lyme Regis. Fourth for the day. By the skin of my teeth the Olympia IV was still in play.

After that things went much better although Anne didn't always think so. When the task was an out and return race to Greenham Common she greeted my cheerful arrival back at Lasham with the words.

"That wasn't fast enough. Go and do it again!" She was right too!

I soon came to terms with my new steed. Its high rate of roll and lack of adverse yaw, thanks to the Frise ailerons, helped to offset the higher circling speed, and suited my own approach to thermal flying. By nature I have always been a frenetic winder, umpteen degrees of bank, pulling hard into the core – and the Olympia IV was just what I wanted. On the climb it seemed to be at no disadvantage, even against Tony D[2]'s Skylark III prototype, unless the lift was extremely weak and narrow. And fortunately the only time that happened turned out to be a no contest day.

When penetration was needed the laminar flow wing came into its own and 'speed to fly' began to make real sense. This method of soaring as fast as possible from A to B, adjusting your airspeed between thermals according to the average rate of climb in the last thermal, had been developed by Paul MacCready in the United States. An excellent article by Nick Goodhart had appeared in a recent issue of *Sailplane and Gliding* explaining how to apply the MacCready calculations to the polar curve of a glider and use it in the air.

That year too the number of speed tasks brought home more than ever the excitement, and the suspense, of racing to a goal. Our early, almost intuitive, final glide computations – say four miles per thousand feet – adjusted for some vaguely estimated tailwind – plus 20% added height for the wife and child! – were slowly becoming more scientific.

Tony D^2 had already followed up Nick's ideas on MacCready and shown us how to use the Cobb Slater variometer with the addition of a hexagonal pencil as a speed to fly director. But his Mark I final glide computer was yet to come.

Until that day those of us who thought about it were guided by another simple rule which went something like this. Is the aiming point – that distant airfield you were so anxious to reach – moving upwards on your canopy as you get closer? – if so you need more height. Is it moving downwards? – increase your speed. Stationary? – you lucky chap! – but beware of downcurrents on the way.

However you approached the final glide there were moments of tension and uncertainty. Perhaps it was late and the convection was already dying, or a gap in the clouds ahead might indicate a downdraught area which could force you to land short. Worse still, sea air penetrating inland on a day with good convection could mean a complete absence of thermals, and a possible headwind, on those last vital ten or fifteen miles.

Failure to complete the course, even by a matter of inches, could be catastrophic. A total loss of speed marks – too awful to contemplate. And for some strange reason the closer you were to success the more marginal it seemed. Then came the magic moment when it was in the bag, when you could start winding up the speed, and there was only a last long dive to the line.

Sheer pleasure and raw competitive emotion filled those last glorious seconds. As the speed rose in final crescendo you felt

CHAPTER TEN   CHARIOTS OF FIRE

absolutely invincible. And if like me you were flying the Olympia IV, with its stiff slippery wing and splendid ailerons, the temptation to ignore any passing turbulence and allow the speed to creep up to Vne^5 was almost irresistible.

My exuberant racing finishes must have rung a bell with Wally Kahn. Choosing his moment with care he addressed me loudly, as we were all waiting in the marquee just before briefing:

"Morning David. How does it feel to be flying the fastest dining room table in the world?"

Typical Wally, and fair comment, for the Olympia IV's natural elegance was greatly enhanced by its sleek and beautifully finished wings. These had been skinned in an attractively grained plywood which might have been selected as much for its appearance as its quality. Hardly surprising for Elliotts first and foremost were furniture manufacturers.

I had a good Nationals lying second throughout most of the contest, until the last day, with Philip Wills unassailably in the lead, and Frank Foster close behind me. Second again, to Steve, on the final triangular race should have clinched my position. Frustratingly it didn't because at that time we dropped our worst day's score and I had failed to work the system! Even so third in the Open Individual Class was good news for the Olympia IV.

Alf Warminger was competing that year. Almost our first gliding encounter since he briefed me to fly that elderly Hurricane at Peterborough more than a decade earlier. His words when we parted company at the end of the contest suggested that he too was aware of the passage of time:

"That was a good contest Dave. If only it could have gone on for a fortnight. One week every two years isn't enough and we're none of us getting any younger. I wish I was twenty five again!"

Good old Alf! In due course there were to be Nationals every year – with lots of Regionals as well – and he's gone on flying for ever. So perhaps by now he's had his fill!

Another Balbo to come - Hildesheim, July 1945.

CHAPTER ELEVEN

A TESTING TIME

Horace Buckingham was delighted with the placing of his Olympia IV in the Nationals and called a meeting to discuss its future development. Present were Harry Midwood who had been the brains and the driving force behind it all, Jim Cramp, Anne and myself.

A fascinating occasion, my first real encounter with Horace, and the future direction of the whole project hung in the balance. My own contribution – and my ability to grasp the relationship between the extrovert, autocratic, boss of Elliotts and the independent creator of his Olympia IV – might well be critical.

Harry had been a real friend in adversity when he came to my rescue in the 1950 Nationals. His considerable abilities were matched by an inherent, if less visible, toughness and he was very much his own man. Horace, of course, had the advantage of controlling all the resources, except the vital design and project management skills needed for the next stage.

The tensions in that relationship had been aggravated because Horace was not in the business of glider manufacturing to make money. His original batch of Eon Olympias, or rather the 100 sets of components from which he assembled finished aircraft to order, had started off as means of acquiring licences for extra timber and keeping his factory filled. Supplies were tightly controlled by the Government in the years after the war.

As for the Olympia IV and Horace's desire to improve the breed I sensed, from the tenor of his remarks, that he really wanted to run a racing stable with the best aircraft and a top pilot to fly it.

Luck in being there at the right time and confounding those who believed that the Olympia IV had problems seemed to have given me the ride. That it was never put explicitly was of no great consequence. Horace and I got on well from the start, and our relationship was always based on trust.

Dora was a great ally. As his wife she took no part in any of the discussions, but Anne and I sometimes joined her for coffee with Horace after our meetings in the factory, and we were always aware of her support.

'D' was one of Constance Spry's inner circle of experts, bandbox smart and highly competent, yet kind and warm hearted, a splendid foil to her buccaneering husband. Her charm and elegance had made its mark on their home, overlooking the Kennet, where the forceful

COMBAT AND COMPETITION

and combative Horace sometimes felt like a bull in a china shop. 'D' was a lovely person and fate smiled on us that day when she took a fancy to the Ince family and to Virginia in particular.

As for the situation in which I now found myself. It would be a marvellous opportunity to become involved in sailplane development and to put my test flying skills to good use. What better way to be doing so than in support of Harry Midwood. I would be able to reinforce his arguments – and to deflect some of the gratuitous, and often conflicting, ideas with which Horace was bombarded by the gliding movement. Between us, in the long run, we might even persuade him to put a developed version of the Olympia IV into production. There was no harm in dreaming!

More likely, and more immediate, was the risk of creating further friction with the establishment. Just over a year had passed since the unfortunate episode of the 'Eagle' and the scars had yet to heal. As a member of the BGA Council I was only too well aware that there was little love lost between Philip Wills and Horace Buckingham. Once we were known to have cornered another perk, and with whom, the reaction would not be difficult to visualise. So what! Gliding was a competitive sport and Horace had opened another exciting door after the one marked 'Eagle' had been slammed firmly shut.

At the first meeting in Newbury we were all agreed that the low speed performance of the Olympia IV must be improved. Perhaps flaps would be the answer. But Harry insisted that there was no substitute for span. The existing wing could be extended to 17 metres and his calculations showed a much better result than with flaps. The longitudinal and directional stability and control characteristics would still be quite acceptable. The extended wing would include larger, higher aspect ratio, Frise ailerons and there would be little, if any, deterioration in the rate of roll. In his opinion an otherwise unchanged Olympia IV, with 17 metre wings, should do the trick.

And so the Olympia 402 was born. It would come to us at Twinwood Farm early the following spring. By then – thanks to the kindness of Ralph Maltby and his wife Heather – Anne, Virginia and I had become weekend regulars at their home in the nearby village of Clapham.

Ambitious plans were afoot to merge the airfields of Twinwood and Thurleigh into a single site for the National Aeronautical Establishment with a vast complex of wind tunnels. Some had already been built, indeed Ralph himself was responsible for the spinning

CHAPTER ELEVEN   A TESTING TIME

tunnel, and others were under construction. But the grand design came to nought and Twinwood was still very much as I remembered it, fourteen years earlier, in the days of 613 Squadron and the Bisleys of 51 OTU.

The N.A.E. Gliding Club – drawing its membership from the ranks of the scientific civil service – bore strong signs of Midwood influence. In the Romney hut next to the blister hanger under the trees, where the Mustangs had once undergone their major inspections, you walked straight into the old crew room. A dark place at best, the new management had turned it into a bar, and had seen fit to make it darker still with a colour scheme of midnight blues and blacks. Empty wine bottles, festooned with wax, stood ready to do further service as candlesticks, and the ugly high pitched ceiling had been hidden behind drapes of fishermen's netting. In the long winter evenings, with a good fug up, it was comfortable and attractive and we enjoyed some rousing parties there in our time.

The longer we spent at Twinwood the more I learned about the Olympia IV and its early development.

It all began in the summer of 1951 when Harry left Avros, to join the Royal Aircraft Establishment at Farnborough, and enrolled as a member of the ETPS gliding section. Moved to Thurleigh, six months later, he decided to travel back there at weekends for his flying. Bill Bedford, on his way to becoming Hawker's Chief Test Pilot – John Sowrey, who was a pupil on No 10 course – and Roger Austin, still a very junior member of staff, were fellow gliding enthusiasts. Each was to play a major role in the story. The irrepressible Sowrey, owner of a gorgeous racing Bentley which he was known to take on retrieves, started the ball rolling by provoking the other three.

"With all the expertise at Farnborough" – he kept saying – *"we can produce the best glider in the world!"*

That was a challenge which Harry could not ignore. Already aware that the use of laminar flow sections might lead to a substantial improvement in performance, he followed up various references and the findings excited him greatly. For a start he discovered that the adverse effect of small imperfections, considered to be a major problem on laminar flow wings, was greatly reduced at the low Reynolds Numbers[1] of glider flight. A thicker section widened the laminar drag bucket, improving the performance over an extended range of speeds, and gave a more gentle stall.

The significance of this last point seemed to elude other designers,

COMBAT AND COMPETITION

including Slingsby, whose projects suffered as a result. Thickening the tips would allow the geometric twist to be reduced without adverse effect on the stall. At high speeds the download on the outer sections would be correspondingly less, with benefits to structural weight, and the gliding angle would be further enhanced. Harry worked out the aerodynamics of a laminar flow wing for the Olympia. The performance was dramatically better. So the team decided to build a pair of wings for the ETPS Olympia.

There were other advantages. Because the wing was thick, and the maximum depth further aft, the D box[2] was larger and stiffer in torsion and bending than on previous sailplanes. So the new Frise ailerons with their reduced trailing edge angle, another feature of the laminar sections, could be made smaller. The control loads would be lighter and the response much better, particularly at speeds approaching Vne.

As the ETPS Olympia still belonged to Elliotts, John Sowrey rang Horace Buckingham to make sure that he had no objection. Horace went one better and offered to build the wings himself. The team decided to carry out full scale tests and Elliotts made up an aerofoil sleeve to their design. This was fitted to a Kite II and flown with a pitot rake[3] to measure the drag. China clay and paraffin were used for boundary layer and transition studies which included the effect of artificial flies. The results were almost exactly as predicted.

After that it would be pleasant to report that all went smoothly until the first flight. Not so. Elliotts started on the new wings. Then they stopped work completely for two years. A strong suspicion remains that people with vested interests in other projects were rocking the boat.

Whatever the reason Horace simply refused to move until Dick Johnson's laminar wing RJ5 had flown successfully in the United States.

The Olympia IV made its first flight at Lasham, where Bill Bedford, assisted by John Sowrey, carried out the tests for its special category certificate of airworthiness. When they were finished Harry took the aircraft up for a brief performance run against Philip Wills in his Sky. Philip was visibly impressed that there seemed to be so little difference between his World Championship winning 18 metre sailplane and the 15 metre Olympia IV.

"As like as two peas in a pod" - he remarked thoughtfully.

After the 1954 World Championships the Olympia IV was returned

CHAPTER ELEVEN   A TESTING TIME

to its designers, who were now operating from Twinwood Farm, and Horace put them under great pressure. He was most unhappy about the rumours which had originated from Camphill and wanted confirmation of the performance as soon as possible.

Stable conditions were essential and it took almost eight months to complete the tests - just five days being suitable during the whole of that time. One flight was typical of the problems which they faced.

Starting even earlier than usual - out of bed at 3 am - to be confronted with an unbroken layer of stratus 200 feet thick, base 800 feet above the ground. The plan - for Roger Austin to find the airfield after the tow and mark it by circling in the tug, while Harry made his partial glides - misfired completely. After release they never saw each other again. Harry broke cloud some miles away and had to land out.

A new technique was used to record the raw data. On each partial glide, the pilot reported his height by radio at 50 foot intervals. Ralph Maltby and his two assistants, one armed with a stopwatch, plotted time against height straight onto a chart. The effect of any disturbance was instantly apparent and the pilot could be instructed to continue his run over a further thousand feet.

The maximum gliding angle of 1 in 33.5 compared with the original design at 1 in 26.5, was a total vindication of their efforts. But the minimum sink was slightly greater than expected and it occurred at 44 knots.

When I joined Harry's test group, after the 1955 Nationals, we carried out pitot rake and china clay/paraffin tests on an inboard section of mainplane. But they showed no evidence of premature laminar separation.

Before the aircraft left Twinwood, Ralph managed to organise wind tunnel tests on one wing, using the aileron as a flap. Intended to confirm their extrapolation of relevant NACA[4] information, to glider Reynolds numbers, this may well have been the origin of the 'no substitute for span' philosphy of the later developments.

The 402 arrived at Twinwood two weekends before Easter. Barely time to sort out any problems and obtain a temporary C of A for an entry in the first contest of the year, the Long Mynd Easter Rally. If it proved good enough there was just a possibility that it might be flown by the British team in the World Championships now only months away.

We got there, but only just. To avoid altering the aileron hinge line, the tip chord on the extended wing had become almost 80%

aileron. Such an aileron had to be right. And this one was not. Elliotts had built in too much camber, the solid balsa wood Frise nose was too large, and there was no mass balance. Harry had an uncomfortable first flight, casting off tow at 400 feet. The ailerons oscillated violently at the slightest suggestion of turbulence requiring both hands on the stick!

By the end of the first weekend Twinwood Farm was littered with balsa shavings, and the cut back Frise balances on each aileron had been covered with almost 7 lbs of sheet lead apiece. It was hardly an ideal solution but at least we had a flyable aircraft. More important the wing tip extensions had reduced the stalling speed by 3-4 knots and the low speed performance seemed much improved.

The 402 was returned to Newbury so that our hasty modifications could be tidied up. It was back with us the following weekend for its special category C of A flight tests – fortunately the weather was kind – and we were able to clear it in time.

The lateral control at low speeds and the rate of roll were better than the original aircraft – and at least 25% superior to the Skylark III. The stall if anything was more docile. Only in a sideslip or spin was the effect of the increased span, with unchanged tail surfaces, apparent – in the form of mild tail buffeting and rudder locking – but this was no problem. It was certainly much less marked than on a Weihe.

The ailerons were still in interim form with excessive camber and upfloat which could only be corrected by rebuilding them completely. So Vne was set at an equally interim 90 knots.

Anne and Harry crewed for me on the 402's first outing and the opening day was anticyclonic, with a wind just east of north. Met gave us the choice of better thermals to the east or waves to the west. But the organisers set distance southwards along a line through Shobdon airfield, near Hereford, so that was that. I crept away in weak thermals, never higher than 1500 feet above the Mynd, and it was certainly easier to hang on with the 402 under these conditions.

Approaching the Black Mountains, under a totally cloudless sky, I hit wave. No mistaking the glassy smoothness and the uncanny climb. A quick 180^0 into wind brought the sun behind me and there was the red and white of another sailplane a mile or so away. It happens so often, you set course and lose sight of each other, perhaps for hours, and then meet up again at a turning point, on the final glide, or almost anywhere en route. Like this wave, in which Philip Wills and I had

CHAPTER ELEVEN   A TESTING TIME

come together quite fortuitously and, as we closed towards each other, we were even at the same height.

It was a gift from the gods. Dead smooth air, and almost wing tip to wing tip we climbed together in that obliging wave, a marvellous opportunity to compare the 402 at min sink against the Skylark III. After several minutes together our relative positions had not changed by one iota. Harry's extra two metres had done the trick! Better still, when we moved off downwind through that invisible wave train, my aircraft seemed to have the edge on the glide.

Going my own way, I parted company from Philip, progressing across the barren uplands of the Black Mountains. Five easy strides into South Wales – head in the non existent clouds – delighted with Harry's achievement.

Crossing the Brecon Beacons I woke up to the fact that the Bristol Channel lay ahead, and I had barely enough height to get across. I decided to call it a day and put down at St Athan. Philip landed at the new Cardiff airport, 4 miles to the east and exactly the same distance from the Mynd. But he was closer to the line and went into the lead.

The difference between us seemed academic at the time – but not so the following day, when I left before most of the field, got caught by a temporary cirrus 'clamp' over mid Wales – and dropped smartly down the order. On the last day, a pilot declared goal, I decided to go for broke and declared Dunstable. Reaching the Chilterns, as the thermals gave out, the Tring gap was too wide to cross on hill lift alone and I landed four miles short. It was enough to let John Williamson, who completed a well judged shorter goal flight to Abingdon, win the day and the rally. But at least the 402 had made second place.

There was no UK Nationals that year, and no sign of any interest from the British Team, but an American from San Diego had been in touch with Horace Buckingham. Bill Ivans was one of the pilots who had been selected to represent the United States. He had heard about the Olympia IV and wanted to fly it in the World Championships.

When Horace agreed Harry and I came up with a plan of our own. After Bill had flown in the World Championships, Jim Cramp would deliver the 402 to Gosselies in Belgium for Harry to take part in the 'Challenge Victor Boin' a one day gliding event. Then the Inces would collect it, go straight to the Wasserkuppe, and compete in the first postwar German contest.

While all this was going on the 402 was fitted with a new pair of ailerons, which overcame the upfloat problem, and the temporary

COMBAT AND COMPETITION

restriction on maximum speed could be removed. We completed the C of A flight tests and there was an opportunity for just one further competitive outing before Bill Ivans took it over.

Whit weekend brought a wonderful spell of weather – and an opportunity to pit the 402 against wider opposition, amongst them Nick Goodhart, Tony D^2 and Philip Wills, all flying Skylark IIIs. Saturday at Lasham dawned clear and bright. By the time we towed off conditions were really booming – with strong narrow thermals – and little wisps of condensation where each one hit the inversion. The task, a 44 mile out and return to the RAF airfield at Andover, had been grossly underset. For me at least it was one of those days when everything came right. Over 4000 feet just before the start – followed by a dive to Vne across the line – and straight into 1200 ft per minute.

From then on it was high and fast, thermals galore, dark glasses showing up the gathering puffs in the sky ahead – hitting each one right on the button – time and again winding straight into the core with those superb ailerons. A perfectly placed thermal at the turning point and a storming second leg merged straight into an 85 knot final glide. Back in well under the hour, and fastest by quite a margin, that task set the scene.

Sunday looked even better first thing in the morning, although there was some strato cumulus hanging around as we rigged. The organisers gave us a 200 km triangle. Turning points were at Dunstable and an old airfield at Stanton Harcourt to the west of Oxford – and for once we were invited to choose our own way to go round. Philip and I opted for Stanton Harcourt first. Nick, Tony and John Willy decided on the reverse and they were the unlucky ones.

The strato cumulus did them down. Nick and Tony were delayed at Dunstable, scratching below it, for almost two hours. As for me, luck was still on my side. I left later than Philip and wasted just half an hour, circling carefully over the network of gravel workings and dismembered runways that marked the first turning point – never in any serious danger – until the sun finally broke through.

Approaching Oxford a gathering upcurrent, above the tree clad slopes and well heeled residences of Boar's Hill, lifted the 402 back into a winder's world once more – strong narrow thermals under a sky studded with fair weather cumulus. On the way home, near Burnham Beeches, I passed Philip who was stuck low down under an area of clag and romped home to win again.

The front forecast for Whit Monday never materialised and it

CHAPTER ELEVEN A TESTING TIME

turned out to be the best day of all. Tony D^2, writing at the time in *Sailplane and Gliding*, obviously thought so too:

Thermals were extremely strong..... and several on end blew us up at 1000 ft per minute. Cloud base started off at about 4000 ft and rose to near 6000 ft by the afternoon. Maximum possible cruising speed was the order of the day, and in the Skylark this is about 80 mph for an average 600 ft per minute climb.

Nick Goodhart, David Ince and I were all released within 5 minutes of each other..... David and I flew to Andover together; sometimes we used the same thermal, but more usually we didn't. There were so many it did not matter.....

Andover was soon reached and then Guildford in the same manner. The 'downs' between thermals were so strong that it made judgement of the final glide difficult back to Lasham..... in the end we were left with 500 ft too much. We all came back together; first David, then myself and then Nick, to land in as many minutes.

90 miles in just under two hours – with a 20 knot crosswind. In one respect, as Tony D^2 pointed out in his article, we had wasted a possible 500 km day towards the Scottish border. But for Harry, Horace and myself Whit weekend was just what we wanted – three wins – on three successive days.

When Bill Ivans arrived at Lasham soon afterwards he was delighted to hear about the 402's performance – and we saw him on his way to St Yan with high hopes. Towards the end of the World Championships we knew that he was lying in the first half dozen and then, one morning, Horace rang to say that he had crashed. The 402 was a write off.

Flying down the Rhone valley, with the Mistral behind him, Bill had been working his way into wave and had been caught in the wild turbulence of a giant rotor. Forced to land his machine had fallen out of his hands, smashing down into a precipitous and rocky field, and he had suffered a badly fractured vertebra.

The loss of our trip to the Wasserkuppe was a bitter disappointment and the end of the 402 was even worse. I would have been happy to see it go into production just as it was but Harry had other ideas. When Horace called another meeting at Newbury he showed them to us for the first time and we were enthralled by his audacity and the simplicity of his proposals.

His drawings showed the original Meise/Olympia fuselage shell with a new, all moving, tailplane. Mounting this on the back of the

COMBAT AND COMPETITION

original sternpost gave a longer moment arm and there was a much bigger fin extending forward along the fuselage spine – changes to compensate for the 17 metre wing. The canopy moulding was wider, and lower at the sides, providing more room and better visibility.

The all moving tail would reduce the trim drag, increasingly so at high speed, and the new design, soon to be known as the 403, had been stressed for inverted flight.

Horace gave the go ahead. But he was adamant that I should not rely on the new prototype for the following year's Nationals. David Carrow solved the problem by persuading his syndicate to offer me their new Skylark III for its first competition outing. Their terms included extensive use of the aircraft to practice on beforehand, and that at the height of the soaring season. It was a most generous gesture and I was glad that my job enabled me to present them with a brand new diluter demand oxygen system.

Some months later, at a cockpit conference in Newbury, there was ample evidence that the 403 was well under way. I offered to give up the Skylark III for the Nationals and commit myself to the 403 there and then. But Horace would have none of it.

"Don't do it David! I have a lot of difficulties at the moment. What you have seen today means absolutely nothing. I simply cannot guarantee that it will be ready."

In fact it was, but only just, exactly four days before the Nationals, when I found myself at RAF Andover, with the aircraft ready to fly and the bearded Tony Goodhart literally breathing down my neck!

Visiting Elliotts at the eleventh hour, he had realised that 403 might still be completed in time, and had somehow persuaded Horace to loan it to him. Now he was full of flap in case I found something which might scupper his chances.

Tony was fortunate. The only immediate difficulty involved the all moving tailplane. 100% mass balancing was necessary to cure a short period oscillation, and this had the further advantage of somewhat reducing the excessive stick force per 'G'. In this state it would be tiring for a competition pilot, circling for long periods in thermals, but that was Tony's problem. So I compromised with non optimised handling, but not with safety, and took the aircraft through its special category C of A flight tests at one CG^5 position. Cleared for contest flying by an experienced pilot, with a maximum speed limitation, it provided Tony with an aircraft for the Nationals.

That year had been threatened by the Suez crisis and the possibility

CHAPTER ELEVEN   A TESTING TIME

of petrol rationing. When the time came all was well. The weather gave us seven good days and a hard fought contest between Tony D^2 who eventually won, Nick Goodhart who was second, his brother in the 403 and myself third and fourth respectively.

Soon afterwards the 403 returned to Twinwood, where its manoeuvrability and the big fin and rudder assembly really came into their own, as I worked up a routine for the National Aerobatic Contest at Dunstable. But slow rolls required considerable care and plenty of practice. Even an experienced aerobatic pilot needed his wits about him.

So it was with something akin to horror that I watched Harry Midwood release from a high aerotow one morning and observed, from the nature of his subsequent manoeuvres, that he was attempting to teach himself how to slow roll!

We had talked it through enough, and he certainly knew the theory, but at the very least he would have been wise to opt for a dual session on the Tiger Moth, before trying his luck on the 403. However Harry is a determined chap and his careful, step by step, approach got him there in the end with relatively little drama.

At Dunstable, where Sandy Powell chief test flying instructor from my ETPS days was secretary to the Lockheed aerobatic judges, they seemed to approve of slow rolls and inverted flying. Although penalised for failing to include a spin I came second to Dan Smith whose immaculate display in a standard Olympia brought him a well deserved win.

Back at Twinwood once more – where we were working on the 403 to reduce the stick free stability and the stick force per 'G' – the pressure was on again. The stalling speed was higher than the 402, there was a suspicion of a premature airflow breakaway over the wing root at high angles of attack, and Tony Goodhart had been unhappy with the low speed performance.

Harry ran some tests and soon established that the thicker wing root (20% compared with the 402's 18%) – introduced for structural reasons – was the main culprit. Reverting to an 18% root section was the first step – and reducing the tailplane mass balance as much as possible, in favour of a bobweight well forward in the elevator circuit, would mean a substantial saving in ballast. Sufficient in total to make good the 403's performance shortfall at low speed.

However by the time we had flown a fully modified tailplane Horace had the bit properly between his teeth. He wanted more

COMBAT AND COMPETITION

performance still! Could the 403, he demanded, cope with a further increase in span? It could, fortuitously, because the airworthiness stressing requirements had just been relaxed, and became 19 metres – the Olympia 419.

This time he was so confident that he started to build three aircraft. Two 419s and a clipped (15 metre) wing 403 with a shortened fuselage, all of which he intended to offer the British Team for the World Championships in Poland the following year.

Whilst they were still on the stocks, we attended some of Twinwood's better parties which featured Ralph Maltby's charming Victorian balloons. Tissue paper creations in the red white and blue of Empire, they were gifts from Messrs Brocks the firework people, who must have thought them a godsend when they turned up amongst some long forgotten stock. For Ralph was an important customer. His wind tunnel consumed vast quantities of artificial smoke.

Ralph could hardly control himself as he read out the the old fashioned instructions:

"Two persons shall stand in an elevated position....." followed by an excruciatingly pedantic diatribe about supporting the sagging tissue walls until the paraffin burner had inflated the envelope.

Pause for much laughter – then Ralph again – "A person shall stand under......" explaining at inordinate length how one must bend down by the burner orifice to light the wick.

Those dreaded balloons were a handful in the lightest of winds. Sometimes we used ladders to ease the strain on shoulders and backs, and to make life easier for the crouching firemen down below. The difficulties were greatly aggravated by the way in which Ralph always insisted on repeating the old Victorian text, like some ham Music Hall performer, reducing his assistants to uncontrollable mirth.

The failure rate was high, but we had some conspicuous successes too. And what could be more evocative, on a quiet moonlit night, than one of those gossamer shapes lifting upwards and away. The flame strong at first, then fading slowly – until it became a mere pinprick of light – lost forever in the mists of time and space.

On many an occasion Anne and I stood apart from the rest, in the dark shadow of that familiar hanger, and watched them go. And the shades of 613 Squadron who had introduced me to the air seemed as supportive and benign as ever.

If the shades of 613 were peaceful, the same could not be said of those elsewhere on the site. For the day came when the Local

CHAPTER ELEVEN   A TESTING TIME

Authority discovered that the gliding club had no running water and they were ordered to do something about it or risk losing their bar licence. Absolutely unthinkable! So they moved across the airfield, to one of the ex Night Fighter OTU crew rooms on the other side, where water was already laid on.

Their new abode had an open plan area at one end and a central corridor, with small rooms leading off on either side. Nothing special about it – yet it could feel mighty queer if you were there alone after dark. Before long it had become a sort of unspoken nightmare amongst the regulars. Until the evening when one of them spoke up and voiced their fears.

"This place gets very spooky sometimes!" he said, and then they all owned up.

To some it was just an eerie sensation. To others it was evil personified. Harry remembers waking in sheer terror, walking down the corridor with his hair standing on end, and rushing out onto the airfield. There were loos much nearer, almost next to the clubhouse, but he simply couldn't face them.

Nobody ever saw the Twinwood ghost, but its presence was real enough. Perhaps the restless spirit of some Bisley pilot who had pranged at night. Or maybe that of the bandleader, Glenn Miller, missing on a flight from Twinwood to Paris one misty November day in 1944. No sense of evil there. But why just the Second World War? For those years were but a moment in the history of a plateau overlooking the river Ouse.

Another, and in its own way, decisive moment was the day when Nick Goodhart arrived with his Skylark III to fly against the prototype Olympia 419.

During the two previous weekends Harry and I had flown the 419 at Thruxton and Andover, found it to be virtually faultless, moved it to Twinwood and, in an intensive two days, completed all the initial tests for its C of A. Tony D[2] had sampled the prototype too and had decided, there and then, to fly it in Poland. Now, with the second aircraft well advanced at Newbury, Nick had come along to evaluate it for himself.

The first step was a comparative performance test, flying a series of partial glides, starting each one in close line abreast and observing the vertical separation at the end of the run. And at every speed the 419 was about 5% better than the Skylark III!

After that Nick had a flight in the 419. Almost certainly he would

COMBAT AND COMPETITION

find the handling superior to that of any glider which he flown before. And what then? Would Elliotts be supplying three out of four aircraft for the British team on this occasion? It seemed more than likely. Philip Wills had elected to fly a Skylark II in the Standard Class and Elliotts were building that special, one off, 15 metre 415 for Tony Goodhart.

But Nick did not chose the 419. In retrospect it is perhaps easier to understand. He was completely at home in his Skylark III, after two year's hard flying, with the aircraft set up exactly to his liking – and the alternative? – a second prototype scheduled to be ready just three weeks before the team's departure date. The uncertainties were just too great.

On the following Friday I was stuck in bed with a dreadful sinus cold. Came the Saturday morning and the trip to Lasham was not exactly welcome, but there was a job to be done. The 419 awaited, its cockpit full of rubber tubing and two newly calibrated ASIs[6], ready for position error testing[7]. My sinus was still playing up. So Harry did the flying while I sat on the ground and fumed. It was classic Buchan's cold spell, blowing half a gale, with lines of shallow cumulus marking the route to Cornwall.

Wally Kahn made matters worse with a story about Nick leaving for Cambridge on aerotow before our arrival that morning. Apparently he had decided to attempt the first 500km flight in the UK. As we were packing up for the day news came through that he had made it with a dog leg flight to Penzance. The straight line distance was 293 miles, a new UK record.

We stood beside the 419 trailer, trying to digest it all, and then a sort of madness set in. This type of weather usually lasted for several days. If Nick could do that in his Skylark III on Saturday – the 419 could do even better on Sunday – even if it was the thirteenth of the month!

A call to our private met man confirmed that conditions would be similar, but not so good, no clouds and the same strong northeasterly wind. In our state of madness it was more than enough.

Shortly before 9.00 am on the following morning I was airborne on tow for Bury St Edmunds. The next couple of hours was a long slog into wind at more than two shillings per mile. Cloud base remained stubbornly around 2,500 ft asl and, as we got further away from Lasham, the sky became totally overcast.

Near Stradishall a few breaks appeared and my spirits lifted, only

CHAPTER ELEVEN A TESTING TIME

to drop into my boots again as the tug started a let down towards Lavenham. This was well short of my intended release, barely exceeding the 500km circle centered on the goal at St Just, and by the time we arrived over the middle of the airfield, at 1,200 ft asl, I was almost beside myself with rage.

Fortunately I ran straight into a rough and choppy thermal and climbed slowly away – drifting off downwind towards Wethersfield and Harlow. Whilst the tug pilot, with his tank nearly dry, dropped down into the circuit and landed.

The first hour soon degenerated into endless circling – struggling to remain airborne – in constant danger of being blown towards the middle of London and far south of track. Then a marginal improvement in conditions allowed a change of heading to starboard and progress across several cloud streets, which brought me to Watford exactly one hour and twenty five minutes from release. Ninety plus kilometres into my flight and less than 65 kph. Nothing like good enough.

At this point, with a sky of thin and flattish cumulus streeting into the distance over the Berkshire Downs, things began to look a little more promising – and I made use of the opportunity, while it lasted, to work my way north of track. Thus providing the basis for a dogleg flight, in case the straight line distance from Lavenham proved insufficient, and at the same time putting the latter part of my route directly downwind. An advantage if conditions deteriorated later in the day.

Watford to Calne took an hour and twenty minutes. A great improvement. But it still left almost 300 kilometres to go, with less than four hours of convection remaining. And Calne itself was almost my undoing. Time to photograph a turning point for that dogleg – and the town would do nicely. Minutes later I was scraping the barrel, almost looking in through the windows of a vast country house.

After several attempts to climb away, each followed by a despairing return to the same thermal source, a tiny cloud shadow drifted across the courtyards and cloisters down below. A proper upcurrent gathered itself together – and I was tossed back to sanity, over 2,000 feet higher, and some miles downwind of Lacock Abbey which I had lately been admiring at close quarters.

As the sun moved into the west and the clouds gradually vanished, the top of each climb seemed like the last of the day. Long heart stopping glides. On and on for miles. Nothing except the driving force of Buchan's boisterous wind. Until another sun trap – tucked away behind some distant hill – betrayed its solitary thermal with a fragile patch of cloud, brilliant white against the blue. Each one a chance of survival.

On the run in I watched the variometer pistons as if they were the stuff of life itself, and the altimeter unwinding – sweating in suspense. Then a mighty surge of lift and the 419 swinging onto its beam ends moving upwards and away.

Four times it happened. Those life giving wind shadow thermals were like stepping stones, across the Mendips, under the southern edges of the Quantocks and the Brendon Hills, and a last one near Tiverton. Or so it seemed. For the brooding uplands of Dartmoor were impossibly far away. Another thirty nail biting miles, until the Tors south of Okehampton stood barring the way ahead. And then, hurdling a lower ridge close to the town, less than a hundred feet above the top, I ran slap into another great hiccuping upcurrent.

My watch read 4 o'clock. By now I had lost all sense of speed. It hardly mattered. Sheer competitive instinct, and a remaining touch of madness, were enough to keep me going:

"On! On!" The unspoken words were like a clarion call – "You're almost there! Hunger, fatigue and the rest are for later!"

And as suddenly it was almost over. The next sun facing slope produced one of the best thermals of the day. Two more giant strides across Cornwall, another climb to over 4,000 ft north of Truro, and I was final gliding towards the most westerly point in the Kingdom. The cramped little fields, stone walls shadowed against the setting sun, were a powerful reminder that Tony D^2 had elected to fly the aircraft in Poland. Perhaps later, when he heard the story, he would understand.

For Anne and Harry it had been a traumatic day as well – as she takes up the story in a letter to her sister in Canada.

At Lasham the conditions were so bad that no one made anything of them until about 3.30 pm - when a few people managed to stay up for half an hour..... Then the tug arrived back having had great difficulty in getting more petrol. To our surprise he said that David had been on his way since 11 am. Harry Midwood and I made a mad dash for the car and trailer and set out on the long trek south west.

We travelled over Dartmoor with this long trailer - thirty four feet of it. The narrow stone walled lanes gave me the willies and I excelled myself by going over a narrow bridge too fast and the trailer wheel ran

CHAPTER ELEVEN A TESTING TIME

perilously along the top of the parapet – while Harry encouraged me with cries of "Keep Going!"

.....arrived at David's field at 11.30 pm and spent until 3.30 am struggling with the trailer which was dragged at times by hand and at times by Rover with a tractor in front down the most miserable farm road in England..... He had landed a few yards from the coast, a distance of 315 miles in a straight line – beating Nick Goodhart's record of the previous day by a good margin.

Sunday the thirteenth had been a day to remember!

The 415 appeared at Lasham a couple of weeks later and presented no problems. Yet in performance terms it was a nonsense. Like building the Olympia IV over again and adding extra weight. Bad luck on Tony Goodhart who would be putting his reputation on the line with it in Poland. But he seemed happy enough with his choice.

After the World Championships we created a hybrid version – mating a long (419) fuselage to the 15 metre wings. With the extra tail volume it turned out to be an excellent aerobatic machine which slow rolled beautifully. More than anything else it helped me to win the National Aerobatic Contest that year. So the 415 was not entirely wasted.

Five or possibly six 419s were built, all of them to Harry's basic design. The first prototype, which Tony D^2 flew in Poland, was bought by the Army Gliding Association. One aircraft went to the RAFGSA and another to Peter Scott. The second prototype was retained by Elliotts and I flew it for several years. And at least one was purchased by the Soviet Union – which acquired a Skylark III as well. Horace showed little interest in creating a market for the 419. He refused to discuss the subject – except to convey the impression that the first batch was made at a loss. And in the end he pitched the price so high that he never sold any more.

Looking back on that period I suppose that the '59 Nationals was critical in my bid to make the British Team. It also happened to be a fascinating and unusual contest. On the first day Nick Goodhart broke the UK goal flight and distance records, to go far into the lead. Then the third day's race, with only two finishers, revealed a serious weakness in the current scoring system. In which, as it happened, Britain was by no means alone. The lucky pair gained a huge points advantage over the rest and the leading places were turned completely upside down.

But to start at the beginning. Nick reached his goal, at Portmoak

COMBAT AND COMPETITION

17 miles north of Edinburgh, on that classic opening day, using a combination of thermal, cu-nim and wave. It was an outstanding flight. Those of us in the leading group behind him ended up around Darlington and Newcastle. Less than 250 miles from Lasham to his 358.

"Never" – as it was said at the time – "have so many flown so far to score so little."

For myself, lying 4th, the position improved after the second day's race to Kidlington and back. I managed to avoid the showers and heavy sink near Basingstoke, made a fast time, and moved up to second place.

On the critical third day our race to the Long Mynd was set into an area of supposedly increasing instability. But the thunderstorms forecast over Wales never materialised. Most of the field ground to a halt around Leominster. But for Tony D^2 and myself, who almost reached the goal, our failure to do so was dreadfully frustrating. It had been cloudless all the way, and I caught my last blue thermal at Tenbury, 19 miles from the Mynd.

Tony joined me on the climb, in his yellow and white 419, and we squeezed every last foot out of the gently rising air. 4200 ft and that was our lot. Reluctantly we set course again, in wide line abreast, flying for maximum distance, hardly daring to touch the controls. To the west of Ludlow a range of wooded hills slipped beneath our wings – sunlit slopes and quarries – a perfect thermal source – and nothing! absolutely nothing!

The landing area and the blister hanger beyond were clearly visible, within easy gliding range, except that the Long Mynd is 1400 ft high. Just one more thermal, even the merest fraction of a thermal, would have been sufficient.

We reached the east face level with the top, not enough wind for slope soaring, just a last few thermal bubbles to prolong the agony. Tony landed first and I followed him into the same field. We stood together looking up at the hill, two solid miles of Mynd separating us from our goal. And as we watched, the silhouette of a Skylark III slid silently overhead – Philip Wills on his final glide. Later that night we learned that Geoffrey Stephenson who started early and Philip soon after him – more than half an hour before us – had been the only ones to make it. Another 500 ft and we would have beaten them both.

Poor Tony, it was much worse for him, he had won the second task after a disaster on the opening day which had put him right down the

CHAPTER ELEVEN   A TESTING TIME

order. And now to be faced with this. He turned to me – the anger visible in his eyes – and for a moment I caught a glimpse of the SAS professional.

"I don't know about you" – he said testily – "But I *had* to get there. I *really* needed those extra points today."

Philip left Lasham on a high note and went off to fly in the Dutch Nationals. After he had gone we flew three more tasks, but the Long Mynd race had put Steve into an almost unassailable position and he defended it well. Even Nick, with the advantage of his epic flight at the beginning, was unable to close the gap. He and I were to remain second and third through to the end of the contest.

Soon afterwards Anne, Harry and I set course for the French Championships at St Yan, with a brief stop at the Paris Air Show. Ours was the equipage to beat them all, over fifty five feet long. The 419 trailer was pretty substantial and we were towing it with an outsize ambulance. Originally ordered by the now defunct Suez Canal Company, Horace had acquired two of them, in near mint condition, and the one which we were using had been converted into a very acceptable motor home. The Suez extras, such as mosquito screens and fans, were still in place. Even the bell was working. To use in extremis if we dared.

Only the loo was missing – a vital necessity on those long open roads across the centre of France. So we cut a hole in the floor near the front of the trailer, with an aluminium flap to keep out the dust, and a big plastic funnel. After due consideration we discarded the idea of a notice – 'Not to be used when the train is standing in the station' – for that would have been illegal!

St Yan had its moments. Winning on the first day, and then wrecking my chances on the second by pushing too hard at the end of a race. It was crass stupidity. Allowing myself to be incited by a gaggle of Breguet 901s which were being flown in true Gallic fashion. We left the last thermal together, with precious little height in reserve, and I failed to accept the superiority of the 901 at high speed until it was too late. Flying one soon afterwards revealed the advantage of negative flap, to become the norm in later years, but that was no excuse.

Day three, going due east, developed into a long sweaty struggle in the Saone valley. Lower and lower. Trapped in a sweltering oven with no means of escape. Crossing the river was little more than a last desperate gamble with barely enough height to reach the nearest ridge on the other side. When I eventually got there, hundreds of feet below the top, running close to a group of houses which clung precariously to the hillside, there was a faint burble of lift. It took an age, gyrating suicidally close to the roof tops which straggled upwards in the murk, until that weak and hesitant upcurrent eventually carried me out of danger.

After that conditions improved by leaps and bounds. Cumulus blossomed, the thermals grew strong, and the high plateaux and long valleys of the Jura vanished from sight as the 419 was drawn up into cloud.

Those thermals over the Jura developed into a series of massive storms, which carried me into the mountains south of Lake Geneva, towards Chamonix and Mont Blanc.

On landing, as a matter of principle, I made my way to the most imposing property in sight, and ended up in strange company. My generous hosts provided a most welcome bath, a temporary change of clothing, and an invitation to dinner. From their conversation they appeared to be a bunch of international financiers and their ladies, American, French and Swiss. All spoke excellent English, and soon, what with their hospitality and my long day in the air, it became difficult to sort out the various nationalities.

But I was not too tired to detect the atmosphere of tension, not to say menace, which haunted the dinner table. As if they were utterly dependent on one another and yet hated each others' guts. Afterwards, with no sign of my crew, I accepted the offer of a bed. But sleep did not come easily, after that sinister dinner party, quite apart from the incessant rumbles of thunder and worrying about Anne and Harry.

At that moment the two of them were struggling in torrential rain, trying to make a 'U' turn on a mountain hairpin. They managed in the end – by chocking the trailer wheels with a tool box, unhitching it and swinging it round by hand – and by some miracle the whole thing failed to go over the edge and into the valley below. Safely past that hazard they arrived at last in a crescendo of headlights and engine noise, and the guard dogs went berserk, but my financiers slept on. Perhaps they were already dead, in a orgy of mutual poisoning which I had somehow escaped!

Our arrival back at St Yan coincided with briefing and there was a mad rush to get ready in time for the next task. Only to find that one of the ailerons had been damaged by a stone on landing the previous evening.

Harry, who had been feeling unwell for several days, missed his

CHAPTER ELEVEN   A TESTING TIME

breakfast in order to complete the repair as quickly as possible. It was too much, coming on top of the round trip to Haute Savoie in such atrocious conditions, and he was forced to throw in the towel soon afterwards. He was back in harness again by the following day, but Anne was left wondering how to cope with a solo retrieve in Elliotts' pantechnicon.

When Monsieur Boissonade, Secretary General of the Championships Organisation – a most accomodating fellow who so arranged his French that we always understood him – heard that she was on her own he produced a stand-in. A rumbustious character, in his late seventies or early eighties, who walked with a stick and still had an eye for the ladies. He seemed to be known as the 'Father of French Gliding' – though whether because of his sexual prowess or in honour of his advancing years was never entirely clear.

It was a hot and humid day and our temporary crew man was insufferable. For a start he kept trying to dry his chief's back, under her shirt, with her own hankerchief. Difficult to resist if you are driving a heavy ambulance, with a trailer on the back, and the perpetrator speaks a different language. Then he resolutely refused to telephone St Yan and the retrieve overshot by miles.

My landing, much too early in the day, was close to a tiny hamlet which gave the impression of being almost totally isolated from the outside world. The sort of place where the inhabitants have been inbreeding for years and are all a trifle odd.

At the village bakery Madame la Boulangere, a pneumatic lady of uncertain age, welcomed me with open arms. Of course I could use the phone. Monsieur was away, and would not be back that night – she lingered over the words – but he wouldn't mind. And of course I must stay in the house until my crew arrived. As the day wore on, and they failed to turn up, she became more pressing. We were a long way from St Yan – which unfortunately was not true! – and Madame Ince might not appear for hours. Never mind, there was a large bed upstairs – and she could make me very comfortable – if I would care to come and see it now?

When the retrieve arrived it was almost dusk and Madame could hardly contain her disappointment. She looked daggers at Anne and, after Anne had told me her story in a brief aside, I looked daggers at the elderly satyr who had accompanied her from St Yan. He was a pain in the neck. We should have left him, there and then, to sow a few more wild oats with Madame la Boulangere. And perhaps, just

COMBAT AND COMPETITION

perhaps, he might have introduced some fresh blood into that strange community!

Fortunately there was more to St Yan than hairy retrieves and unwanted sex. Such as the unbridled enthusiasm and extrovert sportsmanship of the French pilots. Like one previous national champion – 'Old Gravel Throat' we called him – because he spoke the most glottal French you ever heard. After one absolutely disastrous day he was heard to announce loudly during supper –

"Aujourdhi j'acqui zero point," and then he actually laughed.

The severity of task setting was an eye opener. In the sense of being willing to set races which were likely to produce a small number of finishers, or even none, it was much tougher than the UK. Not a bad idea, in those days of lower performance sailplanes, cheap petrol and relatively uncrowded roads. Deliberately putting more stress on your prospective World Championship pilots could be revealing and character forming at the same time. But it needed to be matched by an improved scoring system.

Which set me thinking, particularly in relation to the recent British Nationals and that frustrating race to the Long Mynd. Eventually, chewing it over with Harry, we came up with a formula which increased the points for speed, and reduced those for distance – or vice versa – in proportion to the percentage of finishers. Subsequently I wrote it up in *Sailplane and Gliding*[8] and something not dissimilar, in principle, is still in use today.

My plan to fly in the 'Challenge Victor Boin', on the way home, involved careful planning and 700 kilometres of press on driving. For the French Nationals were due to finish, after a suitable lunch, in the course of one afternoon – and the Belgian contest near Charleroi was scheduled to take place on the following day. That farewell repast continued in splendid and leisurely fashion, long after our planned time of departure, and we urged Harry not to demonstrate the truth of his well worn saying that:

"Time spent in the bar is time saved on the road!"

In the end we made it in 13½ hours, taking turns to sleep in the back of the ambulance, an excellent meal near Rheims and we reached the airfield at Gosselies just before 2 am.

Named after a previous Chairman of the Royal Belgian Aero Club, whose idea it was, Victor Boin was an unusual event – a one day, free distance, contest. The generous cash prizes tended to encourage a good entry, and on this occasion there were 28 starters, French, Belgium and

CHAPTER ELEVEN A TESTING TIME

German. From my point of view this would be an outright sprint, no other word for it, and I wanted to win. There was a pressing need to exorcise the memory of my curate's egg performance at St Yan. The £30 starting money – on top of which they even refunded your entrance fee on arrival – and almost £150 for the winner, would go a long way towards the cost of our expedition to France.

An anticyclone centred over the middle of Germany provided a clockwise circulation with light southerlies at Gosselies which absolutely demanded a track to the north east. With the advantage from my Typhoon days of knowing much of the area like the back of my hand, I planned carefully – to avoid the worst of the damp, low lying, parts – and ambitiously to prolong my flight by soaring the Minden hills at the end of the day.

So much for plans. Twenty first on the launching order meant a delay of forty minutes and, when I came off tow, there were gliders strung out ahead as far as the eye could see. Depressing – until the first thermal rocketed me to well over 4000 feet – and small cumulus, not more than a few hundred feet thick began to appear all over the sky. Ideal racing conditions – and the going was easy – flying straight along the thermal streets and hardly losing any height. In this way I passed a number of competitors who were circling lower down – and, at times, when the streeting was less pronounced, others made excellent thermal markers. Before long I had overhauled most of the field.

After that it was a matter of continuing to force the pace. A couple of fraught moments occurred, when high cirrus damped down the convection, once near the Netherlands/Belgian border and again just short of Germany airspace. But on each occasion the thermals recovered themselves in time. Crossing the Rhine high near Wesel, in thick haze, led to an eventual landing at Emsdetten. About 30 miles short of the Minden hills, but enough to win the day.

The season drew to a close that year, in company with Nick Goodhart, flying glider aerobatics at the Farnborough Air Show. Then, at a BGA Council Meeting in the autumn, John Furlong, reporting as Chairman of the World Championships Master Committee, told us the seeded order for the next World Championships. Anne and I, she had previously taken over the BGA publicity from Wally Kahn, listened with baited breath.

Philip and Steve had stood down. Nick had been selected first, for the open class – myself second, open or standard – Tony D^2 third, open class and Tony Goodhart fourth. I had made the Team at last!

Black Mark Bryan! - Rex Mulliner awards the wooden spoon (for the lowest annual flying hours) to Bryan Greensted. Hunting Clan Xmas Party, 1953.

Wally and I were oil and water - with Bill Worner of Saunders Roe (left) and Wally Monk (right) at a wet Farnborough Airshow.

CHAPTER TWELVE

ELONGATED BALLS

There had of course been much more to life than competitive gliding. Not least the opportunity to play a part in one of the first companies to grasp the true potential of electronics, Elliott Brothers (London) Ltd, which grew and prospered and in the fullness of time became Elliott Automation.

Several years had passed between Ben Gunn's offer to join him test flying at Boulton Paul and the late summer day in 1954 when I moved to Elliotts at Borehamwood. Very different from the independent airline business which had been my life, day and night almost seven days a week, during my time with Hunting Clan.

As base manager at Bovingdon I had shared an office with Bryan Greensted. A tough and irascible character, chief test pilot of Rotol during the war years, he had acquired his air transport background with Skyways on the Berlin airlift. Bryan was technical manager and chief pilot and his arrival at work resembled that of a small tornado, as he bounced in through the door, rotund and radiating new ideas.

But there was a darker side to his character. His liquid lunches were notorious and the results totally unpredictable. Back at base in the afternoon he might work harder, and be more demanding than ever, or the lunchtime session could as easily turn into a lost weekend, regardless of all other priorities.

One visit to Air Service Training at Hamble turned into just that. It ended with a wary Jeffrey Quill joining us to dinner, at the Swan in Bursledon, where we eventually stayed the night. The Quills lived in a large house overlooking the estuary, not far from the Bugle which Bryan and I had left towards mid afternoon, and the atmosphere had been frosty when he arrived home to find the carpets rolled back, his radiogram playing dance music, and the two of us entertaining his somewhat bemused wife. It stayed that way for the rest of the evening, for he knew my colleague of old, but Bryan was rather too well lubricated to notice.

On the following morning we headed for Bovingdon, full of good intentions, until Bryan developed an overwhelming thirst as we neared Windsor Great Park. It took a vast amount of Pimms in the nearest hostelry before he felt able to continue. When we finally got back there was hell to pay. Maurice Curtis, the MD, had been on the phone from London almost continuously since the previous afternoon, getting progressively more irate, and nobody knew our whereabouts.

COMBAT AND COMPETITION

Things became easier when Hugh Cundall joined us from the Air Registration Board to help with the introduction of Yorks and Viscounts. At least there was someone else to share the hazards of Bryan's outside visits. Bad luck on Hugh, his job meant that before long he had acquired the lot – or as near as made no difference – and I had correspondingly greater freedom to concentrate on other matters.

Hunting Clan was fun. There was a sense of achievement as the company built on its trooping contracts to Malta, Gibraltar and Singapore, and won licences for new scheduled services. A Newcastle centred network with links to Bovingdon, Glasgow and Belfast, Amsterdam, Hamburg and Scandinavia came first. Then a West African run to complement the East African Safari to Nairobi and Rhodesia.

As the operations became more complex, and the fleet grew, better methods of aircraft and crew rostering were needed. My good friend Tony Lucking, at that time working with Urwick Orr, came to help. Soon we had decent gant chart displays, together with a flying hours limit calculator and recording system for pilots, radio officers and cabin crews. I looked at other areas – and managed to simplify the WAT[1] calculation for Yorks using high altitude airfields on the Safari routes – whilst Tony, to his surprise, found himself with a totally different project.

It was Bryan's idea. He wanted a work study on the flight deck. Arthur Rusk was the captain. Like all such exercises the crews were deeply suspicious. But Arthur didn't care a jot. He was the original, outwardly scatterbrained, generous Irishman and he had married the most beautiful hostess of them all. They lived in a converted stable block close to the airfield. A delightful pair and their parties were great.

Tony and Arthur got rather more than they bargained for, when their Viking lost an engine immediately after take off, and had to divert into Heathrow under marginal conditions.

"And there was I," said Arthur, "working as if the devil himself was after me – and he was! he was! – and myself full of wicked words. But your Mr Lucking sat there calm as you please with his stopwatch – writing it all down."

In spite of the pressures, and Bryan Greensted notwithstanding, perhaps even because of him, the feeling of fun persisted. We worked and played hard, raising the rafters in many a pub from the upmarket Two Brewers in Chipperfield – where the crews stayed overnight

CHAPTER TWELVE   ELONGATED BALLS

before an early departure – to other lesser establishments in the area. It was like a brief wartime interlude all over again. There were even two ex Typhoon types amongst the senior captains. Bob Hornall, who went on to become senior Vice President of Middle East Airlines, had flown with 245 Squadron and Rex Mulliner had commanded 198, on 123 Wing, alongside Pinkie Stark's 609.

The pressures of impending matrimony had been a sharp reminder about career prospects with an independent airline. For BEA and BOAC were then at the height of their monopolistic powers, and who knew what the future might hold for such as Hunting Clan. So I decided regretfully to look elsewhere.

Elliott Brothers was certainly different. The name of the company meant nothing to me and this, despite their confidently worded advertisement for control system engineers to work on new supersonic aircraft, suggested that they might be short on practical aviation know-how. The positive response to my letter sent on spec – referring to an RAF background, ETPS, and an engineering degree – confirmed that this was so.

Before long I was installed at Borehamwood. In a dark and scruffy works building, fronted by a brick office block, which served as the company's research laboratories. The whole set up had a part worn look about it, suggesting an acute shortage of funds for capital expenditure and non essential maintenance.

In one respect these impressions were correct. For the triumvirate which ruled over Elliott Brothers, Hungarian Jews, brilliant as they were unconventional, were in permanent danger of overtrading. The Chairman, Leon Bagrit, later to be knighted and to become known as 'Mr Automation', was master behind the scenes, rarely seen. In earlier times, when the cash position was even tighter, legend had it that he would strip the company of its component stocks – selling these off one day and buying them back the next – in order to pay the wages. Dr Ross, Managing Director, some time graduate of the Officers' School in Berlin, a cultured, gifted, and eccentric character was the accelerator. Fortunately there was a calming influence too – the Financial Director, balding 'Curly' Herzfeld alias the brake.

The building at Borehamwood – there were others at Lewisham in south east London and at Rochester in the old Short Brothers factory – was a hive of activity behind its seedy image. Divided into separate cells by internal partitions, or sometimes just chalk marks on the floor, it reflected the operational and organisation policy of a dynamic, free

COMBAT AND COMPETITION

thinking, top management. Rapid growth through a proliferation of highly motivated product oriented divisions.

Divisional managers, learning the rules of success and survival, fought their corners, poaching each others markets and people, and the weakest went to the wall. Maybe there was internal strife and unnecessary duplication. By many standards the whole concept was grossly inefficent. But line management was put firmly in the collar and achieved some remarkable results. As a policy for rapid growth, in the circumstances of the time, it was a remarkable success. Later, as the company grew towards maturity, there were modifications, but the proven divisional structure still remained.

My own particular niche was in the Aviation Research Laboratory run by Jack Pateman. There were two main projects, a master reference gyro – MRG 'B' for V bombers and stand-off guided missiles – and an autostabiliser cum autopilot system for the English Electric Lightning. With no specific brief as yet it was the latter which attracted my interest.

Jack was in charge of work on the Lightning and even after he had been joined by Bill Alexander and Ron Howard, an Australian who had come straight to us from Woomera, he kept a firm hold on that project. With the help and support of those three – Jack, whose mind was already beginning to turn strongly in a commercial direction – Bill, lately of Ferranti, full of sound advice – and Ron, the most innovative in flight control systems – I started to get my part of the show on the road.

Bricks without straw. It had to be that way at first. Exploiting the knowledge and the limited hardware arising from the Lightning contract, in order to move in on other projects against established competition. For Smiths and Sperry had been around for a long time and Elliotts were unknown.

Fortunately for the little team at Borehamwood they possessed a unique advantage. The Lightning system was totally different to anything which had gone before. It was fully integrated. The fast response electro-hydraulic actuators were series input, permanently in the control circuit, quite different to the traditional autopilot with its heavy low performance electric actuators which could be clutched in and out at will.

For safety reasons the system had only limited authority. But, for the first time, it had the performance to provide three axis autostabilisation over the full speed range of a supersonic fighter. The

CHAPTER TWELVE   ELONGATED BALLS

associated Mk 13 Autopilot had a very simple attitude hold function – which could be engaged in the midst of any manoeuvre. It featured an approach coupler and an autothrottle to help the pilot cope with flight at and below minimum drag speed. A need which had arisen with highly swept wings.

Elliotts were way ahead, working with full contract cover, and the basic airframe was already flying. From now on, for a variety of reasons, automatic flight control systems[2] would become increasingly important on high performance aircraft, integrated from the start, and matched to the stability and control characteristics of each design. A fundamental change in technology which could only benefit the sales strategy that we were evolving. It was an exciting prospect.

Before taking the next step it was necessary to understand the Lightning system. To wade through the mass of proposals, counter proposals and amendments, which had flowed between Borehamwood, the Ministry of Supply and English Electric, and to debate these with my advisors. An afternoon with the cockpit mockup was time well spent.

A visit to Martlesham Heath, home of the new Blind Landing Experimental Unit, filled in another part of the picture. I was able to try my hand at a Canberra with auto throttle and a Smiths autopilot, flying coupled approaches into the nearby emergency runway at Woodbridge.

Just one more item was needed. A general purpose brochure to leave behind after each visit. A pipe opener on our control system philosophy. Once again I was to be lucky. Bruce Adkins, in charge of the publications department, a bearded ex matelot – to be more precise he was a Cambridge man who had been closely associated with naval radar from the earliest days – proved to be a tower of strength.

We struck up an immediate rapport and from then on nothing was too much trouble. In next to no time he had pulled my copywriting and the other data together, created an elegant logo for the simple window folder which was used for all Borehamwood technical reports, and the brochure had arrived. Better still as my visits created a need for new proposals, and these were developed with the help of my expert advisers, Bruce continued to provide the same fast and immaculate service. Not that he was exactly short of work. He just happened to be one of those busy men who could always find time to help you out.

I had agreed with Jack Pateman to ignore English Electric on my

COMBAT AND COMPETITION

travels. To visit Warton would be preaching to the converted. My input on the Lightning would be through the engineering team at Borehamwood, unless a problem arose which required a more direct contribution. And we would deal with that when it happened. Meantime there were plenty of other advanced projects around.

It was uphill at first. Hawkers were typical. Chief designers of Sydney Camm's stature knew what was good for the customer – and his staff knew that he didn't believe in autopilots for fighter aircraft. If he learned that I was on the premises, and why, he would have me out in next to no time. In any case why should I want to talk to someone at his level? Everyone knew that autopilots were add on items of electrical equipment to be dealt with somewhere down the line in the drawing office.

I sighed inwardly and looked at Frank Cross, the assistant chief designer, as he described the situation. Down in the nearby experimental shop the big Gyron engined two seat supersonic Hawker 1103, or the later 1121, might soon be taking shape. Both seemed to cry out for flight control systems based on the Lightning design but the portents were hardly favourable.

Frank was a good egg. I sensed that he was by no means convinced that his boss was right on this occasion – and he was prepared to listen – but it would be a long haul. We took ourselves off to lunch near Hampton Court, where he revealed his addiction for Mediterranean prawns, and talked over coffee and liqueurs well into the afternoon. It was a start at least.

The same problem arose when we laid on a presentation for Handley Page. This was intended to show them our ideas for automatic flight control on the HP 100, one of four competing Mach 2.5 supersonic reconnaissance bomber designs to OR 330, and start them thinking about Elliotts as a major subcontractor.

Godfrey Lee, who was chief aerodynamicist and from our point of view one of the key men on such an advanced project, refused to come. As I knew him well in the gliding world, I rang and pressed him to change his mind. But he was adamant. Even if Elliotts were proposing a fully integrated control system, which would have to be precisely matched to the aerodynamics of such an advanced canard delta design, the responsibility for its evaluation must still rest with the instrumentation and electrical specialists. It was the add on autopilot complex yet again.

Once the presentation was under away – I got drawn into a

CHAPTER TWELVE   ELONGATED BALLS

discussion about flying the aircraft, on autopilot, through a minature force stick – and it was clear from our visitors' expressions that they were on a different wave length. The arrival of Dr Ross, somewhat bruised and battered about the face, enlivened the proceedings. He was introduced all round and, in response to Jack Pateman's question about his appearance – what Jack actually said was:

"Have you been in a fight Dr Ross?" he explained in torrent of fractured English that it was all the fault of his new car. A Jaguar fitted with automatic transmission.

Starting off for the first time he had put the unfamiliar gear selector into drive and promptly hit the vehicle in front. Irate beyond words he had thrown the selector into reverse and stood on the accelerator instead of the brake. This time he managed to mount the pavement and hit a lamp standard fair and square. In the process he had made violent contact with the windscreen. In his not so humble opinion Jaguar should be sued for producing such a dangerous motor vehicle!

The OR 330 contract went to A.V.Roe and the automatic flight control system to Louis Newmark but it did them little good. The Operational Requirement was too advanced for the technology of the day and within two years the whole project had been cancelled.

Meantime the Aviation Research Laboratory at Borehamwood was on the up and up with two two new contracts. First OR 946 – then, almost in a matter of weeks, an inertial guidance system for Blue Steel a nuclear tipped stand-off missile for the V bomber force.

OR 946 was a new concept. Master reference gyro and air data sources would provide a range of outputs, for aircraft and weapon systems, and would drive a set of new flight instruments to replace the standard blind flying panel. It seemed a good idea at first and another string to the Elliott bow. But the further we got into it the more the display aspects began to look dubious.

The new tape driven ASI/Machmeters and Altimeter/VSIs[3], called for by the specification, could accomodate a much more open scale than any circular dial. But the moving pointer, so essential in providing unambiguous and rapidly assimilated analogue information, had virtually disappeared. Unfortunately this shortcoming could not be overcome without a totally different approach which the Ministry were unwilling to consider.

Dubious or not OR 946 displays were in fashion and our brochures were extended accordingly as my travels continued. A.V.Roe, where

COMBAT AND COMPETITION

a mixed rocket/jet fighter was under development and Peter Sutcliffe from Boulton Paul had become chief aerodynamicist, was next on the list.

When I visited Peter at Woodford he showed me over the impressive stainless steel research prototype which was then nearing completion. A three axis autostabiliser had been specified for the definitive fighter version and I had hopes of it coming our way. But shortly afterwards the Avro 720 was cancelled in favour of the Saunders Roe 177, the expensive prototype was broken up, and it was high time to head for the Isle of Wight.

By happy chance, Pete Wilson, a Naval officer on my ETPS course, had just been appointed Development Project Officer on the SR 177. The design had become a joint RAF/RN requirement, the Germans were showing interest, and the equipment manufacturers were beating a path to the chief designer's door. Looking out across the Solent from his office windows at Cowes, a few weeks later, it seemed an ideal place to work. Especially as it was then, brimming with confidence and enthusiasm.

From my point of view it turned out to be a good meeting, Maurice Brennan obviously wanted to see more of Elliotts, and it looked as if we were in with a chance. An important project too – or so it seemed at the time.

There were other, less encouraging, encounters. Folland Aircraft at Hamble – where Ted Tennant, who had been on Typhoons with 146 Wing, had become chief test pilot – was if anything worse than Hawkers. Their thin wing supersonic Gnat, with AI[4] 23 and OR 946 instrumentation, was a natural for Elliotts. Yet Petter had such a fanatical attitude to weight saving that he simply refused to recognise the need for autostabilisation. Joe Boulger, his assistant chief designer, and I were reduced to all sorts of subterfuges and Ted said that we were wasting our time. He was right of course. The Gnat Mk 2 never saw the light of day.

Glosters, so well placed when I had been involved with them at the end of the war, had become a disaster area. I flew Jack and Eric Priestley, our newly appointed aerodynamicist, over there to talk flight systems on the thin wing Javelin and was deeply shocked.

The design team was almost non existent, quite inadequate for a project on this scale. Lack of contractual or financial cover, and an air of defeatism, met us at every turn. The reality was inescapable. That dusty mock up in the old flight shed was the end the road. Short of an

CHAPTER TWELVE   ELONGATED BALLS

eleventh hour change of heart at Hawker Siddeley our hosts had produced their last design. We accepted their invitation to lunch and cut our visit short as soon as decently possible.

Before setting course for home I took the Auster on a wide circuit towards the Severn estuary. At Morton Valence they were still busy with Meteors and Javelins – but it could only be a matter of time. Memories came flooding back. Frank McKenna at the helm – Mossie showing me round the airfield, I could almost hear his voice again –

"Let me know when you want that accomodation. See you soon." – and he had been dead these last nine years. Killed in a Meteor.

The unfulfilled hopes and ambitions of not so long ago were suddenly hard to bear. And now it was all to end like this. On the trip back, as we bumped along under the summer cumulus, I hardly said a word.

The Buccaneer was a much needed tonic after that final trip to Brockworth and another milestone on Elliott's road to success. Perhaps more than we ever realised at the time, because it survived through all the dreadful cancellations that were to come. No contract had yet been placed but my call to Barry Laight, recently appointed chief designer and another gliding acquaintance, resulted in an immediate invitation to visit them at Brough.

Barry had worked wonders since his arrival there. His was the nucleus of a powerful team. They grilled me on the Lightning, and it was clear that they knew exactly what they wanted to meet Naval Air Staff Target No 39. An integrated system, with full authority autopilot[5], no less, capable of carrying out a programmed manoeuvre in order to 'toss' a free falling nuclear bomb at the enemy.

Barry accepted our invitation to Borehamwood which brought Bill Alexander and Ron Howard in on the act. Soon afterwards Blackburns were awarded the contract and when the flight control system came to Elliotts we were delighted.

The Barnes Wallis episode, in complete contrast, was more like science fiction. It started when Air Marshal Sir Victor Goddard, who had been retained by Leon Bagrit as a defence consultant, appeared at Borehamwood. Sir Victor was a colourful character with a mane of greying hair and an eloquent turn of speech. His arrival on the scene was accompanied by an apocryphal story that he and Sir Frederick Handley Page had clashed regularly, and with violence, over the years. To prove this was alleged to be simple. You asked Sir Frederick if he had christened his new V bomber in honour of Sir Victor – and then

COMBAT AND COMPETITION

moved smartly backwards to observe the results!

What certainly was true, and it emerged early on during the discussions with Barnes Wallis, was Sir Victor's opposition to the idea, then current, of a guided weapons equipped Royal Air Force. As a retired senior RAF commander he could not, and rightly as events have proved, accept the demise of manned military aircraft. He gave substance to this view by referring to all guided weapons as 'Elongated Balls' – lingering sadistically over the words as if to imply certain castration!

Sir Victor was a man of compelling enthusiasms, and his enthusiasm of the moment was a long range, variable sweep controlled, subsonic transport – the Barnes Wallis 'Swallow'. We gazed at the great man, as Sir Victor introduced him to us, and tried to equate his white haired boyish enthusiasm with the developments for which he was famous. The geodetic structure of the Wellesley and Wellington – the dam busting and 'Tallboy' earthquake bombs. The R 100 airship, so much better engineered than its ill fated sister ship the R101, had been in his past as well. It was some record.

By the time he came to Borehamwood, Barnes Wallis had been wrestling with variable geometry for more than 10 years. The first flight trials of his original 'Wild Goose', a ground launched tailless radio model controlled in pitch and roll by wing position, had begun in 1949. He saw it simply as a research tool which would lead to a new generation of aircraft. To the Ministry of Supply it had been the first step towards a new anti-aircraft missile – 'Green Lizard' – and he had gone along with the idea in order to obtain financial support.

He showed us film, airborne and ground shots, of the flight trials at Thurleigh and latterly at Predannock – a disused airfield in Cornwall where Leonard Cheshire, still considering his future after the war, had flown chase in a Spitfire.

'Swallow' was the outcome of this earlier work. With its wingtip mounted engines and revolutionary control system it would form the basis of an outstanding, ultra long range, jet transport. We listened in silence and Eric Priestley, who was nothing if not conservative, shook his head in disbelief and muttered about the aerodynamics giving him nightmares.

Then came the crunch, they were in trouble over stability and control – even without the inertia of wingtip mounted engines – and his friend Victor had suggested that we might be able to help. Furthermore, although this was a key variable geometry project

CHAPTER TWELVE   ELONGATED BALLS

supported by the MoS, Vickers had to pay half the costs. Funding was problematical, our contribution must be on a private venture basis, but success would bring enormous benefits.

Jack Pateman looked decidedly unimpressed. Private venture, almost a dirty word in our language, and the high risk 'Swallow' were not an attractive combination. Jack was unwilling to take it further, but Sir Victor had the chairman's ear and clearly wished otherwise. It was advisable to go through the motions.

By the entrance to the wooden hut at Brooklands, a 'Tallboy' stood erect, its nose a matter of inches from the ground, as if demonstrating the moment of impact. Like the section of racing circuit, which disappeared into the undergrowth towards the members' banking, it seemed to be guarding a host of memories. Inside, surrounded by other memorabilia, were the workshops and laboratory where Barnes Wallis held sway. It was a sad little place. The fading ivory tower of a brilliant and innovative engineer who was difficult to control and had been discarded too soon.

In the low speed tunnel a variable sweep controlled model of the 'Swallow' could be 'flown' manually using a remote control column which functioned in pitch only. None of the Vickers test pilots could manage it and my own efforts, when encouraged to have a go, were disastrous. Yet a contract had been placed with Heston Aircraft to build an experimental, variable sweep controlled, glider – the JC 9.

We were told that one of the technicians on the project could fly the wind tunnel model without difficulty. This hapless man was to be given flying lessons and would qualify for his PPL[6]. When the JC 9 was ready he would make a few low hops, until he got the feel of it, and would then conduct a test programme from a series of 10,000 feet aerotows. It was madness.

When I reminded Jack about my glider test flying experience, and suggested that Elliott's might offer my services to Vickers on the JC 9, he did not take kindly to the idea. He looked me up and down, and paused as he stuffed more tobacco into his evil smelling pipe:

"Look David, you've got more sense than that. Its not on. You're more valuable to us in other ways than messing around and risking your neck in such a damn fool device."

He was right of course but I objected to being defeated by that wind tunnel model and, for the sake of a man who had given so much to aviation, the first manned flights deserved a better chance of success.

COMBAT AND COMPETITION

While we were laying the 'Swallow' to rest there was trouble brewing at Lewisham, in the sales department of the Aviation Division. I was making life difficult for them – or so they thought. The Aviation Division, totally separate from the Research Laboratory at Borehamwood, was run by two managers, working in double harness. Wally Monk, who looked after sales, and David Broadbent who ran the engineering and production unit at Rochester.

Between them they had created a business based on manufacture under licence. Jindevik drone target autopilots, and a range of Bendix instruments, including a fuel flowmeter. Although they were in a totally different line Wally and David obviously resented another rapidly expanding aviation activity elsewhere in the company. To make matters worse their flowmeter production was in trouble and Bill Alexander had been sent to Rochester to sort it out.

Wally was a strange mixture, ambitious and technically naive, a retired Wing Commander who had joined Elliotts from the earlier Ministry of Aircraft Production. Although he still regarded the autopilot as a 'button on' extra and resented the idea of an integrated system, because it was engineering oriented, Wally was shrewd enough to recognise its importance. In true Elliott fashion he used his elbows, demanding that all the aviation sales effort should come under one roof, which should be his and, to my horror, Dr Ross agreed.

Wally and I were oil and water and commuting to Lewisham from northwest London was a bind. But when he tried to break my engineering links with Borehamwood, which were essential on the advanced projects, the writing was on the wall.

During that period, before leaving Elliotts, I attended a Lightning autopilot and OR 946 progress meeting at Warton with Jack Pateman. Some days earlier I had answered an advertisement by Pergamon Press. Robert Maxwell was looking for a marketeer, to attend scientific conferences, around the world, and solicit prospective authors for a new range of publications.

My reply drew a positive response and an interview had been set up, at Pergamon's London office, about two hours before the last train of the day was due to leave for Lytham St Anne's. Catching it was vital, as the meeting at English Electric was due to start at 9 am on the following morning, and I had made this absolutely clear to his secretary.

The whole thing was quite extraordinary. Maxwell put on a pair of very dark glasses and sank back onto a couch beside his desk. Tilting

CHAPTER TWELVE ELONGATED BALLS

it carefully, into a near horizontal position, he clasped his hands behind his head and the interview began. His ambitions were boundless and he quickly made it clear that, if I joined him, he would be buying me body and soul. There would be virtually no limit to my travels or working hours. Holidays were unimportant. In a transparent attempt to pressurise me the interview ran on until I was in very considerable danger of missing my train.

At the end, just before calling up a chauffeur driven car to Euston, he asked me if I was interested in the job. It had been such an arrogant and unfeeling performance that I had already decided not to pursue it and I expressed myself very firmly to that effect. But, give him his due, he got me to the station in time.

The progress meeting at English Electric was equally tiresome. The Lightning programme had slipped and Freddie Page, the chief engineer, was keen to spread the blame. He had wound himself up into a state of righteous indignation about the way in which Elliotts had let them down.

"He didn't wish to point a finger, but..... In spite of all their efforts it had proved impossible to...... The chief test pilot would explain his difficulties....."

It was a tour de force – a splendid piece of play acting – which was difficult to refute.

Jack sat and smouldered throughout the whole performance. He was good at smouldering, particularly at this stage in his career, but today he did so with ample justification. On the way home in the train, brooding, he took longer than usual to fill his dreadful pipe – and then:

"The bastards set us up. That won't happen again if I have anything to do with it. Now David, what are we going to do about Wally Monk?"

But I had gone long before we had time to do anything. To British Oxygen, where there was a new development in aircrew oxygen systems. And when, less than two years later, I next saw Jack again everything had changed.

British Oxygen was a gentlemanly interlude working closely with two charming characters. Jack Foster had flown night fighters alongside John Cunningham, and had subsequently been a member of Aero Flight, at RAE Farnborough, where he had taken part in the transonic research on Spitfires. Air Vice Marshal Carnegie who, prior to his retirement had been CAS[7] RNZAF, was adviser to the main

COMBAT AND COMPETITION

board on matters relating to Government and MoS contracts.

Jack was General Manager of British Oxygen Aro Equipment, BOAE, a newly created subsidiary of BOC to promote Aro Corporation products manufactured under licence elsewhere in the group, and I was to be his Sales Manager.

The three of us shared an office, in the BOC Headquarters Building opposite St James's Palace, and it could be said that the two junior officers treated their colleague with the respect due to his rank! We would have done so in any case, for we respected the man himself every bit as much, but it was also a sensible precaution because our AVM had a short fuse. Fortunately his explosions were relatively infrequent and they were usually reserved for the greater absurdities of those he dealt with in Government or on the BOC Board.

It was the mixture much as before, if in simpler engineering terms. Arguing the case for spherical liquid oxygen converters, in place of high pressure storage cylinders, on all the projects which I had been pushing for Elliotts. There was an obvious need to define a minimum range of standard converter capacities, the quantities in which these might be required, and the manufacturing programme requirements. Allowances had to be made for the possibility of retrofits on aircraft already in service, or on those, which were already well advanced in production.

The MoS were supporting BOAE with an Aro derived stainless steel design, and Normalair with a plated copper converter, in a typical dual sourcing exercise. Yet they could provide virtually no guidance about the likely size of the combined RAF/RN market over the following 5 years. In the end it became a matter of gathering information from a number of sources and making my own projections. Even allowing something extra – for a reasonable share of the demand oxygen regulator market – in competition with a Normalair/Drager design – the results looked pretty thin.

Nevertheless we had high hopes for the lox converter. It was lighter, and safer, than the high pressure cylinders which it would be replacing. And the Aro stainless steel design seemed to be more promising in the long run than the Normalair unit. The main problems were in engineering and manufacture – to achieve the welding standards needed for a consistently hard vacuum, and effective insulation, between the inner and outer shells.

There was a brief look at liquid nitrogen converters as well for fuel tank purging and explosion suppression on the three V bombers. This

CHAPTER TWELVE   ELONGATED BALLS

could have led to a major uplift in sales, but it was much too late in the aircraft programme and would have involved an expensive retrofit for the RAF, and a major investment in ground support equipment.

Ground support equipment was the one aspect of the liquid oxygen converter programme which made the whole exercise more tenable for BOC. Whichever way the airborne systems went, and in what proportion between BOAE and Normalair, BOC stood an excellent chance of getting the contract for any generating plant, plus the storage tanks and recharging trolleys. So the AVM was already hard at work on his MoS contacts whilst I headed for HMS Ark Royal, out in the Channel off the Isle of Wight, to study the carrier environment.

The way aboard was by helicopter, and I found myself in the back of a Wessex with Lettice Curtis, ex ATA and record breaking woman pilot, who was there on some other business from Boscombe Down. The briefing beforehand had included a few words on the only 'safe' method of escape after ditching. Experience had shown that it was vital to wait for 30 seconds, probably underwater, for the blades to stop rotating before abandoning ship. An emergency air bottle and mask, being developed for this very purpose, were not yet available. But that was still the correct drill.

Standing off the carrier soon afterwards, low over a lumpy sea, our blades almost intermeshing with those of the guardship helicopter, we waited for a break in the landing sequence. And I recalled a remark by Peter Masefield:

"You may take it from me that the safest and most reliable helicopter is one with twelve engines and one rotor blade – and even that compares pretty unfavourably with fixed wing!"

And here we were, hanging just above the waves, on one engine, with three main rotor blades, two more at the tail for good measure, and the enhanced possibility of a mid air collision. And there was no emergency air supply. When I gave Lettice a quick resume she was not amused!

As a spectacle of mind blasting noise and sheer brute force the flight deck of a carrier is in a class of its own. From a corner of the bridge I watched in fascination. Captivated by the process of launching tons of Scimitar or Sea Vixen into immediate flight. Seeing the sudden plume of steam – almost feeling the violent acceleration. It needed conscious effort to observe the deck crews and unravel the pattern of activity which might hold the key to the deployment of our liquid oxygen support equipment.

COMBAT AND COMPETITION

The aircraft came back one at a time. Arrowhead shapes, trailing smoke, materialising out of the haze, to hang kite like, on the approach.

Time stood still as the batsman played them in, until each one came crowding in over the round down, impossibly large and fast. Just six arrester wires from disaster. But it was enough. Batsman and pilots had played this game many times before. Flight trials or not, they already had these heavy swept wing fighters taped. Tyres smoked and oleos squashed brutally as they hit the deck and lurched to a halt. Not a single overshoot. It was an impeccable performance.

As for the matter of servicing and recharging lox converters on board ship, which had been the object of the exercise, the indications were that it would be easier than we had expected.

At the time of that visit to Ark Royal, BOAE had some way to go technically, and in terms of product acceptability. But the indications were not unfavourable. There was the prospect of a worthwhile, if somewhat slender, peripheral business for the parent company, developing over the coming years. And the mixed powerplant SR 177 interceptor fighter might well bring additional orders for specialised HTP storage and refuelling equipment in Britain and Germany.

Then in April 1957 the Minister of Defence, Duncan Sandys, who wanted to be rid of all manned military aircraft in favour of missiles, issued his infamous White Paper and almost destroyed the industry overnight. There were some who referred to him unkindly as 'Drunken Sandys' as it became apparent that every fighter project, except the Lightning, was about to get the chop, and the Avro 730 Supersonic Bomber was to be cancelled as well.

When Dickie Martin broke the sound barrier, and his Javelin's shock wave just happened to hit the Houses of Parliament, he made a point for Glosters and said something for the rest of us too. For political ignorance and expediency has done incalculable harm to the British aircraft industry over the years.

But on that fateful April day Sandys was in the driving seat and Sir Victor Goddard's 'Elongated Balls' were in the ascendency. Shortly afterwards Jack Pateman rang to suggest that I return to Elliotts and indicated that the position of manager Guided Weapons Division was on offer. It seemed the obvious thing to do.

However GW was not my scene and before long I was back in the fold – with the task of opening up export markets for Elliott Flight Automation.

CHAPTER TWELVE   ELONGATED BALLS

For Jack and Bill Alexander had long since won their battle with Monk and Broadbent. The aviation activities at Borehamwood, Lewisham and Rochester had been brought together, under their joint management, and had spawned a whole family of divisions. There were already almost a dozen of them, concentrated in a couple of modern multi-storey blocks on the edge of Rochester Airport. Together they had become a highly profitable business and a growing power in the world of aviation.

So far this had been in the United Kingdom only and Jack and Henry Pasley-Tyler, the main board director to whom the Flight Automation divisions reported, were determined to become international.

P-T was a character. Commander RN (Retired) he almost literally strode the quarter deck, addressing all and sundry as "M'boy!" He could talk you off the face of the earth, switching his attention quite ruthlessly when he had something better to pursue, and was a martyr to catarrh and hay fever. Due to his affliction he had a disconcerting habit of stopping in full flood, usually about salesmanship being the origin of all wealth, a favourite topic, to dose himself liberally with the latest in decongestants.

P-T was another accelerator like Dr Ross, if in rather a different mould. Despite his equally eccentric behaviour, most of us respected him for his drive and single mindedness, and recognised his considerable value to us. I met him first, when being interviewed at Borehamwood for the Guided Weapons job, and in formal discussion found him intolerant and demanding. It was a view which I never revised. Yet his behaviour on many other occasions revealed a ready understanding and sympathy for his subordinates. P-T wasn't such a bad type behind the bull.

During my absence at British Oxygen Ron Howard had set up the Transport Aircraft Controls Division and successfully exploited the Bendix relationship to secure the VC10 flight control system. It was audacious buccaneering stuff in the face of fierce opposition from Smiths.

Ron and his team used the basic Bendix PB 20 autopilot computers, and some sensors, with evidence of a licensing deal and back up support, to demonstrate soundly based know-how in the civil field. From this beginning they evolved an integrated system with coupled approach, autoflare, and ultimately autoland, capability. The duplicate monitored channels and the integrated electro-hydraulic controls, were

COMBAT AND COMPETITION

what finally sold the system to Vickers and BOAC. And these owed nothing to Bendix.

The relationship between Elliotts and Bendix, increasingly uneasy as Elliotts had grown more powerful, reached a new low with the advent of the VC10 system. As seen by Bendix – Elliotts had used their hardware, know-how and experience to clamber onto the civil ladder – and had then gone about it their own way to minimise the Bendix share of the project. The situation was not helped by the fact that Wally Monk was now running Bendix UK Ltd, where he had gone after losing his fight with Jack.

My first export assignment, which involved Ron as well, was most bizarre. The Soviet Embassy had made an approach to Elliotts on behalf of a small trade mission, which wished to talk ILS coupling[8] for civil airliners. There was an implied possibility of export sales, which seemed most unlikely, but we were curious about their intentions and security clearance was eventually obtained.

The meeting was held at Borehamwood well away from our military activities. The visitors listened, with ill concealed impatience, as we talked openly about the subject which had been cleared for discussion. As soon as there was an opportunity for questions, they ignored everything that had been said, and turned to something totally different. Radio altimeter cum barometric height locks. It was abundantly clear that they had come, well prepared, to learn as much as possible about the Buccaneer automatic flight control system.

Ron caught my eye and we became absolutely confused! Not only could we not understand their questions, but we suggested that they too had become confused by our description of ILS coupling. Therefore we had better run over it all again. Or perhaps they would like to re-phrase their questions? Which they did, from every possible angle, and we became even more confused! And confusion bred confusion. Until we broke up in complete and polite disorder – with profuse apologies for our lack of understanding. It was all good clean fun.

Soon afterwards Ron and I became the first Assistant General Managers of Elliott Flight Automation.

CHAPTER THIRTEEN

FRONTIERS OF WHAT?

Starting in Europe there was more than enough to do. But where to begin? Sweden seemed a good idea. Their new Viggen project was just at the right stage and, much to our surprise, the local Elliott Automation subsidiary was reasonably well plugged in to the Swedish Air Board. At Saab UK, Roly Moore, Managing Director, and Gerry Alford, his number two, both ex RAF types, helped with the initial contacts at Linkoping, and at Jonkoping which seemed to be more concerned with avionic systems and missiles.

But Sweden was not easy – as was brought home sharply during our very first presentation to the Air Board. At the opening session, giving a rundown on Elliotts, it was unnerving to be faced with an audience which showed no emotion. There was no feel, no feedback at all. It went on like that all day, even the questions were deadpan, but they were shrewd and carefully thought out. One thing at least was clear. They were out to pick our brains.

In the late afternoon we took a select few of them out for a drink. After a time they became animated and 'informal' – exchanging Christian names – and at long last we realised that we had actually made an impact.

There were high hopes for the Viggen. Elliott was a natural supplier with it's Lightning and Buccaneer experience. Yet in the end we had to be content with the automatic test equipment alone. Even so, after we had delivered the prototype, they leaned heavily on the terms of the contract, and the production order went to a Swedish company. Disappointing, but at least a start, a first step on the long export learning curve.

Harry Cook, a keen glider pilot, who had broken new ground with a minature high performance compass and more recently with an electronic variometer, was Manager of the Automatic Test Equipment Division. Harry carried the main responsibility for our first Swedish project. An outspoken and forceful individual, he was in some difficulty dealing with the pedantic Swedes. When it came to contract negotiations they ground exceedingly small. Once, in an exasperated aside, he muttered to me:

"The trouble with these characters is that they haven't had a decent war for ages. It's given them far too much time to think, and be introspective, and work out how to trip us up!"

Before Harry appeared on the scene Bill Alexander and I made a

COMBAT AND COMPETITION

trip to Jonkoping. After a lengthy afternoon meeting we invited the General Manager to join us for dinner at our hotel – and soon discovered that he was a gliding fanatic. When he learned that I had long been bitten with the same bug he began to talk about the marvellous unstable southerly, blowing straight up the country, which had been forecast for the following day. There was a 500km flight to be had, and he could easily take the day off, except that there was no retrieve.

As the evening progressed we toasted each other and drank to the future of gliding. Encouraged by plentiful supplies of aquavit, we hatched a plan. Our meeting with the Swedish Air Board was not until the day after tomorrow. Bill and I would be his retrieve crew, driving back overnight, and the first flight to Bromma the following morning would get us there in time. As a final touch, our pilot, having checked the weather again, would ring me at about five in the morning to confirm or cancel the arrangement.

Whether Bill deliberately encouraged the celebrating to continue, in order to sabotage the whole exercise, is a moot point. But the fact remains that by the time we parted company, the three of us were pretty plastered.

I slept badly, aware of a developing hangover, and dreading the telephone summons. When it came the weather forecast had changed. Our little jaunt was off. I could only heave a grateful sigh of relief and when I called Bill he laughed as much as his fragile state of health would allow.

En route to Stockholm, later that day, we dozed uncomfortably as the little Scandia wallowed around in the turbulence. We were certainly being carried along on a very unstable southerly but the low cloud base, and occasional shower, hardly suggested a 500km day. I often wonder how we would have got on if it had been a boomer.

In aircraft industry terms the rest of Europe boiled down to Germany, France, Italy, Holland and Belgium. Belgium, totally committed to the F104 programme, could be written off. At Gosselies Starfighters filled the assembly lines at SABCA – and those of Avions Fairey on the other side of the airfield. Except for one building where Arthur Talbott, who ran the Fairey subsidiary, showed me a line of fibreglass headstones. He smiled wryly in response to my question – it was shortly after the F104 had acquired a reputation as the 'widowmaker':

"People say we deliver one of these with each aircraft. It's not true

CHAPTER THIRTEEN FRONTIERS OF WHAT?

you know. Perhaps one for every six or ten!" He shrugged his shoulders with an almost Gallic expressiveness.

Fokker was the F104 story all over again, a project in which Elliott had no part, with the faint possibility – coming late in the day – of a few engine instruments on the Friendship.

Back in London, Derek Wood, journalist and writer extraordinary, was a mine of ideas and information. He knew the world of aviation like the back of his hand, and I owe him a great debt for his help then, and on many other occasions over the years. Anne and I had first met him at Aviation Forum, a regular gathering of like minded journalists, at the Kronfeld Club, in a basement behind Victoria Station.

Derek ran Interavia UK from premises little better than a garret alongside the old Daily Telegraph building in Fleet Street. To those in the know it was the hub of a unique information gathering network with Derek at the centre. There were other links – to the Interavia offices in Europe – and in particular to the head office in Geneva – where the Air Letter was published on every working day. The Air Letter was invaluable, an up to date and in depth source of information, for those seeking to keep in close contact with all aspects of aviation.

Derek put me in touch with Ken Powell, a retired RAF Wing Commander, who had set up an aviation agency in Bad Godesburg. Ken had done well. Rumour had it from engine starters and pyrotechnics supplied to the Federal Republic – the origins were obscure and he rarely spoke of the past. Amongst his other interests he represented Rolls Royce as their 'Correspondent'[1] in Germany.

He was paid a small retainer, barely enough to cover the cost of our visits, and it seemed to me that Elliotts were being unduly mean. But Jack was unmoved by my arguments and Ken was hardly Jack's kind of man – wild, volatile and fiercely independent – loyal as the day to those he respected, a bastard to those he did not. So his retainer remained unchanged and I suspect that he stayed with us for the love of the game. Ken was a good friend and an amusing guide and mentor in the re-emerging aviation and defence markets of post war Germany.

The fascination, and the enigma, of Germany was still with me almost fifteen years after the end of the war and I was happy to spend a lot of time there. But there was another, more compelling reason. The German aircraft industry, helped by the F104 programme, was taking it's first tentative steps back into business. On the next major project, assuming that the politicians did not foul it up again, Elliotts

COMBAT AND COMPETITION

must be high on the short list.

Italy, despite the efforts of Dr Alfredo Latour, the Rolls Royce Correspondent in Italy, ably supported by his glamorous Hungarian wife, turned out a dead loss first time round. Fiat, pushing their G91 light fighter for NATO, had no interest in any of our hardware. and Alitalia were too committed to Boeing for the Elliott-Bendix flight system on the VC10, and the new BAC One-eleven, to get a look in.

France was much harder than Sweden, reflecting the divide between Latin and Anglo-Saxon, which always seems at it's worst across the Channel. I was then, and remain to this day, a convinced European. Yet how about the hurdle of Franco-British relations? As Ron Howard once observed:

"Why on earth are the French, who live just across the water, the most foreign and difficult people with whom to do business?"

Ron spoke with feeling. In 1956, just after I left to join British Oxygen, Wally Monk had arranged for him to spend a short time at Dassault. Whilst there he fitted a modified Lightning yaw autostabiliser to the prototype Mirage, correcting what Col Rozanoff, the chief test pilot, described as a tendency to 'shake my backside'. Dassault subsequently abandoned the Elliott design as 'unsatisfactory' and the French 'developed' their own system.

After that my trips to Dassault were not exactly favoured by Jack Pateman. As they were invariably marked by overt requests to reveal all of our work on other projects, and an extreme reluctance to say anything about their own requirements, I soon abandoned the idea. So we saw little enough of the French aviation industry in those early years - and our activities in France usually peaked in the run up to, and during, the bi-annual 'Salon d'Aeronautique' at Le Bourget. This - together with Farnborough and possibly Hanover - had become a key element in creating an image abroad.

Farnborough, halcyon September days, near the end of the soaring season, was a time for meeting and entertaining aviation friends. The afternoons a treasure trove of well loved, well remembered, scenes. Black sheds and Cody's tree - the glint of sun on perspex low down over Laffan's plain - an aircraft shape erupting out of the distance in utter silence - engulfing us all in sudden cataclysmic sound.

All flying life was there. Ted Tennant's virtuoso display with the tiny silver Gnat. Bill Bedford slowly rotating a Kestrel on it's four thunderous columns of hot air. The incomparable 'Bea' winding his pot bellied Lightning into a maximum 'G' turn, twin afterburners glowing

CHAPTER THIRTEEN FRONTIERS OF WHAT?

like the fires of hell. A single Vulcan sweeping upwards into a loop and rolling smoothly off the top – a Victor soon afterwards doing the same – to the sounds of applause. For a moment you sensed the atmosphere of a Roman holiday and then it was gone. Just the reaction of a knowledgeable audience, which had lunched well, proud of it's products and the way in which they were being shown off.

With tea in the chalets came the Black Arrows. Twelve Hunters with a precision matching that of the Queen's Colour Squadron – the best drill unit of them all – filling the sky with their festoons of coloured smoke.

Sometimes there was chance to go visiting. Particularly welcome if there was lunch date for Anne and myself with Sandy and Diana Powell at Lockheeds on the first public day. An event which came to an unhappy end when they made my old friend redundant. There were the chance encounters too, most frequently at Shell, where the chalet bulged with people and the noise was thunderous. It was there that I last talked to Frank McKenna, long retired, looking in on the industry which had been his life.

Another time it was Paddy Bartropp and Ben Gunn. A splendid, deadly combination! Paddy had left the RAF and started a new upmarket hire car service. Chauffeur driven Rolls Royces. A great success in the long run, but hard going at first, and he was looking for help. Sadly the whole thing was way out of Elliott's class. If any of my overseas visitors had arrived at Rochester in a hired Rolls, with Paddy at the helm, Jack would have had a fit and I would have been looking for help. In the early '80s, at an ETPS reunion, after his chauffeurs had all become franchised and self employed with their own cars, Paddy attempted to interest me in his Jet Ranger helicopter, on the same basis, for £100,000. He never stops trying!

On Friday night the company always threw a cocktail party at some interesting spot, like Paul Getty's Sutton Place. Getting there was the problem. You set off, threading your way through the air display traffic, with some vital customer of the moment. An ideal captive audience, but you had to drive and navigate, and keep an ear open for the wives in the back of the car. Throw in the day's refreshments and you were an accident waiting to happen.

Next day, before the great British public descended on Farnborough in it's thousands, the chalet was cool and peaceful. A time when Fred Haskett and I could relax, reviewing the day ahead, whilst Anne organised brandy and iced milk all round. Just the thing

COMBAT AND COMPETITION

for hangovers and uneasy stomachs after the night before. Fred, ex Petty Officer, blessed with the largest conk imaginable and a heart of gold. Until recently manager of the Engine Instruments Division he had become a marketeer and a great ally. Tough and resilient he seemed likely to outlive most of his contemporaries. Yet within a matter of years he was dead. Killed by a massive heart attack. His wife was a character too. At one time she owned the Claverdel Restaurant in Guildford. When he died they were living near Maidstone and she took over his seat on the Borough Council and eventually served as Mayor.

Business and gliding overlapped time and again during Farnborough week. Especially so when friends in the industry, with a shared interest to strengthen the relationship, dropped in for a chat. Better still when Horace Buckingham asked me to fly his Olympia IV in the show.

On balance gliding seemed to be good for one's career, at the very least it did no harm, and it would be increasingly useful as Elliotts moved into Europe.

At the Paris Salon, on the first occasion, we limited our presence to a tour of inspection and a small drinks party. Bruce Adkins, who had moved on from the publications department at Borehamwood to Euratom, suggested an unusual venue in the form of a private museum.

In the end, despite his responsibilities for the promotion of nuclear energy, he became totally involved and agreed to mastermind the whole exercise. It was a generous gesture which we were delighted to accept.

Bruce had changed little since our days together at Borehamwood, except that he had become a committed European. You could tell that he would never abandon the best of the traditions in which he had been brought up. For he remained intensely proud of his country. It was an example which many would do well to follow. Thanks to his organising ability, his local knowledge, and his genuine affection for France, our 'Musee Cocktail,' was an unqualified success.

Two years later we went the whole hog. A good sized stand at Le Bourget, featuring civil and military flight control systems, inertial navigation and engine instruments. Regrettably there was a glaring error in the VC10 brochure which described 'Autoflare'[2] as 'Autofireworks'! My advice, to have the translation checked in France, had been ignored.

CHAPTER THIRTEEN   FRONTIERS OF WHAT?

As the world of the Salon was laughing at our discomfiture on the first afternoon of the show, and I was commiserating with Ron Howard, a familiar voice addressed me in ringing tones. Johnny Button, my Squadron Commander on the Normandy Beachead back in 1944. When I had last seen him, as Air Attache at the Hague, he had been disconcertingly abrupt. Today he was at his most relaxed. He told me that he had recently left the Service and joined de Havillands on the 125. We chatted at length and promised to meet again. But it never happened. The news of his death came as a profound shock and I was glad that our last encounter had been on such warm and friendly terms.

Our second 'Cocktail' was organised by the Hon. John Geddes, the Group PR Manager, in a rather ostentatious hotel. That it was less attractive and certainly more expensive than the 'Musee Cocktail' of two years ago was no reflection on John. Pasley-Tyler, exercising his right as Chairman of Elliott Flight Automation, had demeanded a high profile occasion and he was simply carrying out instructions.

I never discovered how much, or how little, John really knew about the mechanics of his trade, but he was a nice man. Forceful when the need arose - skilled in holding the line between Bagrit and Ross on the one hand and a bunch of ambitious executives on the other - he was a companionable sort who enjoyed the good things of life. Apart from our 'Cocktail', the detailed preparation of which he delegated with great skill, his visit developed into a gastronomic tour.

Paris that year seemed to be be overlaid with images of sun filled patios - John and Anne arguing PR over ice cold Kir and radis beurre - and the thought of more splendid meals to come.

If the aftermath of Farnborough created a sense of euphoria, that of Paris was one of unease - the cost of it all and the impenetrable nature of the French aircraft industry - only a convinced optimist could feel otherwise.

Germany was another story. It showed every sign of becoming more important than France. And in Germany exhibitions were vitally important. But my first visit to Hanover revealed a second rate air show, quite contrary to what we might have expected, a pallid adjunct to the Hanover Messe which is the largest and most prestigious exhibition in Western Europe.

After seeking Ken Powell's advice it was decided to treat it low key. On the first occasion, we took one of the smallest stand units available with Fred Haskett, Fred Pacey, Sales Manager of the Flight

COMBAT AND COMPETITION

Instruments Division, and myself in attendance.

By the time Hanover came round again we had reinforcements. Two new recruits had arrived direct from test flying to look after civil flight control systems. 'Doc' Stuart, an ex naval type from Boscombe Down, had been appointed Sales Manager and his number two, from the Blind Landing Experimental Unit at Thurleigh, was Pinkie Stark. Pinkie and I had only seen each other occasionally since our first meeting at Wunsdorf, just after the war, and now we were heading back there together in my car. Lufthansa was evaluating the BAC One-eleven and the Boeing 737 as alternative Viscount replacements. So Doc and Pinkie were there to promote the One-eleven flight system.

It had all the ingredients of a jolly occasion. Fred Haskett was always good value. Doc, balding and soft spoken, could be mad as a hatter when he was in the mood. Fred Pacey, who had worked with the British Forces Network in Germany after the war, was equally and more consistently crazy. Grey haired and plump, with a wacko moustache, Fred's party piece was to stand on his head and drink a pint of beer. Many a time I watched him, going slowly purple in the face, and wondered whether he would collapse before the glass was empty. But he never did.

So much for the makings. It was Pinkie who, quite fortuitously, brought them all together. He and Doc had been allocated pension accomodation like the rest of us - hotel rooms being almost unobtainable - but they were unlucky. The beds were dirty and the breakfast terrible. Pinkie went prospecting and discovered a splendid alternative on the shores of Steinhuder Meer across the water from Wundsdorf.

Each evening in Doc's white Porsche they guided us over a confused network of woodland tracks to a wooden shack overlooking the lake. Inside, behind the bar stood a black bearded giant of a man, who in times past must surely have been a somebody in the Kriegsmarine[3], surrounded by smoked sausages and sides of bacon and dispensing all manner of alcoholic refreshment with great good humour.

It was a haven of guttering candlelight and human companionship, unspoilt and almost undiscovered, a world away from the noise and crowds of Hanover. A wonderful place to unwind. And when you were hungry his kitchen would produce a massive spread of eels, meat, gerkins, rye bread and butter.

Much later, when the evening reached a certain stage, mine host

CHAPTER THIRTEEN   FRONTIERS OF WHAT?

would remove his prized and ancient blue serge cap from its place above the bar. Then he would make an announcement in ghastly anglicised German:

"Meine Herren! ist wild und sturmich nacht, und ven ist so I put on mein cap jawohl!" whereupon he rescued his piano accordion from amongst the empty bottles and broke into the first of many drinking songs.

I have to say that his cap went on without fail every night that week, and our repertoire of German songs grew substantially, in musical terms, even if the words were mostly beyond us. There was no one to hear in the depths of the forest, with water on three sides, and I often wondered whether we were led into singing some of the forbidden ballads from the Hitler years.

Centrepiece on our stand at Hanover was an electrical signalling system which had been displayed at Farnborough the previous September. The powered controls had been provided by Lockheeds, with the help of Sandy Powell, and the rest, the really innovative part, was an amalgam of Jack Pateman, Eric et al.

A mechanical link connected the pilot's input to the hydraulic jack. In the electrical mode this could be 'declutched' by introducing a deliberate amount of backlash at the base of the stick. As the mechanical system followed up each electrical demand the stick remained centralised within this dead zone and mechanical reversion occurred with the minimum of disturbance.

Although this particular system never flew, its fail safe principles were attractive at a time when the reliability of electrical signalling was in some doubt. Moreover it demonstrated a forward looking approach, and I like to think that it was one of the first tentative steps that contributed to Elliotts' technical leadership in what came to be known as fly-by-wire.

On one of the days we were visited by the head of the German Air Force. As I conducted General Johannes Steinhoff round the stand, and showed him the electrical signalling system, it was impossible not to notice his badly burned face. The result of a dreadful crash on take off, flying Me 262s with Galland's 'Squadron of Aces', in the last days of the war. An interesting man to meet, even on such short acquaintance, and an ex enemy you could not but admire.

That same afternoon we watched the VJ 101 research prototype as it flew past conventionally, before retiring to a safe distance and rotating its massive wing tip mounted engine nacelles into the vertical

COMBAT AND COMPETITION

position. It looked horrific hanging there, for all the world like the twin spires of Cologne Cathedral suspended in the sky.

Some time later we heard that the VJ 101 had rolled uncontrollably during transition, and its American test pilot had managed to survive by the skin of his ejection seat. The news came as no surprise. VJ 101 was the story of the German Aircraft Industry. Fifteen or more years of lost technology, trying to catch up too fast, with inadequate resources.

At a subsequent air show the test pilot, George Bright, visited the Elliott stand and Ron Howard heard his story at first hand. The rate gyros had been reverse connected and when the aircraft started to roll he counted 'black... white... black' and 'GO!' at the beginning of white – in order to eject when his seat was pointing at the sky!

Pondering our future in Germany I took myself off to Bad Godesberg and Ken Powell. We lunched together in the British Club, overlooking the Rhine, and shared the inevitable Mosel to which he was much attached. A pleasant occasion until he noticed Adolf Galland in the centre of an admiring group across the room. Ken worked himself up into quite a state and said loudly that Galland acquired agencies like scalps, for prestige rather than practical reasons, and lived on his past reputation. I took it all with a pinch of salt, because Ken could be very caustic, and everyone knew they were in direct competition.

Finally we got round to the subject of my visit. The main priority would still continue to be Entwicklungsring Sud despite their disaster with the VJ 101 prototype. Its military derivative was said to be short listed for NBMR 3 – a joint NATO[4] requirement. Second would be the Dornier VTOL[5] transport project at Friedrichshafen, on Lake Constance, near the old Zeppelin works.

In addition I would reactivate my relationship with Karl Doetsch – one of the German boffins who had been 'persuaded' to come and work at the RAE after the war. Picked up near Oberammergau, as hostilities ceased, his 'captors' had suggested to him that he might otherwise find himself in Russia. So Karl, as they say, 'chose freedom'. Now back home again he was the new Professor of Aeronautics at Braunschweig University.

Karl had been a 'Flugbaumeister'. One of that rare breed, a highly qualified engineer who was also a skilled test pilot. He had written the first set of German pilot's notes and had developed what was probably the earliest yaw damper to go into production. It was fitted to the

CHAPTER THIRTEEN   FRONTIERS OF WHAT?

Henschel Hs 129 ground attack aircraft and he had tested the concept himself on a FW 190 and an Me 262. The flying side of his career had come to an abrupt end on a flight from Berlin, when his Me 110 suffered a double engine failure and deposited him in the municipal rubbish dump at Augsburg. It must have been quite a prang, because only the tail was left sticking out, and it put him into hospital for months.

During his time at RAE I had come to respect him – in the difficult role which he had to play, almost, but not quite an internee – and to enjoy his company. Of necessity much of his contribution to the Lightning had to be indirect, and unattributable, but I believe it to have been considerable.

Professors are highly regarded in Germany and Karl was no exception. Moreover he had continued to work on advanced flight control systems, almost without a break since 1945. As a result he was in great demand as a consultant, and a potentially valuable point of contact for Elliotts.

When the Viscount replacement exercise was at its height Ron Howard and I visited him to talk BAC One-eleven certification. He and his family received us with typical German hospitality, took us on a tour of the Harz mountains, and looked longingly towards Broken which lay behind the Iron Curtain.

In Karl's early flying days it had been customary, possibly obligatory, to perform aerobatics above Broken's eleven hundred metre peak. Now it was impossible and he made no effort to hide his resentment. He saw it as the brutal obliteration of a youthful and romantic memory. But I suspect it ran much deeper than that.

Our visit did little enough to help the cause of the BAC One-eleven with Lufthansa. They were already against it, for reasons which had nothing to do with the flight system, such as fuselage corrosion below the toilets on their Viscounts. So they bought Boeing and 20 years on seem likely to be faced with similar problems all over again – and BAC got it right on the One-eleven with plastic sealing behind the fuselage stringers!

Gliding was the most constructive aspect of that trip. Karl took us round the workshops of Akaflieg Braunschweig, where the students were building an ultra high performance fibreglass sailplane. He told us that a similar exercise was under way at Darmstadt – evidence of a German led revolution in design.

VJ 101, which I had discussed at length with Ken Powell in Bad

COMBAT AND COMPETITION

Godesberg, was part of the unfortunate saga of common specifications which SHAPE[6] at Fontainebleau was trying to create for general procurement in Europe. NBMR3, for a light strike VSTOL[7] fighter, against which VJ 101 had been tendered, underwent endless revisions and attracted more than a dozen designs from five nations. I spent weeks and months chasing the various contenders.

That search included a number of visits to Italy and several to Fiat, one in company with Ron Howard, where we talked at length with Professor Gabrielli. The results were very fruitful in the long run. Leading to a joint venture between Fiat, Rolls Royce and Elliotts – and the construction of a VTOL hover rig for the G95/4 which performed over 300 hours of tethered flight tests and proved the performance and failure survivability of the control system design.

The G95/4 was subsequently abandoned but much of the system development continued. The prototype quadruplex actuator, exhibited at a subsequent Hanover show, was further improved for a possible installation in the Dornier 31, and subsequently manufactured under licence by Fairey Hydraulics for the Tornado.

Our trip to Fiat had an amusing sequel. On the way home we were scheduled to talk Concorde at Toulouse. This involved flying from Turin to Paris, then Paris–Toulouse, and we were wait-listed on the second leg. A little research revealed that we could catch a train from Turin to Milan, take in the opera at La Scala, and continue by rail overnight via Nice in time for our meeting at Toulouse the next day.

It was too good an opportunity to miss. We cancelled our airline reservations and rushed to the station. At Milan there was even time to visit the cathedral and buy a couple of silk ties before the performance. And 'Carmen' was a very pleasant reward for our efforts.

When we got home Pasley-Tyler refused to sign Ron's expenses, until he explained why it was necessary to go from Turin to Toulouse via Milan. After hearing the truth he took Ron and his wife to Covent Garden!

The NBMR3 project office at SHAPE was another link in the chain, and I chased them too. In the end, with the help of Pete Brothers, then a Group Captain, who was the British representative, I managed to get him and his three colleagues to visit us at Rochester.

We entertained them in suitable style and at some expense, but most properly, in London beforehand. Yet Jack Pateman insisted ever afterwards in referring to it as the 'Night of the four Colonels' – as if there was some dark secret!

CHAPTER THIRTEEN   FRONTIERS OF WHAT?

Perhaps there was in a way. For the separate national identities were a reminder to tread delicately. Yet this was a golden opportunity to explore the background to the various competing projects and their standing at SHAPE. To strengthen the case for Elliotts and calm any fears of excessive British participation with well honed arguments about our joint venture experience. It turned out to be an enjoyable and well matched little gathering and everyone knew the rules:

"Another brandy gentlemen?" (might encourage them to say a little more!)

"Thank you. Yes!" (but you're wasting your time!)

In the end NBMR3 came to nothing. The Hawker 1154 won the day but the French refused to accept the decision. NATO had no central funds to finance the project and any post mortem would have had embarrassing repercussions.

NBMR3, through my international role with Elliotts, had brought me back in touch with Hawkers on the 1154 itself. There was a British Joint Service Requirement. But Hawkers were trapped between the Ministry, which was trying to impose a single design, and the RAF and Navy, whose requirements differed to such an extent that they could not be met in this way. No information whatsoever could be obtained on the avionics fit for the simple reason that the Ministry of Aviation did not know. The 1154 programme was in a complete mess.

However our various contacts with Hawkers on the 1154 paid off in the end. When a three axis autostabiliser was eventually specified for the Harrier the contract came to Elliotts. The result was a very simple system which weighed only $2\frac{1}{2}$ lbs per axis. Even Sir Sydney Camm might have approved.

We devoted a considerable amount of time to the Dornier Do 31, and its Anglo-German derivative to NBMR4, before these two were scrapped.

One member of the family, Silvius Dornier, joined us from time to time on our visits to Friedrichshafen. A pleasant educated man, rather shy, and knowledgeable about the grape. But his interests were mainly legal and financial, so our main contact was Dr Weiland – an enthusiastic mountaineer – and subsequently Dr Schweitzer.

On one visit the latter showed us his simple rig to demonstrate the fundamental difficulties of VTOL flight. A flat metal plate, hinged at the centre in two axes (pitch and roll), operated by a joystick controller. He allowed you to compose yourself, then he placed a large ball bearing in the centre, and you had to keep it there. Simple really.

COMBAT AND COMPETITION

And a brutally effective demonstration of manual control in the hover. Statically and dynamically unstable. Displacement input – acceleration output.

That humiliating unit was there for the benefit of visitors from the Defence Ministry in Bonn and those old or bold Luftwaffe officers who despised the very idea of stability augmentation or automatic controls. For it was still early days in the story of VTOL.

In the summer of 1964 Pinkie Stark, Derek Jackson and I were scheduled for a sales tour in the States – to accompany Dusty Rhodes of BAC, promoting the One-eleven. The combination was good news. Which was rather more than could be said for the programme arranged by the Weybridge Division of the British Aircraft Corporation. For we had twenty plus airlines to visit in a fortnight and several hours flying each day.

The start – we arrived at New York in the early afternoon – was predictable for the way in which it demonstrated how paranoid Bendix had become about Elliotts, and how worried they were about our presence in the States.

They spent so long on the first night explaining why they must support us on every occasion that we ended up rather short of sleep. It seemed as if they might have done it deliberately!

Our presentation on the following day to American Airlines, the biggest and potentially the most important customer on the whole trip, was not helped by their presence. They had insisted on being there, ostensibly to watch points for us first time round, and refused to take no for an answer.

Their tactics were anything but subtle. It was obvious that they had come along to hear what we we had to say, to ensure that any One-eleven flight systems ordered would be supplied by Bendix, and to prevent us from making any sort of progress in their home market.

Afterwards they had the effrontery to suggest that their contribution had been helpful and that they should accompanying us to all the major operators. But Dusty objected strongly. This was a BAC tour, to sell One-elevens, and his management would not agree. In the end we reached a compromise. George Frankfurt from Bendix UK would accompany us, on and off, throughout the trip. Not ideal – but on his own he was always helpful and kept a low profile.

Down the East Coast to Miami for the weekend, where I rang Anne in hospital, to find that our second daughter, had just arrived. The bar was still open and Pinkie called for champagne.

CHAPTER THIRTEEN   FRONTIERS OF WHAT?

It was dark as we moved outside to toast them both. But the clouds offshore were already touched with the gold of another dawn and a cool refreshing shower splashed down around us as we raised our glasses. We were short of sleep again, for the second time in as many days, but it seemed like a good omen for young Ros.

Throughout the following week we pressed on to the west. Dallas/Love Field then Los Angeles and San Francisco. There was a certain amount of difficulty in putting over the Elliott record. Security imposed its own constraints, and most of our audiences, even those with a military background, had never even heard of Lightning, Blue Steel or Buccaneer. But we persevered.

When it came to the VC 10 and BAC One-eleven the emphasis had to be just right – stressing the value of the relationship with Bendix and making it absolutely clear that all the monitoring and failure survival was Elliott. Pinkie did a great job on the two civil systems, talking with full BLEU[8] authority, reinforced by his unique low minima test flying experience and Derek provided the engineering and technical back up.

As Ron Howard put it in a lecture some years later:

To BLEU goes overwhelmingly the credit for bringing to fruition the basic system for making accurate landings on runways, the concept which is now in everday use in both military and civil transport aircraft..... Automatic 'flareout' was first demonstrated in 1947..... In October 1958 BLEU announced that they had completed over 2000 fully automatic landings on several different aircraft.

And Pinkie had been in the thick of it – flying and monitoring the behaviour of automatic systems on a variety of piston and jet engined aircraft in all sorts of weather.

Once at Thurleigh, in a Vulcan, with the Superintendent in the right hand seat, a bank of fog started to drift across the airfield as they joined the circuit. They touched down but could not see the runway and there was no ground guidance. So Pinkie overshot called for a quick GCA[9] from the opposite direction and made a fully automatic landing – downwind – rolling out into the clear where he could steer manually. The fog kept moving, and caught up with them before they could taxi in, reducing the visibility to about ten yards. Jack Shayler was highly twitched by the whole performance, and Pinkie told him that he should have more faith in the trials for which he was responsible.

In the last great London smog, four days in December 1962, all

COMBAT AND COMPETITION

operations at Heathrow were suspended. Pinkie took one of the BLEU Varsities there and carried a series of fully automatic landings, day and night, in Cat3C[10] conditions. This time there was some roll out guidance, a crude head up display, using a zero reader and an epidiascope. When the Varsity returned to Thurleigh it was so blackened and filthy that the whole outer skin had to be treated with a special cleaner. There was much still to be done. But the scene was set. Scheduled blind landing was on the way.

We visited a fog tunnel at the University of California. You sat in an aircraft cabin, suspended on cables like a ski lift, with a suitably scaled lighting system laid out ahead. Artificial fog was pumped through a series of nozzles along the sidewalls of the tunnel, until an infra-red visibility measuring system showed the correct figure. Then the aerial chariot was released, and you tobogganed down the glide slope.

Great fun in a way, and possibly useful in developing better lighting systems for low minima operation. But for us, trying it out in passing, the whole thing seemed highly subjective and open loop. Pilot participation was needed to make it effective but the cost would have been astronomical.

On the way home Pinkie and I found time to look up an old Canadian Typhoon chum, Johnny Brown, a citizen of Toronto.

We got talking about old times and the unsolved mystery of Johnny Baldwin. Commanding 'A' Squadron at Boscombe Down after the war he had arranged for Pinkie to join him. Later, after he was attached to a USAF fighter wing and reported missing in Korea, Pinkie tried to find out what had happened. Only to be faced with a wall of silence.

Eventually he ran an ex Korea POW to earth, a Canadian, who could have been in the same camp as Baldwin – had the latter ever been captured. On detachment to Edmonton, for Arctic trials, Pinkie was given permission to see this man.

"They told me that I could only put one question – and that I must not query his answer. So I asked him if he had ever come across J.R. Baldwin of the RAF while he was a prisoner. He replied, 'No, I did not!' So that was that – and from then on I always assumed that he had been killed."

Pinkie wanted to know more and continued his own investigations. In the end it seemed that Baldwin was flying number four in a section of Sabres. They were letting down in cloud over high ground, and he called a warning to the formation leader:

CHAPTER THIRTEEN FRONTIERS OF WHAT?

"Safety height!"

They all pulled up, and the others returned to base, but Johnny Baldwin was never seen again.

We flew back to a country which was about to put a Labour Government into power, with disastrous consequences for the RAF and the aircraft industry. By the turn of the year the Hawker 1154 and 681 VSTOL freighter had gone. The latter to be replaced by the American C130 Hercules. The RAF and Royal Navy were to have Phantoms. Only the Harrier and TSR2 remained. And the TSR2 – well on the way to production – would be cancelled too in a matter of weeks.

And this was the Government which, in its own words, would work in partnership with industry, and help to generate the white heat of technological change. At first sight, perhaps, that was why Harold Wilson and his merry axemen – unable to see the wood for the trees – continued with Concorde, that most profligate of all white elephants. But the truth is that the Labour Government did try to axe it. The French went to the International Court at the Hague, armed with the treaty, and proved that to do so was illegal. Concorde was saved.

The tragedy was much worse than it seemed at the time. Hidden behind all the visible politics a violent battle had raged within the Ministry before the project got under way. Headquarters wanted the available resources to be concentrated on the development of a big subsonic twin. RAE, mesmerised by the 'frontiers of technology' stuff, wanted Concorde. And it was the RAE that won.

Back in 1961, at the Cranfield Society Annual Symposium, Tony Lucking presented a paper on the Supersonic Transport. Consultant from my Hunting days, and a founder member of the Air Transport Users Association – Tony painted an unmistakable picture of the fallacies of Concorde. Based on the resources needed on earlier projects he showed that an SST would drain the industry of all its civil aircraft design and engineering capacity.

So we lost an all British Airbus, which could have been around years earlier and – apart from the BAe 146 and some major subcontract work for Airbus Industrie, for which the Government can take no credit at all – virtually abdicated from the civil scene.

Yet, in spite of all the evidence, I remain ambivalent about Concorde. To the market orientated General Manager it remains a disaster. But the pilot romantic in me is deeply moved by its elegance and the level of aeronautical achievement which it represents. And,

COMBAT AND COMPETITION

above all, there is pride in our own contribution.

For Elliotts were awarded the prime contract for the autocontrol systems including fly-by-wire, autostabiliser, autopilot and autothrottle, 50/50 in partnership with SFENA[11].

The political manoeuvring which went on beforehand would fill a book. Elliotts, believing that their design leadership had the support of the British Aircraft Corporation and both Governments – and that Sud Aviation alone remained to be convinced – started work on a joint proposal with Bendix and persuaded the Ministry that 25% of the development funding should be allocated to their partner.

But Bendix wanted much more – and the design leadership as well. So they concentrated on the French, and came up with a tripartite deal which included SFENA. Whilst Sud Aviation suddenly started to argue the case for Bendix even more strongly, on the dubious evidence that they were the preferred contractor for the American supersonic transport!

Elliotts moved into top gear. Meetings, official and unofficial, proliferated and we found ourselves rushing between Bristol, London, Paris and Toulouse as if there was no tomorrow. Doc Stuart was given a watching brief, ostensibly liaison with Sud Aviation on all the systems under discussion – in reality to keep an eye on Bendix – and spent many months in Toulouse protecting the company's interests.

It would be pleasant, on this occasion at least, to record that Government had supported British industry in an effective manner. Alas this was not even remotely the case. Unlike the French and Americans, who use their civil servants and diplomatic staff quite ruthlessly, and are frequently prepared to support one company as their chosen instrument, British policy allows no favouritism.

In the horse trading for Concorde this was naive in the extreme. It is a wonder that Elliotts were not squeezed out by the combination of SFENA and Bendix. (Concorde sales in the United States were yet another carrot behind the idea of American participation).

One British diplomat was different from all the rest, Tony Holden, the Civil Air Attache in Paris. Tony deplored the way in which we were being continually outmanoeuvred by the French, and particularly the situation on Concorde. Moreover he was doing something about it.

Meeting him, shortly after his appointment, I had seen how he operated during the Paris Salon and, attending one of his official cocktail parties, had been much impressed. Given sight of an opportunity for British Industry this man would put all his efforts

CHAPTER THIRTEEN FRONTIERS OF WHAT?

behind it. He was even trying to point our inertial guidance people in the direction of various French missiles, although they were right outside his brief.

Thanks to Tony I was able to organise a meeting for Pasley-Tyler and Jack Pateman with a certain General of Aviation, who was reputed to be very influential on Concorde. Flying back afterwards, I kept thinking about the letter which had arrived in the previous day's post. It offered me an appointment as Sales Director in a company which was likely to move away from the aircraft industry – although they had yet to find this out.

I had applied for the position months before, in the early days of the Wilson Government, and now this had come right out of the blue. Elliotts and aviation had been part of my life for a long time. The idea of leaving either was almost unthinkable. Yet there were other considerations.

A few days later I found myself in Jack's office, listening to P–T. I can still hear his words:

"I'm sorry David. We can't all be Managing Directors."

His reaction was so far from the reality of my decision. But there seemed no point in explaining my feelings to him. Had I done so it would have been to savage the politicians for the damage which they were doing to the aircraft industry. For the last crop of cancellations had finally convinced me that I could make a more valuable contribution elsewhere.

Bungy Launch - Falcon I at Long Mynd.

Preparing to Bungy - Espin Hardwick in his Petrel. At left directing bungy crew. John Hickling. Extreme right, Theo Testar.

CHAPTER FOURTEEN

OLD WAR HORSES

Gliding was in a state of change too. A major development in sailplane design and construction was under way in Germany. Its origins lay within the Akafliegs, or Academic Flying Groups, at the Technical Universities. Research prototypes were being built and more than one German glider manufacturer was already involved.

At home, the requirements of Air Traffic Control – as perceived by the Ministry of Aviation – were beginning to have a serious effect on our freedom of operation And, as if this were not enough, the British Gliding Association was involved in a major reappraisal of its function and structure.

The latter had arisen for a variety reasons. The number of gliding clubs was expanding rapidly and the BGA Council was in danger of becoming over large and unwieldy. Philip Wills, John Furlong, Basil Meads and Ann Welch, who were the real power base had been there for a long time. Ann had stood down as Vice Chairman immediately after the 1965 World Championships and for Philip the time was approaching when he too would wish to hand over the reins. Before that, with his usual far sightedness, he had set in motion the first steps towards reorganisation. A study group, headed by David Carrow the new Vice Chairman – which in Philip's own words:

".....is representative of the post war generation and..... as wide a geographical basis as is practicable....."

These were the realities. But the setting, the swinging sixties, was fast developing into a decade of changing values, in which the virtues of free expression and open government would be encouraged as never before. For the autocrat it was hardly a happy time – and the inner caucus of the BGA had been an autocracy for many years.

It is perhaps worth recounting a personal experience which reflects the problems of that era. The details are immaterial and, as an interested party, it would be inappropriate to mention them.

Sufficient to say that the World Championships Master Committee reported one final seeded order to Council for the 1960 British Team in the autumn of 1959 – and a different one early the following year. No explanation was offered and nobody round the Council table questioned the changes. At least not in public. I happen to remember it vividly, because I was present on both occasions, and the second one cost me my place in the team!

At the time it was frightful slap in the face – and Horace

COMBAT AND COMPETITION

Buckingham, when he heard about it, was most upset.

"I'm so sorry for you David. Its all my fault. I should never have allowed you to associated yourself so closely with Elliotts of Newbury."

Afterwards Horace always swore that Philip Wills was behind it all. That setting up the Shaw Slingsby Trust had put him under great pressure to keep Slingsbys profitable and in business. Which in turn made it essential to keep the company's products in the limelight, flying for Britain, and the original make up of the team could have put that plan at risk.

Of course Horace was being quite unfair. Hardly surprising, he and Philip never got on, and it would have been difficult for him to grasp, had he even wished to do so, that the selection process had become much more complex in recent years. In the days of Camphill, give or take a few problems with team entries, it had been reasonable to select a team straight off the top individual placings at the end of a Nationals.

Now there were more contests, some of them overseas, and many record breaking flights to take into account. To make matters worse the World Championships, with Open and Standard classes, were not as yet reflected in the British competition structure.

But, whatever the complexity and the processes involved, the old adage still applies. To be fair and to be seen to be fair. Selection followed by de-selection should never happen to any pilot. Provided that the person concerned remains sane, fit, available and within the law!

Horace's comment on the Shaw Slingsby Trust putting Philip under pressure was nearer the mark. When Major Shaw the owner of Slingsby Sailplanes died in 1959 the trust was created to acquire the share capital and prevent the company from falling into the wrong hands. The trust itself was to be registered as a charity, and the profits of Slingsby would be ploughed back into the gliding movement, like the funds of the Kemsley Flying Trust.

Things began to go wrong almost from the start. Within a year Viscount Kemsley was dead and the KFT was being wound up. So Shaw Slingsby was on its own, the sole and vitally needed source of loans to help the clubs in future, and Slingby's profits were negligible. Worse was to come. The Inland Revenue took exception to its status as a charity and eventually an obituary appeared in *Sailplane and Gliding*, which included the words:

.....the Revenue has now concluded that it cannot continue, on highly

Charles Wingfield in a Slingsby T21.

With 'Fluff' Slingsby, Lorne and Ann Welch - National Championships, 1957.

After the first flight of the Olympia 419 with Horace Buckingham and Jim Cramp.

With Dereck Piggot after breaking the UK distance record, April 1958.

Harry Midwood flying the EON Olympia 403 at Twinwood Farm, 1957.

End of the Line? - ASW 20.

Formation flying with Nick Goodhart - EON Olympias 419 and 415, April 1958. (Photo Charles E. Brown)

National Championships briefing 1963. Left to right seated: Wally Kahn, Rika Harwood, Roger Mann, Hugh Mettam, Dan Smith, ——, Author, Peter Scott.

With Anne - my wife and crew chief. National Championships, 1957.
(Photo Charles E. Brown).

At Lasham with HRH the Duke of Edinburgh, 1987 GEC Avionics National Gliding Championships.
(Photo G.E.C. Avionics).

CHAPTER FOURTEEN   OLD WAR HORSES

technical legal grounds....

That bland statement hardly matched the stand up fight which had occurred in front of an unhappy BGA Council. Philip at his most determined, inclined to ignore the Revenue's conclusions, confronted by Wally Kahn who insisted in no uncertain terms that he was asking the meeting to rubber stamp an illegal act.

So change, when it came about, had to be for the better. And the movement today owes a debt to those who managed it so well. Peter Scott, who else could have followed Philip in such a remarkable double act, sustaining and enhancing the image of gliding with the outside world, and encouraging the innovative process. David Carrow and his study group who were to see many of their proposals turned upside down when Peter and the rest of the Council began to work them over. Yet it was they who had gathered the essential data and provided a starting point for debate.

Not least Roger Barrett who took over the Flying Committee, when John Furlong was eventually persuaded to retire, and threw open the stable doors. You only had to read his regular column in S & G[1], 'Flying Talk' to realise that Roger was determined to communicate with the membership, to find out what they wanted, and to help them in whatever way he could.

But was it all for the best? I look back with affection on those earlier days and wonder. The sense of belonging, of community, within the movement was so much stronger. The discipline - you only have to compare some of the competition briefings, then and now, to see the difference - and the dedication of those in authority.

Perhaps in gliding as elsewhere we have 'progressed' by discarding too much from the past and spurning the lessons of experience. Instead of respecting what is good - and still relevant - and building on that sure foundation with all the advantages of modern thinking and technology.

On the matter of airspace, that most serious of all threats to the well-being of the sport, I am on firmer ground. From the moment when it became a problem in the mid fifties, until his retirement and beyond, Philip's contribution was immeasurable. Nick Goodhart, longest serving Chairman of the Airways/Airspace Committee, was the other principal actor in the piece and together they made a formidable team. Philip, generous with his time, determined not to yield an inch, keeping up a constant barrage on the political front. Nick as always, numerate, immaculately briefed, totally self confident - running circles round the ATC experts who were unfortunate enough to find themselves batting against him.

I know much of this at first hand as one of those who ran the Airspace Committee at other times. A salutary experience, like fighting a series of instant rearguard actions, made worse by the Ministry's nasty habit of introducing each new unpleasantness as a fait accompli.

One of the worst examples, during my first term of office, was the sudden introduction of a 'Permanent IFR'[2] trial in the Manchester Control Zone. As the zone included Liverpool Airport, which in those days peaked for a few days in the summer at a massive 2½ movements per hour, it effectively terminated all sporting flying up the west coast at less than two weeks notice.

Such unilateral action on the part of the Ministry had one immediate result. The various sporting aviation interests of the Royal Aero Club decided to pool their efforts. If need be to take the whole UK airways system apart – on paper at least – and come up with a new and better proposal. In many ways it was a forlorn hope, but there were areas of common ground. A committee of four chaired by Peter Masefield, which included Philip and myself, was given the task, rather like Humpty Dumpty, of putting it all together again.

We met once a month for a working lunch and rapidly homed in on the question of stub airways. Intended to protect climb and descent, around the major airports, they were a major obstruction. Recalling from my days with Hunting Clan that the Avro York had the worst climb performance of all, I acquired a flight manual and started pushing the numbers around. It was easy to see that the Ministry had built in a substantial safety factor. The stub bases were much too low. When I reported my findings to the committee, Peter summed them up neatly:

"You mean that they've allowed for a York on one engine with an elephant on board!"

We put our York back on three engines and came up with a new set of proposals. The stubs were raised and the en route sections pushed up as well for good measure. For a time it looked as if our ideas were making some progress with the Ministry. But in all probability that was just a ploy after their faux pas over the Liverpool Zone.

Before my second airspace stint came round a very grand sounding body, The Civil Aircraft Control Advisory Committee, CACAC for short, had been set up in response to intense political lobbying.

CHAPTER FOURTEEN   OLD WAR HORSES

CACAC was consultative, it embraced all parties with an interest in airspace – the airlines, BALPA[3], the Guilds[4], sporting aviation in its various forms, and the air traffic branch of the Ministry itself.

CACAC was an anachronism. The chairman, the permanent representatives, and the secretariat were all employed by the Ministry. So you found yourself arguing your case before judge, jury, and prosecuting counsel rolled into one.

If the ATC[5] and commercial interests ganged up on you, as happened to Douglas Bader, you were in trouble. The old warrior had come along to argue the merits of 'See and be Seen' – in other words keeping a good look out – as a means of collision avoidance. As an ex fighter pilot he knew what he was talking about, more than most in the room, but it was contrary to their policy, so they refused to listen to him. Then the chairman cut off all further discussion and, to the best of my knowledge, his views were never recorded in the minutes.

At one meeting we were discussing a gliding matter, it may well have been about Dunstable[6] and the Luton Zone, when the same chairman interrupted me rudely with the words:

"You're talking like Captain Goodhart!"

Perhaps it never occurred to him but, in that company, it was more like an accolade!

Ken Wilkinson was chairman of the BGA at that time. When he wished to retire, on being appointed managing director of British European Airways, Chris Simpson became his successor. One day Chris rang up to ask me if I would consider standing as vice chairman. After those earlier years, so often at odds with the establishment, it was like coming in from the cold. Sadly I had to refuse. As marketing director of a newly merged group of companies, which needed a great deal of attention, there were simply not enough hours in the day.

It was Karl Doetsch who had really stimulated my interest in glassfibre, with his preview of the SB6 at Braunschweig, and even more so when he had spoken about Darmstadt. That Darmstadt's long established Akaflieg was developing a 'glass' sailplane as well was hardly surprising. But the rumour that some of the students involved had jobs lined up with sailplane manufacturers suggested that other moves were afoot.

That rumour turned out to be true, and three of them – Klaus Holigaus, Gerhard Waibel, and Wolf Lemke – were soon competing against each other bringing successive generations of glass and carbon fibre, and ultimately Kevlar, sailplanes to the market. And today with

COMBAT AND COMPETITION

a few notable exceptions the designs of Akaflieg Darmstadt – class of '65 – still rule the world.

My last wooden aircraft was a K-6E owned jointly with Tony D[2]. A welcome arrangement although we were still competitive and full of flying. For my business activities, Tony's promotion to Major General, and our family commitments, meant less time for our sport. The launch of 'Euroglide', a second 'National' contest sponsored by the *Daily Telegraph*, was what finally decided us and we were soon in the market for a glass ship.

When the Darmstadt trio produced their first generation Standard Class[7] designs, we decided to look at one outsider as well, Eugen Hanle's Libelle, making a total of four in all. The plastics engineering of the Libelle was outstanding, and it had the lowest empty weight by some 40 lbs. Easy to rig, and delightful to fly, with light responsive controls, and a rear view canopy, it almost won the day. But the airbrakes were abysmal and the sideslip, limited by lack of rudder power, would not have been much help in a tight field landing. So we discarded the Libelle.

The LS-1 was a mystery ship. A brief mention in S & G the previous year, with an unrevealing photograph, and some vague stories about its success in German competitions, otherwise nothing was known about it. Imagine our surprise when a letter to Wolf Lemke, at Rolladen Schneider, produced a four page colour brochure!

They took us to Langenlonsheim to fly an early production version. The tiny strip on the river Nahe, a few miles above its confluence with the Rhine at Bingen, was surrounded by massive dykes. Not a bad place to evaluate its field landing qualities and, sad to relate, they were lousy. Even after the Libelle, the trailing edge airbrakes could hardly have been worse. Almost totally ineffective, except between 75 km/h and 95 km/h. The Achilles heel of a glider which was near perfection.

In the air it handled beautifully, with a 'big ship' feel, which suggested good low speed performance. This seemed to be borne out by the way in which it held its own, thermalling against a Ka-8 and an ASW-12, and the lack of pre-stall buffet implied an efficent wing/fuselage junction. As for the airbrakes, it seemed that help was at hand. The LS-1c, now on the stocks, would have modified Schempp brakes. These, we were assured, would be as good as a K-6.

Three days later I was launched from the Wasserkuppe, nursing a hangover, a shame on such a perfect soaring day. It was Gerhard Waibel's fault. On the previous evening, talking ASW-15, he had kept

CHAPTER FOURTEEN   OLD WAR HORSES

plying Anne and myself with strawberry sekt, and we discovered too late that it was lethal!

Regrettably for Herr Waibel his efforts were to no avail. Tony and I had already flown the ASW-15 which belonged to the RAFGSA[8]. After our visit to Rolladen Schneider it seemed almost certain that we would opt for the LS-1, and Tony decided to give Schleichers a miss. But there had been further modifications to the ASW-15 demonstrator, and I was determined to check them out before we made our final decision.

When it came to the point, they were not sufficient to affect the outcome. The all moving tailplane had been moved higher, so that it entered the downwash – "warning the pilot" – Waibel said –"if he attempted to thermal at too low an airspeed." It seemed a strange idea. In any case, who wants an effect which can best be described as 'stick fixed hunting in pitch.' The static longitudinal stability and stick force per 'G', excessive on the RAFGSA machine, had been remedied. But the handling was still inferior to the LS-1 or the Libelle. The airbrakes, Schempp type upper and lower paddles, were first class with a really useful sideslip to back them up. The ASW-15 had the best field landing capability of all and, for that reason alone, I was sorry to cross it off the list.

I flew the Standard Cirrus on another visit to Germany. A high tow from Hahnweide[9], in the gloom of an anticyclonic October day, with the pepperpot outlines of the castle of Teck shrouded in mist. But the handling was uninspiring and the airbrakes, once again, were not effective.

So Tony and I went back to Walter Schneider, and pressed him for early delivery of an LS-1c with the new long span Schempp type airbrakes. We were lucky on both counts. Our LS-1 arrived in time to make its debut, at 'Euroglide', in May the following year – and the airbrakes were every bit as good as Herr Lemke had promised.

The extra performance soon put a further 460 kms under my belt. It should have been 500 km, but conditions deteriorated sharply approaching the second turning point. On the first leg, over the Cotswolds, I shared a thermal with Frank Pozerskis who was on a flight from Dunstable in his Cirrus. Frank is a character. In his native Lithuania he had even contrived to build his own glider during the German occupation.

Later, destitute, a displaced person outside the gates of Hahnweide, he watched longingly as the first postwar Schempp Hirth sailplanes

COMBAT AND COMPETITION

circled overhead, wondering whether he would ever be able to fly again. Now he runs his own successful timber business, and can indulge his love of gliding to the full. A charming, warm hearted, and modest man:

"The Five Three" – he said in his improbable English, for my number was 53 and this was the first time he had seen the LS-1, "You have wheel down!"

It must have been like that all the way from Lasham. I tucked it up and crept away with an embarrassed word of thanks.

Shortly afterwards I declared an out and return to Lincoln. It was a day of days – high cloud base and small cumulus streeting into the distance.

I scorched off downwind, hardly circling at all. The return leg was even better. Close to the Great North Road, where the runways on some of the old bomber airfields were being dug up for hardcore, dust devils marked a series of splendid thermals. So strong, in their turbulent cores, that they took me to cloud base time after time before the headwind could do its worst. Then it was dolphin flying[10] all the way, with the valuable assistance of a modern electronic variometer and speed to fly director.

At 5,000 ft, to the southeast of Oxford, a new record was in the bag – until everything collapsed over the Thames valley. Drifting backwards, in a series of weak and broken thermals, I called my crew on the radio:

"Tookay – from Five Three prepare to roll – Benson Airfield."

After their acknowledgment came another voice:

"Still looks good over Inkpen if you can make it this way."

No mistaking those emphatic tones – and he was right. I could see cumulus upwind, haloed in the late afternoon sun, far away, beyond the Berkshire Downs:

"Hullo Nick! Not possible now, but thanks for the information."
Then, as the thought suddenly struck – "why are you listening out?" and Nick Goodhart's reply – "Old war horses stir at the sound of the trumpets!"

Old war horse he might imply himself to be. Yet he would become National Champion again in 1971 – with a fourth place, just off the podium, in the World Open Class the following year – a fitting conclusion to a great gliding career.

On the opening day of the 1970 Nationals the LS-1 was the only aircraft to complete the task, an out and return race, from Doncaster

CHAPTER FOURTEEN   OLD WAR HORSES

northwards to Easingwold. It was an unusual flight, working innumerable thermals in an 800 ft height band below 2,000 ft. A real test of the LS-1's low speed performance, and she came through with flying colours.

On the return leg, to the west of York, the conditions improved with some genuine cumulus and I met a few gliders, including Alf Warminger's with which I shared a thermal, but they were all going the other way.

"You given up Five Three?" he said – to which I replied that on the contrary I had already been round the turning point and he would soon be doing likewise.

"Too late for that now – but good for you Dave! and best of luck – you're almost home."

One more thermal, over Sherburn in Elmet, left an easy final glide over the smoking chimney pots of Doncaster and back across the finish line to an empty airfield.

The last task of that contest was a race to Spitalgate near Grantham. Those who went early had the advantage of strong lift to counter the stiff breeze. Ralph Jones in a Standard Cirrus landed out and returned for a relight. Long after we were back at Doncaster he was still airborne, under an overcast sky, fighting a headwind which had become half a gale. Eventually he got there by a combination of skill and dogged determination. Not surprisingly he was very slow and our splendid LS-1 became the highest placed Standard Class entry.

But she was not long for this world. The following year Tony D^2 moved to the Chilterns and sold his share to David Innes. That was a recipe for confusion – David Innes and David Ince in the same syndicate! – and my new partner took it to the World Championships in Yugoslavia on the first of his many appearances for Guernsey.

Early one Sunday morning, while the Championships were still in progress, the telephone rang. It was Ralph Jones:

"Your glider's had a mid air collision with a Nimbus!"

He went on to say that it had happened in a cunim, both pilots had bailed out safely, and David was in hospital with a broken leg.

"When it arrives back in England – you get the bits over to me – I'm going to rebuild the Nimbus as well and we might do ourselves a bit of good!"

On this occasion Ralph was wrong. When the trailer reached Lasham there was only the rudder inside. The souvenir hunters had been at work. It needed a miracle, not a rebuild – and Rolladen

COMBAT AND COMPETITION

Schneider, when approached for a replacement, were unable to oblige for three years.

So we ordered a Kestrel 19 from Slingsbys, but even that could not be delivered for 18 months, and I was without a glider for the following summer. Then I got involved in performance testing on the BG 135 and its owners invited me to demonstrate its contest flying capabilities.

Pat Moore, the 'Windspiel' man, as I remembered him from my first ever visit to the Mynd in 1947, was one of them. To be more accurate he was the driving force behind it. Now a retired Air Commodore, and dedicated as ever to the ideal of the small span lightweight glider, he had set up a design group and they had at last persuaded The Birmingham Guild, an experienced aerospace subcontractor to build a prototype.

The BG 135 started life as a 12 metre – with alternative 15m and 16m variants on the drawing board – but the definitive version was standardised at 13.5 metres span. It was of metal construction, apart from the glassfibre cockpit shell. The parallel chord Wortmann wings were skinned in 30 swg sheet bonded to a rigid foam core, and there was a high aspect ratio butterfly tail.

The airbrakes, trailing edge flaps similar in principle to those on the LS–1a, but long and narrow, were almost perfectly balanced and blew gently shut if the lever was released. They were most effective. The cockpit was roomy and comfortable and the 'midget ship' handling was very pleasant.

The crude performance figures, from our comparative tests, seemed to confirm that the designer's estimates were about right. 33.5:1 at 84 kph was rather good for 13.5 metres.

During the Club Class Nationals at Dunstable it gave me one of the most exhilarating rides of my life. A 190 kilometre race and I took a risk, in the middle of the stubble burning season, by waiting until the rest of the field had gone. (Leave it too late and the smoke could achieve smog-like proportions, blotting out the sunshine and destroying the convection.)

As it was I marked time over Dunstable until the little wisps of cumulus firmed and flattened under the high inversion and I could curb my impatience no longer.

The first leg was easy and fast, working a comfortable height band, using regular, reliable, 9 knot thermals. Ideal weather to match midget ship handling to a winder's instincts. The BG 135 could really hold its

CHAPTER FOURTEEN   OLD WAR HORSES

own against its K-6E competitors in these conditions. And, with that thought, I stepped up the pressure, pulling hard into the cores, working each thermal for all it was worth, accompanied by the constant 'tin canning' of metal skins.

On the second leg, running up to Bedford, the conditions were absolutely superb. Cloud base had risen to over 6000 ft. Cambridge, visible almost 30 miles away marked the track ahead, and the first stubble fires of the day were beginning to stain the air. I could see a field just starting to burn, some miles further on. Ideal for a quick top up, but there was a balloon in the way. The more I climbed, the more it rose ahead obstructing my path. In the end it forced me to go round it and stay legal – but I was too late for that Bedfordshire farmer's thermal.

The day was so good that it didn't matter at all – a heady mixture of consistently strong natural thermals and some absolute corkers blowing up from the burning fields below.

A long fast final glide – the rolling chalk downs and the towns along Icknield Way triggering a mighty series of upcurrents – Baldock, Letchworth, and Hitchin passed in rapid succession. Then the sprawl of Luton and Dunstable in the afternoon sun – the altimeter unwinding – and the finish line ahead. BG 135 was about to win her first race[11] and the best reward of all was to realise the pleasure which that would bring to her designers and above all to Pat Moore.

A barn door day, no doubt about it, yet there had been others far worse in an earlier contest. Including a very marginal one working our way across the Somerset levels, from Compton Abbas almost to Dunkeswell, rarely higher than 1200 feet and she had given me a remarkably easy ride.

So hail and farewell to a competitive little glider. Deserving better than a limited production run of just eight aircraft before the jigs and tools were sold on. But the fibreglass revolution and the endless quest for performance put paid to that.

The Kestrel 19 when it finally arrived could hardly have been in greater contrast to Pat Moore's little sailplane. Over 10 points better on the glide, with a host of modern features – retractable undercarriage, flaps, water ballast and tail parachute – it certainly offered value for money. A typical slippery high inertia glider, with relatively ineffective airbrakes, and interconnected flaps and ailerons which restricted the rate of roll when you selected the landing position. The tail parachute provided a marvellous short field capability. But it was

COMBAT AND COMPETITION

a strictly one shot device and you had to get it right or fall expensively out of the sky.

The extra 2 metres span, added on by Slingsbys, gave a useful improvement in performance – at the expense of rudder locking in a sideslip and increased roll/yaw inertia. On the 20 metre version, still to come, the effect would be even more pronounced and the larger rudder which went with it made the rudder locking worse!

Little did I realise that the Kestrel was to be my last competition glider or, when the time came, that I was flying in my last contest.

I took my leave at 'Euroglide '74'. Good soaring weather and the familiar charm of Nympsfield, overlooking the Severn valley, combined to make it a memorable occasion. Competitors had come from Switzerland, West Germany, Poland, Belgium and Holland – and there was a festive atmosphere about the place when we arrived.

An awkward field landing on the first day, which collapsed the retractable wheel, almost put paid to my hopes of continuing. When Ralph Jones heard about it he insisted on doing an overnight repair. From a competitor lying sixth, who would eventually finish third, to another who had just scored a duck, it was a most generous gesture. I kept him supplied with beer until the bar closed, after which he insisted on finishing the job on his own, working on into the small hours.

In the clubhouse, as I ferried the tankards to Ralph was one member whose presence brought back other memories. Tony Gaze, a New Zealander and a distinguished fighter leader, had been a flight commander on 616 Squadron, the first to be equipped with Meteors, during the closing stages of the war. An accomplished racing driver in his day, he had also represented his native country in the World Gliding Championships.

Years ago when I pranged a Weihe, trying to land in a claptrap mountain area, Tony had come to my rescue.

My back was absolute agony, and I lay flat out on the floor of his very non standard Mk VIII Jaguar estate car, with visions of being stuck that way for the rest of my life. Tony knew the form and he regaled me with stories of motor racing shunts, sore backs and whiplash injuries, and insisted that the recoveries were quick and complete. The most considerate of men, I shall always remember him for his help on a very painful occasion and the fact that he has never mentioned it again.

On the second day, after Ralph's temporary repair had been

CHAPTER FOURTEEN   OLD WAR HORSES

completed, and the gel coat had been given time to set, I made a late start. There were storms around, but they caused no serious problems on track, and I came final gliding home without a care in the world until the moment came to release the water ballast. Immediately there was a terrible cold clammy feeling around the base of my spine which spread rapidly to the rest of my lower anatomy.

Water was cascading out from behind the backrest, in an icy flood, well refrigerated after $3\frac{1}{2}$ hours in the air and several climbs to 8000 ft or more. Thank goodness there had been no need to release it en route!

I climbed out of the cockpit with sodden trousers, to a variety of ribald comments, only to discover that the main jettison hose had not been reconnected after Ralph's efforts the night before. My fault I hasten to add and not his.

The 296 km race, a couple of days later, made up for all that. South from Nympsfield, then east to Lasham, with a dogleg route home and a real cocktail of soaring weather. Recalling that task is to live again through the pressures, and compulsions, and the sheer joy of contest flying.

The familiar tension and excitement, which caught at one's guts, was strong as ever. Different, and yet at the same time strikingly similar to operational flying. So that the sudden gust of an unseen thermal, out on the grid, becomes part of another time and place. Where the air is filled with the crack of a Coffman starters - and ejector exhausts spew oily smoke......

It was a muted start, under a miserable looking sky, shadowed by lumps of useless stagnating cloud. To the west the last vestiges of cumulus disintegrate to nothing as the sea air moves in. Three of us leave together. A Calif two seater below. Alongside, and moving closer, Frank Pozerskis in his ASW 17. The weather stinks. I make the traditional flushing gesture and can almost see his grin.

The first leg is one long battle to stay airborne and the turning point near disaster. The sea air, in full flood by now, pours through the gaps in the Somerset hills. A few rags of cloud drift gently on the breeze, low over the ground, here one moment, gone the next.

Ahead, not far away on the second leg, the slopes of Cranborne Chase rise like a barrier, marked tantilisingly overhead by active and growing cumulus. Gliders appear from nowhere and there are two more Kestrels for company. We circle and sweat, drifting slowly towards the rising ground, barely maintaining height.

COMBAT AND COMPETITION

Then a wonderful, satisfying, kick in the pants. I cram on full aileron and tramp hard on the rudder, trying to override the inertia, skidding wildly into the turn. My love of Wessex is rooted in ancient legend.....

"Stars wink beyond the downland barrows[12]
where Alfred marched to meet the Danes
Far in advance of flinthead arrows
and unaware of aeroplanes."

.....and reaches across the centuries to modern times - a cradle of aviation development in two world wars where the rolling chalky uplands provide some of the finest thermal soaring in the kingdom.

And in sudden change of mood the skies above my beloved Wessex are looking their brilliant best. Time for dolphin flying - into the lift - pulling up straight ahead - sometimes a gentle weave to prolong the climb - then on again. Hurry!... hurry!... hurry!...

4,000 ft and more below the familiar landmarks pass in swift succession. Regimental badges in the chalk above the Nadder valley. Old Sarum airfield. The radio telescope dish at Chilbolton.

A developing stubble fire and the Kestrel is swept upwards in a violent cauldron of turbulence and ashes, blind in the smoke, on instruments. A strong smell of burning and the cockpit is filled with the smuts and bits of straw. The altimeter spins like a dervish and, when I fall out of the top, my private cumulus cloud has pushed well above the inversion.

On the way home, there is a marked change in conditions. More and more fires - the harvest must be going great guns - adding volumes to the acrid sooty curtains which hung rootless and inert above the Berkshire Downs. Visibility was down to a few miles and a layer of dirty decaying cloud spread out overhead, cutting off the sunshine.

A standard Cirrus emerges from the gloom. Together, in silence, we ride the stagnant air, slowing down in the occasional patches of lift, until Nympsfield is almost in range. Almost, but not quite, because there is still the invasive sea air to come and a headwind on the final glide.

A grass airfield below, and with it a hint of brightness in the sky, but I need more height to get home. A sudden hubbub of landing calls on the radio as the failing conditions take their toll. The Cirrus forges on. But I hang back and run into a darker patch of murk which seems to be working. The lift is weak, but sufficent to give a long slow climb on instruments until Nympsfield is in the bag.

The Cirrus must be miles in front. Had I been too cautious taking

CHAPTER FOURTEEN   OLD WAR HORSES

that last thermal? - and almost with the thought there is only the sea air and a cloudless sky ahead.

It was like passing into another world. The last ramparts of the Cotswold plateau and the Severn valley beyond were bathed in brilliant sunshine. On the far side of the river the Brecon Beacons and the Black Mountains loomed dark against the horizon. Smoke from an occasional stubble fire trailed low in the wind, dead on the nose. There was no sign of convection. I check the calculator again:

"Five Three final gliding 10 miles."

Aston Down, the last airfield on track, I'm home and dry. I push up the speed, gripped by the rising excitement of a racing finish. Two miles to go:

"Five Three finishing in one minute!" - release the water ballast.

Another Kestrel, ahead and below, hangs poised at the apex of his vapour trail, as our tanks drain together and we hurtle towards the line at upwards of 140 mph.

The grass floods past, then falls and tilts crazily away. The wheel slams down. Moments later I am on finals, feeling the parachute's hefty drag, floating low across the threshold - and longing for a beer!

Peter Scott was due to present the prizes. It was good to see an old adversary who had packed so much competitive gliding into fifteen short years. He had wasted no time at all. Buying a high performance two seater to build up his soaring and contest flying background with the help of an experienced pilot. Then a personal hanger in which he could keep his glider fully rigged and ready for take off at a moment's notice. A number of the most advanced sailplanes followed, Olympia 419, HP-14, and BS-1.

Peter was National Champion in 1962 and British team squad member in the same year. Due to a prior commitment, as Skipper of the 1963 America Cup challenge, he was denied the opportunity of flying in a world contest. His love and understanding of bird life and nature, his weather lore, his experience as an Olympic yachtsman and wartime MTB captain made him a formidable competitor. A natural who came to gliding late in life and went to the top.

Once, during a long and tedious Council meeting when he was sitting next to me, Peter started to draw. Idly, or so it seemed, yet in next to no time a delightful sketch began to take shape. His Olympia 419 against the contours of the Cotswold edge and the outline of a racing triangle.

"Peter," I said softly, "that would look super on our study wall." But

COMBAT AND COMPETITION

he was already tearing it to pieces!

As we talked that day at Nympsfield, in the Daily Telegraph pavilion, he looked remarkably fit and spry. Almost indestructable.

"Why not come back again Peter?" He looked at me thoughtfully – a glimpse of longing – or was it my imagination.

"Impossible David. I would only be satisfied with a Nimbus, which would be far too expensive, and anyway I have my swimming to keep me fit."

"Oh come on! – You only have to sell a couple of extra paintings."

He just smiled and changed the subject. For the reality was that Peter had moved on to other things.

CHAPTER FIFTEEN

FULL CIRCLE

My job in the '70s took me all over Western Europe, including Germany, where I was responsible for a subsidiary company in the Bavarian town of Waldkraiburg, some 60 km to the east of Munich. A strange place, with its heavily reinforced concrete buildings hidden in the middle of a pine forest, until you delved into it's history. Waldkraiburg had been a major source of munitions production in the days of the Third Reich.

The sales director, Rolf Kliendienst, had been wounded at Stalingrad and was amongst the last to be evacuated by air. He wore an artificial right hand and never allowed his disability to interfere with an active life.

An excellent skier, and a skilled rally driver in his day, Rolf was the most polished and expert motorist I have ever met. With him speed was almost synonymous with safety. A decent loyal man and straight as a die. He must have been a first class NCO in his Wehrmacht days.

One evening, driving to nearby Muhldorf for dinner, while we were still in the middle of the forest, he turned to me:

"Mr Ince, I must show you something special."

We drove on until, approaching the end of the trees, a canal appeared running parallel to the road, and a railway bridge obscured the view ahead. Rolf pulled up just beyond the bridge, alongside a massive concrete wall, like the entrance to some medieval castle. It was built into a high bank, so that it seemed to form part of the bridge approach.

"Here is the door to the flugplatz," he said.

We got out the car and walked amongst the trees. It was an awesome sight. For several hundred yards, leading straight away from the road, the ground was torn and cratered like a battlefield. Huge chunks of concrete lay half buried in the ground, tilted at all angles. Then some gigantic hoop shaped bits and pieces and one which was almost complete, and in situ, like an open tunnel mouth. In the silent depths of that forest, filled with the scent of pines, we were standing on the remains of an undergound airfield.

It could hardly have been better sited, with road, rail and canal access literally on the doorstep. And, for munitions and aircraft, there was Waldkraiburg and the Messerschmidt factory at Weiner Neustadt not so far away. But that was mere speculation. Nobody seemed to know about the intended operational role of that strange airfield, the

COMBAT AND COMPETITION

type of aircraft, or the method of launching and recovery.

Rolf could only tell me the that the Americans had spent weeks and months, and thousands of pounds of high explosive trying to destroy it. Now, so the rumour went, at the height of the cold war, they were sorry that it no longer existed.

Then there was Hermann Kutscha. He was the distributor, based near Heilbronn, for a Belgian Company which had recently joined the Group.

We were introduced to each other at an exhibition in Frankfurt.

"You two will have plenty in common" – they said – "Flying fighters on opposite sides in the last war."

Herr Kutscha was a slight, rather insignificant looking character, hair on the long side exactly so, and one of those droopy Mexican type moustaches. Trying to be with it. If he had been a woman you might have registered mutton dressed lamb. At first sight I wasn't sure that I liked him.

In sheer devilment as we shook hands, and before I could stop myself, the words were out of my mouth:

"A good thing we never met in the air – or one of us might not be here now!"

Later I got to know him rather well. Mainly because he wanted to sell out to the Group, and still continue as Managing Director, and I had to run a rule over his business.

In the air we had more in common than either of us had realised. For Herr Kutscha, the relationship always remained like that on both sides, had been an active glider pilot. But the real eye opener came when he invited me back to his house for a drink. In due course he produced the Book of German Aces, turned the pages to 'K', and their was a younger version of my host staring me in the face. He had flown Me 110s in the Battle of Britain and survived, then 109s on the Western and Russian fronts, and chalked up almost 80 victories. When I handed the book back to him, he grinned, as if to remind me of my remark at the Frankfurt Show.

"So!" I said "You also think that I would have been the one to die!"

Manfred Deckart, manager of the Westphalian Central Cooperative in Munster, was a different proposition. My hotel the night before had been on the northern outskirts of the town. The surroundings looked like an old airfield, and a map confirmed that it was one of the Rheine group which had confronted us back in 1945.

It was a warm summer's evening and I tramped round the

CHAPTER FIFTEEN   FULL CIRCLE

perimeter after dinner and retired to bed in reminiscent mood. The following morning my meeting with Herr Deckart started in a cool if not unfriendly manner, until I happened to mention my airfield hotel, then he really opened up.

What had I been flying, that I knew about the Rheine Group of airfields? Typhoons – then I must have been in his sights, and he in mine, a few times during that dramatic spring more than 30 years ago. He had been called up under age, as a trainee flak gunner, in the last winter of the war and it was enough for him that we had fought on the same sector. From then on he behaved as if we had been comrades in arms!

When, inevitably, we went off to lunch together, he suggested that we avoid one particular restaurant and that we kept our voices down when we spoke in English. No, it was not a question of German antagonism towards former enemies. Munster was a BAOR garrison town and some British squaddies had gone on the rampage the night before. Local feelings were running high.

If British faces were red on that occasion, German ones must have been redder still in the spring of 1983. That was when *STERN* magazine published the first of a series of six articles about the sinking of prison ships by RAF fighter bombers during the final days of the war. The implication conveyed to *STERN's* mass circulation readership was of a cock up, followed by a hush up, as if we were totally to blame. But there was no explanation as to why the wretched inmates of Neuengamme concentration camp near Hamburg had been put on board the Cap Arcona in the first place – nor, as was alleged, why those who managed to escape and get ashore were shot out of hand by the German troops.

The first indication here was a piece in the *Daily Telegraph* one Saturday which described the *STERN* article and questioned its conclusions. Having been involved at the time, I was incensed at what had been published in Germany, and determined to try and set the record straight. My friend Derek Wood was, inter alia, Air Correspondent of the *Sunday Telegraph* at that time. So I gave him a ring and he wrote a pretty forthright column about it, which appeared the next day.

The articles, and the readers' letters, which followed must have been acutely embarrassing to many a decent German. Of course there had been a mistake by the RAF. For the very understandable reason that everything pointed to a final Nazi retreat into a Northern

COMBAT AND COMPETITION

Redoubt, fortress Norway, using all the shipping available. The fact that the Cap Arcona, and two other prison ships, were carrying some 9,400 prisoners on Himmler's express instructions was part of a vain attempt to destroy the evidence of mass murders by the Nazi regime.

Those letters, from eye witnesses amongst the few survivors and British forces on the ground, told a heart rending story. The German troops, mostly SS, had carried out Himmler's vile policy to the bitter end, butchering as many of the survivors as possible. Two large barges, quite independent of the prison ships which had been attacked by the Typhoons, had arrived from Stutthof concentration camp on the Baltic coast near Konigsberg. They were found beached at Travemunde. The ladders had been removed, and the occupants machine gunned at close range. Many of the children had been clubbed to death.

Shortly after seeing these appalling sights, Mills-Roberts, the brigadier commanding 1 Commando, was faced with accepting Field Marshal Erhard Milch's surrender. The latter was unwise enough to do so with the words 'Heil Hitler' and proffered his baton which the brigadier promptly broke over his head.

In the end it was quite clear that the atrocity was German. The shipping strikes went ahead as a result of delays in transmitting the latest intelligence to Air Headquarters and the Nazis did nothing to discourage them. The question remains as to why *STERN* saw fit to publish the story and there have been suggestions of Israeli involvement following Mrs Thatcher's refusal to accept a former leader of the Irgun terrorist organisation as Israeli Ambassador in London.

That sad and sordid episode had a sequel. It led to a call from Dr Conrad Wood, of the Department of Sound Records at the Imperial War Museum.

He visited me at home to record material on the Cap Arcona and went on to do a general fighter ground attack memoir. Which started me thinking about writing a book. But it was lunching with Group Captain Sandy Hunter at Strike Command Headquarters which really got me going.

Sandy also drew my attention to the newly formed Typhoon and Tempest Association. The major catalyst had been 197 Squadron, which had hung together rather well since the war, thanks to the efforts of Derek Lovell. Derek organised a squadron reunion when Allan Smith, their CO during the second half of 1944, was over on a visit from New Zealand. They met in the Tangmere Aviation Museum

CHAPTER FIFTEEN   FULL CIRCLE

at the suggestion of Ken Rimell, a professional photographer, who looked after the publicity in his spare time.

After that there was no holding Ken. Thanks to his enthusiasm, and that of his fellow aviation archaeologists, we had an Association in being and a full blown reunion at Tangmere the following summer.

Great to meet old comrades again, but the two squadrons with which I had served were thin on the ground, and it was kind of 197 to make me an honorary member. That arrangement resulted in a very pleasant trip to Normandy in their company, and a first encounter with Allan Smith 43 years after he had been shot down and taken prisoner.

At these annual reunions Pinkie Stark and I always face the hazard of being invited back to Ben Gunn's place in Worthing. For our old friend's appetite for Scotch is as strong as ever. Ben flew Tempests Vs with 274 Squadron, and Spitfire IXs with 501, but there is no doubt where his loyalties lie.

On the evening of the Spitfire's 50th Anniversary a large party had gathered in the bar of the RAF Club. At the height of the celebrations the door opened briefly – a voice bellowed "Ben Gunn says the Tempest is a better aircraft than the Spitfire ever was!" – and the door closed again.

The scene shifts to a residential area in Worthing on Sea. In the wee small hours there came a thunderous knocking on the door. The occupants stumbled cursing out of bed to find an envelope in the letter box addressed to A.E.Gunn Esq. Inside, on a single sheet of paper, written large, was the word "Bollocks!"

One September day, on my second wave flight at Portmoak, I went straight to 20,000 ft plus over Bishop Hill. My long awaited third diamond was the easiest thing in the world. At the top of the climb the whole of central Scotland, westwards to the Argyll coast, was visible between the stratocumulus bars. There were three of us that morning, above 20,000 ft, with an aggregate age of over 180 years. Geoff Morris in another Kestrel was not far away. I called him on the radio:

"Zero two, this is Kan Kan. I haven't been as high as this for ages. You are at 11 0'clock, 1,000 ft below."

"Kan Kan – I do not have you in sight. A good thing you aren't hostile with 20 mm cannon!"

Geoff, who had flown Spitfires with Fighter Command, was shot down over France and evaded successfully. In the closing stages of the war he was back on a squadron, flying Mustang IVs. Once, when we

COMBAT AND COMPETITION

were chatting in the clubhouse at Lasham, he told me that he had just given a talk to a local group of aviation enthusiasts:

"But you know David there's always that story I can never tell in public."

"What story was that Geoff?"

When he told me, I pondered whether it should be recorded here. So out of context in the world of today. Yet not untypical of the crude humour that helped to preserve one's sanity as a wartime fighter pilot.

"We had a wild Australian on the squadron." - Geoff said - "One day, in the middle of a scrap with a bunch of 109s, his voice came loud and clear through the hubbub on the radio - 'He'll sh*t well tonight! He's got two a*******s!' On the combat film, afterwards, it was there for all to see - exploding cannon shells stitching the bottom of his opponent's fuselage, until the whole thing erupted in flames."

I always think of Wally and Geoff Morris as the doyen of Lasham tug pilots - and would never dare to choose between them - even though I knew Wally much the better of the two. But that was about to change. For three years, as Chairman of the Championships organising committee at Lasham, I was to see a deal more of Geoff and Spike, his wife, who was in charge of Control.

During my first year we were breaking new ground. An Open Class Nationals, and a Regionals, to be run concurrently on the same site, and the first involvement of a very upmarket aircraft industry sponsor. It was fun to be setting up a budget and working closely with Marconi Avionics. For this was essentially the Elliott Flight Automation of bygone days under a new name, now a £ multi million company after years of quite remarkable progress, and the directors were old friends.

Peter Hearne was my main point of contact and the fact that we had been involved together professionally, on many occasions in the past, helped to create a good working relationship from the word go.

At the official opening it was my pleasant task to start the proceedings by introducing Peter, already well known at Lasham, in his guise as a director of Marconi Avionics. It was remarkable how he had followed me into British Oxygen and then Elliotts - and, when I left Elliotts, how he had taken over much of my overseas marketing work.

Now a Director and General Manager of Marconi Avionics, and a past president of the Royal Aeronautical Society, Peter had recently been awarded the John Curtis Sword. Two of the three previous recipients had been in the very front rank of aviation endeavour - Air

CHAPTER FIFTEEN FULL CIRCLE

Commodore Rod Banks and General James Doolittle. It was quite an achievement.

I decided to give his gliding colleagues a run down on Peter in his other incarnation and end up by poking a little fun. I had just retired, to become a consultant, and if our earlier past history together was anything to go by, Peter must be about to retire too!

He responded modestly, suggesting that I must have been talking about someone else, which avoided the need to comment on his future career.

It turned out to be a good week, with six contest days for the Open Class and seven for the Regionals – and for Marconi Avionics too. In a year, as this was, between SBAC[1] displays they had given high priority to their MOD[2], CAA[3], Service, and industry guests. A day out for these people, with glider flights thrown in, was a major reason behind the sponsorship and we simply had to get it right.

So Anne and I had spent many hours beforehand. Integrating Marconi's guests with those on the BGA and Lasham lists, whose goodwill and support was so important to gliding, and attempting to bring groups of compatible people together. It would have been ideal to take the total numbers and spread them equally across the nine contest days. But the majority wanted to come at the weekends and the second Saturday and Sunday, at the end of the contest, were by far the most popular.

Eventually it was the team which organised and marshalled the guests from sponsor's chalet to launch point, and the two seater pilots, who made it all work. Until the last day, when the weather broke, they only lost one scheduled flight, and in total they flew 380 guests.

Looking back on that first occasion was to recognise the very considerable effort involved in organising and running a championships, and the dedication of those who head up each department, sometimes for years on end. A demanding enough task even if you were to tackle it full time.

Yet it had its rewards, working with a marvellous bunch of people, in the satisfaction of difficulties overcome – and, not least, in the constant challenge to do better next time.

Marconi Avionics seemed to be very happy with the results and their sponsorship was firmly in evidence the following summer – with an important difference. Farnborough year and the SBAC Display was less than three weeks after the championships. Chalet and guest flying facilities were not required.

COMBAT AND COMPETITION

But it was still necessary to look after a limited number of gliding guests. So Lasham catering provided a daily buffet and RAF Odiham – through the good offices of Bob Bickers – a 'Tents large, air force tactical, olive drab' in which to house it.

Bob was a tower of strength. An RAF air loadmaster, with a Jimmy Edwards blond handlebar, who helped on the start and finish line. Bob also looked after our airspace briefing and contest task clearances with the civil and military air traffic services. An active member of the Kestrel gliding club he was a 'fixer' par excellence.

Just as well that we were running a very limited visitors' programme, because the contest was held during a period of settled high pressure conditions, at the end of a long hot summer. There was plenty of stubble burning, and the visibility at times was quite appalling. On the fourth contest day there was a mid air collision.

It was a typical pre start line opening situation, with gliders holding close to cloud base. Fortunately both pilots bailed out safely, although not before one of them had half bunted, and descended in an inverted position until he was only 400 ft above the ground.

There was a spectacularly successful rescue operation. The Chief Marshal radioed a non competing pilot flying locally who in turn called RAE Farnborough. Farnborough called Odiham on military UHF, Odiham diverted two Puma helicopters flying locally to search and rescue. Within five minutes of the collision one pilot had been delivered back to Lasham, and the other, with suspected concussion, to sick quarters at Odiham for a quick medical check.

Ralph Jones, flying magnificently that week, had us all confused on another day when he became even more taciturn than usual on the radio, and failed to appear over the finish line when expected. Knowing that he was well ahead of the field he was deliberately delaying his arrival, to make his lapsed time more than 2¼ hours, thus avoiding a derated task. This increased his points lead for the day, even though he lost speed in the process. A cunning piece of glidermanship.

One morning the weather was duff and there was a pilot's meeting chaired by Chris Day, the Contest Director. The previous task had been set with one leg running just upwind of controlled airspace. Bob Bickers reported that NATS[4] had observed the results on their radars and were not amused.

During the ensuing discussion there was a good deal of aggro about airspace constraints. One pilot expressed himself very forcibly saying that the present day restrictions were a nonsense and that he would

CHAPTER FIFTEEN   FULL CIRCLE

break the rules rather than prejudice a competitive flight. It was a dreadful, quite undisciplined, statement coming from an experienced individual. Peter Hearne was horrified. He made no bones about it. Any more of this and he would recommend that his company withdrew its sponsorship.

The discussion grew heated and there was always the danger of a guest or a journalist in the room who might create trouble for the gliding movement if he understood what we were about. I dug Chris hard in the ribs and suggested that the meeting was becoming unconstructive, that we should cool it and move on to other things. A nasty moment and one thing was certain – some guidance on task setting adjacent to controlled airspace must be issued for the following year.

There was another rumpus that week. The penultimate day always involved a final trophy polishing session and an overall review of the prizes. When we looked for the BGA trophies, which are awarded each year in perpetuity, they had not arrived. I rang Barry Rolfe, the Secretary, at home and he confirmed that they were still in the office at Leicester. When I suggested that he might like to collect them himself, and drive down to Lasham, he didn't sound very happy.

I hung up and turned to Bob Bickers for help. Within minutes he was back to say that by some extraordinary good fortune there was a Chinook going that way on a training flight! It would make a landing at Rearsby if the the BGA could get the pots there in time. Barry was much more helpful when I spoke to him again. Perhaps he had registered the likely repercussions of a Nationals prize giving without the BGA pots!

The Chinook was back by mid afternoon with our precious hardware on board. Once again the Odiham choppers had pulled our chestnuts out of the fire. But when I rang the Station Commander to thank him, he insisted that there should be no publicity, or letters from the gliding movement, in case higher authority misunderstood.

The chap who handed out those errant trophies to the winning pilots, on the following day, was a perfect choice. Tom Kerr was on the point of retiring as Director of RAE Farnborough. He had been an RAF pilot during the war, and took quite a shine to gliding, and we to him. Tony Mattin, Chairman of Lasham, and I worked hard on Tom to give it a try. We nearly succeeded too, until he became so involved with the privatisation of the Royal Ordnance Factories that he could not spare the time.

COMBAT AND COMPETITION

Tom's speech to the assembled multitude at prize-giving contained one gem. "I've reached the age," he said, "When your wife says 'Do stop standing like that! Hold your stomach in!' - and you're already trying your utmost to do so!"

Its the sort of remark which makes you look at the speaker's waistline - and Tom wasn't doing too badly. Then, of course, Chris Day and I had to stand on either side of him, Chris reading out the winners' names whilst I passed Tom the prizes. And I was consciously holding my stomach in and wondering what Chris was thinking because his need was greater than mine.

Confound you Tom, I've a terrible memory these days, but I've never forgotten that. Every time I put on a bit of weight, and have to stand up in public, it comes back to haunt me!

By the following year Marconi Avionics had become GEC Avionics. A change which greatly pleased our sponsors - who considered that the dated image, associated with the name Marconi, had become a positive disadvantage in the United States.

After reviewing the previous championships, including racing finishes and marginal final glides, Peter Hearne and I agreed that safety must be paramount. For organisers and sponsor alike there could be no question of tolerating any repeat performance and, even more so, in a year when we were planning on 540 visitors.

Peter, wearing his sponsor's hat, started the ball rolling by firing a warning shot across the bows of the BGA Flying Committee. His message was clear and to the point. Get the safety aspects of starting and finishing sorted out, and reduce the risk of airspace infringements due to task setting, otherwise we shall have to reconsider our sponsorship.

In the end there were new rules and penalties, a procedure for reducing the start line crossing height in adverse conditions, and guidelines for task setters. Peter's letter unfortunately provoked the Flying Committee into a transparent attempt to impose pilot operated starts[5] during the coming season and I was invited to attend one of its meetings.

To argue that this would significantly reduce the collision risk seemed a nonsense. Thermalling close to the start line was by far the most critical phase. Later, when it was seen that the gate could be abolished, there was a real safety advantage. But, for the moment, their proposal did not appear to address the central problem.

Time-base cameras were an essential part of the procedure and

CHAPTER FIFTEEN   FULL CIRCLE

Lasham was urged to purchase them, in partnership with another leading club, for hire to competitors. In order to reduce the initial cost, the Committee had opted for those recording to the nearest minute and could not say when any higher accuracy might become mandatory. Strange indeed for it was the final arbiter in such matters.

I explained that we had been examining pilot operated starts, had conducted trials on an alternative 'ground clock'[6] option and were not prepared to use this method, as a sole source of information, without more rigorous testing and training. As for time-base cameras, there could be no question of such an open ended investment as the Committee could change the specification at any time. Finally, running a Nationals and two Regional classes from the same site, we would be faced with simultaneous pilot operated and ground observed starts, which would further increase the risks of launching an unproved system.

The committee were unsympathetic and continued to press for pilot operated starts. So I left them to continue their deliberations in my absence. We would not change our procedures in 1985.

However we did introduce two other changes. The first, thanks to an old Elliott Brothers colleague working at British Aerospace, was a x 7 magnification gyro stabilised monocular. The 'Steadyscope' proved invaluable. It compensated for 'operator shake' and made the identification of gliders approaching the start line much easier.

The second – an attempt to introduce faster and more efficient scoring, through the services of an up market software house – was a total failure. We briefed them on the BGA scoring system, the data inputs, the requirements for daily and cumulative results. As the picture became more complete I provided them with flow diagrams and we talked about installing TV type displays in the briefing room and sponsor's chalet.

The first indication that there might be problems occurred when they attempted a dummy run, late in the practice week, using the raw data from a training contest. With less than a dozen competitors it took an age, and much senior executive time, to produce a result which failed to match the correct scores! Then the senior executives backed off and, before the Championships were three days old, our scoring was in deep trouble.

Bad enough, at the best of times, with the competitors and the sponsor looking for fast results. But on this occasion we had the Duke of Edinburgh coming to present the prizes and the long range weather

COMBAT AND COMPETITION

forecast was not encouraging. It might well be necessary to set a task on the final day, in marginal conditions, with everyone landing out. The ingredients of a first class scoring nightmare. And we had just five days left.

Tim Newport-Peace ran our internal communications and public address. He could spot problems a mile away and sort them out in next to no time. A most effective troubleshooter – so I pointed him at the scorers.

"Tim! We must get cracking on a fall back plan – even if it means manual processing with pocket calculators."

And Tim produced an instant team of three – one of whom rejoiced, in the nickname of 'Sally the Slide Rule'. They used a programmable calculator worked through the first three tasks and within twenty four hours, aided by a convenient non contest day, they had produced a set of accurate, up to date, results.

The scoring, with Tim at the helm, was back under control. Just as well the way things turned out.

We had reason enough to be concerned about the Duke's programme. Coming by helicopter, direct from carriage driving at Windsor, it was tight, to say the least. Security was a major headache too. Equerry, police, and detectives had descended on Lasham two weeks earlier and laid down the most stringent requirements. Caravans, cars, the glider in which he was due to fly, competitors and public alike, nothing was spared. So different from his visit in 1963.

Then, on the day itself, we did have a task for the Open Class and the conditions were so difficult that none of them got back. The nightmare had started!

When the Duke arrived I presented the contest heads of department and made a mistake – saying of David Carrow that he was Chairman of Lasham during HRH's previous visit. "Oh really," said the Duke and moved on.

Poor David – I felt awful. Tim Finneron, his equerry, said that he hated to have people presented to him in this way.

Then Tony Mattin, presenting a group of Lasham notables, made a similar faux pas with Wally Kahn and we were both in the doghouse with our colleagues.

At the first opportune moment Chris Day and I made for the scorer's office ready to collect the results. Tim and his little team were still flat out on their final checks. Next door we could hear the BGA Chairman, who was holding the fort with the Duke, welcoming him

Germany - Visiting the Harz Mountains with Ron Howard (second from right) Professor Deutsch (right) and his family July, 1963.

Old Warhorses - Members of the Typhoon and Tempest Association at the Bayeaux Museum in Normandy before Flt Sgt Thirsby's funeral, November 1985. (Courtesy Ken Rimell) Left to right: Alec Sibbald 198, John Gerard 197, Tich Halliday 198, George Sheppard 198, Denis Sweeting 198, Doug Castle 257, Basil Tatham 257, Denis Shrobree, Author, Josh Reynolds 3, Malcolm Callaghan, Barry Field, Ken Kneen 175, Chris Thomas.

More old Warhorses - with Mike Bulleid, Pinkie Stark and Ronnie Sheward. Typhoon and Tempest Association Reunion 1987.

CHAPTER FIFTEEN   FULL CIRCLE

formally to the prize giving ceremony. There was a pregnant silence. They were waiting for Chris and myself. The nightmare got worse!

Minutes later – perhaps the longest minutes of my life – we were pushing our way into the crowded briefing room. They hadn't dared to sing 'Why are we waiting?' in front of Royalty and HRH was still smiling. The nightmare was over.

Time for Chris and I to do our double act, as we had with Tom Kerr in the previous year.

"Lunch?" said the Duke, when I passed him the first plastic bag full of gliding goodies – part of somebody's winnings – and I totally forgot to hold my stomach in!

At the end of the championships Chris had been the Director for a long time. He had done a marvellous job. But his new home was too far away and the Lasham Committee thought it was time to bring in someone with current contest flying experience. A 'local man' could combine the role of Chairman and Director once more. I suggested Bob Bickers and offered to put in one more year myself. But Bob was posted to Germany.

My thoughts went back to the pilot operated start controversy of the previous winter. Had my own reaction been just a shade too conservative and fuddy duddy? Was the 'set in his ways geriatric' too much in the ascendancy? It was over ten years since I had last flown in competitions. Perhaps I too was out of touch. At all events it seemed a good moment to stand down.

Those three championships, working with Marconi/GEC Avionics, had a pleasant sequel. Four years later Ron Howard, who had become Managing Director, visited the Championships. In the evening he and his wife dropped in to see us and we had a long chat about old times. He wrote me a letter afterwards, which contained the following passage.

You may not know that our German, Italian, and French excursions paid off extremely well in the long run. The people we got to know in the early sixties gave us the Concorde systems and ultimately, by the seventies, our massive business on Tornado. This was really a superb example of the large outcome which results from doing a good early marketing job.

The Tornado work, and the substantial business which we generated in the USA after 1965, accounts for the majority of our activity. For the last two years GEC Avionics has been the biggest exporting company in the group (around £200 million pa)...... We currently deliver digital

COMBAT AND COMPETITION

computers to the USA at a rate of around 180 per month..... Head up display and air data – in a total of around 12,000 military aircraft, combat, transport and helicopters..... three quarters of their inventory.

Not bad for the little outfit which Jack Pateman started at Borehamwood back in the early 50s!

EPILOGUE

It was quiet and peaceful in the military cemetery below the hills near Villers Bocage. The entrance portico with its massive columns was still wet from a recent shower. Inside was like an English garden - fresh and reverently tended - late roses still in bloom amongst the rows of simple headstones. Each one for a young life cruelly terminated by war.

We moved forward and joined the gathering which surrounded the open grave. Tomorrow's newspapers would call us veterans from the Typhoon and Tempest Association, members of his old squadron and others, come to honour a fallen comrade. Around us stood groups of bemedalled ancients from the Calvados region proudly displaying their tricolour standards, uniformed members of the French armed forces, the British air attache, the RAF Association in France and many others.

The coffin, draped in a Union Jack, with an airman's cap at its head, stood over the open grave. And the Chaplain's words:

"Let us remember the courage..... the sacrifice..... and render homage," as he spoke about Reginald Thursby of 198 Squadron - seemed to encompass a multitude who had died in battle. I never knew Thursby, who was shot down in August 1944. But it felt right to be there when his mortal remains, recovered with the wreckage of his aircraft in a recent dig, were laid to rest with full military honours. For the simple service was an opportunity to remember others as well.

The volleys of rifle fire crashed out in final salute. As the echoes died away there came a wonderful sense of comradeship with those no longer with us and with generations past. An experience which has touched me many times over the years. Face to face with an immortal truth.

"I hear them thus - Oh thus I hear[1]
My doomed companions crowding near
Until my faith, absolved from fear
Sings out into the morning
And tells them how we travel far
From life to life, from star to star."

The gathering round the graveside began to break up. The RAF burial party moved away. The spell had broken. On the right of the line was a tall Flight Lieutenant, wearing an Air Quartermaster's flying badge, matched by a flowing blond handlebar moustache. No mistaking that combination.

The members of 16 Squadron RAF Regiment had been flown in from Wildenrath by helicopter and Bob Bickers, recently posted from Odiham to Germany, had come with them.

Only a matter of weeks since I had introduced him to the Duke of Edinburgh at the end of the National Gliding Championships. The wheel of my flying life had turned full circle once more.

"Good show, Bob" - I said - "Fancy meeting you here! You've really made my day. See you later, at the 'Cocktail' in the Bayeaux Museum, and don't forget I want to hear all about that new glider you're planning to buy in Germany!"

GLOSSARY

CHAPTER ONE
1. "Spitfire into Battle" by Group Captain Duncan Smith. John Murray (Publishers) Ltd.
2. I.O. Intelligence Officer.
3. A.B.T.A. All Bombs Target Area.
4. "France" from Selected Poems by Siegfried Sassoon. By permission of George Sassoon.

CHAPTER TWO
1. "Flying Start" by Group Captain Sir Hugh Dundas. Published by Stanley Paul and Co. Ltd.
2. O.T.C. Officers Training Corps.
3. F.T.S. Flying Training School.
4. M.O. Medical Officer.
5. O.C.T.U. Officer Cadet Training Unit.
6. O.P. Observation Post.
7. K.R.s Kings Regulations.
8. A.C.I.s Army Council Instructions. In this case there was a parallel Air Council Instruction (also A.C.I.) covering the secondment of Army officers for flying duties with Army Cooperation Squadrons.
9. Motley Mounting. Described on page 13.
10. "Don't Keep the Vanman Waiting" by Adam de Hegedus. Published by Staples Press Ltd.
11. O.T.U. Operational Training Unit.
12. Grading School. Described on page 19.
13. I.T.W. Initial Training Wing.
14. E.F.T.S. Elementary Flying Training School.

CHAPTER THREE
1. C.F.I. Chief Flying Instructor.
2. Glide Path Indicator. At the runway threshold. Showed amber if the approach was too high, green if it was on the correct glide slope, and red if it was too low.
3. S.F.T.S. Service Flying Training School.
4. A.F.U. Advanced Flying Unit.
5. Two Stage Amber. The special goggles only admitted amber light. The flares and cockpit lights were both sodium yellow. Nothing was visible to the pilot except the flare path and his instruments. Circuit planning was difficult due to the limited angle of view.
6. P38. Lockheed Lightning. Long range twin engined fighter.
7. Drem Lighting System. Originating at Drem near Edinburgh in 1940. A large circle of lights centred on the airfield - with a 'lead in' funnel - lighting along both sides of the runway and twin glide path indicators.

COMBAT AND COMPETITION

8. Gooseneck Flare. Like a watering can filled with paraffin with a cotton wick in the spout.
9. L.M.F. Lack of Moral Fibre. Hit those who could not cope with the hazards and stresses of operational flying - or those who could cope initially and were eventually overwhelmed.
10. Tac-R. Tactical Reconnaissance.
11. Overlord. Code name for the Invasion of Normandy.
12. Tee Emm. An Air Ministry Publication which taught good airmanship and accident prevention in a light hearted way.

CHAPTER FOUR

1. Pompey. Slang for Portsmouth.
2. G.S.U. Group Support Unit.
3. H.E. High Explosive.
4. +7. Engine inlet manifold - or 'Boost' - pressure in lb/in^2 above atmospheric.
5. A.L.G. Advanced Landing Ground.
6. P.S.P. Pierced Steel Plank. A temporary runway system based on interlocking, lightly corrugated, perforated steel sheets.
7. Servicing Echelons. The Typhoons of 2nd TAF were looked after by engineering units, each of which carried the Squadron Number plus the prefix 6. They were never officially part of the Squadrons to which they were affiliated - presumably to retain maximum flexibility of deployment.

CHAPTER FIVE

1. A.P.C. Armament Practice Camnp.
2. Gustav. German phonetic letter 'G'. Hence Me 109G or Gustav.
3. E.O. Engineer Officer.
4. Brat. Halton Apprentice.
5. F.R. Fighter Reconnaissance. Also shortened to Fighter Recce.
6. Longbow. Call sign of 84 Group Control.
7. Hang Up. Bombs fail to release.
8. Craven A. Nickname for Sqn Ldr Craven the Airfield Controller - from cigarette of the era.

CHAPTER SIX

1. M.R.C.P. Mobile Radar Control Post.
2. V.C.P. Visual Control Post. The Controller was an experienced pilot responsible for directing close support aircraft at targets requested by the Army which, in theory at least, would have been visible from his forward observation position. See also Chapter 8. page 121.
3. Slipper Tank. Belly mounted long range tank.

CHAPTER SEVEN

GLOSSARY

1. C.R.E. Chief Royal Engineer.
2. "Project Cancelled" by Derek Wood.
3. E.T.P.S. Empire Test Pilots School.
4. B.A.F.O. British Air Forces of Occupation.
5. C.F.E. Central Fighter Establishment.
6. S.A.S.O. Senior Air Staff Officer.
7. R.A.E. Royal Aircraft Establishment.
8. M.A.P. Ministry of Aircraft Production.

CHAPTER EIGHT

1. G.G.S. Gyro Gunsight.
2. Hitting Power. Calculations made in recent years suggest that 16 Tornados carrying high explosive bombs could, due their increased accuracy, achieve similar results to those of the 400 Lancasters on the first Peenemunde raid.
3. F.C.P. Forward Control Post. Similar in function to V.C.P. (see chapter 6.) but without sight of the target. Trials conducted by 193 Squadron after the war suggested that V.C.P. with a pilot controller could be very effective. F.C.P. was less so but did not require a pilot in charge.
4. "Flying Start" by Group Captain Sir Hugh Dundas. Published by Stanley Paul and Co Ltd.
5. E.N.T. Ear, nose and throat.

CHAPTER NINE

1. Air Transport Auxiliary.
2. B.G.A. British Gliding Association.
3. Vice Chairman of the B.G.A. and British Team Manager.
4. Press/Publicity Officer of the B.G.A..
5. Breaking Records. That flight set a new U.K. Goal flight record, completed the 6th British Gold 'C', and was the first Diamond Goal flown within the U.K.
6. Weihe. Probably the best production glider available at the end of the war. A Hans Jacobs design like the Meise (Olympia). A few Weihes were 'liberated' from Germany after the war.
7. Derated Days. To minimise the luck element in difficult weather conditions. Essentially the maximum points for the day are reduced in proportion to the soaring achievement of the competition entry, or class, as a whole.
8. Launching Grid. Competing gliders are lined up as in motor racing and launched rapidly once the conditions are deemed to be suitable. The grid is 'rotated' day by day to give every pilot a similar share of early, midfield and late launches during a contest.

COMBAT AND COMPETITION

CHAPTER TEN
1. Burway. An ancient access road to the Long Mynd - still unmetalled in those days.
2. CV Panel. Clear Vision Panel.
3. Unimog. A Mercedes four wheel drive tractor with very large diameter wheels. The Spaniards had short circuited the rear quarter elliptic suspension with a tow bar assembly which was attached to the rear of the chassis and the axle casing! Used for trailer towing and hired out to competitors. The maximum speed seemed to be all of about 20 mph.
4. Diamond Badge. The three diamonds, added to the Gold C badge, are awarded for:- a height gain of 5000 metres, a distance flight of 500 kilometres and a goal flight of 300 kilometres.
5. Vne. Literally speed never to be exceeded. Maximum diving speed in smooth air.

CHAPTER ELEVEN
1. Reynolds Number. A fluid dynamics number which is proportional to density, viscosity, size, and speed. Would be low for a glider.
2. D Box. Formed by the main spar and the 'wrap round' nose aerofoil section forward of the spar.
3. Pitot Rake. A number of pitot heads, arranged in a comb or rake - mounted adjacent to an aerodynamic body to measure the pattern of local airflow velocities.
4. N.A.C.A. National Advisory Committee for Aeronautics. These were N.A.C.A. designated aerofoil sections.
5. C.G. Centre of Gravity.
6. A.S.I. Air Speed Indicator.
7. Position Error Testing. Accurate static pressures are needed for the flight instruments. The error can be measured in a number of ways but gliders are limited to the relatively cumbersome static 'bomb'. Two calibrated A.S.I.s are used, sharing a common pitot, one connected to the aircraft static and the other to the bomb which trails some distance below. Yards of rubber tubing and cable fill the cockpit before the bomb is launched!
8. Sailplane and Gliding - October 1959, p266.

CHAPTER TWELVE
1. W.A.T. Weight Altitude Temperature. Graphs and tables for calculation of the maximum allowable take off weight for any given combination of altitude, temperature, runway length and obstacle clearance on the climb out. A 'carpet plot' developed from them was easier and quicker to use.
2. Automatic Flight Control Systems. The two main reasons for the introduction of these systems on combat aircraft were:

GLOSSARY

       a) lack of aerodynamic damping and adverse roll/yaw coupling with highly swept wings operating over an increasing range of heights and speeds - leading to an autostabiliser requirement   and
       b) the added workload from equipment such as pilot operated radar and guided weapons - creating a need for autopilot assistance.

3. V.S.I. Vertical Speed Indicator.
4. A.I. Airborne Interception (Radar).
5. Full Authority Autopilot. Capable of applying the same control movements as the pilot. On a fully integrated electrohydraulic system, like the NA 39, the electrical demands of the autopilot are fed directly to the power controls which drive the control surfaces and the pilot's controls against the artificial feel.
6. P.P.L. Private Pilot's Licence.
7. C.A.S. Chief of the Air Staff.
8. I.L.S. Coupling. An approach, using the Instrument Landing System, with the autopilot and possibly the autothrottle engaged.

CHAPTER THIRTEEN

1. Correspondent. Rolls Royce seemed to insist on giving their agents this title. Although how their role and remuneration differed in practice was not clear to outsiders.
2. Autoflare. A manoeuvre under automatic control, at the end of a coupled approach, which pitches the aircraft into level flight as it approaches the runway threshold. Lateral control for the landing is carried out manually.
3. A somebody in the Kriegsmarine. He had been a corporal in the Wehrmacht!
4. N.A.T.O North Atlantic Treaty Organisation.
5. V.T.O.L. Vertical Take Off and Landing.
6. S.H.A.P.E. Supreme Headquarters Allied Powers Europe.
7. V.S.T.O.L. Very Short Take Off and Landing.
8. B.L.E.U. Blind Landing Experimental Unit.
9. G.C.A. Ground Controlled Approach.
10. Cat 3C. No cloud base and zero Runway Visual Range - literally Zero/Zero conditions.
11. S.F.E.N.A. Societe Francaise d'Equipment pour la Navigation Aerienne.

CHAPTER FOURTEEN

1. S and G. Sailplane and Gliding.
2. Permanent I.F.R. All aircraft and gliders operating in these conditions must file a flight plan, remain in continuous radio contact with A.T.C. and obey all instructions precisely.
3. B.A.L.P.A. British Airline Pilots Association.

COMBAT AND COMPETITION

4. The Guilds. Guild of Air Pilots and Air Navigators. Guild of Air Traffic Controllers.
5. A.T.C. Air Traffic Control.
6. Dunstable. Site of the London Gliding Club which was being threatened by an expanded Control Zone round Luton Airport.
7. Standard Class Design. Maximum span 15 metres. Retractable undercarriage permitted but no flaps.
8. R.A.F.G.S.A. Royal Air Force Gliding and Soaring Association.
9. Hahnweide. East of Stuttgart. Location of the Schempp-Hirth sailplane factory.
10. Dolphin Flying. Cross country soaring without circling. Came into its own with modern glassfibre designs which, because of their flat gliding angles can use this technique in a wide range of conditions. Glider is pulled up to reduce speed when running into lift and accelerated when leaving it. Effectively a continuous process with the speed varying according to the vertical velocity of the air through which the glider is passing.
11. BG 135 Winning its First Race. Actually equal first with George Lee flying a K-6E.
12. "On Edington Hill" from Selected Poems by Siegfried Sassoon. By permission of George Sassoon.

CHAPTER FIFTEEN
1. S.B.A.C. Society of British Aerospace Companies.
2. M.O.D. Ministry of Defence.
3. C.A.A. Civil Aviation Authority.
4. N.A.T.S. National Air Traffic Service.
5. Pilot Operated Starts. Competing pilots carry time base cameras and photograph the start line as they cross it at the beginning of a race. Thus recording their starting time on film.
6. Ground Clock Option. An alternative (or back up to time base cameras) for pilot operated starts. A large ground clock is set up adjacent to the start line. This is photographed as in 5. above. Ground clocks are usually digital and non numeric in format.

EPILOGUE
1. "All Souls Day" from Selected Poems by Siegfried Sassoon. By permission of George Sassoon.

INDEX

Adkins, Bruce.	199, 218
Alexander, Bill	198, 203, 206, 213-214.
Alford, Gerry	213.
Anderson, Gp Capt	88-89, 113, 115.
Atcherly, Air Cdre Richard	119.
Austin, Flt Lt Bunny	63, 94, 97.
Austin, Roger	173, 175.
Bader, Gp Capt Douglas	237.
Bagrit, Leon	197, 203, 219.
Baker, Bungy	154, 157.
Baker, Wg Cdr Reggie	45-46.
Baldwin, Wg Cdr Johnny	46, 52-54, 66, 72, 111-112, 228-229.
Banks, Air Cdre Rod	255.
Barrett, Roger	235.
Bartropp, Flt Lt-Wg Cdr Paddy	125, 217.
Beaumont, Wg Cdr Roland	216.
Bedford, Sqn Ldr Bill	173-174, 216.
Bickers, Flt Lt Bob	256, 257, 261.
Boissonade, M.	191.
Boulger, Joe	202.
Brennan, Maurice	202.
Bright, George	222.
Broadbent, David	206, 211.
Broadhurst, AVM Harry	48.
Brothers, Gp Capt Pete	224-225.
Brown, Don	155-156.
Brown, Johnny	228.
Buckingham, Dora	171-172.
Buckingham, Horace	166, 171-172, 174-175, 177, 179-180, 181-182, 187, 189, 218, 233-234.
Bulleid, Fg Off Michael	72, 85, 97.
Busch, Field Marshal von	67.
Button, Sqn Ldr-Gp Capt Johnny	1, 43, 52, 57, 111, 219.
Buxton, Capt Aubrey	9.
Camm, Sir Sydney	200, 225.
Carnegie, AVM David	207-209.
Carr, F.Sgt Stan	53, 59, 64-65, 77-79, 88, 95, 107, 110.
Carrow, David	140-141, 147, 180, 233, 235, 260.
Cheshire, Gp Capt Leonard	204.
Churchill, Winston	48-49.
Clarke, Lt-Flt Lt Nobby	17, 68.
Clowes R.D.A.	147.
Cobb, Bert	137.
Cook, Harry	213.
Cotton, Doc & family	157, 158-160.
Cramp, Jim	165-166, 171, 177.
Cross, Frank	200.
Cryderman, Flt Lt Felix	58, 59, 65, 86, 99-100.
Cundall, Hugh	196.

IX

COMBAT AND COMPETITION

Cunningham, Gp Capt John	135, 207.
Curtis, Lettice	209.
Curtis, Maurice	195.
Day, Chris	256-258, 260-261.
Deane-Drummond, Major-Major Gen Tony	164, 165, 167, 168, 178-179, 181, 183, 186-189, 193, 238-239, 241.
Deal, Wg Cdr Johnny	85.
Deckart, Manfred	250-251.
de Hegedus, Adam	15.
Dick, David	136, 140-141.
Doetsch, Prof Karl	222-223, 237.
Doolittle, Gen James	255.
Dorling, Lt Col L.H.G.	12.
Dornier, Silvius	225.
Douglas, Anne (Welch)	145, 163, 165, 233.
Duke, Flt Lt Neville	125.
Dundas, Sqn Ldr Hugh	5, 16.
Eaton, Flt Lt Gerry	67, 79.
Edinburgh, Prince Philip, Duke of	259-261.
Erasmus, Sqn Ldr Derek	69, 72-73, 80, 85.
Ewans, W.O. Jock	83-84.
Farquhar, Sqn Ldr	6.
Finneron, Sqn Ldr Tim	260.
Fishwick, Plt Off Jimmy	97.
Foster, Frank and Pat	160-161, 163, 169.
Foster, Jack	207-208.
Frankfurt, George	226.
Furlong, John	193, 233, 234.
Gabrielli, Prof	224.
Galland, Gen Adolph	221-222.
Garland, Lt-Flt Lt Pat	18.
Garner, Sqn Ldr Pete	125.
Gaze, Tony	244.
Geddes, The Hon John	219.
Genders, Fg Off Jumbo	129, 134.
Getty, Paul	217.
Gibbings, Flt Lt Bob	62, 92.
Gillam, Gp Capt Denys	42, 45, 49, 66, 78, 85, 113, 119.
Goddard, AM Sir Victor	203-204, 210.
Goodhart, Lt-Rear Adm Nicholas	125, 126, 132, 154, 156, 159, 160, 168, 178-179, 181, 183-184, 187-189, 193, 235, 237, 240.
Goodhart, Lt-Lt Cdr Tony	154, 156, 160, 180, 181, 184, 187, 193.
Goss, AC2	71.
Greensted, Bryan	195-196.
Greig, Donald	139.
Gunn, Ben	144-145, 148, 195, 217, 253.
Haigh, Flt Lt Jim	125, 134.

INDEX

Hall, Fg Off-Flt Lt Charlie	43, 59, 64, 66, 76, 77, 97, 99, 100.
Handley Page, Sir Frederick	203-204.
Hanle, Eugen	238.
Hardwick, Espin	141-142, 147.
Harrison, Flt Lt Snowy	86, 88, 89, 97.
Hartley, Flt Lt Geoff	37, 38, 62, 92.
Harvey, Fg Off Len	10.
Haskett, Fred	217-220.
Hearne, Peter	254-255, 257, 258.
Herzfeld, Curly	197.
Hickey, Sgt Joe	53.
Hickson, Lt Ken	125-126.
Himmler, Heinrich	252.
Hitler, Adolph	13, 49, 53, 77.
Hockey, Gp Capt Ron	125, 126, 131.
Holden, Tony	230-231.
Holder, John	138.
Holighaus, Claus	237.
Holmes, Peter	6.
Horn, Doc	51.
Hornall, Bob	197.
Horten, Reimer/Gebruder	162.
Howard, Ron	198, 203, 211-212, 216, 219, 222-224, 227, 261.
Hudleston, AVM	100.
Humphries, G. MacLaren	126.
Hunter, Gp Capt Sandy	252.
Hurford, Lt-Flt Lt David	32-33, 68.
Hurst, Fg Off Bill	65, 83.
Ince, Anne	165-167, 171-172, 176, 182, 186-187, 189, 190-193, 215, 217, 219, 226, 239, 255.
Ince, Rosalind	226-227.
Ince, Virginia	165-167, 172.
Innes, David	241.
Irving, John	37, 62.
Ivans, Bill	177-179.
Jackson, Derek	226, 227.
Jacobs, Hans	132.
Juliana, Princess of the Netherlands	101.
Johnson, Dick	174.
Jones, Ralph	241, 244-245, 256.
Kahn, Wally	146, 155, 169, 184, 193, 235, 254, 260.
Kemsley, Viscount	234.
Kenmir, Charlie	144-145, 148-149.
Kerr, Tom	257-258, 261.
Kilpatrick, Fg Off Killy	47-48, 49-50.
Kleindienst, Rolf	249.
Kronfeld, Sqn Ldr Robert	132.
Kutscha, Hermann	250.
Laight, Barry	203

XI

COMBAT AND COMPETITION

Langille, Plt Off-Fg Off Pete	46-48, 66.
Latour, Dr Alfredo	216.
Laurence, Lt Peter	134.
Lee, Godfrey	200.
Lemke, Wolf	237-239.
Lennox-Boyd, Rt Hon Alan	164.
Lenson, Plt Off-Fg Off Ben	70, 76, 94, 97.
Lovell, Derek	252.
Lucking, Tony	196, 229.
MacCready, Paul	168.
McKenna, Frank	6, 101, 107-108, 111, 114, 117, 133, 203, 217.
Majumdar, Sqn Ldr Karen	34-35.
Malins, Wg Cdr Bill	115.
Maltby, Ralph & Heather	172-173, 175, 182.
Mancus, Lt Dickie	126, 144.
Martin, Sqn Ldr-Wg Cdr Dickie	125, 210.
Masefield, Peter	209, 236.
Mattin, Tony	257, 260.
Maxwell, Robert	206-207.
Mead, Major J.C.H.	9.
Meads, Basil	233.
Midwood, Harry	154, 157, 171-177, 179-181, 183-184, 186-187, 189-192.
Milch, Field Marshal Erhardt	252.
Miller, Glen	183.
Mills-Roberts, Brig	252.
Monk, Wally	206, 207, 211-212, 216.
Moore, Gp Capt-Air Cdre Pat	136-137, 242-243.
Moore, Sqn Ldr Roly	213.
Morris, Geoff	253-254.
Morris, Lt Kenneth	24.
Morris, Rev Marcus	165.
Moss, Llewellyn	128, 203.
Mulliner, Rex	197.
Mussolini, Benito	76.
Nadin, Sqn Ldr Will	142, 144.
Newport-Peace, Tim——	260.
Nicholson, Kit	132, 139.
North, J.D.	148-149.
Ossulston, Fg Off Ossie	25, 27.
Pacey, Fred	219-220.
Packwood, Lt-Flt Lt Lefty	116.
Page, Freddie	207.
Pasley-Tyler, Cdr Henry	211, 219, 224, 231.
Pateman, Jack	198, 200-202, 205-207, 210-212, 215-217, 221, 224, 231, 262.
Petter, W.E.W.	202.
Piggott, Derek	167.
Plamondon, Sqn Ldr Guy	57, 69.

INDEX

Powell, Wg Cdr Ken	215, 219, 222, 223.
Powell, Wg Cdr Sandy and Diana	126, 181, 217, 221.
Pozerskis, Frank	239-240, 245.
Priestley, Eric	202-204, 221.
Proll, Teddy	138, 147.
Quill, Jeffrey	195.
Reitsch, Hannah	161-162.
Rhodes, Dusty	226.
Richardson, Plt Off Eddie	97.
Rimell, Ken	253.
Rolfe, Barry	257.
Rosier, Gp Capt Freddie	109, 117, 134.
Ross, Dr L.L.	197, 201, 206, 211, 219.
Rozanoff, Col	216.
Rundstedt, Field Marshal von	71, 76, 124.
Rusk, Capt Arthur	196.
Sandys, Rt Hon Duncan	210.
Saunders, Wg Cdr Sandy	138-139, 155.
Scheidhauer, Willi	162-164.
Schneider, Walter	239.
Schweitzer, Dr	225-226.
Scott, Peter	187, 235, 247-248.
Shaw, Major J.E.D.	234.
Shayler, Jack	227.
Sheward, Sqn Ldr Ronnie	109.
Simpson, Chris	237.
Simpson, Flt Lt Jimmy	43, 45-48, 52, 58, 61-62, 64, 66, 68-69, 75, 76, 79-80, 85-87, 90-91.
Skorzeny, Otto	76, 161-162.
Slater, Louis	137, 150-151.
Slatter, John	6, 128-129.
Slingsby, Fred	165, 174.
Smith, Sqn Ldr Allan	52, 73, 76, 85, 252-253.
Smith, Dan	181.
Smith, Plt Off Smudger	15-17.
Sowery, Wg Cdr John	173-174.
Spry, Constance	171.
Stanbury, Philip	108, 128.
Stark, Sqn Ldr Pinkie	111-112, 197, 220, 226-229, 253.
Steinhoff, Gen Johannes	221.
Stephenson, Geoffrey	147, 157, 159, 165, 169, 188-189, 193.
Stewart, Lt Ian	26.
Stuart, Doc	220, 230.
Sutcliffe, Peter	202.
Switzer, Flt Lt Bill	48, 49.
Talbott, Arthur	214-215.
Tedder, ACM Sir Arthur	109, 122.
Tennant, Sqn Ldr Ted	202, 216.
Testar, Theo	136, 138-139, 142, 151.

COMBAT AND COMPETITION

Thatcher, Mrs Margaret	252.
Thexton, Mike	97.
Thomas, Flt Lt Neville	45, 49, 61, 71, 78-79, 88, 99, 103.
Thornton, Flt Lt George	115-116.
Todd, Sqn Ldr Arthur	79, 80-81, 83, 84.
Tomlinson, David	27.
Towgood	153.
Trapp, Plt Off Reggie	15, 16.
Turley-George, Sqn Ldr Dickie	126.
Waibel, Gerhard	237-239.
Waigh, Flt Lt Roy	21-23, 27.
Waldron, W.O. Bob	90, 97.
Wallis, Barnes	203-205.
Warminger, Fg Off Alfred	30, 169, 241.
Waterton, Sqn Ldr Bill	134.
Weiland, Dr	225.
Welch, Lorne	153-154, 161, 165.
Wells, Wg Cdr-Gp Capt Johnny	66, 77-78, 85, 108-109.
Westminster, Duke of	31.
Wilkinson, Ken	237.
Williamson, John	177, 178.
Wills, Kitty	163.
Wills, Philip	139-140, 146, 151, 156, 163-164, 172, 174, 176-177, 178, 184, 188, 189, 193, 233-236.
Wilson, Rt Hon Harold	229.
Wilson, Gp Capt Willie	111, 113-114, 133-134.
Wilson, Lt-Lt Cdr Pete	202.
Wingfield, Charles	139, 145-147, 149, 151, 157.
Wood, Dr Conrad	252.
Wood, Derek	215, 251.
Wyse, Plt Off Allan	93-94, 97.

HOW A GLIDER FLIES

A glider flies, like an aeroplane, when the speed of the airflow over the wings produces lift. In an aeroplane this speed is provided by the engine. A glider obtains its speed by following a descending path through the air, using gravity as its motive power.

If the pilot can find and fly in an upcurrent, which is going up faster than the rate at which the glider is descending, it will gain height and the flight will be prolonged. This is soaring.

Traditionally a pilot soars across country by circling and gaining height in rising currents of warm air, called thermals. Having used a thermal in this way he then flies straight, and often quite fast, in the direction he wants to go. During this phase height will be lost and the pilot will be looking for another thermal in which to climb up again.

When the air is moist, the rising thermal upcurrent will produce a cumulus cloud at its top. The pilot uses these cloud markers dotted about the sky on a fine summer's day to seek out thermals. If the air is dry, cumulus clouds do not appear and the thermals are said to be 'blue.' Thermals rise generally to some three to five thousand feet in Britain during the summer. In the winter any thermals that do develop are weak and mostly unusable.

Gliders have flat gliding angles and will travel a long way for little loss of height. Modern high performance gliders, or sailplanes, may achieve or even exceed 1:50 and thus can travel in excess of 50 miles from a height of a one mile - 5,280 feet. In good weather conditions it is often possible for such efficient soaring machines to fly for considerable distances without circling, slowing down in thermals and speeding up between them. This is dolphin flying.

Gliders can also soar in the upcurrents created by wind blowing over a hill. These upcurrents are known as slope or hill lift.

Giant atmospheric wave systems frequently develop over, around, and particularly in the lee of hilly and mountainous regions. They can extend over hundreds of square miles and may sometimes be identified by the lens shaped 'Zeppelin Clouds' well known to mountaineers - hard edged and high in the sky. In moist conditions these 'Standing Waves' may reveal themselves in long parallel gaps, lying across the wind, between adjacent areas of lower cloud.

Gliders can soar in the upward moving areas of these waves. Flights to heights in excess of thirty to forty thousand feet and over distances of many hundred miles are possible.

Acknowledgements to the British Gliding Association.